E.M. Kelly

WAR

A Drew Murphy Post-Apocalyptic Thriller

A Journey Through Hell
Book 2

E.M. Kelly

WAR
A Drew Murphy Post-Apocalyptic Thriller

A Journey Through Hell
Book 2

War
First Edition 2021
Published by: Great Blue Hill Publishing
All rights reserved.

Copyright © E.M. Kelly

Cover design: Aero Gallerie

A very special thank you to my editor.

Dianne Giambusso
&
Jennifer Dinsmore

For my sister, Lea

Slaying Dragons:

One who overcomes addiction to drugs or alcohol,
defeating evil or the Devil

"The Water"

They say certain songs come into your life for a reason.
I definitely agree with that statement, especially when it
comes to the song, "The Water" by Mike Casteel.

It's no secret that I've had my battle with the drink, and
thankfully I'm in a good place now, but there's still more
work to be done. I've had God in my life, but then I lost
Him. I now find myself on this *journey through hell* to find
whatever it is I'm meant to find.

When I sat down to write Demons & War, this song came
into my life. The lyrics combined with the way it was sung,
reminded me of my past. It resonated deeply and stirred
up many emotions.

"The Water" immediately inspired me and was played
repeatedly while writing this book. In fact, I consider it to
be somewhat of a theme song for Demons & War.
I reached out to Mike and expressed how much his song
touched me, then asked permission to use the lyrics in my
book.

I was humbled by the kindness in his response. Although
we've never actually met, I consider Mike to be a friend
and we keep in touch via social media.

I encourage you to check out "The Water" and
Mike Casteel's other songs at:
www.mikecasteelmusic.com

"The Water"

Lord I know that I did wrong
When I chose this road I'm on
Yes I tried to turn around
But every time I'd fall down
It's been years since I've been gone
I think it's time to go back home
So here I stand my head hung low
Lord have mercy on my soul
Take me to the mountain
I want to see the father
Then take me to the river
And cleansed me
In the Water

As I look back at where I've been
I see a life that's filled with sin
I ain't proud of what I've done
But I'm just my daddy's son
And though it hurts me now
I survived it all somehow
So here I stand my head hung low
Lord have mercy on my soul
Take me to the mountain
I want to see the father
Then take me to the river
And cleans me
In the Water

When it's time to lay me down
And they put me in the ground
I won't hurt anymore
Because of trust in the Lord
Now I know I've been forgiven
For the life that I've been living
So now I stand, my head held high
Spread these wings and let me fly
Well I climbed up on the mountain
There I saw the Father
Then I walked down to the river
And he cleansed me
In the Water

And when he had opened the second seal,
I heard the second beast say, Come and see.

-Revelation 6:3

And there went out another horse that was red: and
power was given to him that sat thereon to take peace from
the earth, and that they should kill one another: and there
was given unto him a great sword.

-Revelation 6:4

Chapter 1

Manhattan, New York

New York City did not look the way Glen had remembered. Once full of life and energy, the Big Apple now appeared desolate and frightening as the distant skyscrapers came closer into view. Goosebumps rippled up and down his arms at the sight of the foreboding stillness, nearly causing him to apply the brakes in an instinctive urge to end the journey just shy of his destination.

Yet there was another part of him that wanted to press the accelerator upon finally seeing the much-longed-for finish line. After all, he had been on the road for over two days. The drive from Cincinnati to New York should have taken between ten and eleven hours under normal circumstances. But, like the rest of the survivors in this new world, Glen Daniels knew these weren't normal circumstances.

The drive had been slow, with long stretches of highway heavily congested with wrecked or abandoned vehicles, especially whenever his trip brought him near a major city. In those areas, he followed a path just wide enough for him to squeeze his car through. At one point, he rubbed tires with big eighteen-wheelers or had traded paint with various car fenders. Somewhere just outside Columbus, Ohio, he had lost his right-side mirror to a blue Chevy Malibu. The control wires that moved the mirror were the only things left in its place. The way they hung made him imagine his car was some sort of creature, hidden underneath a shell, and he couldn't stop glancing toward the thin tentacles as if expecting them to reach for him.

Perhaps Glen's imagination was really a defense mechanism his subconscious used to shield his sanity from the horrors he had witnessed in those congested areas, like the one he was now entering. It was all the other vehicles, the ones that weren't moving, that were the real fright. So many had been abandoned in the middle of the highway. The worst were the ones with occupants who were as lifeless as their vehicle's engine. He tried to keep his eyes forward whenever he passed them by, but there were just too many and Glen witnessed firsthand that the unexplained virus did not discriminate against race, gender, nor creed.

Worse still, and the most maddening parts of this road trip through hell on Earth, were not the cars without corpses blocking his path, and not the cars with corpses, but the corpses without cars. The numerous dead lying in the middle of the highway. Glen dared not leave his own car to move the bodies out of his way, having been unsure if they were still contagious. His SUV was high enough off the ground, so his best option had been to drive slowly over such obstacles. He had shut his eyes each time he did so and tried to convince himself they were merely speed bumps, but the sound they made when his car drove over them was not the same thump that reminded him of speed bumps. This was more of a squish.

Glen had cringed and tensed up with every scrape and screech caused by his forcing his way in between other vehicles. But that other sound, that squishier sound, would haunt his memories forever.

Coming face-to-face with the aftermath of the plague that had spread across the globe should have been, and probably would be, enough to give him nightmares for the rest of his life. Instead, it was the broken mirror with the hanging wires that gave him the creeps. Glen almost laughed at his own absurdity.

Some activity ahead brought his attention back to the present. Up on the right, four men dressed in coveralls and work boots used a backhoe and chains to remove cars from the roadway, and Glen slowed his SUV to a halt to wait for them to finish. A small wave of relief came over him. They were the first living people he had encountered since his departure from Cincinnati. And the fact that they were working to clear the roads felt like a good sign. It was like in a massive blizzard. When it hits, everything shuts down. But when you finally see the plows going up and down the roads you know the worst is over, and it won't be long before things are back to normal.

Still, he was too paranoid to get out and talk with the men. As much as he wanted an update, especially one that might bring some good news, the thought of the sickness kept him from leaving the safety of his car. He wouldn't even roll down his windows. The men at work didn't seem to have a desire to speak to him either, paying mind only to their task at hand. And he could tell they didn't take any chances, noticing they all wore filtered masks.

Once they removed the last car, the driver moved the backhoe off to the side and climbed out. He was older than the three men who worked the chains and, as he stepped down onto the asphalt, he looked toward Glen's SUV and tipped his hat, as if to both thank him for waiting and to signal that he could proceed forward. Not sure what else to do, Glen just smiled and waved awkwardly as he slowly drove forward.

From this point and heading toward the city, the highway now had a wide enough path for him to drive without the fear of debris, and he was more than thankful for the brave construction workers. No more close calls trying to fit through gaps barely wide enough for his car. No more corpses. No more squishing. Glen glanced over to his right and fixed his eyes again on the wires, dangling from where the side mirror had been. Though they still gave him an uneasy feeling, he smirked and gave them the finger, as if the improved road condition was his own personal victory with which he could taunt his adversary. "Take that, jackass," he said aloud.

The wires only fluttered in the wind. Glen's smirk turned to a grimace, and he redirected his eyes forward, willing himself to ignore them.

It was the solitude. He was sure of it. The solitude of the past two days; it was playing tricks on his mind. Why else would he eye the stupid side-mirror wires with suspicion? Why would he feel like they were a menacing creature, not an immediate threat, but something patiently waiting for him to exit the safety of his cocoon before ensnaring him in its death trap? "Stop it!" he snapped at himself suddenly. "They're just fucking car parts!"

It was more than solitude, he decided. It was the job. He was nothing without it. As a top news anchor in Cincinnati, Glen was revered and respected in his field. He was untouchable. But the suspension had taken that status away. All because that intern slut had to open her mouth and go public with their private affairs.

Before her, Glen had been careful with his infidelities. But he supposed, inevitably, he would eventually slip up. The more often he screwed around, the more likely he'd get caught. It's not like he wanted to make a habit of cheating, but given his position, so many young hotties had admired him, and he had thrived on the attention. It had made him feel powerful. But, in the end, it was his own ego that led to his downfall. He wooed and seduced the intern to satisfy that ego until she was completely head over heels. But, of course, he wouldn't leave his wife for her.

Glen supposed that when she got pregnant she'd thought that would be enough to get him to file for divorce. Now, on the road, he'd had plenty of time to think about it, and he suspected she had tampered with the condom she'd given him. That crazy bitch had most likely planned to get pregnant. And when he still wouldn't leave his wife for her… well, hell hath no fury like a woman scorned, as they say.

He would have gladly funded her privately, would have been able to support her financially with no problems. But she just had to fuck up his world and rat him out to HR, then text his wife to boot. Within days, his world had been flipped upside down. Suspended from his prestigious position. Kicked out of his house.

Then the sickness hit.

Glen supposed, looking back, he should be thanking the girl. If it hadn't been for her interfering with his perfect life, he might have gotten infected in the newsroom with everyone else. Instead, he'd been holed up safely in the apartment he'd temporarily been staying in. Thanks to her, he was still alive. Thanks to her, there weren't many left alive with his experience, which was most likely why he had received a call from Mr. Williams at WTFH with an incredible offer to report on the aftermath of the crisis.

In the end, it looked like karma was on his side after all. A sex addict he may be, but his addiction had saved his life. As far as Glen was concerned, he was one lucky son of a bitch. He dreamed of gaining even more fame from this new opportunity, and made a note to himself to get the most expensive bottle of scotch and raise a toast to the intern. She was probably among the dead now, may she rot in hell. He'd find himself a new pretty young thing soon enough. With society having crumbled, he doubted he would have to worry about HR again.

Glen's attention was quickly back on the road once he rounded a corner. His eyes widened at the view before him and he jammed on the brakes, bringing the car to a halt. The road before him now led straight into the city, and on both shoulders, as far as he could see, were stacks of bodies. Some were draped in sheets while countless others were exposed.

Thousands of carrion birds perched on the piles of corpses, picking away at the bloated, open remains of men, women, and children. Their constant pecking caused blood to ooze into puddles that seeped into the street. Glen could see a thin film of yellow-and-green pus floating on top of the little crimson pools, like pollen at the edge of a lake.

Suddenly, vomit rose from the depths of his stomach. He finally dared to open the window just in time to hurl the contents of his digestive system out the side. It ran down the driver's door and spattered onto the street below. Some chunks hit the edge of his door and seeped down the inside, wedging into the space between his door and his seat.

The foul smell of his bile was nothing, however, compared to the intolerable odor of death from outside, which had now penetrated the interior of his car. Glen took in the sight of the horror before him again. Some bodies had rolled off the massive piles and ended up in the roadway. They looked like overcooked hotdogs, except the griddle was black asphalt. Glen forced himself to roll the window back up, preferring the scent of his own puke to that of the decaying sea of corpses.

All he could do was sit in shock, his car idling, staring straight ahead at the cold stone cement buildings off in the distance, which rose up from the ground like tall tombstones. The city was one vast cemetery. He knew the death toll was catastrophic, but the impact of that knowledge was nothing compared to seeing it firsthand.

Taking a deep breath in an attempt to get himself together, Glen put weight on the accelerator. He had seen enough. All he wanted was to get to the safety of the news station and be done with this nightmare of a drive.

Suddenly a bright flash of white light exploded across his vision. Glen slammed on the brakes again and closed his eyes, shielding his face from the intensity with his forearm. When he reopened his eyes his vision was blurred, and it took some time before the impression of the whiteness started to wane. Even when he could finally see to some extent, he continued to blink rapidly, trying to clear the remaining white spot from his sight.

"What the heck?" he cried aloud, his body shaking from the fright of the unexplained flash. At first he feared the end of it all, his mind entertaining the idea that the military had just detonated a weapon of mass destruction for some god-unknown reason, and he half expected the shockwave to hit at any second. But there had only been the flash of intense light; no sound. After several seconds, Glen breathed a sigh of relief when all remained still.

Before he could drive forward again, the idling SUV suddenly lost power, and the engine shut off. Frantic, he turned the key several times and forcefully pressed on the accelerator, but his car showed not even the slightest sign of life. Was it an electromagnetic pulse? God, not an EMP; not now. Not when I'm so close!

Exasperated, Glen stopped trying to resuscitate the SUV. Exhaling with frustration, he smacked the side of the steering wheel and leaned his head back against the headrest. The once-lively engine was now dead, and the only sound was his own breathing.

Suddenly, staring at the ceiling of his car, Glen's eyes narrowed as a curious realization came to mind. He realized his breath was the only sound he detected. Not just within the interior of the SUV, but everything around him was at a complete standstill. The notion itched away at his consciousness, and his left hand, as if it had a mind of its own, pressed the button on the door to lower the window. Nothing happened. "Duh," he said to himself. No power meant no power windows. Instantaneously, his left arm pulled the lever to open the door.

A bit of paranoia still endured in his blood, as if the air itself was contaminated with the microscopic germs of the virus, but if he couldn't get the car started, he'd have to get out anyway.

Standing just outside his car door, he realized his strange notion was confirmed. There was no sound anywhere. No distant sound of the road crew he had passed, not the slightest gust of wind, and not one croak from the thousands of carrion birds. Almost afraid to look, Glen slowly scanned his surroundings. The birds still sat perched upon the sea of bodies, but they were as still as statues. To his astonishment, even those airborne had frozen in place in the sky. It was as if he were in a video that had just been paused, and only he was unaffected.

Just as he decided the still-frame world before him was merely the result of a nervous breakdown, in his peripheral vision Glen noticed one other thing beside himself that was moving. He turned and fixed his sight on someone in the middle of the road, coming toward him. Rubbing his eyes again, a deep foreboding fear washed over him. The figure appeared to be a shadow of a man. His eyes widened as he recognized the thing approaching; he had seen it before, when he left his apartment complex.

In a panic, Glen jumped back into his car and locked the doors. His heart was pounding so hard he could feel his pulse banging away in his neck. He repeatedly tried to start the engine, not taking his eyes off the thing as it closed in. It was different somehow. Now it had eyes. Red, devilish orbs that burned with the color of molten lava.

"Fuck this!" Glen blurted out, forcing himself out of his hysteria as he opened the door, ready to get out and run for his life. He had only gotten one foot onto the pavement when the unexplained happened. A strange whipping noise, the only sound besides his elevated breathing, came from his right. Instinctively, he turned toward it and, to his utter horror, froze as the thin wires dangling from the broken side mirror started flailing in all directions. And they were expanding, growing from inside the SUV like vines on steroids.

Glen wanted to move, but his mind was slow to process the unnatural occurrence and it happened so fast. With incredible force, the wires whipped against the passenger window and broke through. Shattered glass sprayed everywhere, some small shards hitting his face and embedding themselves into his skin, and he cried out from the sting.

Before he could react, the wires wrapped themselves around him and tightened their grip upon his throat and wrists. He tried to fight back, but the rubbery tendrils lurched him forward, slamming his face against the steering wheel. The impact caused the tiny fragments of glass to dig deeper into his skin, and fresh blood shot from his nose, which had taken the brunt of the hit. In an instant, the monster wires yanked him back flush against the seat and forced him to turn to face the driver-side window, his cheek now flush with the headrest.

The figure approached Glen's car, and suddenly the driver-side window rolled down on its own. And then, like back at his apartment complex, Glen heard a voice. "Chosen!" It seemed to come from everywhere, but it sounded like a whisper.

"Not chosen!" Glen shouted, overcome with fear. "Not me!" No matter how hard he struggled, the demonic magic that possessed the innards of the SUV's broken side mirror kept him wrapped up the way a spider wraps its prey in webbing just before feeding. Thin trickles of blood ran down his face from the multiple glass pieces sticking out of his skin.

The dark figure raised its arm and reached into the car. A long black talon uncurled from the end, which slowly crept toward Glen's face. It gently touched the top of his forehead and traced his hairline, down his face, past his ear, and across his jawline. It felt like molten rock was tearing open his face. Just as it reached the bottom of his chin, the talon turned and jabbed upward, piercing the skin. An intense jolt of electric pain shot through Glen's whole body, followed oddly by a feeling of euphoria. His vision suddenly disappeared, and all he saw was a purple hue that fluttered between dark and light.

The talon wiggled and pulled free. His vision returned, followed by an intolerable feeling of both excruciating pain and fulfilling ecstasy that seethed throughout his body. The paradox of the two polar and simultaneous sensations was unlike anything he had ever known. The veins in his neck bulged and Glen felt his bladder release, followed by a raging erection.

Glen's eyelids closed. When they reopened, his pupils were black as olives.

He gazed upon the ominous figure and into its glowing red eyes. It pointed at him and spoke a word which seemed to come from its hidden mouth and the heavens above.

"War!"

Another bright flash exploded from all directions. Glen's mind struggled to break free of the delirium that clouded it, and he let out a high-pitched, blood-curdling scream.

Suddenly, his vision returned. Frantically, he patted himself all over and jolted his head in multiple directions, trying to see everything that was happening all around. But, to his surprise, there was nothing. The dark figure was gone. The windows were unbroken and rolled up. The thin cables were back in their place, dangling from where the side mirror had once been.

Glen adjusted the rearview mirror and checked himself. No blood, no glass pieces in his face. No black eyeballs. And he could hear the engine of his SUV running idly. He scanned the road ahead to see the birds in motion. The paused video had resumed to once again follow the natural rules of time. It was as if he had only had a nightmare, and his screaming freed him of it.

Glen laughed nervously, almost hysterical as tears welled in his eyes.

It was just a dream. It had to be. Get a grip on yourself, Glen.

With an uncontrollable, quivering hand, he finally shifted the car's gearstick to D and slowly drove forward, continuing toward his destination.

Within minutes, he had almost fully convinced himself that the entire ordeal had truly just been a dream, but he shifted in his seat uncomfortably, unable to understand why he had an erection, both pleasant and painful, yet with a burning sting festering inside his hardened manhood.

He sat upon a red horse and he brought War.

Chapter 2

I-95, Florida

Drew Murphy sat on a cold steel guardrail on the side of Interstate 95, a bottle of booze in his hand as Cassandra attended to his wounds. With a thousand-yard stare, Drew reflected on what the hell had gone wrong as his mind played out the events of the past month.

First, a heated argument with his wife, Annabelle, regarding his drinking, where she called him an alcoholic and then told him she wanted a divorce. Next, a phone call from his mother's best friend, informing him that his mother had suffered a massive heart attack, and he needed to get down to Florida fast. After catching the first flight out of Boston, he had arrived to the sobering news that his mother had passed away, missing his opportunity to say goodbye. His world seemed to be shattering with every passing moment.

Then, after boarding his return flight home, an explosion at the airport prevented takeoff. Drew and another passenger had commandeered a truck, intending to drive home. As if things couldn't get any worse, a plague of biblical proportions had then spread across the country, killing millions. Society quickly crumbled. Drew realized it had become every man for himself after Brad, his traveling companion, was shot and killed over a pack of cigarettes.

After his death, while stocking up on supplies, Drew had seen the dark silhouette of a man in a sporting goods store. The apparition left Drew uneasy, with a sense of foreboding.

Continuing homeward, the roads had become impassable due to deserted cars, many with decaying corpses inside, forcing him to go by foot. While gathering more supplies at a rest stop on Interstate 95, Drew came upon a man from Maine also trying to get home to his family. Traveling together, a bond had formed between Drew and Steve. Venturing off of the highway in search of food and supplies, they discovered the side roads were passable and not littered with abandoned vehicles. Back on the road again, and with a new set of wheels, they continued north.

One night, they had stopped and set up camp next to an old farmhouse. Early the next morning, Billy, an adventurous little boy living in the farmhouse, ventured over to meet them. Drew befriended the young man, discovering he was a carefree soul. After a brief encounter with Billy's family, they continued their quest for home with instructions from Henry, Billy's father, to avoid certain areas, having heard reports of people being shot on sight.

Coming across a roadblock, the men discovered the reports were correct as a bullet pierced their windshield, almost killing Steve. Ditching the car, they then used the train tracks to make their way home, hoping to avoid further trouble. On their way, they encountered a group of college kids who had luckily survived the sickness. Pulling on Steve's heartstrings, the two men took the kids under their wings. The only problem was that the kids were unwilling to help search for food, clean up, or do anything, expecting Drew and Steve to do it all.

Taking a swig from the bottle, Drew recalled the events of the past two days, which weighed on him the heaviest.

While searching for food, Drew had come upon a liquor store and then spent most of the day drinking and stewing over the kids and their inability to lift a finger to help. They never pulled their own weight, which was a huge pet peeve of his.

Returning late that afternoon with a belly full of booze, Drew had been drunk and looking for a fight.

Watching Drew stumble back into camp infuriated Steve, after all their discussions about staying sober and Drew promising not to drink again. Having had enough, a fight then ensued and quickly escalated as the students jumped into the mix. Soon, Drew had been arguing with just about everyone. The heated exchange ended with Steve telling Drew to leave, which he gladly did to rid himself of those free-loading college kids. Seething with anger, Drew picked up his pack and weapons and set out on his own. Feeling free from the burden of having to take care of the kids, he walked away, unknowingly leaving Steve and the six college students completely defenseless.

The next morning, after sobering up, Drew had headed back to apologize to Steve.

Taking the walk of shame and apologizing for his drunken actions was something Drew was very familiar with. Head hanging low as he walked back, Drew thought of what he would say to Steve and started rehearsing it to get it right, something else he was very familiar with. Drew's head snapped up when he heard gunshots off in the distance, from the area of his friend's campsite. A wave of fear had washed over Drew and he increased his pace, realizing then that he hadn't left the group with any weapons.

Approaching the camp, Drew saw Steve fleeing toward the tree line with four armed men chasing him. Moments later, the chase ended as the men caught up to Steve, knocking him to the ground. They began assaulting Steve and looked about to kill him unless Drew killed them first. Making quick work, all four marauders soon lay dead.

While Drew tended to Steve's wounds, Steve had been overcome by his emotions, sobbing uncontrollably as he explained how he had been returning from collecting firewood when the group of men attacked at first light. Steve described standing there in shock as he watched one man shoot the boys, execution-style, while the others raped the girls. Then, he explained how one man spotted him and he had escaped only by the grace of God until his guardian angel arrived. Listening to Steve recall what had happened to the kids set fire to an anger deep inside Drew.

Back at the campsite, Drew had found the bodies of Greg, Jim, and Shawn sprawled out on the ground, facedown, all shot execution-style. Next to them lay Renell and Jessica, both stripped, raped, and shot. Drew suddenly realized that one girl was missing. Cass. Searching the area, neither Drew nor Steve had found her body. Standing there, Drew could see only one conclusion; the men had taken her with them, which meant she was probably still alive.

While loading his weapons and preparing to head out after her, Cass had come running toward them, surprising Drew and Steve. She explained that the two men who had taken her had become frightened when they heard shots and the screams of multiple men. Using that to her advantage, she'd broken free and run off.

Drew figured the others would come looking for them, wanting vengeance for their murdered friends. He'd been right. That night, a large group of men came hunting for them. One by one, Drew killed them off, sustaining only a grazed gunshot wound to his left foot until being shot in the arm by Chad, the leader.

With that evil shadow thing by his side, Chad had stood over Drew, taunting him. But, before Chad could kill Drew, one of Chad's surviving men turned on him, killing the leader instead.

The dark apparition had then disappeared in a fit of rage.

Taking another swig from the bottle, Drew now found his mind going back to when he'd found the kids' bodies.

Seeing dead men didn't bother him - hell, he'd killed plenty himself. Men who had deserved it. But women; he had never before seen a woman killed like that. What bothered him the most was the vision of the girls, with their innocence on full display, violated and humiliated, their eyes lifeless. Drew's fist tightened around the bottle as the faces of the girls on the ground changed, morphing into the faces of his wife, Annabelle, and his daughter Stephanie.

Cass pressed a bandage against the wound on Drew's foot, sending a shooting pain up his leg and bringing him back to the present.

"Hurt?" she asked.

Nodding, Drew took another long pull when, from out of nowhere, a wave of overwhelming fear washed over him. Perspiration covered his forehead and his palms felt clammy. Questions began swirling around his mind. Questions about his wife and daughter. Were Annabelle and Stephanie safe? Do they have enough food? Are they able to defend themselves? Are men going to rape and kill them, like they did Jessica and Renell? Can Annabelle keep them both safe? If so, for how long?

All were questions he could not answer. Looking down at the bottle in his hand, Drew knew that no matter the alcohol proof no bottle would rid the fears now plaguing him.

The carotid arteries in Drew's neck bulged, and a loud thumping sound formed inside his head. He began rubbing his temple as the thumping quickly turned into pounding and his blood pressure skyrocketed. Suddenly, there was an immense pressure inside his chest; it felt heavy, like someone was sitting on it. *What the hell is happening to me?* Drew thought as he put a hand on his chest. To top it all off, he was now finding it harder to breathe.

Steve stood with his back toward his friends, upset. More so at himself than at Drew, for he had failed to help his friend quit drinking. Not just a friend, but someone who had saved his life several times. Yet Steve couldn't help but be angry at his friend because he had promised not to drink again, but there Drew sat, drinking straight from the bottle. He would not watch his friend drink himself into a stupor, not this time, so he turned his back and began walking away.

Grant watched Steve walk off and then turned back to Drew and noticed his cheeks had become flushed, while his eyes seemed to stare off into nowhere, as if he was deep in thought.

Drew opened and closed his mouth, trying to rid the weird taste that had formed inside. It was the one that usually arrived just prior to throwing up. He felt his stomach gurgle and he then let out a burp. *Not now*! he said to himself at the thought of getting sick. Not knowing what to do, he closed his eyes and took a deep breath, hoping it would help. It didn't.

He tried relaxing, but his mind only made it worse. With both eyes closed, all Drew saw was both his wife and daughter's small frames lying on the ground. Even though Annabelle had always given him a run for his money when horsing around, he had never tried to overpower her into submission. It had always been the way lovers play, not trying to hurt each other or make them cry out in mercy. But, Drew knew, men like the ones he had encountered wouldn't be playful. They would be hostile and cruel. They would take what they wanted by force. No matter how many times Drew had allowed her to beat him, Annabelle could not take on men with that mindset— not unarmed, anyway.

Drew tried to swallow, but a lump had formed in his throat, making it hard to do so.

Slowly, the bottle slid gently from Drew's hands, perspiration covering his palms, but Drew never noticed, his mind having traveled a thousand miles away, to home.

Cass sat on the ground, bent over and cleaning Drew's foot, as the bottle of booze slipped and struck her head, dumping alcohol all down her back.

"What the hell, Drew!" Cass screamed as the bottle smashed on the black asphalt, sending shards of glass everywhere. Standing up, she rubbed the back of her head, glaring at Drew.

Drew's spinning mind finally caught like smoking tires on a hot blacktop. Standing up, his big body momentarily swayed side to side before sitting back down.

"Whoa, big fella. What's wrong?" Grant asked concerned and called out to Steve.

Hearing his name, Steve turned back toward his friends.

Cass bunched up her shirt and began ringing it out, "Damn it, Drew!"

"Drew, are you okay?" Steve asked. "Did you drink too much? Are you going to be sick?"

Searching the faces of his friends, Drew slowly spoke, his voice shaky, "I need to save my family. I need to get home."

"What's gotten into him?" Steve asked as he looked from Grant to Cass, who was back to rubbing her head.

"Serves you right if you get sick," Cass said as she turned and walked toward her pack to get a dry shirt.

"I need to get home. Now!" Drew said again and stood up. Instantly, a wave of searing pain shot across his wounded foot. Staggering, Drew sat, or perhaps fell, back down.

"Maybe you need to sober up first," Steve said, looking to Grant for affirmation.

Taking a deep breath, Drew composed himself and stood up again.

"Drew, you need to sit back down. I'm not done with your foot," Cass said, wearing a new shirt and holding a bottle of hydrogen peroxide.

Drew sat down.

"Thank you," Cass said. But before she could tend to Drew's foot, he pulled on his boot.

"Drew?" Cass gasped.

Before anyone could say anything, Drew grabbed his half-full pack and slung it over his shoulder, wincing as the strap grazed the wound on his arm, and started hobbling down the road.

Both Cass and Steve scrambled to gather their supplies.

Grant stood there, perplexed, and asked, "What's going on?"

Cass stood next to Steve, leaning over her pack. "What the hell has gotten into him?" she asked.

Steve grabbed his pack and slung it on. Having seen it before, he knew what had his friend so riled up, fear.

Chapter 3

Stoughton, Massachusetts

It had been a long day. Stephanie had been fussy and had kept asking for her daddy. It broke Annabelle's heart to watch her daughter stand in front of the living room's bay window clutching her woobie and waiting for her father to return. She didn't know how to tell her little girl that her daddy wouldn't be coming home, not ever. Glancing over her shoulder, she saw her mother, Susan, standing behind her in the kitchen, one arm across her chest and the other hand covering her mouth. Annabelle could tell, by the look on her mother's face, that her heart was aching for her granddaughter. Drew might have been a drunk, but even Susan, the most outspoken member of the family, couldn't say that he hadn't been a great father.

The sun had set and the cold was settling in. Susan rubbed her hands together, trying to ease the pain from the arthritis, which flared up when cold weather was upon them.

"Do your hands hurt, Mom?" Annabelle asked.

"Yes, they do," Susan replied, continuing to rub her hands. "As you get older, your body is able to predict the weather."

"I'm sorry you're in pain, Mom."

"It's not your fault, dear," Susan said before looking out the kitchen window, as if she could see the pending cold. "I think we should leave the generator running for a few hours tonight."

"Are you sure? We discussed how much louder it sounds at night, hence why we turn it off at dusk. We don't want to draw attention to it."

"I know, but I think the temperature is going to plummet, and we should try to keep the house warm for a little while longer in hopes it will last through the night. If it was just us then I'd say turn it off, but we need to keep that little girl of ours warm."

"But, what do we do when we run out of gas? The worst part of winter is still a ways off."

"I know, Annabelle," Susan said. "I just wish your father had had the fireplace fixed. The handle for the damper broke off, and it's stuck in the closed position."

"We can pack up some supplies and head to my house. My fireplace works fine."

"But you also live on the main drag, so there's more of a chance of being seen by people passing by in search of food and warmth than there is on this little side street."

"I know, Mom, but we need to do what we need to do to survive."

"Annabelle, the one thing your father taught me over the years was to play it safe. I didn't always listen to him, which resulted with me constantly having egg on my face, but by the grace of God I am going to heed his advice now."

"Mom, playing it safe will wind up getting us killed. We will need to take chances if we want to survive."

Susan scowled at her for defying her father's advice.

"If there's one thing my husband has taught me is that you need to adapt, improvise, and overcome. I never really knew what he meant by that until now, because I have never really been challenged until now. Before, you and Dad always looked out for me. You stopped me before I reached any serious pitfalls in life. But now we're both trapped in a huge pitfall; and not just us, but Stephanie as well, and she can't get herself out alone."

"Fine. Tomorrow I'll venture out in search of gas for the generator."

"Mom, you don't have to do that."

"Yes, I do," Susan said, turning and walking down the hallway toward her room, a ritual she always did when she was mad at being proven wrong.

Annabelle felt her frustration rising. The one thing she hated most about her mother was her pigheaded stubbornness. Her father had also hated it but, like him, she loved her mother, which meant she would have to deal with it. Against her better judgment, Annabelle made her way downstairs to the basement. As she descended, the sound of the running generator grew louder.

It had been years since the last time she had been down, back when her father was still alive. To her astonishment, it still looked the same. There was a tool bench on the back wall, which was still nice and neat, just how she remembered it as a child. To the left of the bench was the door that led out back. Standing there for a moment, she felt she could still see her dad working at his bench, tinkering with one thing or another. He had seemed to enjoy taking things apart and trying to find out how they worked. It was his hobby, his passion. It was his escape from life, especially when Susan had her ladies' nights, for card games or her Intimate Book Club, which were three or four times a week, and he had retreated down to his area, where he could be alone and do the things he liked.

She remembered sitting on the bottom step, listening to the Red Sox game on the radio that hung from a large nail above the workbench. She didn't know much about the game, but the excitement in the announcer's voice was intriguing, especially when the bases were loaded and the sounds of the fans cheering grew in intensity. Her father would turn and put his back against the bench, then close his eyes and listen. "Here comes the pitch," the announcer would say, followed by the crack of the bat, and the crowd erupting in a roar. A smile would appear on her father's face, his eyes still closed tight, as if imagining he was there.

The announcer would shout "It's going! Going! And, it's gone!" as the ball sailed over the Green Monster.

Opening his eyes, her father would do a fist pump, then he'd look over at her and wink.

Annabelle turned and looked at the step where she had sat as a little girl, but there was nothing there now, just an empty stair tread. Turning back, she looked to where her father had stood; again, there was nobody there. A deep sadness at his loss washed over her; combined with the sadness from the loss of her husband, and watching Stephanie wait for her daddy to return earlier, it was becoming too much to bear.

Adapt, improvise, and overcome, she heard the words as if Drew had been listening to her thoughts.

Reaching up, she wiped away the tears that had formed before stepping over to the door and opening it. The cold air rushed in, biting at her hands and face, causing goosebumps to form. The sound of the running generator was deafening, as it sat right outside the back door. Glancing at the fuel gauge, she saw that there was still three-quarters of a tank left. Stepping back into the basement, she closed the door and quickly headed back upstairs.

Annabelle lay in bed, snuggling Stephanie close, enjoying the heat her tiny body emitted. Another wave of sadness washed over her, and the tears flowed as she remembered how Drew would snuggle her at night. She especially remembered how much heat his body gave off, and what it was like having her very own personal furnace right there under the covers. She missed him terribly, even the smell of booze that had permeated from him.

Thinking back to the last time she had seen her husband, she remembered how she'd been so angry with him for being drunk, which she now regretted — not for calling him an alcoholic, because he was, but for the manner in which she'd said it. If she had known that would be their last night together, and the last time she would see him alive, she would have taken him by the hand and led him into the bedroom to make love to him one last time and then cuddle him all night. Drew was a good man, and a good husband, but he could become such a belligerent drunk. She had feared their future together because of his drinking, but now she feared what was to come without him. If Drew were there with her, he would keep her and Stephanie safe no matter what. She also knew her husband was one tough son-of-a-bitch, and would have done anything to protect them. How she wished he were here now. She'd give anything to feel that security again.

Stephanie shifted and nestled closer against Annabelle, who placed a loving kiss on her forehead and then tucked the blankets over the back of her neck to keep the cold from nipping.

Annabelle laid her head down on the pillow and let sleep take her.

There was a loud bang from down the hall and Annabelle slowly opened her eyes, reaching out to feel for Stephanie and make sure she hadn't climbed out of bed. It wouldn't be the first time she'd gotten into mischief in the middle of the night. Feeling Stephanie's warm body, Annabelle laid back down. Lying there half awake and half asleep something dawned on her, the generator was no longer running.

That's odd, she thought. She'd checked it just before bed, so it shouldn't have run out of gas. She hoped her Mom hadn't gone down to shut it off and then fallen while coming back up the stairs.

Annabelle sat up, put on her robe, cinched it tight, and stood up. The floor was cold to the touch. She missed her slippers on the first attempt to slide her feet into them, but was successful on the second try. Making her way around the bed through the darkness, she found the doorknob—also cold to the touch— and opened the bedroom door. Rubbing the sleep from her eyes, she started down the hallway toward the kitchen. Halfway down the hall, she noticed beams of light dancing across the kitchen and living room. Realizing what they were she stopped, but as her weight shifted from one foot to another, the old wooden flooring let out a loud squeak.

The beams instantly stopped moving.

"Hello?" Annabelle called out before realizing it probably wasn't a good idea. *Shit*, she said to herself.

Whispers came from the end of the hall, and she slowly backed up. Suddenly, a head covered in a black cap poked out from around the corner, followed by the beam of a flashlight. Annabelle raised her hands to her face to block the blinding light.

"Hello? What are you doing in my house?" she asked.

There was a bright flash, instantly followed by a loud bang. Annabelle knew the sound of a gunshot and took off running back down the hallway, bursting through the bedroom door and slamming it shut. Quickly, she locked the door and grabbed her nightstand, sliding it in front of the door just as a bullet splintered the molding.

Chapter 4

Rockefeller Center, New York

High above the New York skyline, sunlight cascaded into the oversized executive office, filling the room with a natural warmth. Mr. Williams sat in his plush leather chair, clutching his chest. For the past couple of days he had sat there, staring out the window. Every day had brought the same, but the other day he had felt a glimmer of hope when he noticed people milling around, down in the streets.

Not everyone has died, he thought to himself, thinking back to how bad it had been in the city once the plague hit. People brought the bodies of their loved ones out to the curb, leaving them there to be picked up. At first, teams of men in white, space-type suits came around and collected the dead, loading them into military-style trucks. After a few days, the trucks and the men stopped coming around, but the bodies continued to pile up. Before long, the stench of death was insufferable. The government activated the National Guard in every state, and ordered them to surround the major cities to stop the infected from escaping. For the first time since the colonization of the country, orders came down from the top to shoot unarmed citizens. America, the greatest country on the planet, had officially crumbled.

Mr. Williams was in the news business, and bad news sells; but sometimes, even the media turned a blind eye to atrocities carried out by its own government. Deep down, he knew that if he had allowed reports to air of the military shooting unarmed citizens, then sooner rather than later, he would have been staring down the barrel of a gun.

I should have reported it, he thought with regret. The pain he had felt before the sickness was now back, and so was his fear of dying. Except now it was unbearable, but there was nothing he could do. Silently he prayed, promising he would do anything to make it go away. Anything.

Thirty-five stories below, Chris stood at the control booth, staring out at the news desk. The vision of Bethany dying right there, just feet from the control room, haunted him and replayed in his mind. It was by far the worst thing he had ever witnessed. During the height of the sickness, Bethany had gone to the local hospital and interviewed sick patients and staff. When she and her cameraman returned to drop off their footage, Chris, the new station manager, asked Bethany to fill in, as the scheduled anchor had called out.

Chris knew he shouldn't have asked, but she had firsthand knowledge of what was happening out there. She looked horrible, but he knew Bethany felt invested in the story and wanted to deliver what she had witnessed sweeping the country. It was a decision Chris regretted, as Bethany had died on live TV in front of millions of viewers; she died without dignity. Mr. Williams had called down to the control room to tell Chris to keep the cameras trained on her, knowing full well she would die, and said that if he took the cameras off of her Chris would be out of a job. The old man was more concerned about ratings than he was for the safety of his staff.

Chris knew that it was a decision which had kept him alive. If he had cancelled the live feed before Bethany died, Mr. Williams would not have invited him to stay, and Chris would have been out on his own with all those infected people.

Mr. Williams was a bit of a survival nut, and had confided to Chris that he feared the end of the world was coming, so he'd had the floor beneath his penthouse office turned into several shelters. As far as Mr. Williams knew, if the world went to shit, there was no better place than being thirty-six stories above the ground. Being a billionaire, and owning the building, had allowed him to do whatever he wanted. Owning his own media company meant that after whatever apocalyptic event hit he would be there to report on the rebuild, and then Mr. Williams would control the flow of news. By controlling the news, he would profit from sponsors looking to get their product in front of surviving viewers.

Chris turned his attention to the electrical panel, and the huge problem that he didn't know how to fix. When the power in the city had gone out, the generators in the building had switched on. Designed to give a limited amount of power to the studio, most of the power diverted to Mr. Williams survival shelter and office, high above. The problem Chris now faced was that the generators did not produce enough juice to amplify their signal. Using a satellite phone, Mr. Williams had contacted a famous news anchor from Cincinnati, Ohio, who was now making his way toward the newsroom. The old man wanted the studio ready to broadcast once Glen Daniels arrived.

The problem was that they needed more power to run the newsroom and transmit the signal. What good was a news program that couldn't broadcast? Chris worked out the problem in his mind, and the only conclusion was to get the power to the city restored. He needed full power for everything to work properly. Hell, with enough juice, Chris could beam the signal up to their satellite and broadcast worldwide. The only problem was he knew hardly anything about electricity, never mind how to restore it to the whole city.

"Is that the only way?" Mr. Williams asked as Chris described the problem.

"Unfortunately, yes. We just don't have the power," Chris replied.

Suddenly Mr. Williams again felt the sharp, stabbing pain in his chest, causing him to wince as it took his breath away.

"Are you okay?" Chris asked, concern filling his voice as he watched perspiration form on his boss's forehead and the old man's cheeks grew flush.

Reaching into his desk drawer, Mr. Williams pulled out a pill bottle and, popping the top off, dumped the last pill under his tongue. A look of dread set in as he stared at the empty bottom.

"What's wrong? You don't look so good," Chris asked, rising to his feet.

Leaning back into his chair, Mr. Williams took a few deep breaths as the pill worked its magic. After a moment the color in his cheeks reappeared, and his clammy look disappeared. "I'll be fine. A bit of indigestion is all."

"Are you sure?" Chris asked.

"Yes, no need for concern. Our eating habits haven't been…" and, after a brief pause, he said, "Should I say, the healthiest."

"I know, sir. It's packed with preservatives."

"Once the city is back up and running it will be fish, salads, and healthy food again. Now, why don't you check to see if our friend has yet arrived. He should be here any time."

Chris turned and walked away. As he reached the door, he turned back to look at Mr. Williams, who waved, so Chris left, heading for the elevator.

Once Chris left, Mr. Williams grabbed the bottle of nitroglycerin and shook it, hoping there was a pill he had missed, but as he'd known, there was nothing inside. A dying man will do anything for a reprieve on life, but he knew there would be none today and his shoulders hung low as he put the bottle down on the desk.

***

A few days before the sickness hit, Mr. Williams had found himself in the downtown hospital's emergency room after experiencing severe discomfort in his chest. At first, he'd thought it was indigestion, but the pain soon worsened. It felt like someone was jabbing a knife into his chest, and his shirt became soaked in perspiration; beads of sweat ran down his forehead, dripping off his nose.

Instinctively, he clutched at the pain rooted deep inside his chest—he now felt light-headed as pain radiated down his left arm. Overwhelmed by thirst, he stood up to get a cup of water, then instantly had to sit back down. His breathing had become labored, and for the first time in his life he feared dying. Not knowing what else to do, he sat back down in his leather chair and pressed the button on his phone to call for his assistant.

"Help," he gasped, mouth dry.

Within seconds the door burst open, his assistant rushing in. She dialed 9-1-1, and provided the dispatcher with his symptoms, then provided the code to the elevator that made it go straight to the penthouse— no stops.

The paramedics arrived and inserted an IV, putting him on oxygen. Once in the ambulance, the medic called the hospital and requested the use of nitroglycerin. The ER doctor approved the request and the medic reached into a cabinet, pulling out a small bottle.

The medic had lifted the oxygen mask from his face and said, "Open your mouth and lift your tongue. I'm going to give you some nitroglycerin."

Watching as the tiny pill dropped into his mouth Mr. Williams had thought, *What the hell is that little thing going to do?*

The pill landed under his tongue and he closed his mouth.

"Leave it under your tongue," the medic had said, putting the oxygen mask back on.

Within seconds the pill dissolved, causing him to feel light-headed as the pain in his chest started to dull.

"Better?" asked the medic.

"Yes," Mr. Williams said, the relief in his voice.

"Gotta love the nitro. Why don't you lay back and relax? We'll be to the hospital soon," the medic said as the siren blared to get through the bustling city traffic.

Mr. Williams took deeper breaths, inhaling the oxygen. Suddenly, he did something he'd rarely done. Reaching out, he'd grabbed the medic's arm and when the medic looked down, Mr. Williams said, "Thank you!"

"Just doing my job," the medic replied.

After a few hours of lying in the ER he'd finally met with a cardiologist, who asked all sorts of questions, from his family history to his diet— which didn't exist now, and never had. The cardiologist told him he would perform a cardiac catheterization, and then described the procedure. "I will insert a small needle into a vein in your wrist, then feed a tiny camera up through your arm and into the heart, where I will look around."

"Will I be awake?" Mr. Williams had asked.

"Somewhat. We will use a conscious sedation on you."

"What does that mean?"

The doctor chuckled, as if he knew the question was coming, and said, "You will be awake but sleepy, and you'll slip in and out of consciousness, but you'll be able to answer our questions."

"Oh, I see."

"Do I have your consent to perform the procedure?"

"Yes."

"Great! One of my assistants will be down with some paperwork for you to sign, and then they'll bring you upstairs to the cath lab."

"Thank you," Mr. Williams said for the second time today.

"All right. I'll see you upstairs."

After the procedure, all he'd wanted to do was sleep, and when they brought him back downstairs to his room, he'd fallen into a deep sleep.

The next morning, the cardiologist had come in and provided him with the results of the test.

"We found a sixty percent occlusive blockage in your heart. We believe this is causing you the pain and discomfort in your chest."

"Will I need surgery?" Mr. Williams asked.

"No. We typically do not perform surgery unless it is seventy percent or more blocked, plus your blood pressure is extremely high."

"So, what do we do?"

"We treat it with medication and diet. I'll write you a prescription for nitroglycerin, and one for your blood pressure. I suggest you follow up with your cardiologist as soon as possible. If left untreated, you could potentially die."

The next day they'd released him from the hospital, and his driver had picked him up and dropped him back at the office. His assistant made an appointment with the best cardiologist in the city, and two days later he'd met with her. She had graduated from Harvard Medical School and was the absolute best at what she did. After reviewing the reports, she'd believed his heart was worse than the hospital believed it was.

"I'm not sure I agree with the hospital cardiologist. What's today, Tuesday?" she'd asked.

"Yes, it's Tuesday," he'd said.

"I'd like you to rest for a few days, and then I want you to undergo a stress test."

"Okay."

"A stress test will determine how your heart works under physical activity. We will look at the blood flow and the movement of your heart muscles, and this will help us determine the best course of treatment." She looked at her schedule and said, "How does this Friday the thirtieth sound?"

"Sounds perfect."

"How are your prescriptions?" she'd asked as she searched his paperwork.

"They gave me one for my blood pressure, and some nitroglycerin in case the pain comes back."

"It looks like he gave you a month's supply. That should hold you over until after the strength test, then we'll reevaluate your prescriptions. If you can't make the appointment, please call us; we'll phone in a new prescription until you can reschedule your appointment."

Then, on the morning of the thirtieth, Mr. Williams received a phone call from the cardiologist's office stating they had cancelled his appointment for later that day due to the epidemic that was sweeping the city.

***

Now, the room suddenly grew cold, and Mr. Williams thought he saw a shadow move across the room.

His left arm felt like it was on fire, and the pain in his chest grew worse. It was so bad it now took his breath away, causing him to wince in pain every time his chest expanded, eventually causing his breathing to become shallow.

"Please, God, make it quick," he said aloud.

The room continued growing colder, and Mr. Williams thought the end was finally here.

"Is this part of death, oh Lord?" he said out loud. "Does everyone feel cold when they die?"

The old man could feel himself dying. His consciousness was leaving and as he lay there, fading, he thought he saw another shadow move across the room. Then he heard a whisper.

Do you want to live?

"Yes," Mr. Williams said, breathing a dying breath.

Do you really? The voice asked.

"Yes," he repeated.

Will you live for me?

"Live for you," he mouthed.

Open your eyes, the whisper said.

Slowly, his eyelids fluttered open and a rising pressure coursed through his body. A pounding rose from inside his head as his blood pressure skyrocketed. The pounding was so intense he could barely keep his eyes open.

Open your eyes, the dark voice commanded.

The pain in his chest intensified, and there was now a burning sensation— along with a stabbing. He closed his eyes, welcoming the darkness, asking it to take him and end his misery.

Open! The voice boomed, filling the room, causing the thick glass windows to vibrate.

Mr. Williams's eyes shot open, fear coursing through him. On the other side of the desk stood the dark silhouette of a man with molten-red eyes.

"I'm going to hell, aren't I?" Mr. Williams asked as his bladder released at the sight of the pure evil being standing before him, soaking the front of his pants in warm urine.

Live for me and I will let you live forever, the entity said.

The silhouette came around the desk and stood before him, inches away.

"A demon has come for me because of my wicked ways," Mr. Williams said, as he watched one of its arms reach toward him.

Slowly, the appendage began to spin, and Mr. Williams's eyes widened as a hand formed and started to protrude from the blackness until it was inches from his chest.

An intense jolt of pain shot through his body, arching his back; his heart felt as if it would explode from his chest. He screamed out in agony, but he could make no sound — just silent cries. A single tear escaped from the corner of his left eye before both eyes rolled up into the back of his head and his final breath escaped him— everything had gone dark.

Chapter 5

Paxton, Nebraska

Bill Johnson sat on the front porch with a glass of cold lemonade that his wife, Maureen, had just poured. For the past few hours he'd worked at repairing the windmill, which needed greasing to keep working and create electricity for the house and barn. Along with the windmill, they'd also had solar panels installed behind the house three years ago to help offset the rising electricity costs.

The screen door creaked open and then slammed shut behind Maureen as she came out to join her husband and enjoy the cool weather. The heat from the stove kept the kitchen cozy, but sometimes it could become a little too stuffy for her liking.

"How far do you think he's gotten?" asked Maureen, referring to their salesman, and friend, Stanley, who'd had the luxury of being with them the day the FAA had closed all the airports.

"Boston is a long way from here," he said before taking another sip of his drink. "And the carnage he described seeing on his first attempt before returning, well, I guess that's going to add some time to his trek home, especially if it's like that the whole way."

"Well, he hasn't returned, so he must be doing okay," she said.

"Or he's already dead."

"Bill!" she yelled, hitting him with her apron. "He's our friend, how can you say that?"

"I'm just saying, is all. You saw how bad it was on the news."

"I know, but I don't want to think about it. He was a nice man."

"Don't you mean, *is* a nice man?"

"Yes, *is*," she said, straightening her apron.

"I'm just concerned about all the major cities and towns he has to cross through before reaching home. People act like monsters to one another when society collapses."

"Oh, hush," she said, whipping him again with her apron.

"I gave him those guns, so he should be all right," he said, placing his hand on her lap. "He's a resourceful man; he'll be fine. Try not to think about it, is all."

She gently tapped his hand and said, "I can't help it," then stood up. "Go wash up. Dinner should be ready in a few minutes," she said, turning and walking into the house, the screen door slamming shut behind her.

Bill took another long swig from the glass and looked out at his crops, which he knew he would soon need to be harvested.

I just hope there is a society left to sell them to, he thought, before carrying his glass into the house.

After dinner, Maureen snuck out onto the porch, making sure the door didn't slam behind her, to have a smoke. It had been a while since she'd had one, and for some unknown reason she'd been craving one all day. Pulling a cigarette from the pack, the sweet smell of the old tobacco filled her nostrils. The pack was probably a year or so old, and the butt tasted the way the pack smelled when she placed it between her lips. The old lighter sparked right up, and she drew in a deep breath of smoke, filling her lungs. It tasted good, and she instantly felt a rush as the nicotine hit her system.

Sitting there, smoking, helped wash away the stress of the day and calmed her nerves. In the morning, Bill planned on venturing into town. They were low on supplies, and after days of discussion they'd decided he would head into town to look for supplies and to see who, if anyone, in town had survived. Bill had wanted to take the boys, but she'd given a hard, "No." There was no way she would allow her two babies to risk their lives over simple, everyday supplies they could live without if they had to— but soap would be nice, as they all stank.

They showered with just water, which as Eben put it, was like rinsing a dirty dish before putting it in the dishwasher. They only got so clean, and soap helped with the "stuck-on", smells, as he called them. The boy was right, water itself did not wash the stink off from working all day in a barn with animals.

Besides the supplies, Bill wanted to find out how bad it was out in the rest of the world. They had crops to harvest soon, and if there was no one left to buy the crop, they wouldn't have to rush trying to get them to market. Nor would they have to plant next season, other than what they would consume for themselves. She guessed the only good thing about the sickness was that there were no more bills to pay, and chuckled to herself that she no longer had to write out a check for the mortgage. They wouldn't receive any more threatening letters from the bank.

Taking another haul off the cigarette, she scanned the darkness before her, hoping someone they knew was still alive out there.

Tilting her head back she exhaled, blowing smoke into the night sky. The stars were in full view, and she searched them, trying to find the different constellations as she had as a child, when something on the horizon had caught her eye. The stars seemed to dim in a certain area, appearing as if a wave of heat had passed in front, the way the road shimmers on a hot day. She thought it might be water evaporating and rising into the night sky, and took another drag from the cigarette.

A piece of tobacco stuck to the tip of her tongue and she tried spitting it out, but it wouldn't budge. Bringing her hand up to her mouth, she licked the tip of her finger to transfer it off her tongue. But still it stuck. Using her fingernail, she scraped it off, looking at it before wiping it on her apron. When she looked back up, the hairs on the back of her neck stood up.

Off in the distance, a pair of bright red lights appeared in the middle of the field, piercing the darkness. Maureen sat still as a chill of fear ran down her spine. Time seemed to halt as the pair of glowing red orbs grew closer. The cigarette between her fingers burned down to the filter, and the long bit of ash fell onto the porch. Fear turned to fright as Maureen realized what the red glowing things were: eyes.

Hello, Maureen!

She heard her name as if someone had whispered it from the nearby crops.

Maureen tried to move, but couldn't. She was frozen in place.

Chapter 6

Decatur, Illinois

Stanley drove with the 9mm in his lap and the rifle leaning across the console, the barrel toward the floorboards. He didn't know guns. Hell, he didn't know the difference between caliber and millimeter. All he knew was how to point and shoot.

He had been driving for days, and no longer knew which day it was. It was as if time had been obliterated. The miles dragged on, his mind filling the long gaps of time in an endless fear of what lay beyond the windshield. Snaking his way through the abandoned cars reminded him of the brutal traffic back home in Boston, except those cars had sat idling with living occupants inside.

Thinking of home, Stan thought of the slalom course he drove nightly, trying to avoid all the neighborhood kids' bikes and toys left out on the asphalt of the cul-de-sac where he and his wife, Carol, lived. They'd never had children of their own, but all the kids in the neighborhood had made up for that. They used their yard as the home base for most games they played, and Carol would bake cookies and other treats for them to snack on. In return, they would help her weed the garden and assist her with things around the yard.

The porch light was usually on for him when he returned home from work, and Carol always met him at the door with a wet, slobbery kiss, excited that he was home. She'd hated when he was away on business, as she thought the house didn't feel like a home until he returned.

A large amount of abandoned cars barring the road up ahead brought him back. But there was a gap between a couple, an old Dodge truck and a compact Toyota. Making his way toward the opening, he pulled himself up using the steering wheel, hoping it would give him a better view and help him judge if he could make it through. Stan had figured there'd be enough room to squeeze through, but there was not.

The left side of his bumper rubbed up against the Dodge and the car slowed. Still thinking there was just enough room, Stan gave the car a little more gas. But as he did, there came a cracking sound as the plastic bumper twisted and began to splinter and break apart. Stan pressed his head against the windshield, trying to see if there was enough room, when the twisting turned to screeching as the plastic gave way and metal rubbed against metal. He gave a little more gas, hoping the car would break free, but it just rocked in place as the two vehicles caught on each other.

Then came a loud bang.

The car jostled, then the front left side dipped as air escaped from the pressurized tire.

"Damn it!" Stan shouted, slamming his palm against the steering wheel at the thought of being stuck in the middle of nowhere with no help.

After a minute, seething, he looked around at his surroundings. The car to his right had a body slumped over the wheel.

I'd better get out of here before that becomes me, he thought, thankful the car was an older model, with crank-down windows, because he'd somehow managed to sandwich the car between the Dodge and the Toyota and had no way of opening the doors.

Once outside, Stan began searching the surrounding vehicles for any supplies that would aid him on his journey. Several cars held nothing useful, one was completely empty, and in another was a pack of smokes in the front console. It had been a long time since Stan had smoked and, after quitting years ago, he'd vowed to never smoke again. He remembered looking at that last cigarette and saying, "My last one," before sparking it. The clock would be reset today.

After searching for most of the day, Stan found a new set of wheels. It was a black Ford truck, and he lucked out as it had a full tank of gas. During his search, he'd come upon a small convenience store, which thankfully hadn't yet been looted, and stocked up on water, beef jerky, chips, and candy. *Never has a Snickers bar tasted so good*, he thought.

Across the street from the store was a gas station, with two mechanic bays. Stan now walked over, hoping it too hadn't been looted. If he were to make the long journey home, he would need plenty of gas; otherwise it would take him a month to walk. He poked around in the clerk's office before checking out the bays. The smell of gas and grease filled his nostrils and the layer of Speedy Dry covering the floor crunched under his feet. Standing there, he remembered breaking down, years ago, and requiring a tow to a local gas station. It had taken most of the day for his car to be fixed, and while sitting and waiting he'd watched the attendant check the amount of gas in each of the underground tanks. The man lifted each of the covers then lowered something into the tank, which Stanly presumed was a weighted measuring device, then marked his findings on a clipboard.

After a brief search behind the counter, Stan found something similar to what he'd seen that man use, along with a crowbar. Heading over to the tank covers, he used the crowbar to lift a cover to one of the underground tanks. To his surprise, it didn't open directly into the tank, the way a septic tank did. Instead, there was some sort of connection that the pipe from the truck must have connected to, allowing the gas to go into the tank and preventing rainwater from getting in.

Unfortunately, there was no electricity to run the pumps, so getting the gas out was going to be a problem.

Stan went back into the building, hoping to find something to help with his predicament. The only thing he found that was of use was a portable gas can, which was probably used for those unlucky folks who'd run out of gas. His foot was tangled in the air-compressor line and reaching down to free himself, an idea hit. He disconnected the line, grabbed the gas can, and headed for his new wheels.

Stan drove around until he reached a neighborhood. He watched the curtains move in several houses, and getting out of the truck took balls.

Knowing most people now stayed away from others worked to his advantage. He quickly ran from backyard to backyard, searching sheds for gas cans. Most sheds housed lawn mowers, and had gas cans used to fill those mowers. He grabbed both empty ones and ones with gas in them, running them back to the truck each time he found them. Before long, he'd filled the bed of the truck.

Stanley then drove to a different neighborhood and, before exiting, cut a length of the air hose. It took most of the afternoon but, using the length of hose, he siphoned gas from cars parked in driveways. After several hours, he'd managed to fill all the tanks. He stunk of gasoline, but he didn't mind because he now had enough food and gas to get him home.

Returning to the station, he cleared a spot on the floor of the clerk's office and prepared to bunk for the night. He closed the door to the mechanic bays to block the smell.

After a good night's sleep, Stan woke up just before sunrise. As he stepped up into the truck, he turned and looked at the assortment of gas cans in the back. They were too visible, and he needed a way to cover them up. Thinking a tarp would be perfect, he headed back into the station, checking all the compartments and drawers, but his search came up empty. Realizing there was nothing there that would suffice, he headed back to the neighborhood he'd visited yesterday. He thought of searching the sheds again, but then he imagined a tarp flapping over the back of the truck, and besides the obvious noise factor there would also be the added visual alerting others to his presence.

Slowly, he drove through the neighborhood, hoping something would catch his eye and sure be it, something did. One of the homeowners had put out and an old mattress and box spring which had discolored from the weather. Stan pulled the truck over to the side and felt the mattress, fearing it would be waterlogged, but it was not. After a brief struggle, the mattress soon lay in the back of the truck, covering most of the tanks.

Stan pulled out another Snickers bar and picked up the atlas. After a few minutes spent orienting himself, Stan marked his position on the map and plotted his course home. He placed the black magic marker in the cup holder, realizing it was critical to keep track of where he was in case a road was blocked and he needed to turn around. Taking another bite of the Snickers, he headed out on his long trek.

Most roads were passable, except for the few where he had to backtrack and find a new way. Before long, he had made it to Columbus, Ohio. Going through the city, he noticed the main road appeared to be rather clear, as if someone had pushed the abandoned cars off to the shoulder.

He stopped twice to gas up, once before reaching the outskirts of New York City, and once more after passing through. Stan knew it was now a straight shot up I-95 through Connecticut and Rhode Island, bringing him into Massachusetts, to home.

Chapter 7

Orlando, Florida

Kendra slowly trudged through the streets of Orlando, still unsure of what had happened. She knew she had been on the verge of death; the drugs had worked quickly into her system. She could see the other side, a warm light at the end of a long tunnel. She had felt at peace. But then something had happened, and the warm light became cold and started to drift away.

She remembered little of what happened afterward. At some point, she awoke to find herself sitting on the edge of her bed, just as she had been when temptation had taken hold and she had finally given in. Or given up. Either way, she had taken the syringe and filled it up with the good stuff, then she'd filled her veins. One last trip before the end.

And why had it mattered? She had figured she was going to die anyway. Everyone else had. At first, she had been safely locked up in her apartment, with plenty of supplies to survive until the pandemic passed. But then Hector had screwed all of that up. Why did he have to break in; was it just to get a piece of ass? Just had to try to get his jollies off before biting the big one? But, as one ill turn deserves another, Kendra had screwed up his plans by putting a bullet in his head. It was self-defense, after all. Sorry, Hector, but even escorts have their standards.

Yet that didn't matter. Hector had been infected with the virus, and she had made contact with his blood and guts when attempting to move his dead, fat ass out of her apartment. It was a sure bet she had contracted it, and all she could think about was how all those people had suffered terribly. God, it was awful. Looking back, Kendra may have denied that shithead her snatch, but she had still done him a favor by ending his life quickly. You're welcome, Hector.

Ending his life quickly…

And that's when the idea had come, or temptation did. The way she had seen it, she would have rather gone out feeling high as a kite than to suffer the symptoms of the cursed plague. Kendra recalled how, in that moment, she would've done anything not to have to go. So, overdosing on heroin had seemed like a good idea.

She had taken more than enough to do the job, and she recalled again that warm light. The… something dark… something terrifying. She couldn't quite remember. It was still a mystery how she'd ended up sitting on her bed, as if she hadn't taken the hit. But she had. The empty syringe that had been sticking out of her arm was proof. Yet, somehow, between injection and the moment she'd felt herself succumbing to the proverbial abyss, all had returned to normal.

Almost…

Not everything was exactly the same. For one thing, Kendra no longer felt concerned or worried about the virus. She recalled the anxiety that had sprouted in her heart while Hector was breaking down her door, how it had bloomed into sheer terror when she saw the yellowish green pus oozing out of every opening, even his eyes. Then, after she had shot him, Kendra remembered the never-ending fear within, when she knew she would have to attempt to push his carcass out of her apartment without physically touching him. And how, when she had slipped on his blood and pus, and when it had splattered all over her, how that fear had immediately morphed into full-blown panic.

Yet, when she'd come to, after her heroin trip that never was, those survival instincts were no longer there. It was almost as if, beyond her own control, her body had risen from the dead.

She still couldn't explain it. It was as if she had been compelled by some force that came not from within, but from an outside, almost alien, influence. Or so it had seemed to Kendra. And, when she had confidently exited the apartment, she stepped right over Hector's lifeless corpse, not a care in the world over having killed him. As she passed by, all she had regarded him with was a curious glance. Maybe even a smirk? Or a carefree, goodbye, Hector.

Now she was casually walking downtown, in the middle of what was normally a busy street. She wasn't sure where she was heading. Again, it was as if something else was guiding her, though she was not in command of moving her feet forward. She would turn the heads of countless people as she passed, a beautiful, enchanting seductress, if those countless had still been among the living.

She turned her head left and right, regarding the mucus-covered corpses lining the sidewalks no longer with terror or sadness, but with a strange, disconnected wonder. This new sensation intrigued her. She still had conscious thought, but it felt cold and empty. As she continued down the street, Kendra wondered if she'd become a zombie. But that couldn't be right. Zombies liked to eat brains, and she herself had no appetite whatsoever.

Everything felt strange and unreal, yet she felt no fear or anxiety about anything that may come. Eventually, Kendra had altogether forgotten about trying to solve the mystery of how she had recovered from her overdose. She even stopped concerning herself with where she was heading, or why her body was kind of on autopilot but also kind of not.

Instead, she focused on looking upon her surroundings with new eyes. Listening with new ears. The world was different. There was no sound, and the city reminded her of an early Christmas morning. At least the silence, anyway. For a moment, she closed her eyes and imagined children lying in their beds, dreaming of Santa, and not stacked in piles in the streets.

The thought of the holidays, and of children, brought a brief wisp of her former self back, and for a moment she thought she felt not complete sadness, but a hint of it. Somehow the realization that she would now never experience motherhood hit her; she may not be dead, but she wasn't sure she was altogether alive either. Was this purgatory? Goddamn you, Hector.

No. Kendra knew that, if it truly was purgatory, it was her lust and addictions that had led her there. Even if Hector hadn't inadvertently sped up the process, she would have ended up paying for her sins eventually.

Suddenly, a small piece of her, deep inside, felt like screaming, *How did I let this happen to me!*

But a much larger piece of her, the new Kendra, knew it would be pointless. If she could speak, her voice would only dance in an echo around the city buildings, like a bullet ricocheting off metal.

She also wished to collapse and weep, but no one would hear her cries. No one would play the knight in shining armor, come to save her from herself. No one ever had…

No one had saved her from her drunken stepfather and his friends, and she'd never forget the lust in their eyes whenever they had looked at her; would never forget the foul stench of their sweaty palms, one covering her mouth to silence her while the fingers of the other went exploring; would never forget how he'd watch nearby, finishing his bottle of rum, waiting for his turn.

No one had then saved her from the hardships that followed after she'd run away.

Who could blame her for leading a life built on sex and drugs? A life of chemical escape from demons that never stopped haunting her. If she were truly in purgatory for her sins, then whatever higher power was in charge could go screw itself.

Kendra opened her eyes, and a sudden, foreboding gust of wind dried the faint bit of wetness that had formed at the corners. Whatever sentiment that had almost brought her back to her former self— her weaker, more pathetic self— was squashed as quickly as it had come.

The coldness returned, and she welcomed it.

As she continued to walk, it didn't take long before she forgot she'd ever felt anything, even sadness or anger.

The countless dead surrounding her were not of concern though they were at her feet. They were literally beneath her. She pressed on, letting go of it all, enjoying the numb state of this emotionless utopia. It was better than any drug she had ever tried. She'd never known such freedom could exist. Thank you, Hector.

Just as these thoughts came, Kendra felt that alien urge inside her again. It was the same urge that had compelled her to walk, without her making the conscious effort. It buzzed through her mind with such force she dared not ignore it, for she somehow understood that to do so would only intensify it. The outer influence spoke to her, making only one command: *New York.*

Kendra now knew where she was walking, or where her legs were carrying her at least. But she didn't seem to care, nor did she have any apprehension about the unknown future ahead. Whatever force was guiding her, be it of nature or of the supernatural, must also be responsible for bringing her back, for granting her this gift of being numb to the world. In return, she would follow it without question.

Walking on, she passed into a darkness that formed like rain clouds passing in front of the sun, enveloping everything in shadow, except these shadows were pitch black and, when she passed through, everything — everything — disappeared.

Chapter 8

Crescent City, Florida

Billy was upset. He wanted to go with his father and uncle into town, but his mother wouldn't let him. Heck, she hadn't let him out of the house since he'd got caught trying to sneak out. Instead of going, he sat on the couch sulking, his elbows resting on the back, and looking out the window. "Shucks," he said out loud as he watched his father drive off. Henry caught a glimpse of his son's pouty face in the rearview mirror as he headed for the store.

"Hey Henry!" said a friendly voice from behind the counter as he walked in.

"Hey, Cap," Henry responded as he looked around at those inside.

"How's the family?" Cap asked.

"They're good."

Cap looked down at the counter. "Did you lose anybody, Henry?"

"No. We all made it through. How about you?"

"Margaret and Phillis are good. Thank you for asking."

"Have many people have come in?" Henry asked, looking around the store.

"People are trickling in," Cap's brother, Doug, said, looking away from the static on the TV he was working on.

"How bad is it?" Henry asked.

"It's bad," Cap said. "We've started a list of those we lost on the wall over here. We're up to one hundred and seventeen dead so far."

Henry's eyes bulged. Each number represented a person who'd had a name and, being such a small town, he probably knew most of them, if not all.

"The sheriff was in the other day and he said he's been driving around checking in on folks. Said he had just come from the McGrath's, and that all nine of them were dead. Said he could see them through the window of the front porch. They all died cuddled up together. The youngest was just six years old."

"The McGrath's were good people. Betty-Sue grew up with them," Henry said as he walked through the vacant produce section.

"We're all out of produce," Cap said, pointing out the obvious.

"Are you looking to buy some?" asked Henry.

"Have you been working the farm?"

"Yeah. We put Grandpa and Billy on lookout while my brothers and I work the farm. I have some crops ready to harvest."

"What do you have?"

"I have sweet corn, broccoli, celery, and cucumbers. Potatoes should be ready soon."

"I don't have the money to pay you right now, but once they sell I can, or we could barter?"

Henry thought about it for a minute and asked, "You got toilet paper?"

"Some."

"I'd be willing to trade goods," Henry said. "As long as it's within reason."

Cap nodded in agreement. "We might be on the barter system for a while, until the economy can get back on its feet."

"Okay. Put some of that toilet paper aside for me and you've got yourself a deal. I'll be back in a couple days."

Henry watched as Billy used all of his might to push on the clutch. The gear caught, and the front of the tractor hopped off the ground.

"There you go, son," Henry said as he patted his boy on the shoulder. "Now, turn the wheel and avoid that grove of trees up ahead. There's a ditch behind them, and we'll never get this here old tractor out if we drive into it. Keep turning the wheel and head straight for the barn."

Driving the tractor was hard for an eight-year-old boy, but he knew Billy was glad to be out of the house. His talk with his wife, last night at the kitchen table, worked because she finally let him outside.

Ever since he'd snuck out to meet those two men a few weeks back, Betty-Sue had forbidden their son from leaving the house. She'd even had Grandpa nail the window to the sill to prevent him sneaking out again. Henry had thought it a little over-the-top, but it was easier to say nothing than deal with her wrath. However, after venturing into town and finding out that others had survived, Henry insisted he would need his son's help with the season's harvest if they were to have produce to barter. God only knew how much his ass yearned for actual toilet paper. And, come hell or high water, he would get his hands on some.

It had been a long day, and it was clear Billy was exhausted. This morning he awoke earlier than he could remember him doing in a while. It was hard for him to contain his excitement about his Dad's venture into town. Last night over dinner, he'd listened as Henry relayed what he'd seen in town. People had finally started venturing out in search of food. They wore masks and bandannas over their faces, to protect themselves from the sickness. Most people were armed, and spoke to each other from several steps away. One store even had a dead body inside, and someone had spray painted STAY AWAY on the front in big red letters.

Hearing about Cap and his gun-toting brothers protecting the store from any potential looters had enthralled Billy. He'd always loved going into the store because it had a wild-west look and feel. The first time he'd entered the store, he'd asked Henry why it looked that way, and what that funny smell was. Henry had explained the store had been passed down from generation to generation, and had been the first store built in town and so the odor was from the old wood flooring. Learning the owners were walking around with loaded guns had reminded Billy of those gunslinger Westerns his Grandpa loved to watch, and had imagined aloud how it added to the store's feel.

Henry then told his family how surprised he was to see the store still had both dry and canned goods. "They have soap, soup, and even toilet paper!" Henry exclaimed. He explained he had made a deal with Cap, and that they would deliver fresh fruits and vegetables the day after next.

"There is one other thing," Henry had said. "Before I left, Cap warned me to keep a vigilant eye out for thieves. He said a band of young men has made camp on the outskirts of the Prather's farm. Cap said, at first, they were just stealing the crops to eat, but then they started stealing them to sell. Next, he said they tried breaking into the house. Thankfully, old man Prather's boys were home and shot those folks dead. Cap said we can't trust no one and, I tell ya, I believe him. It was scary going into town, especially with everyone wearing masks, as it was hard to tell who was who."

After dinner, Billy had sat on the front porch with Grandma as she rocked in her favorite chair. They had pulled first watch together, but he knew that was because it was still daylight. Once night fell, they both had to be inside.

Picking up a handful of pebbles, one by one he tossed them at his mother's statue of the Virgin Mary in the flowerbed next to the house. If he hit it just right, he would be rewarded with a hollow clunk sound.

Grandma's eyes glossed over and her chair slowly rocked to a stop as she fell asleep.

Waving his hand to see if she really was asleep, Billy had turned his head, peering into the window and checking to see if the coast was clear. Standing up, he crept over to the shotgun resting against the porch railing. Checking again to verify Grandma was asleep, Billy reached out and picked up the weapon. The long, black barrel had been cold to the touch, and it was heavier than he'd thought. Grandma adjusted in her chair, startling Billy, and he put it down. Fearing he would get caught, he took his seat. Leaning back in the chair, he rested his head against the side of the house and scanned the horizon, searching for any unwanted guests. Secretly, he wished someone would show up so he could use the shotgun and blast them. He was old enough to defend his family, he told himself.

Sitting there under the open window, Billy had listened to his parents and uncles talk.

"I wonder how those two men are doing, and if they made it back up north to home?"

"It's funny you should mention them," Henry said, "I thought of them today while in town."

"Oh, really?"

"After seeing most everyone packing heat today, I wondered if those two men Billy had snuck out of the house to meet had made it home yet, or if they had run into their demise at the hands of others."

"Hopefully not," his mother said. "They seemed like good men."

"That they did, and Billy was fond of the big guy, too," Arthur, his father's brother said.

"His name was Drew," she said.

"That's right, Drew. He was a man who looked like he could handle himself in a tough situation," his father replied.

Later that night, Billy lay in bed, sore and tired. Muscles he hadn't used before twitched from the day's strenuous work. The Spider-Man night-light on the opposite wall emitted a dull light. As he fell deeper and deeper into sleep, he dreamed about the shotgun and its long black barrel…

Downstairs, Henry sat sipping the last of his favorite whiskey, wondering if Cap had any liquor in the store's backroom.

If there was one thing he looked forward to bartering for, it was toilet paper. His ass itched and burned something fierce from having to use sheets of paper to clean his backside.

With eight people in the house, toilet paper had been one of the first comforts to go and his bum required some TLC from soft, two-ply sheets.

Wiggling his butt into the chair, he tried to sooth his inflamed anus, but nothing seemed to work. The whiskey helped a bit, but now he was out.

Henry's older brother, Arthur, had been fidgeting with the TV, trying to find a signal, when he caught sight of his brother and burst out laughing.

"Hey, keep it down! You're gonna wake Billy and Betty-Sue."

"Sorry," he said before bursting out in laughter again.

"What the hell is so funny?"

"You!" Arthur said. "You should see yourself wiggling your ass in that chair."

"It's not funny!" Henry said, clearly mad at his brother for laughing at his predicament.

Arthur, seeing it made his brother upset, only laughed harder. "Why don't you drop your trousers and scoot your ass across the carpet like a dog!"

Henry saw the visual in his head, couldn't control himself, and soon both men howled with laughter.

The men were making so much noise they drowned out Billy's groans...

Billy's head shook and jerked on the pillow as his eyeballs danced under their lids, racing back and forth in their sockets. He was in a cold, dark room except for a small pinhole of light far off in the distance. It appeared as if it was a peephole of some sort, and Billy could feel something watching him. The hair on the back of his neck stood on end as he heard a deep, dark voice whisper his name from deep within the darkness. "Billy!"

His heart pounded in his chest as he scanned the vast blackness for an exit, but there was none. In fact, there were no walls; nor could he see a floor or ceiling, either. He just hung there, in the nothingness.

"Oh, Billy boy! Are you going to let me in?" the evil-sounding voice asked, followed by a bone-chilling laugh. "Hahaha!"

Billy's fight-or-flight reflex kicked in, and he began flailing, trying to escape, but there was nowhere to go and nothing to grasp onto. He was trapped in an unforeseen cell, hovering like a helpless astronaut in an endless void.

"My, my, is someone afraid?" the sinister voice asked.

In that moment, the fear did set in and Billy's entire body went rigid. His tiny nostrils flared vigorously as he hyperventilated.

"Billy!" the scary voice whispered, now sounding like it was right next to him.

Billy spun around and around, trying to see the evil thing that was calling his name when he glimpsed a pinhole of light.

"Over here, Billy," he heard another voice say. It differed from the evil voice. This sounded like a muffled child's voice, and seemed to come from the light.

"Where are you?" Billy called out.

"I'm here."

"Where?" Billy cried out again.

"In the light. Come to the light, Billy," the childlike voice called.

Billy moved his arms and legs, as if swimming, and the light grew closer.

"Where do you think you're going?" boomed the sinister voice, which sounded further away now.

Billy looked over his shoulder and into the infinite darkness, then looked back at the light, which was growing warmer and brighter.

As he approached the light, a small hand reached out, took hold of his arm, and pulled him into the light.

Billy felt himself grow heavy as he passed through.

"Wake up, Billy," the childlike voice said. "Wake up."

Billy's eyes fluttered opened. Sweat covered his forehead, soaking his hair and pillowcase. Breathing heavily, he lay there for a moment, thankful the nightmare was over. Billy hated the dark, he feared it. Always had. The pounding in his chest slowed, and he noticed his room was brighter than usual. Spidey always provided enough light to break up the shadows, but it seemed brighter now. The room basked in a warm light, not quite as bright as that when the bedroom light was turned on but brighter than normal. Just then, Billy heard a voice. The same voice from his dream.

"Vroommmm! Vroommmm! Momma, come look at this."

Slowly, Billy shifted his gaze to the left while reaching up and rubbing away the sleep. He felt the wetness of the pillowcase and his eyes opened wide as he heard the voice again.

"Cool!"

Rolling over, Billy sat up on one elbow, surprised by what he saw.

A bright light was emitting from the center of the room. It came from a little boy, who sat playing on the floor.

Billy raised his other hand to block the light.

"Watch out for the evil man," the little boy said.

"What?" Billy asked, turning his head from the light.

"Watch out for the evil man," the boy repeated.

"Please turn down the light so I can see," Billy requested.

The bright light dimmed as asked, and Billy could now clearly see the little boy standing in the center of his room. He looked a few years younger than him and had bright red hair, which the boy pushed from his eyes.

"I love butterflies," he said.

"What are you doing in my room?" Billy asked.

"I don't know," the little boy answered, looking scared.

"How did you get in here?" Billy asked, sitting up and sliding his feet into his slippers.

"I don't know," the boy answered again.

"Where do you live?" Billy asked as he stood up.

"I live in the warmth of the light."

"Why are you here in my room?" Billy asked.

"I'm here to warn you about the evil man."

"What evil man?" Billy asked as he eyed the boy, trying to figure out how he had gotten into his room.

"Oh look! A black butterfly," the boy said as he bent over and reached for something.

Billy looked but saw nothing, then asked, "What are you reaching for?"

"The dark man will manifest. Something evil is coming. Don't go downstairs," the boy said.

"Why can't I go downstairs? What's happening down there? My grandparents are down there!" Billy said, the excitement creeping into his voice. He turned toward the door, quickening his pace.

Before Billy reached the door, a bright flash filled his room. It was like looking into the sun and he fell to the floor, covering his eyes.

A while later, Billy awoke in the dark, still on the floor. His knee hurt. Sitting on his bum he brought his knees to his chest and rubbed them, sore from when he fell. He could feel a bump under his pajama pants. He vividly remembered his dream. It had felt so real, like it actually happened.

Scared, he stood up and put the light on. Searching the room, he looked for any sign of the little boy but found none. Standing still, he remembered what the boy had said: "I'm here to warn you about the evil man, and to not go downstairs."

Fearing something had happened to his grandparents, Billy raced to the door and down the stairs. He barely touched the steps, his legs were working so fast. He reached the bottom and rounded the corner, racing down the long corridor that led to the kitchen and his grandparents' room. He slid to a halt as he passed the entrance to the kitchen and noticed his grandparents sitting at the table.

"What's wrong, Billy?" Grandma asked as he entered.

The smell of fresh-brewing coffee filled his nose, followed by the wonderful aroma of freshly spread strawberry jam.

"Oh nothing, Grandma," Billy said. It must have just been a dream, he thought.

Chapter 9

Upper West Side, New York

Peter Bane sat at the kitchen table, his head hung low. That morning his wife had opened the last can of food. Removing the piece of fat from the beans, she'd divided them evenly among her family and placed the bowls on the table.

The first week after the sickness hit was the scariest, but also the easiest. Keeping the children safe had been their number one priority. At first, staying cooped up was easy, but as the weeks passed it became harder and harder to keep the children from going stir crazy. Having become accustomed to being outside— from going to school to seeing their friends and going to the park to play; to all the activities they did to keep their children occupied— it all no longer existed. Not to mention there was no TV to watch. In the weeks following, both Peter and Cindy laughed, remembering how hard it had been trying to keep their children entertained during a snow day, which had been easy compared to this, and how for the children it had felt like living in prison.

Now, the discussion they'd been having for weeks finally arrived. There was nothing left, both the fridge and the pantry were empty. Tomorrow, his family would wake up hungry and there would be nothing to eat. The days following would bring on starvation. They would be lucky to survive three to five days but after that, death would come a-knocking. Peter couldn't stand the thought of watching his family die one by one, knowing that dying from starvation is a horrible death. Grabbing his bowl, he stood up, walked over, and put it in the sink. Looking around the barren kitchen, he'd never thought his life would end like this.

Sighing, he moped down the hall and into his bedroom, locked the door, and lost it. Tears formed in the corners of his eyes, and once they started rolling down his cheeks, they did not stop. Sniffling, he wiped the snot that hung from his nose before running a hand through his salt and pepper hair and crumpling to his knees. Wailing, his chest heaved up and down as he begged God to spare his family and to provide food for them, swearing he would do anything to keep them alive. Anything.

They lived in a quaint apartment in a pleasant part of the city, but you wouldn't know it now as the streets looked like something out of a post-apocalyptic nightmare. Peter had already scavenged all the other apartments in the building. First, he'd ventured down to the parking garage and noted the empty parking spots. Being a tradesman, he'd used his battery-operated drill to bore a hole into the door of the apartments that corresponded to the empty parking spots. Peeping through, he'd then checked to see if there were any bodies inside before breaking down the door. What food he'd found in his building, and the surrounding buildings, quickly dwindled.

Desperate times bring out the best and, unfortunately, the worst in people. For his wife, Cindy, it had brought out the worst. As their food supply dwindled, Cindy feared death. The fear had consumed her to the point that she started lashing out at Peter and the children. She did nothing in the search for food, expecting him to do it all. All of her women-are-equal-to-men rhetoric went out the window once put to the test. She even slapped him across the face, calling him a coward and a pussy for not being able to find food. She questioned his manhood by telling him a real man would provide for his family.

Kneeling on the floor of his bedroom, he thought back to a time when he'd feared nothing. But age has a way of replacing courage with fear, or maybe logic replaced stupidity, he didn't know. Neither of those factored in here. This was survival.

Peter knew what he needed to do, and started rocking back and forth on his knees until he had mustered himself up enough to "man up" and go out in search of food.

Standing up, he made his way down the hallway toward the living room. Passing his children's bedrooms, he glanced in and saw their frail little bodies, deprived of energy, and a lump formed in his throat as he envisioned them dying from starvation there in their beds. A renewed sense of determination filled him, and he knew he could not afford to come back empty-handed. He headed to the closet and put on his coat, winter hat, and gloves.

"I'm going out to search for food," Peter said to Cindy, who was lying on the couch, and walked out the front door.

Closing the door, he turned and headed down the hallway. He was halfway down the hall when he heard a door creak open and his wife's voice call after him. Turning, he saw Cindy standing in the doorway, her cheeks glistening from the tears running down her face.

"Be safe. Come home to me. I love you," she said.

Peter turned and walked back to her, determination still on his face. She closed her eyes as he raised his arms, fearing he would strike her. Grabbing her by the shoulders, he pressed her hard against the wall. He almost feared he would finally explode and tell her off for the evil things she had done and said. But, as forceful as he was in pushing her against the wall, he brushed his stubble against her cheek and gently kissed her.

It was the first time he'd kissed her since he'd caught her cheating a few months ago. The image of her in bed with another man was burned into his memory. It was one of those things; the damage was done, and he'd wanted to leave, but there was no way. Neither could afford to live on their own. Cindy didn't work, and with child support and alimony he'd never get by alone. It was cheaper to stay married. The entire ordeal had broken his spirit, and caused him to feel less of a man.

Reaching up, she grabbed his cheeks with both hands, kissing him passionately, like they had when they first fell in love. All the animosity and disdain washed away, and he rested his forehead against hers and looked into her eyes. "I love you!"

"I know."

"I'll be back with food."

"I know you will."

With that, he kissed her again and walked away.

"I love you! Be safe," she said, closing the door.

Years' worth of memories came flooding back, like from when he was a lineman and had to head out in snowstorms and Nor'easter's. Much like now, it was a life-or-death situation. He'd answered the call to get the power turned back on during storms. There were even times when a call came in to turn the power off in order to save a drunk driver who had wrapped themselves around a pole, and the fire department needed the power cut to make the rescue. It was calls like that, drivers and families trapped in burning cars, which drove him to apply to work at the plant. The rush to get the power back on was still there, but there were no dead and dying people involved. No more torrential rain or long, bitterly cold nights climbing poles in order to replace them, along with transformers and downed wires. Before the pandemic, he'd had a cushy job riding a desk in a cozy office. Being station chief did have its perks.

The 10023 gang was a gang that plagued and terrorized the Upper West Side. Using their zip code as a logo, it symbolized their turf, their streets.

Most of the gang slept during the day, spending the nights out on the street selling drugs, stealing, and harassing people at local businesses.

The sickness hit on a Friday morning. As many members were falling asleep, people out in the city were falling dead. By the time they awoke in the late afternoon, the city was already at a standstill. Like everyone else, they'd spent the weekend cooped up. Then on Monday morning, they'd found themselves running low on supplies.

The gang had sent the newest members, those awaiting initiation, out into the streets to find food. Walking up to the front door of the grocery store, they shot out the glass before loading several carts with food and pushing them back to their crib.

The days turned into weeks, and soon the stores were running low on supplies. The leader took over several properties, and sent his youngsters out onto the streets to find and capture whatever seemed vital.

As the sickness died down, word spread that the 10023 had hoarded lots of food. People ventured out, desperate. At first the gang accepted ass and grass for payment, but as time passed on they realized both held nothing significant for resale.

With supplies again running low, the minions had to go further out into unknown territory, crossing paths with civilians and other gangs roaming the streets, searching for their own supplies.

Peter searched building after building, but all were picked clean. At some point, he unknowingly ventured into the 10023 territory and had found himself cornered by three gang members. They approached from all sides, and before he could raise his fists in self-defense they'd knocked him to the ground and kicked him unconscious.

When Peter came to, he found himself tied to a chair. Blood dribbled from his nose. Crimson drops clung to his mustache before dropping to his crotch, staining his jeans.

"What are you doing in my neighborhood?" asked a gangbanger, his 9mm handgun pointed at Peter.

Looking up, he scanned the room and couldn't help but notice the shelves on the back wall were stocked with food, along with several dead bodies in the corner.

"I'm searching for food for my family," Peter said as he noticed a shadow glide across the back of the room.

"Aww, he's searching for food," said the second member before a third punched Peter in the back of the head. The blow stunned him before the pain brought him back to reality.

"So you think you can just come and steal our shit, man?" asked the member with the gun.

Peter winced as the pain in his head throbbed; he could feel a lump starting to form.

"Answer me!" he shouted.

Peter looked up as the man raised the gun over his head. "Answer me, I said!"

As he brought the handle of the gun down, Peter thought he saw a pair of glowing red eyes circle the back of the room just before he felt the impact.

"Bitch, you came into the wrong neighborhood!" the second man said.

"What have I gotten myself into?" Peter said as blood trickled down his forehead.

"Gonna make you wish you never woke up this morning!" one of the bangers said, punching Peter in the face.

Suddenly, Peter heard a voice, like a whisper, inside his head.

You run the power plant here in the city, correct?

Not sure if the voice was real or caused by the pain, but he felt compelled to answer. "Yes," Peter said out loud.

"Look at this dumb motherfucker!" said the gun-toting member. "Yes, what?" He punched Peter again.

If I help you, will you help me?

Just wanting it to be over, Peter replied, again out loud, "Yes."

"You have got to be the stupidest bitch left on Earth," the man punching him said, preparing for another.

Will you do exactly as I say? In exchange, I will let you live.

Peter's left eye had started to swell shut, and blood gushed from his nose and mouth. Two of his teeth had been knocked out. Between punches, Peter looked up and saw the blackened silhouette of a man, with glowing red eyes, standing near the bodies in the corner. Believing he was hearing the voice of Death itself, Peter said, for the third time out loud, "Yes."

"Know what, just kill this motherfucker!" the man punching him said to his friend with the gun.

You heard the man. Do it! a booming voice said, filling the room.

The three gang members looked around, trying to find from where the voice was coming. The ominous figure moved behind the man with the gun and reaching out a black arm, touched the thug's shoulder.

The gangbanger began screaming at the top of his lungs as pain coursed through his entire body, as if it were an electrical current. It must have been intense as urine soon stained the front of his pants and globs of shit fell onto his Nike's, leaving a stain on the white-and-red material before slopping onto the floor.

The two other gang members stood there, looking on in disbelief. Behind their friend stood some dark, shimmery form with piercing red eyes.

Peter sat watching, and could not believe what he was seeing.

The screaming man's arm started moving, until it was pointing the gun at the guy who had been punching Peter.

"Hey, Troy! Don't point that at me, man!" he said, stepping back and raising his arms.

The shadowy figure cocked his head to the side and the gun went off. Bullets tore into the man's chest, killing him.

The other gang member took off, running for the door.

But the evil presence shifted with unbelievable speed, and the screaming gunman turned with him. Troy's arm shot across the front of his body, causing the pitch of his scream to momentarily change. The gun fired in rapid succession. Four bullets found their mark, slamming into the back of the man running away, who also fell, dead, his body sliding to a halt.

Troy's body started twitching and shaking, his screams becoming so loud they hurt Peter's ears. The man's eyeballs bulged out of his head, and blood streamed from his nose. His screams turned into a high-pitched whine, which stopped suddenly only to be followed by a distinct pop as Troy's brain exploded inside his head. His lifeless body fell to the floor, gray brain matter oozing from his nose and ears like melted butter on top a pile of hot mashed potatoes.

Now Peter, I need you to go turn the power to the city back on, the voice said.

Chapter 10

Manhattan, New York

Glen blinked a few times and the black started to fade from his vision, moving from the pupil and gathering in the inside corner of his eyes. It felt like he had been sound asleep, and someone had woke him up in the middle of the night. His eyes burned from the flash, and the small puncture wound under his chin ached.

Glen reached down to his crotch and felt the wetness from him pissing himself, but felt something else, too: a full erection. He felt horny, the horniest he'd felt in a while. Looking around at all the dead bodies, he questioned how he could feel this way right now, especially since the act of sex was to create life and, well, he was surrounded by the opposite.

Glen looked to his right and noticed the ominous black figure standing off to the side of the road, its menacing red eyes staring at him. Turning away, he hoped it would be gone when he looked back— but it was still there.

The dark presence raised its arm and pointed at the tall buildings straight ahead.

Grabbing his bag, Glen exited the car. As soon as his shoes touched the ground, they became stuck in the slippery red current of blood. Looking down, Glen realized the blood had once been a vast river, but it had now crusted over. Tiny red rivers flowed through the cracks created within the layer of drying blood, reminding Glen of the beach after the tide receded when the water left little rivulets in the sand as it rushed away.

Glen found his footing and made his way carefully across the road. Gently, he placed each foot until sure it was sturdy, then he carefully transferred his weight from one foot to the next, trying his damnedest not to fall into the sea of blood.

When he was within a few feet of the roadside, he looked up to find the best place to cross. In some spots, the bodies were stacked four or five high.

Finding a place up ahead where the bodies were only two high, he started making his way over.

Furrowing his brow, Glen turned his head away from the disgusting sight of the black crows picking at the dead. The sound of their beaks pecking away at the flesh made his skin crawl. Smaller birds swooped in and attacked the hordes of flies that buzzed from body to body. The sound of their tiny wings flapping together created a loud constant buzz.

Leaving the dumping grounds, Glen turned onto Madison Ave and headed for the News Center. The only sound here was his footsteps echoing off the buildings. A memory came flooding back, from the last time he'd been here on an interview. It was ten years ago, and he had been doing the early morning broadcast at his local station when he got the call.

Joel, the station manager, had called him into his office once the morning report ended. Glen had been getting ready to meet one of the interns at the hotel down the street for some morning sex before heading back to the station for his lunchtime shift. Sandra, his wife, was at home sleeping as she worked nights as an ER nurse. Being on opposite shifts didn't help their relationship, and had made their sex life nonexistent.

Joel approached him as he exited the studio and said, "We need to talk. Can I see you for a moment in my office?"

Glen's heart raced, his palms sweating, and he wondered if Amber had told HR about their affair. He had quickly scanned the newsroom, searching for her, and caught a glimpse of that tiny little ass of hers as it exited out the back door to the parking lot. Glen swallowed hard and loosened his tie as he walked into Joel's office.

Joel motioned for Glen to sit. Fearing he was getting fired, Glen had literally sat on the edge of the seat.

"I just received a call," Joel said.

Glen hung his head low, wondering how he would explain the affair with Amber. His mind filled with different scenarios he could use:

She seduced me. Have you seen that ass?

Luckily, he didn't need to explain about the affair.

"I received a call from New York, and they want to see you right away. They have an opening coming up for the weekend morning show and they're calling all potential candidates to come in and interview," Joel said.

Glen couldn't believe his ears. "Really?" he'd asked.

"Yeah. They want you up there this weekend to meet with the cast and crew. Take Friday off and drive up there."

Glen now passed by a convenience store he had stopped at on the morning of his interview; all the windows were smashed, the inside ransacked.

He remembered the old man behind the counter, with a red turban and gray beard. The man had asked, with a thick Indian accent, if Glen was a news anchor.

"Well, actually, I'm here to interview for an opening. How did you know?"

"You look like a news anchor," the man had replied.

Glen took that as a sign he had the gig. If a local merchant thought he belonged, then hell, he belonged.

The memory faded, and Glen didn't feel any excitement like he had that day. He felt fear.

The walk down Madison Avenue had reminded him why he was here. He was to be the fresh face for the nation as it rebuilt, and he hoped the public would come to love him. He would deliver the news and make people feel safe.

In his heart, Glen was a good man, but he couldn't help himself when it came to the sins of the flesh.

Some time later, and a ways down the road, Glen heard shouting, and it sounded as though two men and a woman were arguing. There was then a loud, distinct gunshot, followed by the woman's screams, which were quickly silenced by another shot.

Making his way further down the street, Glen heard one man screaming from the side street up ahead. "You two-timing whore! Why did you cheat on me?"

As Glen approached the intersection, he spotted the woman's body lying on the ground and, after a few more paces, saw the man's body. Continuing quickly on, Glen could still hear the man talking to himself, although he couldn't see him as his voice bounced off the buildings and echoed down the desolate road.

Stepping over several bodies, Glen crossed to the other side of the street and onto the sidewalk. Pulling his coat tight he looked down, wanting to pass the scene without incident.

"Hey, man!" Glen heard. Turning his head, he saw the man leaning up against the side of the building at the edge of the side street.

"Where you are going, man?"

Glen dug his hands deeper into his coat pockets and trudged on.

"I'm talking to you!" the man shouted as he kicked off the wall and started after Glen.

"Did you fuck my girl, too?"

Glen tried to ignore the man, but could tell he was gaining ground.

"Get back here! You can't just fuck my woman and run off! I own these streets and you gotta pay for the pussy I provide!"

Turning his head, Glen looked back at the man, who was now pointing a gun at him.

"Pay up, motherfucker! I'll shoot you dead!"

Glen turned back, scoping out the area, looking for a place to run, when the dark apparition appeared up ahead, its eyes glowing red-hot. It moved fast, speeding past and creating a breeze similar to when a big truck drove past.

"What the fuck is that?" the man cried out.

The dark thing moved with impeccable speed.

"Fuck you!" the man yelled as he fired two quick shots. "Fuck yyoooouuuuu!" the man cried as his body went soaring through the air.

Glen turned back and watched as the man's body sailed backward and bounced off a car. The windshield cracked, and the driver's side front-end quarter-panel caved in, the impact causing the handgun to skid out into the road as the man's body rolled to the ground. Screaming in pain, the man tried to stand, but the femur in his right leg had snapped and one end now protruded through his torn pants. The man frantically looked down at his leg, then back up to the entity bearing down on him. As the presence closed in, the thug tried to scurry over to the handgun. Just as the darkness was on him, the man reached for the gun, held it up to his head, and pulled the trigger.

The man's lifeless body was now sprawled out in the street. The entity bent over, as if smelling its victim, and then turned back toward Glen, who was surprised to see it now had a more defined, human-like outline, and that its darkness had begun to fade, yet its eyes were still the color of molten lava.

Glen stood there, shocked by what he had just witnessed.

The thing, whatever it was, also stood there, staring back. Glen tilted his head to one side, trying to figure out what it was.

After a moment, it again raised its arm and pointed. Glen swore he could see the outline of its face, and that it now had a mouth, which suddenly opened. A sound escaped, louder than a whisper, and when it reached his ears he heard a single word: *Studio.* It was followed by another command: *Now!*

Glen immediately turned around and began walking. He had forgotten about the cold until a frigid blast of wind hit his face. As he walked, he realized something: he was no longer afraid. There is a certain amount of fear everyone has when they go into a big, unknown city; and even if you're from the city, some parts still scare you. Glen had been scared up until the point he'd realized that the thing was protecting him. Straightening his back, he walked a little taller, knowing he had his own demonic bodyguard. The thought of no one being able to hurt him got his imagination going, and he forgot about the cold again as he walked.

The city seemed smaller. Well, maybe not smaller, but faster to navigate. Without all the people crowding the sidewalks and cars lining the streets, he was making good time. After a twenty-minute walk, Glen reached the news studio.

Upon arrival, he found the studio's front windows had been covered up from the inside, and there was a sign taped to the glass which read, *Glen, go around back.*

Glen again felt uneasy as he rounded the corner, heading toward the back alley of the building.

Cautious, he made his way down the alley, stopping every few feet, listening. Creeping toward the end, he poked his head around the corner and saw the alley was empty. He stepped out.

From inside, Chris looked up as the flashing red light of a motion sensor caught his eye. A man had come around the corner of the back alley, tripping it, and now stood in the middle of the lane. A smile washed over Chris's face.

Glen just stood, staring down the empty alley. He looked up when he heard the buzz of a camera moving above him, and he looked directly at it and then smiled and waved.

After a minute, Glen heard the lock turn and the big brown door creaked open as a young man with a ragdoll hairstyle stepped out.

"Glen Daniels?" the man asked excitedly.

"That's me," Glen responded.

"I can't believe you're finally here. The studio is all set and ready to go. Come on in."

Once inside, Glen glanced around, concerned, and unsure of what he would find. Had looters gotten into the studio through the smashed-out windows at the front of the building?

Chris led him down a long hallway that came out to the studio.

Scanning the studio, Glen looked at the anchor desk and then over to the control room.

"We never lost power. Well, technically we didn't. There's a backup generator that has kept the lights on. I'm told the power to the building is being restored. Mr. Williams is kind of a survival freak. He has a stockpile of supplies and he's committed to getting the station back on the air." Chris said this all in one breath. Glen supposed it had been months since he'd last seen another person other than Mr. Williams, and couldn't contain his excitement.

Glen walked over to the anchor desk and stepped up onto the raised platform. It looked exactly as it had the last time he was here. He eyed the top, looking for any stain left behind from when Bethany died, but he didn't see a trace. It looked a little worn, though.

"Mr. Williams had me scrub that spot every day since he called you. I used bleach and a whole assortment of cleaning products. It's nice and clean."

Glen ran his hand across the spot. The table had a rough texture, except where it had been scrubbed. The surface there felt smooth. He pulled out the chair and looked at the seat. It was clean.

"Mr. Williams made me replace the chair. If you don't like it, we have a bunch of different ones down in the storage area."

Glen sat down. The chair felt nice. He looked straight ahead at the camera. He missed it. He missed telling the news. Glen had always loved how a great anchor could captivate an audience. They could make a person hold their pee, waiting for the story of the day. It was a unique power. The power of influence.

Over the years, Glen had grown tired of commenting on the news but he enjoyed reporting it. He had no interest in being part of the story, but the norm had grown so that a reporter put their own two cents in about the story. It felt fake, like one was trying to persuade the audience. Glen wanted to be great like Cronkite. One whose emotions came through as they read the news. It was how to make a powerful statement without words. The raised eyebrow. The teary eyes. People reacted to how he told the news, not his perception of it.

Glen wanted to change the world.

"There's something I want to show you," Chris said, making his way into the control room. "Mr. Williams had me create a video package for your first broadcast. Wanna see it?"

"Sure!"

Standing behind the panel, Chris pushed several keys and, after a moment, the large screen hanging on the wall came to life.

"This is incredible!" Glen said as he watched the monitor. "When did you film this? I didn't see any of this on my way here."

"I didn't film it," Chris said, looking over his shoulder as if to make sure they were alone.

Glen thought about it for a minute and, realizing he had seen no one else in the studio, asked, "What do you mean? Who did then?"

Chris rubbed his palms on his pants and looked over his shoulder again. His gaze scanned the studio beyond, but he must not have seen anyone, because looking back at the monitor again he said, "It's archive footage."

"From when?" Glen asked, "Because it looks current."

"Last year. They filmed it when they redeveloped the theater district."

"Okay, but why use old footage?"

"Mr. Williams thought it best to give the viewer the impression that things are getting better."

"But they're not. It's pretty bad out there. Trust me, I know," Glen said as he sat down and put his elbow on the table, resting his head in his palm.

"Did you really drive all the way from Ohio?"

"I did."

"What did you see?"

"A whole lot of death," he said.

"What's a lot?"

Glen slid his fingers across his forehead, until his middle finger and thumb rested on his eyebrows and the palm of his hand covered his eyes. Slowly, he began rubbing and pinching his eyebrows, shoulders hung low, and then said, "Trust me, kid, you don't want to know."

Chris then showed Glen to the suite he had prepared for his arrival. It wasn't much, but it had the creature comforts of home. There was a queen-sized bed up against the far wall; a laptop on top of a desk in the corner of the room; and in the opposite corner a small vanity with large, clear bulbs surrounding the mirror, with a stack of skin-tone make-up and a mason jar full of brushes.

"It's not much," Chris said.

Looking around, Glen said, "It will do."

"You must be starved," Chris said.

"I could use something to eat," Glen said as he patted his stomach.

"Well, I'll let you get settled in while I head downstairs and prepare something for you to eat."

"That would be perfect. Thank you, Chris."

"If you need anything, just let me know."

"I do have a question, though," Glen said.

"What is it?"

"When do I get to meet Mr. Williams?"

"You'll meet him at dinner. He's resting now."

"He's resting? I'd thought for sure he would have greeted me when I arrived."

Chris looked cautiously around, then said, "How do I say this? He's old and not in the greatest of health. Plus, he's cranky."

Glen chuckled. "I've heard that about him."

Chapter 11

I-95, Florida

"Steve, come on! He's almost out of sight!" Cass shouted as she slung her pack over her shoulder and started walking, but stopped after a few steps.

Grant stood there, not knowing what to do. One minute they'd been talking, but the next Drew was on his feet and hauling ass down the road. For a man who had just been shot, he was moving.

"Does he really think he'll be home tonight or something?" Steve asked, cinching up his pack.

"No, but at that pace he might be there tomorrow," Grant said with a chuckle.

With everything that had happened in the last twenty-four hours, it surprised Steve to hear Cass snicker at Grant's comment. Looking down the road and seeing Drew cresting the horizon provided him with an uneasy feeling. The last time he'd watched his friend disappear over the horizon, the group had come under attack and he'd watched his young friends be executed.

"Come on, Steve," Cass said again, this time giving chase to her guardian.

The first hour was the worst. Drew's foot was killing him, but he didn't care about the pain or that it was bleeding. Hell, he didn't care about those he'd left behind. All he cared about was getting home to Annabelle and Stephanie. They were his life; they were what mattered.

They were what kept him alive. Like always, he followed his gut, and his gut was telling him that they were in danger. It didn't matter that he had another seven hundred and fifty miles to go. He would push on. Push on through the pain.

Deep inside, an old anger rekindled, burning hot. Wincing with every step, Drew still didn't care. He recalled all the horrible things that had happened to him as a child, things he'd thought would kill him but only strengthened him. Slowing briefly, he pondered if he had suffered through all that to be here now. To use it as fuel to survive. Yes, to survive. Drew Murphy was a fighter, and that is what he would do. Fight and survive.

"Damn you, Drew!" Steve said under his breath as he slung on his pack.

Grant followed, but only because it was the way back toward the retreat.

The sun was now high in the sky, and Drew was still a speck on the horizon. Every few miles, they'd find a small discarded bottle of booze. Discarded fuel cans. Like a trail of breadcrumbs. But they all knew how that children's fable ends. Steve couldn't help but be impressed because even with his injuries, Drew maintained a hefty pace.

It was late afternoon by the time they caught up to Drew, who was sitting on the fender of an abandoned car. He'd depleted all of his anger for the day, but Cass' was in full roar, knowing what had happened to her friends and upset at having to deal with this new life. It was anger that had been raging inside, just waiting to be released.

Steve arrived a minute later, panting and searching for his canteen.

"What's your problem?" she screamed when she was ten feet away from Drew. He looked up, took a long pull off a bottle, sucking it dry, then rolled his eyes before chucking the empty into the woods.

"So, you're just gonna abandon us?" Cass screamed as she dropped her pack and knelt down in front of Drew.

Drew had now cupped one hand inside the other, resting his chin on them.

She opened her pack and pulled out the medical supplies, then laid them next to Drew's blood-drenched foot.

"Well?" she asked, looking up into his eyes. Steve knew she was hoping to find an answer, expected to find guilt or shame, or at least hoped she would. But he knew she found neither. What they both saw was something dark, a fierce intensity behind those blue eyes of his. They stared at them, piercing through them like they weren't there. Like they didn't exist. Cold eyes. Like the eyes of a shark before it attacks.

"Jesus, are you drinking booze or jet fuel?" Grant asked, stopping next to Steve.

Drew looked up with those same burning, intense eyes.

"Whoa!" Grant said, as if he had been punched from the hard look Drew gave him.

Cass finished tending to Drew's foot and then they made camp at the side of the road. Drew wanted to push on, but exhaustion was setting in. They had pushed themselves hard today, and now their bodies were paying for it. Plus, it would soon be dark, and with the cloud cover overhead, there was no light from the moon, making traveling at night impossible with all the hidden obstacles.

Drew stated that the sooner he went to sleep, the sooner he would wake up and could continue on his way home. Grabbing a can of beans, he scarfed them down. Once done, he bunked down for the night and within a minute was out cold.

Steve and Cass spoke with Grant for a little while. Eventually, he looked up and saw the sun would soon set.

"I should get back to my wife," Grant said.

"What will you say when you get back?" Steve asked.

"I don't know yet," Grant replied.

"You can't tell them the truth," Cass said, poking a stick at the empty can of beans.

"If you do, there'll be a lot of resentment toward you because you lived and their spouses did not," Steve said.

"I'm not sure what to do. But I need to do something," Grant said, standing up.

Both Steve and Cass also stood and Cass stepped toward Grant, giving him a brief hug. Steve held out his hand and Grant accepted it, and the men shook hands. "You know you and your wife are more than welcome to travel north with us."

Grant nodded and said, "Tell the big guy goodbye for me, please."

"We will," Cass said.

"Goodbye," Grant said. He then turned and walked away.

Cass stood next to Steve and, leaning over she rested her head on his shoulder as they watched Grant disappear, swallowed up by the horizon.

"Jesus, that man can snore," Cass said, looking over at Drew lying in his sleeping bag.

They both chuckled.

"Come on, we better start a fire," Steve said, and they walked off to the side of the road in search of firewood.

Chapter 12

Stoughton, Massachusetts

"Hey, man, I thought you said they'd be asleep!" one boy said excitedly, standing in the kitchen.

"Well, if you weren't so loud, she wouldn't have heard us," replied another.

"Let's get what we came for and get out," said a third boy.

They finished tossing the food from the freezer and the pantry into their pillowcases.

"Okay, let's get outta here," the leader said.

The four boys took off, running down the stairs into the basement.

Outside, another boy waited. Assigned generator duty, he'd disconnected it and gotten it ready for transport, which he had done with ease. His grandfather used to have one, and he'd helped with it during those cold New England storms. He was standing in the basement doorway, watching for his friends, when he heard gunshots followed by what sounded like a herd of elephants coming down the stairs. Flashlight beams danced across the walls and ceiling as the four boys came pouring into the basement.

"What happened? Did you shoot someone?" the boy waiting asked, clearly scared.

"No, they were warning shots. Did you finish disconnecting the generator?" Tommy, the leader, asked.

"Yeah, it's all set. I'll need a hand carrying it, though."

The five boys exited through the back door. Two grabbed the generator while the rest hauled off with the loot. They would eat well tonight.

Everything had happened so quickly. Susan woke up to the sound of a gun, and before she could get out of bed she heard the heavy footsteps of people running down the cellar stairs and out the back door. She went over to the window and peeked through the blinds, spotting the boys running from the house and laughing. The last boy, carrying a gas can, turned to look back to make sure they weren't being followed, his flashlight illuminating his face.

"Thomas Welch," Susan said out loud as she watched the boys run into the darkness, until she could no longer see their dancing flashlight beams.

Tommy Welch lived diagonally across the street from Susan. As a child Tommy would come over and hang out with Howie, her husband. Tommy's dad hadn't been around much as he'd traveled a lot for work, so the boy clung to any male attention he could get. As the boy grew older, he mowed their lawn for spending money, but then in his teenage years he'd gotten involved with the wrong crowd. Before long, Tommy was getting into trouble both in and out of school. Howie tried talking to him, but Tommy wanted no part of it and told Howie to fuck off and that he wasn't his father. Howie had scolded the boy, telling him he was lucky he wasn't his son, because if he was he'd knock some sense into him. Tommy just laughed. Ever since then, Susan had had a dislike for the boy.

Susan turned and ran to her daughter's room. She tried the door, but it was locked.

"Annabelle, it's me. Mom. Open up!"

Annabelle unlocked the door, letting her mother in, and together the three women, including her mother, huddled in the corner, draped in a comforter. After a period of time, Susan said, "I don't hear anything. I think they all left."

Annabelle pulled Stephanie closer as her mother stood up.

"Mom! What are you doing?"

"I'm going to see if they're gone," Susan said, exiting the bedroom and closing the door behind her. As soon as she entered the hallway, she was hit by a blast of frigid air. Slipping into her room, Susan grabbed her flashlight and made her way down the hall. As she passed the basement door, she felt the cold air creeping in from down below.

Slowly making her way into the kitchen, she swept the flashlight from left to right, checking to make sure no one else was in the house.

Her heart sank when she rounded the corner and saw the freezer door hanging open. Hoping there was something left, she looked inside. Empty. Grabbing the handle of the fridge, she pulled open the door and shone the light inside. Standing there, tears welled up and streamed down her face. The only things left were the condiments on the door. *They even took the butter*, she thought.

Standing there in her nightgown, fear turned to anger. Storming down the basement stairs, she found the back door wide open. The molding had splintered from being pried open, causing a long, thin white strip of wood to tear off; it hung haplessly, tiny pieces of wood peppering the floor.

Susan searched her late husband's work bench until she found what she was looking for. Picking up a hammer in one hand she reached into one of the mason jars sitting on the sill of the bench with her other, pulling out a few long nails. Next, she found a length of two-by-four. Then, resting the flashlight on the bench, she aimed the beam at the door and nailed the piece of wood across the door, rendering it useless.

"Mom, what are you doing?" Annabelle called down.

"I'm making it so they can't get back in," Susan shouted, putting the hammer back on the bench before heading up the stairs.

Annabelle stood in the doorway, holding a hand in front of her face to block the light from her mother's flashlight.

"Did they take the generator?" Annabelle asked.

"Yes, and all the food from the upstairs fridge and freezer."

"No!"

"Yup and they wiped out the pantry, too."

Just before dawn, they heard their generator start up. Susan looked out the window just as the lights flickered to life inside Tommy's house.

Chapter 13

Rockefeller Center, New York

Sitting there, staring into the blackness of whatever was before him, the entity released its finger from Mr. Williams's shoulder. Taking a long, loud draw of breath, life returned to what had been nearly dead. The pain that coursed through the older man's body finally ended, and he felt lucky to be alive.

Do as I say, Mr. Williams heard, knowing it came from the entity.

Searching it with his gaze, Mr. Williams saw no real features other than it appeared to look like a silhouette of a man with glowing, red-hot eyes. Wisps of darkness rose from it, which reminded him of solar flares escaping from the sun, except instead of being bright they were of the darkest black, like the depths of space. Swirling, they ascended then, without warning, banked downward, as if being sucked in, and disappeared back into the larger mass. The light surrounding the visitor appeared to fade and discolor, as if it were being consumed by the specter.

Do as I say, it commanded.

"Yes," Mr. Williams said dryly.

The entity reached out its arm and touched Mr. Williams again, placing its hand on his chest, just above his heart. Tiny sparks formed inside the dark appendage, which slowly began to spin. At first, they were barely noticeable, but as they spun faster and faster the lights grew in intensity. The rest of the being kept its solid, black onyx color. The reflection of the swirling lights danced across the room, like that from a disco ball, and the air inside the room churned, causing the papers on the desk to slide off.

Using its other arm, the shadow figure reached out and placed its index finger above the pill bottle. An individual spark shot out from the swirling lights. It streaked across the demon's chest, down its other arm, and exited the tip of its finger. Mr. Williams heard a clink as a tiny white pill bounced off the bottom of the plastic bottle. One by one, sparks launched across the darkness of the presence, filling the container. A few pills landed on the desk, spinning to a stop, while others rolled and fell to the floor.

Take every day or die, Mr. Williams heard.

"Take every day or die," he repeated as he picked up a pill and placed it under his tongue.

The twirling lights inside the figure's arm slowed. As they came to a stop, the sparks burned out and dissipated. Once they were gone, it removed its hand from Mr. Williams and stepped back.

The pounding in his head subsided as his blood pressure dropped, leaving him light-headed and woozy. Mr. Williams leaned back in his chair and, after a moment, the feeling passed. Sitting there, he noticed something different. It took a second to realize what it was, but then it hit: He felt great. Better than he had in years. Both the pain in his chest and his anxiety had disappeared. It was incredible; the fear, and the dread, of dying no longer existed.

Live for me and I will grant you immortality, the being said.

Looking at the shadowy form and staring into its molten eyes, Mr. Williams said, "I live for you."

The entity moved around the room, and as it moved Mr. Williams heard the voice say, *Electrician. Woman. Coming.*

"There's an electrician and a woman coming?" Mr. Williams asked.

Yes

"I take it the electrician is coming to fix our power problem?" the old man asked.

Yes

"I'll let Chris know to let them in," Mr. Williams said as he reached for the phone. When he looked back up, the form had vanished.

Getting up, Mr. Williams walked over to the window and looked out over the city. The sun warmed his face and he basked in it for a moment, glad to be alive. Whatever that thing was, he knew it had given him a new lease on life.

Glen finished unpacking and sat down at the vanity in his room. Gazing around, he was glad to finally be here and looked forward to getting back to work. Glimpsing himself in the mirror, Glen stared at his reflection. He looked like shit, and felt like it too. He felt the overwhelm wash over him as his mind went back to what had happened, and the things he'd seen, while making his journey here. Holding his hands up to his face, he wept, thankful to be alive. After a few moments, Glen composed himself. Wiping the tears from his eyes, he grabbed his toiletries and made his way into the bathroom to take a long, hot shower.

Chris returned to the control room after showing Glen to his suite. He had started reviewing the video news package that would accompany Glen's opening monologue when something on the monitor for the back alley caught his attention. It appeared as if the sunlight had dimmed and night had fallen, yet all the other monitors around the building were displaying daylight.

"Isn't that strange?" Chris asked out loud.

Just then the phone rang, startling him. Picking up the receiver, he held it to his ear.

"Has he arrived yet?" Mr. Williams asked, sounding back to his old self again.

"Yes, sir. He arrived a little while ago. I showed him to his room, and he is unpacking."

"Good. I want to meet him as soon as possible," the old man said.

"That's good because he was asking to meet you."

"Once he's done unpacking, give him the code and send him up."

"Yes sir," Chris responded.

"Oh, and one other thing. There should be an electrician and a woman arriving soon. Tell the electrician what you told me regarding our power issue, and show the woman up to my suite when she arrives."

"A woman?" Chris asked.

"Yes," the old man said, then hung up.

Chris put the phone back in its cradle and looked back up at the monitor. The back alley was now pitch-black, and he wondered if the camera had malfunctioned. Pressing the power button, he hoped it would reset and fix whatever the problem was. Counting to ten, he pushed the button again. The monitor displayed the same darkness. Chris had stood up to go and manually inspect the camera when a flash on the screen caught his eye. Looking back at the monitor he watched the darkness fade, as if the sunlight was consuming it. He was transfixed on the darkness, which was constricting and disappearing like water down a drain.

Focusing on the black spot, Chris didn't notice the beautiful woman standing in the alleyway. It took a few seconds for his mind to catch up, as if time had somehow slowed down— or even stopped.

Movement on the screen took him out of his daze, and it felt as though he had suddenly awakened from a deep sleep. The gears in his mind started turning. Grabbing his keys, Chris made his way toward the back door.

Chapter 14

Rockefeller Center, New York

Kendra was in shock. One moment her body was walking down a street on the outskirts of Orlando, and the next moment she was surrounded by skyscrapers. The temperature went from balmy to downright freezing and, although she couldn't feel it, she could see her own breath. She couldn't feel anything at all because everything she ever was, was now no more. Now, she was just mere consciousness, reduced to self-aware thoughts, capable of thinking but nothing more.

Her physical connection to the world was gone, severed and taken away by the needle. She no longer made assumptions about where she was, for now she knew. She had heard stories about this place before, from children she'd grown up with who went to Sunday School classes at the local Catholic church. She'd also seen it in a movie once, but this… this was real; her existence was trapped, confined to a place with no others, to pay for the sins of the flesh. This place, her cell, was where she always knew she'd end up. Welcome home, she thought. Welcome to purgatory.

Kendra's body stood looking down an alley, at dozens of tall buildings dotting the horizon. It too was deserted and silent, just like Orlando had been. She heard the creak of a door, and her body started moving again.

The back door of the studio swung open, bathing the hallway in natural light. It took a second for Chris's eyes to adjust to the sunlight, which felt good on his face, especially after being cooped up indoors for so long. *My Lord!* Chris thought as the stunningly beautiful woman stepped into view. She was slightly shorter than him, with a full head of luscious auburn hair and the most stunning emerald green eyes he had ever seen. Her skin was a pasty white, reminding him of the mother on the TV show *The Munsters*, which he used to watch as a child sitting in his grandfather's lap.

"Hey, I'm Chris," he said, his voice cracking like it did when he was a teenager.

Instantly, she noticed the man's eyes staring at her chest, eyeing her up and down. Many women hated men ogling their breasts, but she'd never had a problem with it, especially given her line of work. Hell, she wouldn't have worked as a stripper if she minded men staring at her.

But now it stung, and she knew what those women had felt. For the first time, it felt as if she was being seen, but not being seen, at the same time. Now, she realized what those women meant. Before she'd had control over men once they'd seen her, but now she had none. She was just a piece of meat to this man. Something he probably wanted to have his way with, and then discard like trash. To Kendra, it had always been about money and control. Now she had neither. All she had was herself, just like when she was a teenager and her stepfather and his friends had had their way with her. As she'd grown older, she learned to understand the dynamics of control and then flipped it, taking her life back. Yet now, like then, she no longer had control. She was a prisoner in her own body. Trapped in her own head.

"Down the hall and to the right," Chris said, watching the woman's backside. Closing the door, he slid the deadbolt and scurried after her. As she turned the corner, he glimpsed her side profile and stared at the curve of her breasts. They looked amazing, and he thought back to the last time he'd seen a nice rack.

Bethany immediately popped into his head, and his excitement rapidly diminished. She was the sexy news anchor who'd used her looks to her advantage. It was an added bonus for the male viewers, as Bethany was a winning trifecta: intelligent, sexy, and talented. Using her charm, she could get a story out of anyone who was reluctant and did not want to be interviewed. She'd also died at the news desk, live on TV. Recalling watching her die of the sickness, then having to scrub her blood off the anchor's desk, really took the wind out of his sails.

Mr. Williams had just finished introducing himself to Glen, when Glen caught sight of Kendra and froze in place, his mouth gaping open, staring at her with immediate lust.

Seeing the look on Glen's face, Mr. Williams turned and damn near had another heart attack. Thankfully, he'd gotten a fresh supply of pills because, if not, his heart wouldn't have survived the excitement he felt in that moment at the sight of the woman. She really got his blood flowing.

It had been months since either of them had seen a woman, never mind one as sexy as the one before them now.

A smile appeared on Glen's face as he looked her over from top to bottom. Kendra's auburn hair hung over her shoulders, and his eyes followed the contours of her body. The natural formation of her hips led his eyes to her pubic region, which looked very enticing in her skintight black leggings, and he was instantly aroused.

"Our friend said to expect a woman, but by God, I wasn't expecting anything like her," the old man said, adjusting his tie.

Chris circled around the room, never taking his eyes off Kendra, as he stood next to Glen and Mr. Williams.

Kendra watched as the three men stared and ogled her body.

Even though physically trapped, her mind still worked, and she sized up the men standing before her. The brown, shaggy-haired one — who let her in — was one of those men she knew she could control and bend to her will. Years of working at the strip club had provided her with a keen sense on how to read a man. The other one, the short-haired blond one, dressed in the expensive suit, exuded charm and charisma, and was clearly the type who knew what he wanted: sex. She could read the telltale signs of a ladies' man a mile away, and he fit the bill. A living definition.

The old man stood there, staring, his mouth open like some dumb fish. Believe it or not, she had seen a lot of men like him back in the strip club. Rich men who lacked personality and who usually had a small prick; hence why, in life, they lived large, literally trying to make up for their shortcomings.

The dark thing appeared next to her and placed its hand on her back. She felt pain, like an electrical shock. Even in her little prison, she felt it. It was the first thing she'd felt since the day the darkness had enveloped her. Reminding her that she was still cognizant and alive, the pain waned to a dull numbness. Either way, it reminded her that she was in hell. Living hell.

She tried slapping herself in the face, wanting to wake herself out of this nightmare. As the pain coursed through her, what was left of her anyway, her hand shot up and she succeeded.

The dark thing pressed harder, intensifying the pain, and she screamed internally.

She watched as the well-dressed man sauntered over, a whimsical charm about him. That smug, I-can-have-any-woman-I-want bravado. If she had control over her own body, she would have put him to shame. She saw him for who he was and what he was — weak. To him, women were a conquest. She'd seen it a million times: Men trying to prove something with their dicks. She knew all men weren't that way, just as all women weren't sluts like her. It was a choice. Something she now regretted. Something that had been forged from abuse. She had taken control of what others used to take from her; and she didn't do it because she had to, but because she wanted to. It was her escape mechanism. It was her taking back her life.

She felt the numbness coursing through her for a brief time, allowing her a sliver of control. If she was able to feel again, could life come back to her body? Kendra realized when the thing touched her that she may be able to regain control.

Her body seemed like it was working from muscle memory because she could tell it had just leaned against the doorframe. Looking down, she watched as her arms crossed underneath her bosom and lifted up her tits. Then her body slid to the right and slightly bent as she moved, exposing her cleavage.

"Hey, Glen," said a cold, sexy voice.

It took her a second to realize it was her own voice speaking. It sounded weird, like when you heard yourself on a recording or in a video. That constant conversation she'd been having with herself, while trapped inside her head, did not accompany a voice. Hearing her own voice, while not speaking, was hard for her to understand. It took her a second to realize that the evil thing was using the numbness to control her. Was there anything it could not control?

The woman brought her index finger up to her mouth, gently sucking on it.

Glen was frozen by her sexual lure and prowess. Pulling her moist finger out of her mouth, she slowly reached out and pressed it against Glen's lips, then slowly started circling his lips with the tip of her finger.

"Do you like?" she asked.

"Yes," Glen said, starting to feel excited.

Mr. Williams was focusing on her chest, and Glen noticed her supple nipples poking through the thin material of her shirt. "What a beauty It has bestowed upon us," he said, just above a whisper.

Looking out of the corner of his eye at the old man, Chris wondered who the "It" was. Then he noticed his boss was licking his own lips and that the older man's hand was moving inside his pants pocket.

Disgusting, Chris thought. *I'm better suited to be with her instead of blondie there, or Mr. Old crusty over here*, he added, adjusting his trousers and trying to hide his own semi-erection.

Kendra felt the numbness turn to tingles, followed by a strong electrical current coursing throughout her body as the entity behind her applied more pressure to her back. Inside her head, it sounded like TV static that had been turned all the way up. It cut right through her, drowning out her voice inside her prison cell. The sound was incredibly annoying, and prohibited her from thinking. It felt like she was being bounced from wall to wall inside her tomb, robbed of her ability to focus.

Kendra clung to nothingness, hoping it would end soon, which it did.

When it finally stopped, and she had her thoughts back, she looked out of her eyes and saw the blond-haired man leading her down the hall and into a bedroom, closing the door behind them.

Chapter 15

Harlem, New York

In pain, Peter sat watching as small, entrail-like tubes snaked toward him from the dark entity. Eyes wide, Peter noticed tiny dots of light starting to swirl around inside its appendages. He watched with bated breath as one of the protuberances headed straight for him; one brushed up against his knee, and an immediate numbness ran down his leg. It continued making its way around his waist, heading for the plastic zip tie cuffing his hands together. The demon's eyes grew with intensity, and a bright light streaked through the appendage. As it shot through the tube-like limb, Peter noticed the light had a tail, reminding him of a comet or shooting star, and the way it streaks across the night sky.

Peter sighed in relief, his hands now untied. Rubbing the red indentations on his wrist, Peter looked up at the entity before him. The other tubular appendage slowly rose into the air, looking like a King Cobra prepared to strike — which it did. With impeccable speed, it shot straight at Peter's head, striking and attaching itself to his left temple.

Hello Peter, Peter heard inside his head. *I have let you live, and now I need you to help me.*

There was a sharp, stinging pain where the tentacle-like thing attached to his head.

Don't, Peter heard inside his head as he thought of reaching up and tearing it off, followed by a burning pain that coursed throughout his body.

Relax and this will go more easily, Peter then heard. Closing his eyes, Peter took a deep breath and tried relaxing his body. As he did, the burning sensation waned.

Memories started to appear in his mind and, after a minute, Peter realized it was not he who was thinking them, it was the entity going through his memories. His memories flipped, faster and faster, as if they were pages in a book. The memories then stopped, and Peter found himself recalling his wedding day. The images spun again, stopping at the birth of his children.

Inside his head, Peter heard his instructions. First, he was to pick up the gun on the floor before him to use as protection. Then he was to load up the shopping cart in the corner with food and supplies for his family, and get a good night's rest. But first, he was told to head over to the WTFH studio and figure out a way to restore the power. In the morning, he was to pack up and head over to the news studio, where he and his family would make a new home.

Peter was then told to oversee the restoration of power and help ensure the station could broadcast. The tentacle then detached itself from Peter's head, leaving a bright red mark on the side of his forehead.

Reluctantly, Peter picked up the pistol, on which were small gray pieces of brain matter. After wiping it clean, he tucked it behind his back, into his waistband. Then, Peter loaded the carriage and headed out.

Cutting down Park Avenue brought Peter directly to the studio. Making his way around back, he parked the shopping cart across from the back door and rang the bell.

The chime for the back entrance scared Chris, who was sitting at the control panel piecing together different videos. Making his way toward the back door for the third time that day, Chris found it funny that he hadn't seen anyone in weeks but now people were coming out of the woodwork.

"Hi, I'm Peter. I was told you have an issue with your power?"

Chris stood there, staring.

"You should see the other guy," Peter said realizing how he looked with his beaten and bloody self, which was exactly how he felt.

Chris looked over his shoulder at the shopping cart.

"It's food and supplies for my family," Peter said.

"Any tools?" Chris asked.

"Not with me."

"How do you plan on fixing our problem?"

"I'm here to scope it first. Plus I don't think the problem is with the building but with the underground power lines, either that or the plant itself is down, killing the power to this grid."

"Oh, really?" Chris said, poking his head around the door as if he could see them.

"How long have you been here?" Peter asked.

"Since the sickness hit," Chris said, then seemed to realize he should invite Peter in as he added,. "Please, come in."

"Can you show me to your electrical rooms?"

"Sure," Chris said. "Right this way."

Peter followed the younger man down the hallway, noticing the lights were on. "I guess you have a generator?" he asked.

"We do, but it doesn't have enough juice for us to broadcast. We've been using it ever since the power went out. I think it's tired now," Chris said.

Peter rounded the corner of the long hallway, and his eyes widened. Standing still for a moment, he gazed around in awe at the newsroom before him. He had seen them on TV before, but the vast size was lost on the screen. Off to his left were workstations, a lunchroom beyond them, and the scenery to his right was impressive. The anchor's desk sat on a raised platform, with four large cameras spaced out in front. Past the cameras, Peter could see the control room, which had a large control panel and over a dozen TVs on the side wall.

Peter inspected the power rooms, and everything looked good. Walking around the building, he found nothing out of the norm. He then asked Chris for a pen and pad of paper, and set out, walking each block in a grid pattern, searching for any obvious problems and seeing if the power was on in any of the nearby blocks.

Peter spent the rest of the day scoping out the area, then headed back. He reported what he'd found to Chris, who picked up the phone and spoke for a moment, then said, "Mr. Williams would like to see you upstairs."

Getting off the elevator, Peter could sense something sinister, and upon entering the office noticed the black shadowy thing standing next to the old man, who sat at the desk.

"Ah, you must be Peter. My friend here told me to expect you. I'm Mr. Williams and I own the station."

Peter said hello, but couldn't take his eyes off the form in the room.

"What's the situation with the power?" Mr. Williams asked.

Peter broke his gaze from the apparition and looked at the man in the chair, explaining what he had found and telling Mr. Williams he would need between ten and twenty men to restore the power to the building. Explaining what it would entail, Peter also informed them that the power plant was probably offline, and he would need to get it back up and running.

Mr. Williams looked to the force in the room, then nodded. Peter assumed the figure was speaking to the gentleman in private, as it had done with him.

"What do you think the timeline will be to get the power restored here to the studio?"

Peter thought about what he'd have to do. The first priority would be to get into the plant, then to get the tools and equipment to make the repairs, and then to get the plant up and running. "A couple days, maybe less, depending on how many helpers I have," Peter responded.

"Okay," Mr. Williams said, after looking at the shadowy form.

"What about the men to help me?" Peter asked.

Mr. Williams stared at the specter for a few moments and then said, "Go home tonight. Feed your family, and in the morning bring them here. We'll have one of the suites set up. After that, head over to the plant and we'll have men waiting."

"All right," Peter said, noticing the kid who'd brought him upstairs never looked at the presence. He wondered if he couldn't see it.

"Will you please show our guest out?" Mr. Williams asked Chris.

"This way," Chris said, turning and walking out of the office.

The sun was just starting to set when Peter arrived back home. His wife and children were excited to see him, and elated he had successfully found food. Cindy tended to the wounds on his face, then they all ate well and went to bed with full bellies.

Later that night, something happened that hadn't happened in years. While lying in bed, he felt his wife's fingers on his back. Soon, they made their way across his hip and down the front of his pants. Cupping his penis, she slowly stroked him until he was erect. Rolling onto his back, she kissed him passionately before removing his pants.

Climbing on top, she then took him inside her and rode him slowly until they both climaxed.

Drifting off to sleep, Peter couldn't help but feel thankful for all that had happened that day. From being saved to having food to feed his family and to the happy ending to the day. He knew he owed it all to the dark phantom— none of it would have been possible without it. Looking forward to getting back to work, Peter fell into a deep, sound sleep.

The next morning, Peter did as instructed and packed up his family and headed for the studio. He explained that he'd met someone, leaving out the detail of who, for his wife would surely assume he was crazy, and that these people needed his help to turn the power back on— and to keep it on— so they, in exchange, could stay in the secured building with food and supplies.

Peter arrived at the studio on time, and Chris showed the girls to their new suite. Upon arrival, they found Mr. Williams waiting for them and it surprised Peter at how well Mr. Williams treated the kids. He was expecting more of a Scrooge, but he turned out to be like a Bob Cratchit.

"There is a group of men already waiting for you down at the plant," Mr. Williams told Peter.

"Wow, that was fast," he replied.

"Our friend works in mysterious ways," Mr. Williams said with a wink.

"You ain't kidding."

"Good luck."

"Thanks," he said, and with that Peter kissed his wife and kids and then headed down to out.

Coming around the corner, Peter found fifteen men standing in a circle. They had been discussing how they'd survived the plague, and the Shadow Man. It, as some referred to the figure and He by others, and how that, in their worst time, it had seemed to appear, providing an opportunity to get out of whatever life-threatening situation they had found themselves.

The rugged men looked up as Peter approached.

"Are you Peter?" one of the men from the circle yelled.

"Yes," Peter responded, not sure how they knew his name.

"We've been sent to help you," the man yelled back.

Peter walked toward the group and two men stepped aside, creating a hole in the perimeter of the circle.

Peter stood in the middle, slowly turning, looking at each man.

"You all know why you're here, right?"

A few men answered "Yeah," while others nodded.

"Does any man here have experience working on power lines?" Peter asked.

Every man shook their head.

"Well, I can tell you that in a month's time some of you won't be here anymore."

One man gasped while another said, "Okay. But we're under the dark man's protection. We can't die."

"That's right, or we'd already be dead," said a scrawny, middle-aged white man.

"I can't speak for him, but I can tell you this is a numbers game and we always lose numbers. No matter how good men were, we lost them. And, before you speak up again, I'm sure it was him, the dark man, that came and took those men," Peter said.

"You got that right, mister," a big black man said.

A skinny white kid, who looked like he'd just come off a seven-day binge, said, "He ain't gonna let us die. He's our new god."

"Damn straight," said another man.

"Yeah. I never believed in that long-haired hippie Jesus, anyway. My dark friend saved me when no one else would. He's the real Messiah," said another.

"It doesn't matter what we think. We all made a promise to be here today. I say we keep it in exchange for tomorrow," Peter said.

"Right on, brother," said a Latino man, who fist bumped the man standing next to him.

"Well, we've got some training to do before we can make repairs and get the power back online. I'll give you a tour of the plant, and show you how things work in the power industry. After that, we'll begin your training on how to repair the transmission lines," Peter said.

Peter finished giving the men the twenty-five cent tour. Most could barely read, let alone understand something as complex as a power plant, so it was pointless to waste time explaining. Plus, he figured most would die from electrical shock.

After the tour, he led the men to a secure area and then through a series of doors. They passed a break room and entered a large locker room, lined with wooden cubbies. Each bin held a tool belt and an assortment of tools and equipment. Peter began giving his crash course on how to restore the power.

Chapter 16

Paxton, Nebraska

Maureen woke the next morning, those glowing red eyes staring from the crops burned into her mind's eye. Worse was the sound of that haunting voice saying her name, which still rang around inside her head.

For some strange reason, the voice had seemed familiar but she couldn't put her finger on where she'd heard it before. She looked down and found her hands were trembling.

Trying to convince herself she had not seen what she'd thought last night, Maureen told herself she must have nodded off and it had just been a dream. Yet, staring at the ceiling, those red eyes seemed to be everywhere she looked— like when a flash goes off and all you see is the white ring of light. Getting out of bed, she dressed and headed downstairs to start breakfast.

Bill soon returned from the barn and sat down at the kitchen table. Breakfast was served every morning at eight: bacon, eggs, toast, and a cup of black coffee. Even though the rest of the world had stopped working, there was still a lot to do on a farm. The animals needed feeding, and their stalls cleaning. If the end of humanity really was here, they could survive for quite a while off of the animals and the crops.

The clang of silverware, and her husband and two boys chewing, were the only noises in the kitchen. The red stove light was on, indicating the surface was hot. Maureen couldn't help but stare at the glowing light. It reminded her of what she'd seen last night. Her entire body flinched as the light doubled and now two red lights were staring at her.

The lights, burning red-hot, grew in intensity and Maureen slowly backed away from the oven. The ruby eyes grew larger.

It must have been bad nicotine, she thought, backing up to get away. She backed up until she bumped into Bill's chair, knocking the eggs from his fork.

"Um… Excuse me," Bill said, stabbing another forkful.

"Oh, sorry, dear."

"Are you okay Mom?" Caleb, the older of the two boys, asked.

"Yeah, it was probably just old nicotine," she said out loud.

"Nicotine?" Bill asked.

"You don't smoke, Mom," Eben, her other son, said.

Realizing she'd spoken out loud, Maureen quickly thought of something to cover her slip. "Oh no, dear, I was thinking about the book I'm reading."

Bill looked at both boys and raised his eyebrows, causing them both to laugh.

"Oh stop, you," Maureen said, hitting her husband playfully with her apron. Looking back at the stove, there was now just the one light.

How old were those cigarettes? Were they laced? she wondered, still trying to force the images, and the voice, from last night from her head. But they kept popping up, and she had an overwhelming feeling she would see them again.

"Well, wish me luck!" Bill said after breakfast.

"Good luck, Dad!" both boys said in unison.

Maureen handed him the lunch she'd packed and kissed him goodbye. Bill grabbed one of his handguns and a rifle, and headed out to the pickup parked next to the barn. The screen door slammed behind Maureen and the boys, who had come out to wave goodbye from the porch.

Bill gave a *toot-toot* of the horn as he drove away, dust following the truck down the dirt driveway.

"Okay, boys, back to your chores."

"But, Mom, we already finished them," Caleb said.

"Yeah can't we go play, Mom? Please!" asked Eben.

"Oh, okay. But be back for lunch."

Both boys shot back into the house and up the stairs to finish their video game, which had been on pause since early this morning.

It was a little after ten when Bill arrived in town. Pulling into the grocery store parking lot, he was surprised to find it full of cars and people.

Chapter 17

Jacksonville, Florida

Grant hurried down the dirt road toward the retreat. He wasn't fully sure what to tell the women once he returned, but he knew he couldn't tell them the truth. How would that go over? *Sorry, all of your husbands are dead because they were a bunch of murdering rapists.* Yeah, that wouldn't work. He decided he would tell them that Chad had discovered a warehouse full of supplies, and he'd sent some of the men to find vehicles to load up and bring back.

He walked inside the lobby, where three women sat as lookouts. Two stood up to greet him, asking if the rest of the men were back.

"No, they'll be back tomorrow morning," he responded.

"Why so late?" one woman asked.

"Well," he paused, trying to get his story straight, "Chad found an enormous warehouse full of food, and the other men are searching for trucks to load up and bring it back here."

"What did they find?"

"Anything good?" another woman asked.

"I'm not sure. You know how Chad is. He sent me back here to tell you all that they wouldn't be back until tomorrow," Grant said.

While Grant had been walking up the driveway, one woman had run off to tell his wife, Sara, he was back, and they told him this now.

"Chad sent you back to tell us this?" asked the woman, still sitting.

Grant turned toward her, not seeing Sara walk up behind.

"Well," Grant started, then paused again, trying to think of an answer, his hand nervously rubbing the seam of his pant leg. "It was Robert's idea. He said he didn't want to listen to his wife bitch when he got back, and he suggested to Chad that I come back."

The three women all began laughing as they couldn't stand Erica, Robert's wife, the constant worrywart.

"Please don't tell his wife I said that," Grant begged, which caused the women to laugh harder.

"We won't say anything," the woman sitting said. She then stood up and said, "Come on, girls, we should tell the other women not to expect their men back tonight."

The women walked past Grant, and he turned to watch them go. Surprised, he did a double take at the one standing behind him wearing sunglasses, and it took him a minute to realize it was his wife behind the shades.

"Everything okay?" she asked.

Grant looked nervously around and said, "Yeah, fine," then asked, "Everything okay here?"

Sara and Grant were not only married, but together they also ran a successful business. They may have been at a low point in their marriage, hence the couples retreat, but that didn't mean they didn't know when something was up with the other.

"Let's go to our room so we can get you changed out of those filthy clothes," Sara said, taking her husband by the arm.

Once inside, Sara closed and locked the door.

Grant turned, staring at her.

She looked at him, and he knew she instantly saw it in his eyes. "What happened? Where are the other men?"

"Dead."

"Why are you wearing sunglasses at night?"

Sara looked as though she wanted to make a joke about the eighties song, but didn't. Instead, she asked, "All of them?"

"Yeah," he answered. "Take off the sunglasses."

Hanging her head low, she reached up and slowly removed the shades. Her left eye was bruised black and blue, and the lid was puffy.

"What the hell happened?" Grant asked.

"Food is running low, and a few women are beating up others and taking theirs."

"Are you okay," he asked, walking toward her.

"I'm fine. It just hurts a little."

Grant reached up and slid his fingers through her hair, pushing it back to get a good look at her face. "It looks like they used you as a punching bag."

"It's not that bad; some of the other women are worse. Sally, the lady with the purple hair, well, they broke her nose and knocked out a couple of teeth."

"Jesus," he said as he ran a hand through his hair and sat down on the edge of the bed.

"How?" Sara asked.

"How what?" Grant asked, looking up at her.

"How did the men die?"

Grant told her everything, about Chad, the college kids, the rapes, and the murders. Then he told her about Drew. Told her how this massive, muscular man had killed them all. He told her about Steve and Cass, too, but the only thing he left out was the shadowy demon because he knew she wouldn't believe him.

"What are we going to do when the men don't come back?" she asked.

Right then and there Grant made a decision. "We won't be here. We're leaving."

"Leaving? Where are we going to go?"

"We're going to travel with Drew and his friends for a while.

"Are you serious? We don't even know those people."

"Don't worry; you'll like them. But Drew, well he takes a little bit of getting used to."

"Getting used to? You want me to run off and join people who take 'a little bit of getting used to'?"

"Well, you can stay here and be those bitches' punching bag."

"Not funny!"

"Do you trust me?"

"Come on. That's a silly question, given the circumstances."

"Sara, you don't know what I saw, what those men did. If other men like them were to come here, we have no way of defending ourselves. These people I just met have weapons, and they have one badass motherfucker who knows how to fight."

"I don't know about this."

"Do you trust me?" he asked again.

"Do you remember why we came here?" she asked in return.

"Yes, I do. To save our marriage and now we need to leave in order to save our lives."

She simply stared at him.

"I know things haven't been great between us lately, but I'd never put you in harm's way. Deep in my gut, I know we have to do this. We need to leave now. These people aren't going to wait forever."

"But, what about all the other women here? Shouldn't we tell them?"

"No. Some of those women are crazier than the men!"

Sara couldn't help but laugh. "True!"

"Pack your bag. We'll slip out the side entrance while everyone is down in the dining hall and hearing how the men won't be back."

Five minutes later, they made their way through the side entrance of the retreat and toward the tree line.

Chapter 18

Crescent City, Florida

Billy yawned as he drove the tractor back to the barn. The early mornings and vigorous work was catching up to the boy, when he usually had endless energy. Up ahead and on the left was the grove of trees his father had warned him about. The last thing he wanted to do was get the old tractor stuck, and have to spend time that could be used for sleeping instead being used to remove a tractor. Driving was new to him, both exciting and scary at the same time. It was harder than he'd thought, and he now knew what his mother meant when she yelled at his father to keep his eyes on the road.

He watched for all the bumps, which he feared hitting because his uncle had told him that, if he hit one the wrong way, he could be thrown off the tractor and squashed by the big knobbed tire. His uncle's words had stuck: "You noticed there's no seat belt on that thing, right?"

Billy wasn't sure if he'd been serious or just trying to scare him. Keeping one eye on the ground in front of him, Billy looked up to make sure he was far enough away from the trees when a silhouette of a man resting against one caught his eye.

Henry, sitting next to Billy, reached into his pocket and pulled out his pipe. Looking down, he packed a pinch of tobacco into the bowl.

Billy didn't remember seeing the yard decoration this morning when they drove past heading out into the fields, and wondered how it had got way out here.

"Hey, Dad, look!" Billy said taking a hand off the steering wheel and pointing to the trees.

Henry, patting down his coveralls searching for his matches didn't hear the boy over the noise of the engine.

Billy stared at the silhouette and he even thought he saw it move.

Finding the book of matches in his front pocket, Henry tore one from the pack.

Billy couldn't take his eyes off the black object, which still appeared to be moving. Doubting what he was seeing, Billy tried to rub the dirt and sweat from his eyes. *It is definitely moving,* he thought.

Just as Henry struck the match and it came burning to life, glowing red eyes appeared on the darkened form. Billy's mouth dropped open as fear filled the boy.

"Billy, look out!" Henry shouted, tossing the match and reaching for the steering wheel.

Billy looked up just as the front tire crashed into a large hole made by an oversized rock that had been pulled up while tilling. Only holding on with one hand, Billy's buttocks left the seat and his feet went sailing behind. The toe of his boot bounced off one of the rubber nubs on the tire. He screamed, fearing he would be squashed just like his uncle had warned.

Henry clamped down tightly on the pipe and thrust himself into the seat. Grabbing the steering wheel with his right hand, he leaned over and scooped Billy up with his left arm just as his son's grip slipped from the wheel.

Almost falling, Billy again screamed out in fear and closed his eyes, waiting for the black wheel of death to run him over; he hoped it would be quick.

With a heave, Henry hoisted his son up, the boy's tiny legs flaying like a rag doll's up and away from the tire before his tiny frame came crashing down into Henry's lap. He slammed on the brakes.

"I got you, son," Henry whispered into Billy's ear.

Billy, trembling with fright, turned and hugged his father tight, sobbing into his chest.

After a moment, Henry said, "Let's not tell your mother about this."

"Okay, Daddy," Billy said, clutching his father tight.

Henry drove the rest of the way back with Billy in his lap.

After parking the tractor, they both headed in to clean up for dinner. On his way inside Billy passed his uncle, the one who had told him to watch out for the tires, and felt him staring.

"Close call with the tire, huh?" his uncle asked.

"No!" Billy said, pouting.

"Oh, yeah," his uncle said with a chuckle, "Well your face says otherwise."

After dinner, Billy told his parents he was tired and kissed them goodnight before heading upstairs to take a shower and climb into bed. As soon as his head hit the pillow, he was out cold.

"*Billy*"! the deep dark voice whispered. "*Wake up, Billy.*"

Billy stirred, tugging the covers over his head, expecting to dream about the boy and the bright flash of light.

"*Wake up, boy!*" the sinister voice demanded.

The voice scared Billy, and he pulled the covers tightly over his face.

He then felt something touch the mattress, like it did when his father sat on the edge of the bed to have one of those talks when he'd done something wrong.

"*Wake the fuck up!*" the voice shouted.

He was terrified. The image of an evil man then filled his mind, and he felt a pain in his bladder. Tightening his legs in an effort not to wet himself only caused it to worsen.

Billy felt something grab hold of the covers, the sound reminding him of one of his cat's claws catching on a blanket.

"Get out here!" the voice growled.

The little boy's heart raced, his chest heaving rapidly up and down as his lungs worked overtime.

Reaching down under the covers, he grabbed his knees, pulling them tight to his chest to keep far away from the beast at the end of his bed.

Billy then felt something tighten around the blanket and start tugging fiercely. The thin material began to stretch and tear, causing strands of fabric and dust to fill the protective shelter. Billy choked and coughed on the particles. Unable to breathe, the blanket slipped from his grasp. With a violent yank, the cover went sailing across the bedroom.

Billy opened one eye a tiny sliver, exposing his gaze to a dark, shadowy silhouette of a man standing over his bed. It had glowing red eyes the color of molten lava. Billy opened his mouth and attempted to scream, but nothing came out; it felt like he'd lost his breath. Clenching his fists, he tried filling his lungs, but again nothing happened. His chest seemed to tighten instead.

Gasping for breath, he opened and closed his jaw, trying to draw in much-needed air. His eyes widened as panic set in.

The evil man leaned over him, staring into his eyes. Inches away from his face, Billy felt a chill emanating from the blackness of its face. For the second time that day, he felt sure he would die. The figure reached toward Billy with its claw-like hand. Still gasping for air, Billy began flailing his arms and legs, trying to squirm away. Terrified, his bladder released. Hot urine stained the front of his underwear, seeped out the seams, and dripped onto the sheet and began pooling on the plastic mattress protector.

Desperate to flee the razor-sharp talons, Billy kicked out to keep them away. Growing closer and closer, one talon touched his leg, piercing deep into the meaty part of his calf and sending a shot of searing-hot pain through his body. It was so intense that his lungs finally drew in a huge breath of air.

Inching forward, the demon reached for the child with its other arm.

Digging his left heel into the mattress, Billy used all his might to push himself away. As he pushed off, a wave of pooled urine went sailing off the bed and splashing onto the floor. Vaulting backward, Billy screamed as the talon tore his muscle away from his leg, exposing the bone beneath. With a thud, his head and shoulders slammed into the headboard, knocking him unconscious.

Betty-Sue and Henry awoke to the sound of their son screaming bloody murder, followed by a loud thud. Henry was out of bed and down the hall in the blink of an eye. It had been a long time since he'd had to go running to his son's room.

Whipping open the door, he hit the light switch. Light filled the room and he saw his son crumpled against the headboard. As he stepped forward to reach for Billy, he felt something warm and wet underfoot. Before he realized what he'd stepped in, he slipped and lost his balance. Both his feet shot out from underneath him and he landed hard on his back, slamming his head against the floor. His hair and the back of his shirt were both soaked with warm piss.

Betty-Sue came running at the loud crash and turned the corner to find Henry getting up off the floor, the back of his shirt soaking wet. Henry then got to his knees, grabbing his son and pulling him in close.

"Is he okay?" she asked, stepping around the puddle of urine.

"I think he had a nightmare and wet himself," Henry said as he looked over his son's body.

Billy slowly opened his eyes and looked up at his father.

"Daddy, I saw the evil man."

Chapter 19

Rockefeller Center, New York

Glen lay face down on the bed, breathing heavily, beads of sweat covering his back. Kendra lay next to him, motionless like a statue.

"My God, that was good," he said, rolling onto his back, the sheets absorbing his sweat. This had probably been the longest stretch he'd gone without sex, but thankfully that had just ended.

"Did you enjoy it?" he asked. "I've been told I'm fantastic in the sack."

Kendra just lay there.

"You don't say much, do you?" he asked, thinking back to the different interns he'd slept with who wouldn't shut up afterward. "It's nice. You're not like all those other women. It seemed like they'd fucked me hoping it would get them a better position at the station, or at least a pay raise. They couldn't just fuck to fuck, no strings attached."

He looked over, but she just laid there staring at the ceiling. Reaching over, he grabbed her nipple and gave it a hard squeeze.

"Damn woman! Most chicks jump or slap my hand, you must really like it rough."

He leaned over, cupped her breast and, taking her nipple into his mouth, bit down.

Kendra didn't flinch.

"Jesus, I could get used to this," he said, rolling over onto his back again. "A woman who will let me do whatever I want to her and doesn't talk; I must have died and gone to heaven."

Glen, tired, closed his eyes. Laying there he felt something was different with his manhood. He'd never remembered his junk feeling hot or cold, but now it felt like it had been chilling in a fridge and ached like his fingers and toes did when exposed to the cold for too long. Reaching under the covers, he placed his palm over his piece and found it, cold to the touch.

"Hmm," he said out loud, rolling onto his side and putting his hand on her pubic hair, then inserting his middle finger into her vagina. "What the hell?" he said, pulling out his finger and looking at it. "Your pussy is as cold as ice."

He brought his finger up to his face, sniffed it, and immediately gagged. "Shit, when's the last time you showered?"

Sniffing his finger again, he felt bile rise into his throat. The smell reminded him of the foul stench of roadkill that had sat for a few days in the scorching sun.

He gagged two more times before having had enough. Whipping the sheets off, he headed into the bathroom and hopped into the shower.

After, he came out to find his bed empty and figured she had gone to take a shower. Awoken and refreshed from the hot shower, Glen got dressed and headed downstairs.

Arriving in the newsroom, Glen sat down at the anchor's desk. There was one red light on in the back of the studio, powered by the generator. Adjusting his posture, he looked straight ahead into the camera and turned his head slightly to the right, showing off his best side. Sitting there, he imagined all the people tuning in and watching him from home. He couldn't wait to become the face of the nation as it was rebuilt. *Everyone will know my name, and women will throw themselves at me*, he thought.

He wanted to be like Cronkite, a newsman with a distinguished career delivering the news and connecting with his audience. He did not want to be like Rather or Williams, becoming part of the story, and especially not like Lauer— which almost happened to him, except on a smaller scale. Then, the end of the world had happened and here he sat. Now he would be the face to lead the country, and the world, out of the darkest time man had ever seen.

Glen's mind went off on a tangent, and he started thinking about how books would be written about him— minus the whole sleeping with the interns part— and he imagined they'd probably even make a movie.

Suddenly, all the lights in the studio came back on. Computer screens powered up, the TVs in the control room came to life, and the cameras before him turned on.

Chris, who had been sleeping on the console in the control booth, woke up. "Yes!" He looked around in amazement, fist pumping the air, and shouted, "We're back in business!"

Looking through the control room window, Glen witnessed Chris's excitement and couldn't help but smile. They were on their way to starting over.

"Hey!" Chris said, exiting the room.

"Hey!" Glen said, excited, looking around. "Power's back on."

"I guess he was the right man for the job," Chris said out loud.

"Who?"

"Peter. The guy Mr. Williams found to turn on the power."

"Don't you mean the Shadow Man?"

"What?" Chris asked, looking perplexed.

"You know, the thing."

"What the hell are you talking about?"

"Are you serious? You haven't seen it?"

"Are you messing with me?"

"No, I'm not messing with you. It protected me on my way here."

Just then the buzzer for the back door sounded. Chris raised his eyebrows and turned, clearly thinking Glen was losing his mind, and made his way back to the control room to see who was at the door.

"You really haven't seen it?" Glen asked, as Chris exited the control room, wanting to finish the conversation.

"No," Chris said, walking down the hallway.

A minute later, Chris returned with three men and one waved to Glen as he entered the studio.

"Hey," Glen said, waving back.

"This is Peter, the guy who turned the power back on," Chris said.

"Great job, Peter."

"Thank you."

"Peter, let me ask you a question," Glen said.

Peter stopped, looked at Chris, and then looked back at Glen.

"This is Glen Daniels. He's the news anchor here," Chris said to Peter.

"What do you want to know?"

"Have you seen the Shadow Man?" asked Glen.

"Oh, not this again!" Chris said, throwing his arms into the air.

"He hasn't seen it, or can't," Glen said.

"You can't see it?" Peter asked, looking at Chris.

"Not you, too!" Chris said, rolling his eyes.

"That thing, the Shadow Man, as he called it," one of the men with Peter said, "It saved my life."

"Me, too," said the second man.

"Okay, I'm done with this," Chris said, turning to Peter. "You know where the electrical rooms are," he said and walked back to the control room.

"He really can't see it?" asked the second man.

"I guess not," Glen replied.

The three men had started walking away when Glen called after them. "Hey, thank you for all you do! I appreciate your hard work."

"Sure, no problem," one of the men responded.

Best to be nice to everyone from now on, Glen thought, *otherwise they might say bad things about me and I don't want that in the book or movie.*

Chris sat down at the control panel and picked up the red phone. A moment later, the old man answered.

"The power is back on," Chris said.

"Perfect! How long before we can broadcast?"

"Peter is here now working on that. Once I get a time frame, I'll let you know."

"Did you finish working on the video packages?"

"Yes. They're all loaded and ready to go."

Chris heard the old man take a deep breath and slowly let it out.

"Thank you, Chris. Let me know when we're all set up and ready to go live. I want to come down and watch our triumphant return."

"Will do," Chris said as the line went dead.

Chris pressed a button and a sequence of colored bars appeared on the monitors in the control room.

Chapter 20

Jacksonville, Florida

Drew woke up groggy and sore. In the middle of the night he'd rolled over onto his wounded arm, and laying on the hard ground didn't help with the healing process. His mouth was dry and felt like it was stuffed with cotton. The sun had started poking through the trees, and the brightness didn't help the hell of a hangover he had going. It had been a while since he'd felt like this. Squinting, he held a hand up to his brow, trying to block the sun.

Letting out a big yawn and a stretch, Steve looked over at Drew and noticed he was awake. Steve rose, went over to his pack, and retrieved three aspirin and a bottle of water, then made his way over to Drew.

"I figured you could use these," Steve said, handing Drew the aspirin and water.

"Assuming I have a hangover?" Drew said in that sarcastic tone of his.

"No, because I assumed you were sore from being shot."

"Oh, right. Sorry," Drew said. "I thought you were going to give me another lecture about drinking."

"Nope. Do what you want. It's your life."

Drew hung his head, but after a moment looked up at Steve, wondering if his friend could see the hurt and pain he carried with him. It was an invisible weight that wore him down.

"I'm sorry about yesterday. I have this feeling something bad is going to happen to Annabelle and Stephanie, and I need to get home."

"I understand. Apology accepted. But you'll need to apologize to Cass. She thought you'd abandoned her."

"I didn't, but I will apologize."

"Your family will be fine," Steve said. "I know they will."

"Thanks," Drew said, popping the aspirin into his mouth and swallowing with a gulp of water. "I don't want to drink anymore. I just want to get home to my family. I want to change."

"Change is good."

"Can you help me, please?" Drew asked. "I don't want to live like this anymore."

"Of course I will," Steve said, reaching out and putting a hand on Drew's shoulder.

A wave of relief washed over Drew, and he felt a small amount of hope bloom deep inside.

"Thank you," he said with tears in his eyes.

Just then, Cass stirred. Wiping away the tears, Drew looked over and only then noticed Grant, and someone sleeping next to him.

"Who's that?" Drew asked, nodding his head toward the sleeping woman.

"That's Sara, Grant's wife. They're going to travel with us," Steve said.

"Okay. When did she arrive?"

"Last night when..." Drew wondered if Steve had almost said, "passed out," but had decided it best not to phrase it like that. "You were sleeping," he finished.

Drew nodded and thought, message received.

"You hungry?" Steve asked.

"Starved," Drew said, getting up.

"I'll get breakfast started. We'll need a healthy meal to give us the energy needed for getting you home to your family."

"Hey, kiddo," Drew said, walking over to Cass and sitting down next to her.

"Hey," she replied, rubbing the sleep from her eyes.

"I'm sorry I just took off yesterday," Drew said, his head hung low. "I couldn't shake the thought that my wife and daughter were in danger, and I have this overwhelming feeling that I need to get home as soon as possible. I don't want you to think I was abandoning you, because I wasn't. You're very special to me."

Cass looked up at Drew, her gaze meeting his. "Really?"

Drew smiled. "Yes, I mean it. You're very special to me, and I'll never leave you again."

Cass sat up and wrapped her arms around Drew's neck. "Do you promise?"

"I promise."

"Okay, I forgive you. But never leave me again. You and Steve are all I have left. Plus, you are my guardian angel."

Drew wrapped his powerful arms around Cass and gave her a loving embrace, the way a father would to his daughter. He thought it funny, just the other day he couldn't stomach the girl, and now he couldn't envision her not being around. Knowing what she'd gone through and how he hadn't been there to protect her weighed heavily, but he would never admit it. Yet he swore to himself he'd never let it happen again.

She gave him a peck on the cheek before closing her eyes and resting her head on his shoulder. In that moment, Drew suspected it was exactly what she needed: a sense of comfort from a strong, loving embrace. It was also something he needed as well.

Drew felt eyes upon him. Looking up, he found both Grant and Sara staring. Instantly, he noticed her bruised eye. She must have felt Drew lingering on her beaten and bruised face, as she smiled awkwardly and ducked away.

After watching the exchange between Drew and Cass Grant sat up, kissed his wife, and wrapped his arm around her. Sitting there, for the first time in a while, all five travelers felt a small semblance of comfort.

Steve continued making breakfast and coffee and, before eating, Grant introduced Drew to Sara. Over breakfast Drew filled everyone in on his fear that something bad was going to happen to his wife and daughter, and that he felt he needed to get home as soon as possible.

After breakfast everyone packed up, and the group set out down the road.

Stopping for a bathroom break, Grant followed Drew into the tree line. Both men stood a few yards apart to relieve themselves, and Grant looked over his shoulder to make sure the coast was clear.

"You okay?" Drew asked, noticing Grant in his peripheral vision.

"I'm just keeping an eye out for that dark, shadowy…"

"Don't," Drew said, finishing nature's call and then turning toward Grant, cutting him off.

"Do you know what it is?"

"Are you serious? How the hell would I know?" Drew responded in an angry tone.

"But, we both saw…"

"Stop. Don't say another word. We don't know what we saw," Drew countered, speaking just above a whisper. "But, whatever it was, we keep it to ourselves. Cass's sanity is hanging by a thread right now. And Steve? If he finds out, he'll retreat into his Bible and probably never put it down. They've got enough on their plate as it is, and we don't need to add this to their list of shit to worry about."

Grant hesitated, but then finally nodded to show he understood.

"Don't bring it up again," Drew said, and walked back toward the road.

Steve watched both men. Their demeanor seemed different. It appeared as if Drew might be angry with their new traveling companion, and he wondered if he'd been drinking again.

The women exited the tree line from across the road and after a moment the group set out again.

Steve led the pack, walking a full car's length ahead, deep in thought. Clearly, the conversation he'd had with Drew the other day had just been a joke to him, and Steve was angry with himself for believing Drew would change—especially since he'd already promised not to drink. Given the first chance, Drew didn't just fall off the wagon, he drove it into the trees and jumped off at the last minute before it splintered into pieces and the wheels came spinning off. I honestly thought he was the type of man who would keep his word, but apparently he's not, Steve thought. Instead, he's the type who will tell you whatever you wanted to hear.

Deep down inside, Steve could feel his anger swelling as they walked. I bet he's drinking again for sure, he thought, but then a memory popped into his head. It was something he had learned, and even taught others: relapse, it happens. Not only does it happen, but it is often part of recovery. Suddenly, his anger dissipated. How could he blame Drew if relapse was part of the process? Turning, he looked over his shoulder at Drew, who was limping, wincing at the pain in his foot. Resentment crept in and Steve's anger returned, but not with Drew— with himself. How could he be mad at him, especially with everything they had just gone through? Single-handed, Drew had saved their lives. Slowing his pace, Steve allowed the others to pass and for Drew to catch up.

"What's wrong?" Drew asked as he limped up beside his friend.

Steve looked at Drew and saw he was in rough shape. His face looked like life had kicked him squarely in the teeth, leaving him dazed, except there were no bruises or swollen eyes. Steve was close to Drew, but thankfully couldn't smell any booze on his breath. Looking at his friend, he realized it wasn't the booze he needed to worry about, it was the look in Drew's eyes. It was a look Steve never thought he'd see on the face of one of toughest men he had ever known: trepidation.

Clearing his throat, Steve said, "I'm sorry."

"For what?" Drew asked.

"For not understanding."

"Steve, you have every right to be upset with me. I told you I wouldn't drink, and I did."

"I know, but… relapse is part of recovery."

"So you've said."

"So, I'm finding it hard to stay mad at you."

"I really do want to stop drinking, but sometimes it's just so hard."

"It's like a crutch."

"Yes, it is," Drew said, taking a deep breath and letting out a lengthy sigh. "My wife is right, I'm just an alcoholic. I'm a no-good husband and father."

"You're a damn good man, Drew, but you have an ugly side when you drink," Steve replied, putting a hand on his friend's shoulder. "We'll work on the drinking part together."

"Okay, bud. Thank you!"

"Now, I know this isn't something you want to hear, but you need to put your trust in a higher power," Steve said.

"Listen," Drew said, stopping. "God gave up on me a long time ago."

"Drew," Steve said, standing in front of him, "just because you believe in a higher power doesn't mean it has to be God. For me it is, but for you it could be anything. It's about believing in something bigger than yourself. Something that you can ask for help when the urge to drink comes."

Drew's mind turned to his family and how he would do anything to get back to them, including giving up alcohol.

"All right, Steve, I'll give it a shot."

Chapter 21

Stoughton, Massachusetts

Annabelle was trying to sleep, but the sound of their generator running at the house across the street kept her awake, along with the sound of her mother milling about in the room next door.

She's probably searching for candles or more blankets, she thought.

Stephanie had fallen asleep, wrapped up in extra blankets to help fight off the cold. At some point, exhaustion or the cold, or maybe a little of both, finally brought sleep.

In the middle of the night, Annabelle awoke to the sound of muffled screams. Frantic, she reached out for Stephanie, releasing a sigh of relief when she felt her warm little body under the covers next to her. *It must have been a dream*, she thought, laying her head back on the pillow, her heart rate now returning to normal. Staring up at the ceiling, she watched as a reddish-orange hue danced across the room, then heard the generator sputter and die.

She was trying to figure where the bright colors were coming from when she heard popping, like that of wood in a fireplace. The glow intensified, brightening considerably until the whole room was illuminated.

A choked, blood curdling scream filled the night air.

Hopping out of bed, Annabelle ran to the window, stuck her fingers between the blinds, and pushed them apart. At first, she had to turn her head away from the intense glow of the raging inferno that now consumed the house across the street. Shielding her eyes with her other hand, Annabelle saw fire shooting out of the windows and heavy, thick, black smoke pouring from the attic and roof vents. It was mesmerizing, fascinating to watch, and she couldn't believe how fast it was spreading. Hearing her mother's quickened footsteps, Annabelle turned away from the window just as her mother began pounding on her door.

"Annabelle! Wake up! You're never gonna believe what's happening across the street."

Annabelle hurried to the door and opened it before the banging woke Stephanie.

"Did you see?" Susan asked before the door was fully open.

"Yes, Mom. I saw."

"Isn't it great! We won't have to worry about them troublemakers anymore."

Annabelle just nodded.

"Aren't you happy, dear?" Susan asked.

Annabelle shook her head, and a deep sadness washed over her as memories of Tommy came flooding back. She recalled when the Welch's had first moved in, and she'd met Ruth and Mac out in their front yard while Tommy sat playing on the grass. Ruth had waved hello, introduced herself, and asked if Annabelle had any experience or interest in babysitting. Telling her she did, Ruth offered her a job three days a week, watching Tommy after she got home from school. She'd also babysat every other Friday night, while Ruth and Mac went out for dinner and dancing. They'd leave a twenty on the table for her to order pizza, and always let her keep the change along with her fee. As a child, Tommy was well-behaved and hardly gave her any trouble. He would cuddle up next to her while watching cartoons, pizza sauce all over his face, and fall asleep in her lap. She'd always had a soft spot in her heart for Tommy, even when he'd wanted nothing to do with her when he became a teenager. Eventually, he'd started hanging out with the wrong crowd and found himself in constant trouble, both at school and with the police. He was no longer the young boy who'd warmed her heart.

"Well, I'm glad they're dead. That little troublemaker tried to kill you," Susan said.

"But he didn't."

"Well, they could have killed me or, even worse, Stephanie."

"Again, they didn't."

"No, they just took all of our food."

"Did you ever stop to think that they were hungry, too?"

"Why didn't they just ask then, instead of stealing from us!"

"I guess we'll never know now, will we?"

"I guess not!"

"And now we won't be getting back any of our food and we lost the generator too."

A horrified realization washed over Susan's face. "Oh no!" she said.

Not wanting to argue with her mother at this late an hour, Annabelle said, "The generator, and all of our supplies, were in the house."

"And that's exactly why your father put it outside. That and because of the noise."

"I assume because of the carbon monoxide too, Mom," Annabelle said closing the door and crawling back into bed.

Lying in bed, her breath visible in the air, Annabelle wondered what they were going to do for food. It had been a long night, and she was exhausted. The air was still, and the smoke rose straight up into the night sky. The fire raged and within minutes there was hardly anything left, except an empty shell. After a while, the glow from the house across the street died down and the room returned to darkness. Unable to sleep, she tossed and turned, but her mind would not stop worrying over their situation.

Adjusting her pillow for the umpteenth time, an idea hit. It was daring, but desperate times call for desperate measures.

Hearing her mother's heavy breathing, which wasn't as bad as her dad's snoring had been but still noticeable, Annabelle got out of bed and got dressed. Gently, she removed Stephanie from bed and carried her into her mother's room, placing her daughter next to her grandma.

Then, she went into the kitchen and scribbled a quick note, telling her mother she'd gone in search of food and would be back.

Her nerves were shot and Annabelle dreaded heading out into the dead of night, but she needed food to keep her daughter and her mother alive. Knowing she had a pantry full of food at home, she had to try.

Grabbing a flashlight and a carving knife, Annabelle slid the knife into her back pocket before slipping out the front door. Once outside, she was met by a cold drizzle and the distinct smell of smoke. Walking across the street, she approached the once-existing house. The flames had died down, and smoke rose from the charred pieces. The pungent stink of decay hung in the air. A lump formed in her throat, knowing Tommy had been in there along with all of the supplies he'd taken, and now there was nothing left. Everything had been incinerated.

Circling her way around, she noticed the far back corner of the house remained somewhat intact, and there was a small section where the outside paint was still visible. Moving the beam of her flashlight further up, Annabelle gasped at the sight of a charred arm sticking out an open window.

How awful, she thought, *to make it that close but not get out.* If her mother were here, she would say it served them right.

Annabelle continued to make her way around the property. Glancing over at her mother's house, she thought of her daughter and mother sleeping inside and wondered what they would do if there was a fire? Forcing the thought from her mind, Annabelle made her way back across the street and climbed into her car.

Sitting there, feeling the cold material of the seats through the back of her pants, it dawned on her that this was the first time she'd been outside since it had all started. Fearing the car wouldn't start, she put the key in the ignition and held her breath. To her surprise, the sedan started right up. Backing out of the driveway, she proceeded to head north down the road toward home. The town seemed deserted, although everything pretty much looked normal until she reached the center of town. Police barricades blocked the intersection, forcing her to turn left.

She drove cautiously, turning down side streets, trying to bypass the road closures. Her trek brought her past the grocery store, and she slowed the car to a crawl. Pulling into the parking lot, she noticed three empty cars in the lot.

Slowly, she drove past the front of the store, astonished to see the glass door and windows had all been smashed out. Inside was completely dark. She swung the car around and parked right in front of the door, using the headlights to illuminate the interior of the store. She watched for any movement, then waited a little longer, but didn't see anything.

Pieces of tempered glass crunched under her feet as she exited the car, and the cold air nipped at her nose. Looking down, she noticed she'd parked across the fire lane, then realized it didn't matter because, even if the building caught fire, no one would be coming to put it out— just as no one had come out to the Welch's.

Making her way toward the busted door, she poked her head inside and yelled, "Hello!"

She waited a moment, listening. After a few seconds, she stepped inside the store. Grabbing a cart, she headed toward the aisles, but was shocked to find the shelves completely bare. Every aisle was the same; there was nothing left. Not even a can of olives.

Abandoning the cart and turning around, she made her way back toward the front door. The headlights were blinding, causing her to put a hand up to block the beams of light. Suddenly, the light on the left went out and came back on— followed by the right.

"Hello!" Annabelle shouted, knowing someone had passed in front of the car. "Hello!" she repeated, her hand still up to her face as she passed through the checkout lane.

The car door swung closed as Annabelle exited, and she heard the gears change just as she reached the driver's side door.

A young woman in her early twenties, with frizzy blonde hair, sat behind the wheel. Annabelle made eye contact, and the woman's eyes looked like those of one deranged.

Pounding on the window, Annabelle screamed for the woman to get out. With a quick glance over her shoulder, the woman began backing up, and Annabelle jumped back to keep her feet from getting run over.

The car sped backward and screeched to a sudden halt. The woman slammed the gear into drive, pressing hard on the accelerator. The tires spun and chirped against the pavement as the car raced away through the parking lot and out the exit.

Annabelle watched as the red taillights disappeared down the road.

Chapter 22

Paxton, Nebraska

Bill had been gone for the better part of the day, so Maureen sighed in relief when his pickup rumbled down the dirt driveway. Wiping her hands on her apron, she headed out to greet her husband. Standing on the porch, Maureen allowed the dust cloud to settle before venturing down to the truck.

"Hey, Babe," he said exiting the truck and wearing a smile.

"How did it go?" she asked, happy to see he wasn't angry.

"So, so," he said, removing his hat.

"I don't understand?" she said, confused as to why he would smile considering his given answer.

Bill glanced around the front of the truck to make sure the boys weren't around, causing Maureen to do the same.

"I went into town, and a lot of folks have died."

"Really?" she asked.

"Yeah, most of the west side of town was wiped out. I guess Jenny Gates' newborn came down with it and Jenny went from house to house, looking for something to treat the baby with, and infected everyone."

"How awful!" Maureen said, holding a hand up to her mouth.

"I ran into Jose Rodriguez, he bought the Smith farm a few years back, and he said people are looking for food. He asked if we had any crops."

"What did you say?"

"I told him we did."

"Why?"

"Because the man is hungry and wants to feed his family. He offered to help us with the harvest in exchange for food."

"I didn't mean it how it sounded. I meant, aren't you worried about him telling others and them bringing the sickness here?"

"No. He and Doug Reynolds said there haven't been any recent cases."

"How can they know that?"

"Well, people have been checking in at town hall. They have a list of survivors going, and each week people check in. They also provide a list of those they'd had contact with, so they could start contact tracing."

"Oh, well, that's good."

"Now, if someone comes down with it, they can quarantine those people."

"What about supplies? Were you able to get any?"

"I was," Bill said, reaching into the back of the truck and pulling out a cardboard box along with bar soap, deodorant, shampoo, toothpaste, toilet paper, laundry soap, and dish detergent.

"How?" Maureen asked, thrilled to take a shower to clean the filth from her hair and skin.

"I bartered for food."

"Really?"

"Yeah. Apparently, we're the only ones in town growing crops. Everyone else either died, or didn't have help to work the land. I told people to come over and help themselves."

"Why, William, I am so proud of you helping your fellow man," she said, grabbing him by the cheeks and planting a big, wet kiss.

"Old man Carson offered us two of his cows for meat, in exchange for alfalfa to feed his other cows," Bill said, beaming from his wife's kiss.

"Did you accept?"

"With our freezer dwindling, I accepted his deal if he threw in a few chickens. Eggs are good protein, especially for our growing boys."

"Yes, indeed."

"I'm gonna need those boys' help harvesting the crops. I want to store some for us, and we'll need to bring the cattle into the pen closer to the house. We don't need any thieves stealing them."

"Okay, Bill."

Looking down, Maureen couldn't believe Bill then said what he did, knowing there would be pushback.

"I also want to train both boys in how to shoot."

"Bill," Maureen said, putting her hands on her hips.

"Now, I know you're opposed to it, but there might come a time when the boys will need to defend the farm, or the house, and I'd rather them know how to handle a weapon."

The thought of people, hungry people, coming over to get food really left little argument as she knew starving folk would do desperate things. "Okay," she finally said. "But you better train them right."

"Of course I will."

"Well, come on in and get washed up. Dinner is just about ready.

"Oh, Maureen?"

"Yes," she replied turning back around.

"I got this for you too," he said, and pulled a pack of cigarettes from his pocket.

Chapter 23

Manhattan, New York

The air had become crisp, so Stan put the window up. He had reached New York City, and now saw several work crews removing abandoned cars from the roadway. There was even a crew working on restoring power, tinkering with the top of a telephone pole.

Pressing on, he saw the iconic George Washington Bridge on the horizon. A few minutes later, he passed through the desolate toll booths. An electronic billboard, which ran off solar power, was flashing a grim reminder of what had happened: The Sickness is Spreading. Avoid Others.

A minute later, he crested the center of the bridge, staying to the left as the overhead signs instructed him to continue on I-95 North. He had traveled through New York more times than he could remember, but not once had there been no other cars on the road. It had usually been bumper-to-bumper traffic, and he found the lack of motorists eerie.

The road was windy, and every now and then he'd pass an abandoned vehicle. Stan figured staying in the center lane was best, as it provided the opportunity to swerve to either side of the road to avoid obstacles if need be. The road was a lonely place, and at times could be frightening, but he pushed on. Knowing he was only five hours from home excited him, and he couldn't wait to see his wife.

Shortly after crossing over into Connecticut, the alarm indicating low gas sounded. Pulling over to the right, he exited and removed several gas containers from the bed of the truck. He dumped each can into the tank, chucking the empties into the back again. Tightening the cap he smiled, knowing it was the last time he'd need to fill up.

Hopping back in, Stan subconsciously checked his rearview mirror before pulling out onto the road. A minute later, he was back to cruising speed, his next stop home.

Chapter 24

Rockefeller Center, New York

Kendra's body made its way to her room. Once inside, it stripped down and stepped into the shower. How she wished she could feel the warm water rinsing her clean of the sweaty man who'd mounted her and conducted his business. She felt worthless, and it seemed she was being punished by God. She hated this purgatory; it felt like she was being forced to relive her childhood over again with yet another man taking advantage of her body and having his way with her.

Remembering back to being a young girl, and the feeling of the grotesque weight of her stepfather's friends on top of her, the way they'd handled her frail body, and the violence felt by their angry, lusting thrusts. Praying to God became useless, because clearly God either ignored her prayers or He didn't exist. Instead, she would find a spot on the ceiling to focus all her attention on until the man's act was complete; which was what she'd done today, staring at a spot on the speckled white ceiling tiles.

In the shower, Kendra reflected on the events that had just happened. Lacking all control over her body and not being able to enjoy the feeling of being alive, Kendra did something she hadn't done in over twenty years: she prayed. She begged Him to make it stop, to end the misery that had become her life. As soon as she ended her prayer, Kendra felt a sharp pain.

It came from her thighs. It was a pain she was familiar with; a pain caused by having a man on top of her. Some men, usually the ones with a small pecker, would drive their bony knees into her thighs, which hurt like hell, as they tried to get their little tootsie roll inside. She would typically laugh about those encounters, because if it wasn't for that pain she wouldn't have felt anything at all — especially not from their tiny pieces.

But today she welcomed it. She welcomed the ability to feel, even if it was pain, because it meant she was still alive. She'd also felt something else. A wet feeling. If she could have smiled, she would have, and felt a moist tear run from the corner of her left eye and roll down her cheek.

Stepping out of the shower, Kendra caught a glimpse of herself in the mirror, and was horrified. She looked like hell with her eyes sunken into her head. Her reflection looked like that of a zombie, not the vibrant woman she was.

After drying off, Kendra's body dressed itself and headed downstairs.

Chapter 25

Crescent City, Florida

For the second time this week, Billy woke to see the evil man at the end of his bed. This time, thankfully, he didn't wet himself, but the man threatened to kill him and his family.

Reject the light, the ominous form said. Its fierce red eyes growing in intensity.

Billy lay curled up in a ball, hiding from the thing that now haunted him. For the past couple of nights, he'd switched beds. The first night he slept with his parents, but Henry wouldn't allow him a second night in their bed. He'd told Billy he was a big boy now, and he had his own bed for a reason.

The second night, Billy had lay in his bed after his parents kissed him goodnight and shut off the light, too scared to sleep. Listening to his parents converse in their room, he'd hoped the evil man would not return. But it hadn't take long before he'd heard the loud, chainsaw-like sound of his father's snores; he wondered how his poor mother could fall asleep next to that every night.

Scanning the room for any signs of the nighttime visitor, Billy had waited a few extra minutes, ensuring his father's snores would drown out the sound of his sneaking down the hall. He made his way past his parents' door and down the stairs. Slowly, he crept down the first-floor hallway toward his grandparents' room, then grabbed the knob and opened the door. His grandparents differed from his parents, in that they both slept in separate beds at opposite sides of the room. The door creaked as Billy opened it, and a beam of light from the kitchen sliced through the dark.

Grandma had rolled over and saw him standing there, then smiled and patted the bed. Billy tiptoed across the room, trying not to awaken his grandfather, and climbed into bed with her, snuggling against the warmth of her housecoat. For someone who always complained of being cold, to Billy she felt pretty warm.

He'd slept with his Grandma for a few nights, until the other night when he was trying to sneak down the stairs and the wooden step creaked under his weight. Instantly, he froze, and before Billy could get to the bottom his father had opened his door and caught him. Henry then stood there, pointing back down the hallway toward Billy's room. Hanging his head low, Billy turned and walked back up. Just before turning into his room he looked down the hall at his father, who was still standing there, watching him, then nodded to indicate he should enter his room.

Billy had thought about how he could keep the evil man away, and decided to leave the light on. He'd stared at the ceiling and, before long, sleep took hold and he drifted off to sleep.

A presence startled Billy awake. Eyes still closed, he felt it, though he could tell the light was still on. Slowly, he opened his eyes and instantly the hairs on his arms stood on end. Looking straight ahead, he stared into the red eyes of something purely evil. It stood before him, wearing a black robe with a hood that covered the back of his head. This time it had a face, but it looked waxy and fake. It reminded Billy of how his Aunt Martha had looked in the casket after the cancer took her.

Reject the light or die! I will kill you right where you lay and then kill everyone in this house, it said. The evil man's face began melting away, the skin around the jawline splitting and blood pouring from the cracks. Crimson liquid splattered onto the mattress as chunks of skin started sliding off its cheeks, landing on the bed with a loud, wet slop.

Billy's eyes widened as some little drops of blood bounced off the mattress then turned into red fire ants. They seemed to roam aimlessly and then, as if on cue, they all stopped, turned, and started marching toward him. The pieces of skin started squirming, and tiny legs with sharp claws protruded from the mass. Brown fur began to cover the blobs, and a long pink tail sprouted from the end of the bloody mass. Rolling over, little beady black eyes formed, along with long, pointed teeth. The rat-like creatures shook, sending tiny droplets of blood sailing through the air. Then, before the droplets could land, they sprouted wings and turned into flies. Soon the room buzzed with little bugs sporting razor-sharp teeth. Some swooped and dove, feasting on the ants, while others started chasing their own kind, devouring them mid-flight. The rat-thingies scurried across the bed, their tiny claws getting stuck in the fabric of the blanket.

Billy froze in fright as the man's face completely melted away, leaving nothing but a black hole. The faceless man bent toward Billy, who stared into the void that had once been the man's face. It was the darkest thing he'd ever seen, and the infinite nothingness was mesmerizing. The boy's eyes then widened at what appeared to be tiny sparks shooting across the blackness, which filled quickly, swirling and spinning. Billy felt as though he was staring into the night sky, in what had been the man's face.

Billy momentarily broke his gaze and noticed all the ants were looking to the faceless man; as were the rats, who sat on their haunches. The flies swirled around in the room, mimicking the tiny sparks.

Billy again stared at the sparks, which were now spinning faster and faster. Then what appeared to be an arm started growing from the center, but it was a tiny vortex that spun like a tornado. With each revolution it spun faster and faster. The growing arm snaked its way toward Billy, and the rats and ants looked up as it protruded out above. The black flies now circled the spinning appendage, still keeping in sync with the sparks.

Small black talons formed at the end of the growing form.

Pressed up against the headboard, Billy had nowhere to go. The thing was coming for him, and he went cross-eyed as it reached closer to his face, stopping an inch from his nose.

Billy was suddenly filled with fear and hatred. His heart felt heavy and his soul weak, and worse as the thing came closer. His face became flush, and the blood in his cheeks started tingling. They felt numb, like when he went to the dentist and they'd given him novocaine.

The ants and rats were now in his lap, the blanket that had covered him no longer visible. They seemed to sway in unison, watching the talon of the dark, spinning mass.

Then came a bright flash— the brightest light Billy had ever seen. Instantly, the black appendage turned to stone, like black onyx. The light intensified and the stone shattered. The shards absorbed the light and then began glowing, white-hot, before bursting and turning to dust. The light turned the ants and rats into ash in an instant, and it appeared as if a nuclear weapon had been detonated on his bed, incinerating them all.

The evil man's left arm shot up, and burying his face in the crook of his elbow, as if by magic, he disappeared.

Billy looked to the light coming from the corner of the room. Standing there was a man dressed in a white robe, who held his hands out toward Billy. Instantly, love and hope enveloped the boy, and his smile beamed from ear to ear. He felt as if he had just woken on Christmas morning to discover every single toy on his list under the tree, plus more.

"Don't be afraid, my son. You are under His protection and no harm shall come to you," the man in the white robe said. "Sleep now."

Billy felt himself grow tired and he slid down under the covers. Before the boy drifted off to sleep, he opened one eye, checking to see that the ants and rats were truly gone.

He felt at peace then, and sleep took him.

Henry awoke from a deep sleep to sound blasting from the TV downstairs. Slipping his feet into his slippers, he headed down to investigate. Rubbing the sleep from his eyes, Henry leaned against the banister at the bottom of the stairs for support and found the living room basked in multicolored light.

Dave turned from the TV when he heard the squeak of the fourth stair tread, which annoyed them all. Every house had one, usually a step near the top or the bottom of the staircase. Taking the last step onto the hardwood floor, Henry rubbed his eye with one hand and scratched his groin with the other, then gave his brother a what-the-fuck-are-you-doing look.

"What?" Dave asked.

"Turn it down. Billy and Betty-Sue are sleeping."

"Sorry. I thought I heard something on one of the national channels."

"Sounds like static to me. Loud static."

"I'm sorry," Dave said as he turned the TV down.

"Go to bed."

"I can't sleep."

"Well, try."

"Now I won't be able to. I think I heard something," Dave repeated, looking at the TV. "Maybe things are getting better."

"That old TV probably doesn't even work. Where did you find it?"

"I found it in the back room, while I was looking for blankets for Mom. She's afraid we'll lose power, and then we won't have any heat. She's worried Dad and Billy will be cold."

"We create our own power, with the windmills and solar panels."

"I don't think she understands how they work."

"Probably not."

Dave turned back toward the TV.

"Well, why don't you give the TV a rest and try again in the morning."

"I'll try for a little longer. I think the tube may be blown, but hopefully the sound still works. I'm gonna tinker with it a little. Dad has several old TV's back there, so I'm hoping to get one of them working."

"Fine. Suit yourself but keep it down and don't wake the house."

"All right, Henry. Goodnight."

"'Night."

After Henry left, Dave lifted the old TV off the stand and put it on the floor, then headed to retrieve another old set. It took just a minute to change out the wires from one TV to the other.

Here goes nothing, Dave thought as he turned on the TV, flipping to the channel he thought he'd heard something on earlier.

"Oh my God!" Dave said out loud at the sight of the words 'Please Stand By' in front of the colorful bars.

Chapter 26

Rockefeller Center, New York

They'd finished their last dress rehearsal, and Glen now felt comfortable using the foot pedal under the anchor desk to control the teleprompter. It took a little getting used to, as his previous employer had someone control it for him from the booth, but Chris would be tied up with putting the segment pieces up in the window so they would display on the screen next to Glen. All Glen had to do was stare into the camera and read the words from the prompter, which reflected onto a one-way piece of glass in front of the camera. Controlling the speed with the pedal, if he wanted he could even scroll forward or backward at a tap of his foot. The camera placement ensured Glen appeared to be looking right into people's homes, connecting directly with the viewer through their TV.

"I think we're ready," Chris said, the excitement building in his voice.

Glen gave him the thumbs-up and stood. Glancing to his left, he noticed Kendra behind one of the large floor cameras at the back corner of the newsroom.

Glen instantly felt aroused at the sight, and reached into his trousers to adjust his growing member.

"How much time before we go live?" Glen asked out loud, knowing Chris could hear him because the newsroom was mic'd to the control room, allowing them to communicate.

"I'll call Mr. Williams and find out what time he wants to air," Chris said into the microphone, broadcasting his response into the newsroom.

Glen sauntered over toward Kendra, whose body looked enticing. Leaning his elbow against the wall, he used his most seductive voice. He was horny again, itching for some action; after all, he was a sex addict.

"Came back for more?" he said.

Kendra's head slowly turned toward him, and a half smile appeared.

"He wants to go live at five o'clock," Chris said into the mic as he hung up the phone receiver. Pushing a button, Chris removed the 'Please Stand By' screen and replaced it with the WTFH logo, a map of the United States behind it.

Glen looked down at his watch. It was only a little after three in the afternoon. "Okay, I'm going to head upstairs to freshen up before our triumphant return," he said.

"See you in a few," Chris responded, then disappeared, no doubt to double and triple check that everything in place and ready to go.

Glen moved in closer to Kendra and reached out, grabbing her by the buttocks and pulling her in close, then pressing his semi-hard cock against her leg and squeezing both buttocks while planting a kiss on her luscious lips. After a moment, he led her by the hand up to his suite to fulfill his sexual desires.

An hour later, Mr. Williams called down to Chris, making sure everything was set and ready to go. After, he turned toward the entity and said, "It's time. Shall we?"

The wraith turned and headed for the door, and Mr. Williams followed.

Chapter 27

Pooler, Georgia

The group walked down the sunbaked asphalt. Cass had her arms out to her sides as she tried to walk solely on the divided yellow line. Laughing, both Grant and Steve followed suit, which left Drew and Sara walking by themselves on the shady side of the road.

"Nice shiner you got there," Drew said.

Now Sara understood what her husband had meant by Drew taking a little bit of getting used to but to her, there was no need, as she was already used to it. Growing up with three brothers had seen to that; unlike Grant, who was an only child, so sarcasm was something he wasn't around much.

"Thanks," Sara responded, her own tone sarcastic.

"Did he do that?" Drew asked, nodding toward Grant.

"No, he's never raised a hand to me."

"Chad?" he asked.

"Nope, his wife."

"Did you give as good as you received?"

"I wish. I was sucker punched for a can of soup."

"Campbell's?"

She chuckled. "No. Progresso."

Now he chuckled.

"Grant told me you're an EMT and were in the Marines. And that you're trying to get home to your family," Sara said.

Drew thought of Annabelle and Stephanie, and hoped he could make it home before something horrible happened. But this damn walking was going to take forever.

"I am. I was, and I am."

They walked a few paces and she asked, "Where were you when the sickness hit?"

"In Florida. My mother had a heart attack and died just before the news broke."

"I'm sorry."

"It's okay," he said, then asked, "Where were you?" It reminded him of the weeks following 9/11, and how people had asked each other the same question.

It was the first time Sara had been asked that question. After a moment, she began to speak. "A few months ago Grant and I barely spoke, and when we did it was usually yelling. Like most couples, our relationship had hit a downturn and we were on the brink of separating."

"Oh, really?" Drew said, thinking about his situation with Annabelle.

"One of my friends mentioned a couples' retreat that her sister and her brother-in-law went on, and how it supposedly helped. I figured it was worth looking into, that it couldn't hurt. I spoke to Grant about it, and he agreed to go. He said he, too, wanted to save the relationship."

"Well, that's a good thing," Drew said.

"That's what I figured," Sara said, fixing the hair that fell into her eyes. "We're lucky enough that we own our own business and can take time off whenever we want."

It was winter back home up north in Boston, and Drew wasn't used to the heat of the south at this time of year. He wasn't sure if it was the heat, or being dehydrated from all the booze, but he was parched. Reaching into the side pouch of his pack, he pulled out his water bottle and took a long swig. After, he gestured the bottle toward Sara, who waved the offer off.

"Our first day there we had a huge blowout regarding what to do that day. Grant wanted to do the confidence course, and said he thought the thrill of it might bring us closer by working together to get through. I wanted to take the class where couples made a meal together, because it was designed to show the non-cooking partner in the relationship all that went into preparing and making a meal. I thought it would be good to start off the week showing him all the work I put into making meals, because God knows he can't cook, so I'm the one always forced to do it unless we do take-out. He made a snide remark, asking if they had a lawn-mowing class where he could sit down and watch me push the mower under the blistering sun and point out the spots I missed, as if I did that to him."

"Both going for the full role reversal, huh?" Drew said. Sara either didn't hear him or decided to ignore the comment because she kept on talking.

"The arguing became worse on the second and third days. I literally packed my bags, and was ready to leave when the sickness hit. I'd just finished packing my toiletries and had come out of the bathroom to find Grant standing in front of the TV. I told him he could Uber home and to give me the keys. Then I figured he was being coy with me because he just stood there, staring at the TV. I yelled at him a second time and he turned to me, looking concerned, before turning back to the TV. We've been together long enough to know each other's looks, and what I saw was his scared look."

"I asked him what was wrong, and after a minute more of staring at the TV he looked down at the bags in my hands and told me we couldn't leave. I told him he had to be kidding, and to hand over the keys. He brushed past, not saying a word, walked to the door, and checked the deadbolt. I put my bags down on the edge of the bed, went over to the TV, and my mouth dropped open. The local news was reporting that the roads, from Jacksonville to Tallahassee, had been closed due to the sickness. They showed footage from all across the country."

Drew remembered that day, sitting on the plane, as the entire plane had gasped and everyone stared at the TVs located in the back of the seat in front of them. A commotion had broken out in the front aisles of the plane just before the explosion.

"I asked him how this could have happened, and he said he didn't know and called me 'Babe'. I love it when he calls me that, and he hadn't done it for a long time. There's nothing like a tragedy to put things into perspective."

"Very true," Drew said.

"I told him I was sorry and that I loved him, and he told me the same before grabbing me in a loving embrace, which I enjoy so much and had missed. All the animosity and trouble seemed to wash away with that embrace.

Drew couldn't wait to hug and kiss Annabelle when he got home, and hoped the same would happen for them.

"The moment was disrupted when the manager started pounding on our door, asking everyone to come down to the dining room as there was a situation."

"Were they kicking you out?" Drew asked.

"That's what we thought, too. But Grant suggested we go down and see what they had to say."

"How did that go?"

"Not well. The manager, his name was Paul, told everyone what was going on and that we all had to leave."

"Oh boy."

"A few of the couples left. They wanted to get home to their children and families.

"I sense a 'but' coming."

"But, some couples didn't want to leave. Like us, some didn't have children to go back to, or their families lived far away. One woman stood up and said that we should stay put, because the sickness wasn't here as no one was sick. The manager said absolutely not, and that no one was staying. There was a young couple, must have been newlyweds, and the wife was pushing her husband to speak up. When he finally did, he asked about a refund and that's when things got ugly."

"Let me guess, the manager didn't want to issue refunds?" Drew said.

"Bingo!"

"What a dick."

"Well, he got his. A blonde woman stood up and shouted that it wasn't right for the retreat to be kicking them out and not even be issuing a partial refund. He told her he didn't care and to get out. That's when that guy Chad stood up and beat the guy to a pulp."

"Oh, that guy!" Drew said, rolling his eyes.

"After, we went back to the room to try and decide what to do. We put on the news, which said the virus was spreading from person to person. We had all been there for the better part of a week, and as no one was sick and no one new had shown up, we decided it was best to stay put until whatever it was blew over. Eventually, we ran out of food and Chad decided to put himself in charge."

"No one tried to stop him?"

"Most of the couples were already on a rocky road, and Chad used that to his advantage. By planting doubt in some people's minds, he then used that as a way to get them to turn on their partner. He didn't seem that smart to me, and I thought for sure someone else was calling the shots and pulling all the strings— just like a puppet master. Eventually, Chad became an evil overlord followed by his little minions."

"Unfortunately, whenever there is a group of people, someone always wants to lead."

"When the supplies became sparse, Chad sent the men out to find more. Every time they returned with food, they also came back with weapons they had found. Just before they left in search of you, Chad got some of the men all worked up into a tizzy. Grant told me that Chad told them they should kill all of you for what you did to the others."

"I killed them for what they did to those college kids!" Drew said, his anger washing over his face.

"I know. Grant told me what Chad did to your friends. I'm awful sorry. He was such an angry, cruel man. Grant also told me what Chad planned to do to the women when he returned," she said, placing her hand on Drew's arm. "Thank you for stopping him."

Drew looked over at her, confused. "What?"

"Thank you for killing him so he couldn't rape all of the women at the retreat."

"Is that what Grant told you?"

"Well, he said you killed all the men. Is that not true?" she asked, confusion in her eyes.

"It was your husband who took care of Chad."

"Wait, what?" Sara asked, shocked. "Grant killed Chad?"

"I see he's humble, too," Drew said, looking at her.

They were walking in step and Sara looked down, as if trying to process the information. "I know he's an adrenaline junkie and loves jumping out of planes, hence why we opened our own skydiving business, but he's never been one prone to violence."

"Well, he emptied the gun into Chad's back while Chad was on top of me."

"Wow! My husband is a badass! Who would have known?" she said, surprised.

Drew stopped short. Sara took an extra step or two, then stopped and looked back.

"Did you say you own a skydiving business?"

"Yeah, back in Putnam County. We have three planes and six part-time instructors."

"So, you own planes?" he asked.

"Yes, three," she repeated.

"Do you know how to fly?"

"No offense, but I wouldn't own one plane, never mind three, if I didn't have my pilot's license."

Drew dropped to his knees and hastily removed his pack, setting it down on the ground. Unzipping the flap, he reached in and pulled out his atlas and immediately started flipping through it.

"Where are you?" he said out loud, frantically turning page after page. Finally, finding the one he was looking for, he folded the book in half and began scanning the page with his index finger.

"Yes!" he shouted, loud enough that the others heard him and stopped in the middle of the road to turn around.

"What is it?" Grant asked, looking at Sara.

"I don't know. We were talking and he just stopped," she said.

After a few seconds, Drew looked up and asked, "Do you both know how to fly?"

"Yes," Grant answered, looking to his wife.

"There's an airport less than five miles from here," Drew said, pointing to the map.

"What kind of airport?" Sara asked.

"I'm assuming one that has planes," Drew answered.

"Is it an international airport or private?" Grant asked.

"Because if it's international, that will have mostly jetliners, and we're not licensed for those," Sara added.

"I doubt someone will be there to check your license when we board," Drew said.

"Oh, I like this guy," Sara said with a smile.

"I thought you might," Grant replied.

Drew looked from Sara to Grant and then back again, waiting for an answer.

"You do realize that flying one of those jetliners requires more in-depth training because there's a huge weight difference and it's more complex to fly."

"Okay, got it. This looks more like a private airport to me. It's small and nowhere near a major city," he said, handing over the map while still marking the location with his finger.

Both men studied the map.

"That's definitely a private strip, which means we can fly basically any plane there."

Chapter 28

Statesboro, Georgia

The group made its way toward the airfield. If there was one thing Drew could do that impressed Steve the most, it was his ability to navigate by map. In the age of GPS, map-reading was a skill few people now possessed, but Drew was a professional. He had passed both day and night land navigation in the Marine Corps with flying colors. Given a destination, a compass, and a map, Drew could find anywhere X marked the spot.

Both Steve and Grant were intrigued by how Drew held the compass on the map and looked through the aperture. Looking through the slit in the cover of the compass, there was a tiny wire, known as a sightline, which Drew would line up with a landmark corresponding to the bearing where he was heading. Drew would find something that he could see— a rock cropping, a colorful tree— something that stood out. Even if Drew had to divert around a body of water or a cluster of rocks, he always stayed on course by making his way toward the object he had spotted. Once there, Drew would shoot a new sightline. Sometimes, because of heavy vegetation, Drew would move only fifty to a hundred yards and then shoot a new line of sight.

"The airfield should be right behind that grove of trees," Drew said, pointing.

They made their way through the trees and, as they exited the tree line, they were greeted by an eight-foot chain-link fence standing between them and the runway.

Drew paused at the sight before him, recalling that the last time he'd climbed a fence was to get out of an airport.

Shortly after that, Brad, his first official travel companion, had been shot and killed over a pack of smokes.

The group quickly scaled the fence, except for Drew who grunted in pain as he dug his wounded foot into the fence for a toehold. He groaned again, landing on his bad foot. After a moment they headed toward the hangers on the other side of the runway. Limping, Drew led the way with the rifle at the ready, followed by Cass, who had the shotgun shouldered and ready to fire. Behind Cass were Grant and Sarah, and they were followed by Steve, who held the pistol out at arm's length, covering the left side. There was no sign of anyone, but they weren't taking chances. They moved quickly. Swiftly.

"There!" Sara said, loud enough for Drew to hear as she pointed toward a hangar that had the name, Eddie's Skydiving, written across the top. Below it read, Jump, and Gravity Takes Care of the Rest.

Reading the sign, Drew chuckled. *No shit*, he thought.

Keeping up their pace, they crossed the tarmac, trying to limit their time out in the open, and reached the hangar moments later.

"Stay here. I'm going to circle the building to make sure the coast is clear," Drew said.

He was halfway down the right side of the building when he looked back over his shoulder and saw Cass following.

"What are you doing?"

"I'm going with you."

"Why? I'll be right back."

"In case you haven't noticed, the safest place is with you."

Drew rolled his eyes and shook his head.

"Don't even!" she said.

Remembering what had happened to her boyfriend and friends the last time he'd left her alone, his conscience got the better of him. "Come on, then!"

They made their way to the end of the building, and Drew poked his head around the corner, taking a quick glance and then pulling back.

"Is someone there?" asked Cass.

"No, but the back door is open."

"What do we do now?"

"Stay here. I'm going to take a look inside." He knew Cass would protest, and he was ready for it. "You stay here and cover me in case someone comes out."

"Okay," Cass said, surprising Drew as he'd thought for sure she would argue.

Staying low, Drew made his way toward the open door. Tilting his head, he peeked inside.

A large yellow plane with Eddie's Skydiving written on the side in bright red lettering, appeared to be the only thing inside the hangar. In the back-left corner was an office, the door open giving Drew a view right inside; it appeared empty as well.

Drew signaled for Cass to come to him, and he walked inside.

By the time Cass rounded the corner and entered the door, Drew was already inside the office.

"Anything?" she asked, walking up.

"Nope."

"Want me to let the others in?" she asked, about to walk away.

"Hey Cass!" Drew called out.

"Yeah?" she asked, appearing in the doorway again.

"Let's check out the inside of the plane first," Drew said, looking out the office window at the aircraft.

"Really?" she asked.

"Yeah, no Trojan Horses today."

Drew circled around the tail wing and opened the fuselage door, scoping out the inside. "All clear. You can let the others in."

Cass removed the latch from the center of the two enormous doors and pulled one open. "Come on in," she said to the others, pushing the door all the way open.

Sara walked into the hangar, and her eyes opened wide. "Damn! Grant, look. It's a Twin Otter!"

"Wow! She's a genuine beauty!" Grant replied.

"Is it a good plane?" Drew asked, coming around the nose.

"It's one of the best skydiving planes made. It's a twin-engine Viking Air DHC-6," Sara said, admiring the machine.

"Is that good?" Steve asked.

"Yes. It's like the Cadillac of skydiving planes," Grant said.

"Is this what you own?" Cass asked.

"I wish," Sara said.

"These things have a price tag of about seven million dollars," Grant said.

"What do you fly?" asked Steve.

"We have two Cessna 182 Skylanes and an older Cessna 172 Skyhawk," Sara said proudly.

"How much do those cost?" Cass asked.

"A little over one million for the two Cessna 182s. The 172 was a gift from my dad before he passed," Grant said.

"Oh, I'm sorry," Cass said.

"Thank you," Grant replied.

"He's been dead for about five years now. He wanted his son to follow his dream, which Grant has done," Sara said, wrapping her arm around her husband.

"That's nice," Drew said in that sarcastic Boston accent of his. "But how far can this thing fly?" He thumbed over his shoulder toward the plane.

"Well, if memory serves me correctly, it can fly around seven hundred nautical miles. Maybe a little more," Sara said.

"And how far is it from here to Boston?"

"Well, we crossed over into Georgia, so my best guess is that it will be close," Grant said.

"It will be close?" Steve said, now sounding like Drew.

"We'll just have to jump," Sara said, with way too much excitement for Drew.

"Did she say jump?" Cass asked.

"I did," Sara said, smile wide. "Don't worry, we'll probably make it there, anyway. But, if we don't, you'll love the jump."

"Well, I hope we make it all the way," Cass said.

"I second that," Drew said.

"Come on! Really? Are you scared to jump, big man?" Sara asked, slapping Drew on the shoulder.

Drew was no longer a fan of flying, especially given what had happened the last time he'd been on a plane.

An hour later, they had fully fueled the plane and completed the pre-flight checklist. Both Sara and Grant provided a quick introductory lesson on how to jump from a plane and use a parachute.

Once aboard, Drew, Cass, and Steve sat in the back, with Sara and Grant sitting in the cockpit. Drew closed his eyes and leaned back against the seat. The plane had some real pep, and Sara provided a smooth takeoff.

***

Drew calculated they had been flying for almost two hours, so he made his way to the cockpit to find out how much longer.

"Where are we?" Drew asked.

"Somewhere over Connecticut," Grant said.

"Sorry we couldn't get you closer," Sara said.

"No worries. We can make it to my house in a day or two, depending on what we encounter."

"Drew, listen, I know you said you didn't want to jump, but we're getting low on fuel and any potential area we find to land seems to be blocked," Grant said.

"I'm okay with losing a wing on landing. It beats jumping," Drew replied.

"You have a real fear of heights, huh?" Sara asked.

"Yeah, that and sharks."

"So, landing in the ocean is out then?" Grant joked, but his smile quickly faded when Drew shot him a glare.

"I'll tell the others," Grant said, getting up from the co-pilot seat.

Drew sat down in Grant's seat and looked out the window.

"First time in a cockpit?" Sara asked.

"In flight, yeah," Drew said.

Behind them Grant called, "Good news. We're almost there."

"Thank you, Jesus!" Steve said.

"Well, there's bad news too," Grant said.

"What?" Cass asked, sounding frightened.

"We're low on fuel and there isn't any place to land, so it looks like we're gonna have to jump," said Grant.

"Did he just say we have to jump?" Cass asked, her tone now one of sheer terror.

"We could not locate a road or highway with a long enough stretch to accommodate a safe landing. Most roads are either clogged with abandoned cars, or have debris in the way. The only clear roads seem to have high, overhanging tree canopies, which we could never clear. Plus, with the telephone poles on either side of the road, it doesn't allow enough room for the wings."

Suddenly, the low fuel alarm sounded.

"So, it's Plan B then," Sara said.

"Great!" Drew said sarcastically, making his way to the back of the plane and sitting down.

Steve put his hand on Drew's shoulder and said, "Are you ready, big guy?"

Drew hoped the look he gave clearly indicated he was definitely not ready. Jumping from a perfectly good airplane was not a great idea, he thought, and he'd rather take his chances clipping a wing on landing. He was thankful his old unit hadn't been airborne, because heights scared him shitless. Hell, he didn't like going above the third rung of a ladder. His heart was pounding, and fear really took hold once Grant opened the door.

Just then, the plane sputtered and stalled, dipping a little before evening out.

"If we're doing this, we'd better do it now!" Grant shouted as he ripped off his headset.

Cass sat holding onto the shoulder straps of her chute, wanting to say a prayer, but she didn't know any. She had always laughed at religious people, but now she wished she had known any prayer to help her survive this. Closing her eyes, she tried to bring one to mind, but the only thing that came was one she'd always seen on TV and in movies. She remembered it had something about walking in the shadow of death, but couldn't remember the rest. Damn! She cursed, figuring it served her right for picking on those who believed in God. "I'm sorry," she whispered out loud.

Just then, Cass felt a hand on her shoulder and a slight wave of relief washed over her. It felt almost as if God had heard her.

"Repeat after me," Steve said, one hand on her shoulder and the other on Drew's.

Cass wiped the hair that was now whipping everywhere from her eyes and nodded.

Steve spoke slowly, and the noise of the wind inside the cabin seemed to disappear. Drew looked up at Steve just as he began to speak.

Dear Jesus, lay your Wounded Hand
  Upon my weary head,
And teach me to have courage
In the paths that I must tread.
  Bless me, and bless those whom
   I love,
And give us grace to see
  These crosses bravely borne by us
Will keep us close to Thee.
And if at times a shadow falls
  In unexpected ways,
Put Your gentle Hand in mine
And guide me through the days.
So bless my people, one and all,
With Thy protecting grace,
And impart to them Thy Wisdom
Ere they meet Thee face to face.

Tears formed in Cass's eyes, as in Drew's, and he immediately wiped them away, blaming it on the wind from the open door. But it was hard to ignore the calming effect the prayer had on him.

Before fear had a chance to creep back in, Sara emerged from the cockpit, adorned with her parachute and wearing a look of determination. The plane was now gliding and would soon drop like a rock.

"Why haven't you jumped yet?" Sara shouted as she put her hand on Cass's shoulder, indicating for her to stand up.

"Are you ready, hun?" Grant asked Sara.

"Yeah," she replied.

"Remember what we went over, count to five and go after the person in front of you. Pull the cord once you exit the plane," Grant said as Sara dove headfirst out of the airplane.

"Holy shit!" Drew said.

"You're up, Cass," Grant said.

Cass made her way to the door, looked back at Steve, and then jumped out.

"Come on, big man, you're next," Grant said to Drew.

"Steve. Send Steve next," Drew said, his voice shaking.

"Steve, you're up. We're running out of time. Jump."

Steve made his way to the door and held on to both sides of the hatch. The air rushed past, and it appeared as though excitement washed over him.

"Jump!" Grant shouted.

Steve looked back at Drew.

"Jump!" Drew yelled.

Steve adjusted his shoulder strap, then jumped.

"Big man, it's now or never my friend."

Drew looked at the door and then up at Grant. "No!"

"Are you crazy? You're the toughest motherf'er I know. Now jump!"

Drew pushed back into the seat. Whatever prayer Steve had said had apparently worn off or gone out the door with him, because fear had gripped Drew again.

"We gotta jump now!" Grant shouted.

Just then the plane was no longer gliding and had started to free fall, with the nose dipping toward the ground.

"Hell with this!" Grant shouted, then jumped out the door.

Drew was frozen with fear. Besides sharks, a fear of heights was the next biggest thing on the list of things he was afraid of.

Steve looked up from underneath the parachute and found the plane above him. He watched as it dipped, leveled off, then dipped again. A wave of relief washed over him when he saw someone exit, then his heart sank when after a few seconds no one else emerged from the fuselage. The plane was going down now.

Well, this really sucks! Drew thought as the plane began to nosedive. There was a moment when his stomach made that flip like when you ride a roller coaster. Fear was controlling him, and he dug his feet against the floor and pressed his back as hard as he could into the side of the plane. His mind began to race, and Drew found himself lost in another memory…

A young Drew stood on a ladder with a can of canary yellow paint. He didn't understand why his father wanted to paint over the dark brown color of the house, which actually looked nice. But his father had insisted, and every day after school that spring he'd had a brush in one hand and a gallon of paint in the other. Painting wasn't so bad, even after school, but being screamed at sucked. All he could think of was Daniel LaRusso from the movie The Karate Kid and the famous line, "Paint the fence" — but there was no lesson to be learned here. Daniel didn't have to stand on an old, rickety wooden ladder with his asshole father below him shaking it, trying to make him fall off. Yet, the old man screamed louder and louder as the paint spilled.

"How about I bang your skull off the side of the house! Will that wake you up from your stupidity? You dumb fuck of a son!" his father had yelled.

Tears streamed from a young Drew's eyes. "But Daddy!"

"Don't 'but Daddy' me, you lazy fucking 'tard!" his father yelled as he shook the ladder harder.

"Daddy!" he shouted, afraid of falling.

"Get down here!"

Drew had put the paintbrush into the gallon of paint and made his way down. He'd hung onto the rung with one hand as the other clutched the paint can. Paint sloshed from side to side as Drew's father rocked the ladder back and forth.

He wasn't as scared of falling as he was of his father getting hold of him, which was inevitable, since he was standing at the base of the ladder.

Drew clung to the rung, stepping down one at a time, trying to block out his father's voice and the threats he shouted from below.

It was like a game of cat-and-mouse as Drew lifted his foot, trying to escape his father's grasp but, as usual, his father wrapped his long fingers around Drew's ankle and violently yanked.

Now, Drew tried to breathe, like he had when he hit the ground after being pulled off the ladder, the force of the impact causing him to lose his breath. Drew tried filling his lungs, but the air wouldn't move in either direction. There was a sharp, burning pain on his right side, just under the shoulder blade. He had landed on a rock, which protruded from the ground and had dug into him like a nail being driven in by a hammer. Fear crept in, as his breath seemed nonexistent. There was a small sucking sound coming from his mouth as his body tried desperately to pull in oxygen.

With the pain and inability to breathe combined, a young Drew definitely thought this was the end, panic setting in.

Like when a child and not wanting fear to control him, Drew was finally able to catch his breath and rolled onto his side. Lying there a moment, Drew did nothing but breathe. It felt like someone had hit his reset button and he was waiting on the green light to go. Slowly, his eyes began to focus, while feeling returned to his extremities as blood that had been pulled into his core to preserve life again now pumped throughout his body.

Drew found his bearings and realized he wasn't lying on the ground at his childhood home, but was up against the fuselage of the plane. His mind was trying to catch up to the fact that he was on a plane plummeting toward the ground and that he needed to get out and get out now!

He lunged for the door, grabbing the handle with one hand and the frame with the other.

Drew knew he was in a grave situation, one growing worse with every passing second. Still, he managed to pull his knees to the side of the door and stuck his head out.

He glanced down and was in awe at what he saw; the world without violence or death. No struggle, just peace and serenity. There was vast green scenery below, growing closer by the second, and he contemplated riding the plane down to what would be its final resting place. He saw the ocean and a windy road that snaked along the coast. In just a few seconds it will all be over, he thought, closing his eyes. But, as soon as he did, he saw himself as a boy lying on the ground gasping for air, his father standing over him.

"Fuck this," he said, opening his eyes and hurling himself out the door.

The tail of the plane zipped past, almost cutting him in two.

Frantic, Drew searched for the ripcord with his injured arm, finding it pressed up against his shoulder strap, pinned against it by the velocity of his fall.

Chapter 29

Stoughton, Massachusetts

With the store empty and her car stolen, Annabelle had one of two options: either walk back to her mother's empty-handed or head for home and hope no one had looted her house. If she went back to her mother's now they'd still be in the same predicament tomorrow but, if she went home, she had the possibility of returning with food. The decision was clear; home it was. Plus, she could use Drew's car to drive back.

Thankfully, the drizzle had stopped, but the temperature was starting to drop and the rain-soaked ground began to freeze.

The grocery store was a little over a mile away from her house. Swinging her arms as she walked, Annabelle tried to get her blood pumping, hoping it would help keep her warm. She found she needed to pay closer attention to her footing, as she had already slipped twice. The last thing she wanted was to fall and hurt herself. *I'll have to drive back slowly*, she thought.

A little more than halfway home, Annabelle reached the steepest part of the hill. She was taking her time when she heard a cough. Scanning the area, she then noticed a man standing on the front steps of the house at the top of the hill. The end of his cigarette caught her attention, burning bright with every draw. For those brief seconds it illuminated his face, and she knew it was a man by his thick black mustache. Continuing to walk, she kept her eye on the man and was thankful when he dropped his cigarette and opened the door, the glass glinting in the moonlight, and stepped inside. Passing the house, she turned when she heard voices coming from where she'd seen the man smoking. Looking over her shoulder, she spotted three men now exiting the front door.

"Hey baby! Where did you go?" a voice yelled.

"She was just there," Annabelle heard one of the men say.

"Quick, get in the car," another said.

Fear and panic set in, and Annabelle picked up her pace. At one point, she was sliding across the slick pavement like she was ice skating.

She heard the car backing down the driveway, then heard it skid, followed by a thump and the sound of plastic shattering as it crashed.

"Keep going! Keep Going!" she repeated to herself out loud. She was almost to the curve in the road, which led to a straightaway, and her house was about a quarter mile down to the right.

A minute passed, and she heard nothing.

Then came the sound of spinning tires. Frightened, her mind racing at the thought of what they might do to her if they caught up— because she knew they were coming after her. Looking left, Annabelle saw the headlights sway through the trees as the driver tried to keep the car on the slick road. The lights straightened out, then the car's engine raced as it began to gain speed.

Her heart was pounding as she made it to the other side of the curve; she could see her mailbox at the side of the road. *Almost there!*

Suddenly, the car came around the curve, its headlights flooding her and the whole road in light, and the engine revved again.

Shit, I'm not gonna make it! The headlights were closing in.

"Come here, bitch!" someone yelled from the car.

At the last second, she jumped into the brush on the side of the road and the car skidded to a halt. The back door whipped open and a twenty-something male jumped out.

"Come here sunshine!" the punk yelled.

Annabelle scurried, on her hands and knees, over to the base of a large tree.

"We're going to have some fresh pussy tonight!" the man said as he shone his flashlight at the brush.

Her left knee hurt from landing on a rock. Reaching down, she felt a tear in her pants, and wasn't sure if the wetness on her fingertips was blood or from the damp ground.

"Come here, bitch! You can't hide from us," the man said, his flashlight beam growing closer.

Twigs snapped with the man's every step, and he was almost on top of her.

Annabelle was shaking. She had never before feared for her life like this. She'd heard about people having to make split-second decisions, and now she was actually faced with one.

The man stopped and she could hear him breathing.

Holding her breath she closed her eyes, hoping he wouldn't find her.

After a few moments, thinking he'd moved on, Annabelle opened her eyes and found herself blinded by the man's flashlight.

"There you are, sunshine," he said, reaching down and grabbing her by the hair.

Annabelle screamed.

"Now comes the fun part."

Scared, she reacted. Reaching behind her, Annabelle pulled the knife from her back pocket and thrust it upward into the man's groin, then yanked it out.

The man let go of her hair and reached for his groin, blood seeping through his fingers. The man's breath began to quicken and his hands fumbled as he tried to stop the bleeding, but it streamed down his leg and into his boot.

"Oh my God! Oh my God!" the man mumbled as he tried to turn and walk away. Stumbling, he fell to one knee and dropped the flashlight, which landed between his legs. His upper body began to twitch and shake. "No! No! No!" he said, unzipping his pants and trying to get his hand directly against the wound. The front of his underwear was soaked in blood. Shimmying his pants down, blood squirted from the artery, which had been severed. Pale and lethargic, the man fell forward, landing next to the flashlight. Steam rose from the blood that had begun pooling in front of the flashlight lens, basking the area in crimson.

The other two men got out of the car.

"Yo Rex, you find her yet?" shouted one.

"Hurry up! I want me some pussy," the other shouted.

Clenching the knife, Annabelle crawled away, looking over her shoulder as she went. Her hands were freezing, and her pants were drenched.

Pausing, she heard the other two men find their friend.

"Rex! Are you okay?"

"We gotta get him outta here!"

Laying on her belly, she watched both men pick up their friend and drag him back to the car. The flashlight of the man she'd stabbed, Rex, was left behind, illuminating the bloody mess as the car drove off.

Annabelle took a minute to catch her breath and let her heart rate come down. Wondering if the men would come back, she decided it was best to get moving.

Looking around, trying to figure out exactly where she was in relation to her house, the passing clouds above parted, allowing moonlight to cascade down and reveal her location. She was near the power lines which abutted her property. There were only three houses on this side of the road after the curve, which also happened to be where the power lines crossed the street.

Now knowing where she was, she spotted her house through the trees and followed the trail beneath the power lines until she was parallel to it.

Making her way through the trees, she came out right in front of the back gate of the fence surrounding her property.

Finding the hide-a-key under the fake rock, she unlocked the back door and made her way over to the sink behind the bar. Dropping the knife into the sink, she removed her wedding rings and put them down on the counter then washed her hands. Using paper towels she dried her hands and headed upstairs. Once in the kitchen, she opened the pantry door and let out a sigh of relief as all the food was sitting on the shelf, right where she'd left it.

Annabelle washed the blood from her hands in the kitchen sink, finishing just as the water pressure died off.

Using the backpack, she loaded it up with food. Once full, she walked down the hall to Stephanie's room and opened her closet, looking for the other backpack they'd left.

Hmmm… that's strange, she thought, *I remember putting it in here.*

After a moment, it dawned on her that Drew had probably taken it with him when he left for Florida.

Oh no! she thought, *that means he took his car too!*

Walking back through the kitchen, she opened the breezeway door and saw the empty driveway. "Dammit!" she said out loud, knowing that she'd be walking back to her mother's.

Pacing the kitchen, trying to figure out what to do, she came to the conclusion that she would just have to carry it back. With that, she grabbed a few plastic shopping bags from under the sink. As she started loading up the bags, she realized they crinkled a lot, and it probably wasn't the wisest decision to head out carrying something that would make so much noise; plus, they weren't that strong and would probably end up breaking on the journey home.

Unsure of what to do, she headed back down the hallway toward her bedroom. The flashlight beam swung side to side, reflecting off the glass of the picture frames that lined the hallway. She stopped and looked at one from last year. All three of them were smiling and happy. Reaching up, Annabelle kissed her fingers and then placed them on Drew's face.

Crying, she walked into her bedroom and sat down on the bed. She was overcome by emotion from all the recent events, and being back home and seeing Drew's face, knowing her husband would never be returning, was too much. Her cries became uncontrollable, her shoulders heaving up and down as tears streamed down her cheeks.

She noticed one of Drew's sweatshirts on the end of the bed. Grabbing it, she brought it to her face. The scent of Drew filled her nostrils and she began to weep again. "What am I to do?" she sobbed, putting her head on the pillow. "What would Drew do?" she asked herself.

Tears continued to flow, absorbing into the pillowcase. The wet spot began to spread, and she felt the wetness against her face. Sitting up, she stared at the pillow. "Oh my God!" she said out loud and, after a brief moment, she began laughing and said, "Thank you Drew!"

She put his sweatshirt down and then picked up the pillow and removed the case, doing the same for every case on the bed.

Chapter 30

Paxton, Nebraska

Maureen lay in bed, her eyes heavy, but sleep would not come. Bill was sound asleep next to her, his snoring in full swing. She wanted to punch him to have him roll onto his side, but it really wasn't his fault, much as the way it wasn't her fault when her period came when the boys slept over at their friend's house, leaving them alone for some well-needed intimate time they couldn't then have because of "Aunt Flow."

She looked over at her husband as he slept, the man who loved her and who, during those heavy *flow* times, had held her and snuggled her close on the couch while they watched Netflix, ate popcorn and other snacks together — which was not good for either of them. Yet he loved her for her, and not for her vagina, bleeding or not. For him, being with her when he could not be *with* her, was special. It was love, and he had always loved her.

Maureen was thankful Bill wasn't like her father, a man she'd tried desperately to scrub from her memory; just the vilest of human beings. She wondered how her mother had put up with him, and then realized he must have shown her love like no other had no matter how fucked up their relationship was.

But now Maureen had this man, this snoring man, who loved her for who she was. He never woke her and told her to roll over, even when many a night she had caught herself snoring and woke with a dry throat or found a puddle of drool on her pillowcase. He'd never complained to his friends about it, much less anything at all she did, yet she'd complained to all her friends about the many things he did.

Right there in bed, remorse hit. She felt she needed to be punished for how she'd treated her husband, and now she demanded that she be punished.

As she lay there, she wondered if it was the cigarettes or the wine talking, possibly a combination of both, or if it was just her conscience being honest. She figured she could always differentiate herself from her *true* self and the *drunk* her, but right now it didn't seem like she could. Suddenly, she felt tired and closed her eyes. Within mere seconds, sleep took her.

Maureen woke in a strange place. A chalky taste filled her mouth, and she craved a glass of water.

Dehydrated, she moved her tongue, trying to bring moisture to her mouth, but it felt as if something was removing the moisture from the air and her body. She glanced over at the nightstand next to the bed, looking for water. There was none. The only thing on the table was a pumpkin. Staring at it, she noticed the color was fading and it was wilting and collapsing in on itself. Devoid of moisture, the pumpkin dried out and withered away.

Her hands itched, so she scratched at them. Flakes of dried skin fell from her hand, followed by an excruciating pain. Looking down, she screamed. Clumps of skin dangled from her fingertips. Muscle tissue, cartilage, and bone were all exposed, yet there was no blood. Her hand appeared the same way chicken did when peeled from the bone.

Screaming, Maureen jumped from bed and made her way toward the bathroom to get a towel to wrap around her hand. Focusing on the wound, she watched as blood began rising to the surface. She quickened her pace, darting across the room. The floor beneath her bare feet felt cold, which was odd since the bedroom had wall-to-wall carpeting. Before she had time to process this, she slammed into the wall; her wounded hand hitting first. The impact knocked her backward, onto the hard linoleum flooring.

"What the hell?" she yelled. How did I miss the bathroom door, she thought, having walked to it several times each night?

Grasping her wrist, she looked down at her hand, which now dangled, limp. She tried wiggling her fingers, but they would not move. Each finger felt weighed down, as if filled with sand, then came that numb, tingling feeling, like what would happen if she'd slept on it wrong.

Getting to her knees, she called out for Bill.

"Bill!" she screamed at the top of her lungs. Holding her injured hand, Maureen rose to her feet and called out for her husband again. But standing there she realized she was not in her bedroom; well not the one she'd gone to sleep in. It was a place she was familiar with, but hadn't seen in years.

Looking around, she couldn't believe where she was, she was in her childhood bedroom. Unicorn and flamingo pictures covered the wall above her bed. Then she heard voices in the room with her, and slowly turned around. Against the back wall was her brother's crib, but it was empty except for a small white, fluffy blanket. Scanning the room, she saw her brother sitting in the corner, talking to a sheet hovering in the air, two holes cut out for eyes.

Slowly, Maureen made her way toward her brother, who sat with his back to her.

As she approached, the air in the room became freezing cold. She heard her brother's little voice, and could see his breath as he spoke to the ghost.

Goosebumps covered her body, and she felt genuinely frightened as a black, tentacle-like arm reached out from under the sheet, heading straight for her brother's head.

"No!" Maureen screamed, lunging to snatch her brother from the thing's reach.

The blackness behind the eyeholes in the sheet turned a sinister red, and Maureen froze in place. Fear was powerful, powerful enough to stop someone in their tracks.

Clicks and clacks came from beneath the sheet.

What the hell are you? Maureen thought, trying to move. But she was powerless over her own body.

All she could do was watch and listen. She was a spectator, and nothing more.

Her brother sat on the floor, wearing only a diaper, his curly golden locks hanging down to his shoulders.

The tentacle moved closer and closer to the boy's head while he sat playing, unaware or unafraid of the thing before him.

Maureen watched as her little baby brother reached out and grabbed hold of the sheet, then started tugging.

The red eyes disappeared for a moment as the cutouts slid down, but the radiant glow pierced through the sheet, illuminating it in crimson.

Out of the corner of her eye, Maureen saw a little boy with brown hair appear. A gray feather with a white tip protruded from the back of the child's head. Lifting up his hand, the boy pointed at the ghost with his index finger.

Maureen's eyes shifted back to the sheet, which fell to the floor. She expected to see some kind of monster, but underneath the sheet was nothing but darkness.

How can that be? Maureen thought, still unable to move.

The tentacle protruded again from the darkness and continued toward her brother's head. Tiny spikes began poking out of the appendage, as if searching for its prey. Her little brother looked at the tentacle, then reached up with his left hand. Suction cups unfurled, exposing razor-sharp teeth at their center. Suddenly, a bright flash filled the room. It was so intense that Maureen closed her eyes and held her hands up to her face.

I can move again, Maureen thought. But she could not see. Everywhere she looked, all she saw was the afterimage of the flash.

"Agh!" Maureen screamed as she felt cold hands grab her arms. Flailing, she tried to free herself from the grasp that held her down.

"Maureen! Maureen!" She heard her husband's voice.

Slowly, she opened her eyes and found herself staring at the ceiling light. Bill's face appeared, and she felt the grip release her.

"What happened?" she asked, sitting up, rubbing the bright image from her eyes.

"You were having a nightmare and thrashing around," Bill said.

"It was just a nightmare?" she asked, her voice trembling.

"Yes," Bill said in a soft tone, trying to calm her down.

Tears welled in her eyes.

"Are you okay?"

"No!"

"What was it about?"

"I don't want to talk about it. I'm sorry I woke you. Go back to bed. I'm going downstairs to get a drink," she said, and then disappeared from the room.

Chapter 31

Mystic, Connecticut

Drew was scared shitless, and thought he was actually going to piss his pants. He did not like the feeling of falling— at all. Instinct kicked in, and he remembered what Sara and Grant had told them before boarding the plane.

"Once out the door, watch your altitude and deploy your chute at five-thousand feet," Grant said, and Sara reiterated his words.

Drew looked at the altimeter on his wrist; he was already at forty-five hundred feet, and dropping.

Grabbing hold of the ripcord he said, "Here goes nothing."

Drew floated down, slowly recognizing where he was. They were indeed over Connecticut, as Grant had said, but now he knew which part: Mystic, Connecticut.

Drew had been here several times before, and was excited to see a familiar place. Turning, he aimed for the desolate parking lot located between the Mystic Aquarium and the little shops next door. He had been here just last summer when he and Annabelle had made the drive down, passing through Providence, Rhode Island and continuing south on I-95 until they reached the Rhode Island and Connecticut border. The Aquarium was just over the Connecticut border.

Just before his feet touched the ground, Drew released the pack strapped to his left leg. As it hit the ground, a hard gust of wind blew, causing Drew to drift from where he'd wanted to land on a soft patch of grass between the two parking lots. Now, he'd be forced to land on the hard asphalt of the steak restaurant parking lot. Straightening his legs but keeping his knees slightly bent, Drew prepared for impact. Sand and other debris littered the lot, and his feet slid out from under him as he touched down, causing him to land hard on his ass; otherwise, he would have stuck the landing on his first jump. Getting up, he rubbed his backside, which didn't hurt as much as his pride did when he noticed both Sara and Cass walking toward him.

Great, I'll never live this down, he thought.

"Are you okay?" Sara asked as she approached. "The wind caught hold of you at the last moment, but you handled it well."

"I'm fine," he said, giving a wave as he checked to make sure the weapons were operable; they had made a loud clang upon hitting the asphalt.

"Wasn't that so much fun?" Cass asked, her face beaming with happiness. Now on the ground, she was singing a different tune from when they'd been in the plane.

It was the first time he had seen her smile since losing her friends, and he didn't want to spoil the moment by telling her how scared shitless he'd been the whole way down and that he could use a moment to collect himself. He also didn't want to remind her she needed to be scared of their new surroundings. *Let her have the moment,* Drew thought. *God knows when the next good one will come.*

Drew removed the parachute, and gave the weapons a once over. Other than a small nick on the barrel of the shotgun, both seemed operable.

"There they are," Sara said, pointing toward the back lot of the Aquarium.

As the men approached, Cass asked, "Where have you been? Drew beat you down."

"Haha," Steve said. "Someone here wanted to prove how good they were at landing and landed right where they said they would, which was right inside the Aquarium, and we've spent the last few minutes trying to get him out."

Grant chuckled.

"You never could pass up a great LZ, could you?" Sara said, planting a big kiss on Grant.

"LZ?" Cass asked.

"Landing Zone, hun," Sara said between kisses.

"I see someone has found a new spark in their relationship," Steve said.

"I think you're right," Grant said as he grabbed his wife by the waist and kissed her again. "I love you," he said between kisses.

"I love you too," Sara replied.

"There's plenty of hotels around here. You two want to get a room?" Drew asked.

"Very funny," Sara said, placing a last kiss on her husband's cheek.

Steve slowly made his way next to Drew and said, "Big guy, don't forget they're trying to help get you back to your beloved wife and daughter, so how about you cut them some slack."

Drew instantly felt an inch tall.

"Yeah," Steve said, seeing Drew's face.

"Hey guys, I'm sorry. Go ahead and suck face," Drew said.

"Really?" Steve said.

"I mean, enjoy each other. Just keep it G-rated in front of the kid," Drew added.

"Kid!" Cass said. "I'll have you know I've probably had more sex this year than you've had your whole life." As soon as the words left her mouth, she instantly started crying. "Greg!" she cried out, bringing her hands up to her face.

"See, I was trying to avoid that," Drew said as he slapped Steve on the shoulder.

"Oh, I see," Steve replied.

Cass walked over to Drew and buried her head into his shoulder, and wept.

"Guys, maybe now isn't the time," Steve said as he made his way toward Grant and Sara.

"I feel awful," Grant said.

"Me too," Sara said.

"Don't," Steve said. "Enjoy your happiness. Given our current situation, we can use all the hope we can get."

With that being said, Grant reached out and gently pinched his wife's ass.

Sara turned, held her hand to her mouth and said, "Why, Grant, do you like my ass or something?"

"Or something," he replied, as Sara fell into his arms. They laughed and kissed again.

Whatever good memory Drew had from this place dissipated as he noticed a truck bearing down on them.

Chapter 32

Mystic, Connecticut

Stan was approaching Exit 90 on I-95 North, crossing the Mystic River Bridge. He would be crossing into Rhode Island soon and was looking forward to seeing home when on the horizon he noticed a parachute floating down.

Slowing the truck, he leaned forward, pressing his chest against the steering wheel and kinking his neck to look upward. To his amazement, he noticed two other chutes floating down, watching as a fourth deployed.

"What the heck?" Stan said out loud as he saw an airplane fall from the sky. Slamming on the brakes, he stepped out of the vehicle and watched as the aircraft plummeted to the ground. Within seconds, black smoke rose from behind the trees in the foreground.

I hope everyone made it out okay, he thought, just as he spotted a fifth chute descending from above.

Turning his attention back to the first chutes, he noticed that they'd all landed off to the right of the exit and knew they were either in the Mystic Aquarium parking lot or near the quaint little shops he and Carol loved to visit.

Getting back into the truck, Stan headed up the road and exited the highway, taking a right at the end of the ramp.

His excitement grew when he saw three people in the parking lot of the steakhouse, which was a must-do when visiting the area. The thought of their well-done steak tips filled his mind, causing his mouth to salivate and reminding him how hungry he was.

Driving past the restaurant, Stan took the next left toward the entrance to the shops and steakhouse. Rounding the corner, he noticed a lip-locked couple intertwined in each other's embrace.

Before he reached the group, a large muscular man dropped to one knee and took aim with a rifle.

Stan slammed on the brakes and stuck both arms out the window. Slowly, he reached down and opened the door from the outside and then stepped out of the truck with his arms raised above his head.

"Are you guys okay?" Stan asked. "I saw your plane go down and stopped to see if you needed help."

Drew stood up, lowering his weapon, and approached cautiously.

"I'm Stan," he said as the brute of a man came close.

"Drew," the man said, stopping before him.

Stan was delighted. "It's been a long time since I've seen someone else."

Drew must have picked up on his accent and he then asked, "Where are you from?"

"Quincy, just south of Boston."

"I know exactly where that is. I live in Stoughton."

"No way, we're practically neighbors. Is that where you're heading?"

"Yes," said another man, coming up behind Drew and looking over his shoulder at Stan."

"I'm heading that way if you want to hop in. It will be tight, but there's plenty of room in the back. There's even a mattress."

"How lucky are we?" asked a third man, stepping next to Drew and offering his hand.

"God works in mysterious ways," said the first.

Drew glanced over at him, then back at Stan and said, "The religious one here is Steve. That's Grant." He used his thumb to point sideways. Looking over his shoulder, he added, "That's Sara, Grant's wife. They're the two lovebirds of the group, and that's Cass." The girl waved.

"Where were you coming from?" Stan asked.

"Florida. You?" Drew asked.

"Nebraska."

"You drove the whole way?" Grant asked.

"I did. We can talk on the way if you like. I'm heading home to see my wife."

"So is he," Steve said, nodding toward Drew.

"And his daughter," Cass said, approaching the truck.

Stan went to get in the truck but stopped. Slowly, he turned back to face the group.

"What?" Drew asked.

"I should warn you, I have a rifle and pistol up front with me. I don't want them to take you by surprise."

"No worries," Steve said, lifting his shirt up and exposing the handle of the pistol tucked into his waistband.

With that, the group climbed in and headed up I-95 toward Massachusetts.

Chapter 33

Stoughton, Massachusetts

Susan's eyes fluttered open, and she found herself in a strange sun-filled room. Climbing out of bed, she was met by warm, comforting air, which felt good on her hands which no longer hurt. Looking around the room, it felt like she had been there before, but she couldn't put her finger on where it was. The scent of Jasmine oil filled the air, and that triggered a distant, fond memory. Then it hit her, and she knew exactly where she was. This had been a week of firsts. It had been her first plane ride. First time to Florida. And the first time to Disney.

It was here, in this hotel suite where she'd spent her honeymoon... and what a joyous week it was. This room held many a first, too: first time sharing a bed with a man, first time seeing a man naked. And it was the place where she'd lost her virginity.

She'd spent every day, for the rest of her life, with that man, until his passing.

The smell in the room had changed, and now the aroma of sizzling bacon and freshly baked cinnamon buns filled the air. The hotel was known for its gourmet food, and her mouth salivated.

She made her way from the bedroom, passing an oak-framed mirror hanging on the wall. Glancing at her reflection, she saw herself as she was now; wrinkled skin and gray hair. *How awful,* she thought, continuing into the small foyer. The hallway beyond led to the front door, beyond which dark and cold air crept in from the darkness beyond. Goosebumps formed on her arms and legs, and she looked back over her shoulder toward the warmth of the hotel bed.

Cold air wisped toward her, like the way it does when a freezer door is opened on a blistering summer's day. Beyond the darkness, Susan felt something watching. Something evil. Something vile. Something that scared her.

Behind her, she heard her husband's voice. "We should move here. It's always sunny, warm, and there's plenty of fresh fruit and vegetables. Heck, we could find a nice place to settle down."

"Henry!" she cried out, excited. Her heart raced and her palms felt sweaty at the thought of seeing him again now. She hurried back to the bedroom, hoping to find the man she loved, but when she came around the corner, Henry was not there. No one was there. Confused, she searched the room, even got down on her knees, her old joints cracking, and looked under the bed. She'd just heard his voice; she knew she had.

Before getting up, she heard it again. "Florida. Go to Florida, Susan."

Hopping to her feet, she searched the room again, then took a step to her right and looked down the hallway.

Go to Florida Susan, she heard again, but this time the voice came from beyond the cold darkness.

"Henry!" Susan cried out, falling to her knees.

Florida, she heard again.

Suddenly, while staring down the hallway, a pair of glowing red eyes appeared within the darkness, and Susan became taut with fright.

Florida, Susan heard again, before waking in her frozen bedroom.

Heading down the hallway, Annabelle walked back into Stephanie's room. Using the flashlight, she searched for extra warm clothes for her daughter to wear and grabbed her snow boots from behind the door to keep her little piggies warm. She didn't see the car that was used by the men who'd tried to attack her drive past, stopping when they saw the light dancing around the room.

Once she finished packing the clothes, she headed to the kitchen to pack some food. The pillowcases were strong and held the contents well, but the cans of soup and bottles of water were getting heavy. She needed to distribute the weight over her shoulders so she didn't have to carry everything with her arms. Thinking she heard a car door, she stood still in front of the kitchen island that was covered with food to pack. After a few moments, she'd figured it was just her imagination and continued packing.

Then came a loud bang and the sound of wood splintering. The front door flung open, crashing into the wall, followed by heavy footsteps. Annabelle looked up as two men walked into the kitchen.

One had a thick black mustache, bloodstains covering the front of his shirt and pants. In his right hand, he wielded an aluminum baseball bat. The other man was balding, fat, and held a tire iron. Both stared at her, wide-eyed, and the one with the bat spoke first. "You killed our friend, you bitch!" he spat out.

"Yeah, all he wanted was a little fun with you," said the fat one.

"Now it's time for payback!"

Trapped, Annabelle stood with her back to the sink as the two men stood on the other side of the island, which led into the living room and hallway.

Facing two men who wanted to rape and murder her, that little voice inside her head piped up and asked, *What would Drew do?*

"What would Drew do?" she asked out loud.

"What?" the fat man said, tilting his head and confused by the question.

Annabelle looked down and, in that split second, saw a can of peas. Before she knew what she was doing, she reached out and grabbed it. Back in high school she'd been the pitcher for the girls' softball team and, cocking back her arm, she rocketed the can at the man. Hurdling through the air, it smashed into the nearest man's face, the lip of the can digging into the bridge of his nose and splitting it wide open.

The man crumpled to his knees, dropping the tire iron, which clanged as it hit the tile floor, and then clutched at his face with both hands. Blood poured between his fingers.

"You crazy bitch!" the other man said, lunging at her with the bat.

Grabbing another can, she whipped it.

The man dodged, but his foot got tangled up in the legs of a stool in front of the island and he fell hard, the bat clanging to the tile floor.

Annabelle, seeing her chance, jumped over the man holding his nose and bolted down the hallway. As she ran, she remembered playing hide-and-seek in the house with her husband and daughter. Drew would run down the hall, flick on Stephanie's light switch and slam her door, but would then quickly turn and hide behind the bathroom door across the hall. Seeing the light on, Stephanie always headed straight to her room and, as she passed, Drew would reach out and grab her.

Running to Stephanie's room, she opened the door, dropped the flashlight, and slammed the door shut.

"You're dead!" one man said, and she heard him get up and make his way down the hall.

Annabelle still had the knife in her back pocket and reached behind her to grab the handle. Taking the bait, the man walked past the darkened doorway and flung open Stephanie's door.

He stood there a moment, trying to find her, not knowing he was backlit by the flashlight.

With one swift motion, Annabelle pulled the knife from her back pocket, took a step forward, and brought it over her head. Holding it with both hands, and using her forward momentum, she plunged the knife downward, stabbing him right at the base of his neck. The blade pierced the man's spinal cord, and became lodged between cartilage and bone. No longer having control over his body, the man fell forward, slamming into the door and sliding down, then crashing onto the floor.

Annabelle, still holding the knife as the man fell forward, could not stop her own momentum and fell on top of him, driving the tip of the knife through the front of the man's throat. Laying on top, she shivered at the horrendous gurgles coming from the dying man. The body twitched twice, and then both the twitching and the gurgling stopped.

Climbing off, she picked up the flashlight and then heard a loud bang from the kitchen. Slowly, she made her way back toward the kitchen. Halfway down the hall, she saw the other man's legs sprawled on the floor. Approaching, she noticed marks in the blood, indicating he'd slipped trying to get up. She spotted blood dripping from the granite island countertop and shinned the light on the perpetrator's head, illuminating a nasty gash.

Annabelle stood there for a moment, shocked. The only sound came from the man on the kitchen floor, now taking weird, short breaths that didn't look or sound good. Catching her own breath, she flipped the hair out of her face before searching the man for his keys. She then quickly finished packing up the pillowcases, and loaded them into her new wheels before driving off.

Chapter 34

Rockefeller Center, New York

"Are you ready?" Glen heard in his earpiece.

Sitting at the news desk, Glen looked up at the digital clock hanging below the camera and nodded his head.

Chris glanced up at the monitor for camera one which was located in front of the news desk, and noticed Glen was ready to go. "We're live in 3...2...1," Glen heard in his ear.

At the press of a button, Chris introduced the video he'd created for their triumphant return, which replaced the SMPTE rainbow-colored bars.

Glen heard Chris in his ear again as the 'On-Air' light came on. "This is the first live broadcast after the worldwide pandemic. The film is rolling, and the timestamp is in place, marking mankind's continued evolution of endurance and survival. And it will be you leading this new world as we rebuild," Chris said.

A smile washed over Glen's face. His lifelong dream to become the number one anchor in the business was not only coming true, but now he surpassed that goal by becoming number one in the world.

Mr. Williams pumped his fist as the monitors in the control room displayed the video airing live, which was being broadcast worldwide through various satellites.

"Twenty seconds until the package ends," Chris announced into the mic.

With his foot on the pedal to control the teleprompter, Glen waited for the light on top of the camera to change.

Sitting there, he counted down the seconds in his head when suddenly something surprising happened. Glen felt himself getting aroused. It was more than just aroused; he had a full-blown erection.

Shifting in his chair, he accidentally tapped the prompt button for the teleprompter, causing the words to scroll up.

"What the hell is happening?" Mr. Williams yelled.

Glen tried wiggling to adjust his manhood and ease the pressure as it began pressing up against the inside of his pants. *What the hell!* he thought. *Not now!*

"I think he froze up," Chris said.

"No shit, you don't say!" the old man retorted.

Glen heard Chris's voice in his earpiece again, "Are you okay?"

Arching his back, Glen reached into his pants on live TV and moved his erect piece to the side, so it was no longer pressing up against his belt and zipper.

"You good?" Chris asked.

Glen nodded and gave a thumbs up sign with his right hand. He tapped the rollback button on the footpad with his foot and the teleprompter started over again.

Glen took a deep breath and started. "Good evening, America. I'm Glen Daniels and I come to you live from New York City." A lump formed in his throat, causing him to pause. He had rehearsed the speech several times, yet the levity of the situation hit him all at once.

"I'm not quite sure what to say," Glen said. Looking down, he noticed the chemical stain left on the desk from cleaning up after Bethany died and a lump formed in his throat.

"Glen, you okay?" Chris asked into the mic.

Taking yet another deep breath, Glen wiped the tears from his eyes, and after a moment, he spoke.

"I never thought I'd see this day," he said, ignoring the teleprompter.

"My friend and colleague Bethany Rogers died right here at this desk, live on the air," Glen said, as he moved his notes, exposing the stained desktop.

"Get a close-up of that!" Mr. Williams shouted to Chris, who toggled the camera above the news desk and zoomed in on the blotchy stains.

"She died doing her job. She died trying to warn you, the viewers, of the danger that was spreading. While visiting several hospitals in the city, she interviewed many doctors, nurses, and patients, trying to understand how the virus spread. Unfortunately, she too became infected. I honor her by picking up the torch and carrying on. Like Bethany did, we will bring you the news - just the news. The days of journalists and reporters putting their own 'two cents' on a story and spinning it to fill their narrative is over."

Glen's shoulders rose and fell as he took another deep breath, then looked back up towards the camera. Tears welled up in his eyes until they spilled over, running down his cheeks. Sniffling, Glen wiped his nose using his thumb.

"I'm at a loss for words over all that we've endured." Glen used his thumb to wipe his left eye. "All of us have lost friends and loved ones, but we're still here," Glen said, "And I guarantee they would want us to push on."

He sat up straight in the chair and took yet another deep breath. "The time of the virus has passed. We must not be afraid to go out, and we cannot hide forever. But, it's okay to be cautious, and if you prefer, wear a mask around others. Get out and connect with others who have also survived. We must help our neighbors and accept help from others when offered, if we wish to survive."

Glen took another deep breath and continued.

"We will have tough days ahead, but we will also have good ones. Strive for the good days. Do your part as a human to help your fellow man. Together there's nothing we cannot do."

Glen paused and looked around at the empty the newsroom. "This studio was once bustling with people working hard to bring you the news. It will take time, but I expect to see fresh faces around here soon!"

Staring into the camera, his top lip began quivering, "And like here, you will meet fresh faces too. I promise I will be here for you every day. I...," Glen stopped himself, "No, that's not right, I mean *We*. We will bring you the critical news you need to stay informed every day and beyond. We will be here for you as well as the new faces you meet."

Glen glanced at his papers, searching for the right words to say next. *Unity not diversity*, he thought and looked into the camera. "No matter where you are on the globe, you are not alone. We are all in this together. From this day forward, we will no longer be separated by race or creed. We are all human and the human spirit can endure anything!"

"This message will repeat at the top and bottom of every hour, so others who tune in may discover it. Twenty-four hours from now we'll be back on with another live broadcast."

Scrambling, Chris typed and scrolled until he found what he was searching for. Pushing a button, a world clock appeared on the screen.

"Currently, it is 5:00pm here in New York. Please note the time difference based upon where you live, as we will see you tomorrow at this same time. Until then, take care of yourself and help others who are less fortunate."

He finished with, "This is not goodbye; this is until tomorrow."

Chris pushed another button, and the new global logo displayed on the screen. Using the same station letters, Chris came up with a new acronym for WTFH:

World **T**ogether **F**inding **H**ope.

In the control room Mr. Williams sighed in relief. "I thought for sure he was going to screw that up," he said. But damn, he turned it around."

Chris smiled and nodded. "He did good. Real good"

The dark entity stood next to Mr. Williams; happy its plan was coming together.

Chapter 35

Paxton, Nebraska

Maureen sat on the porch rubbing the cold from her fingers and hands before reaching into the fresh pack of cigarettes that Bill purchased on his trip into town. Pulling one out, she placed the filter in her mouth and sparked up. Staring down at the lit end, she watched as it glowed red hot, then turned ash gray before a thin line of smoke trailed upward.

The smoke filled her lungs while the taste of tobacco clung to her tongue, which brought back memories from when she picked up the habit.

She was fifteen years old and in immense pain. First, her father backhanded her, followed by a heavy punch to her left side. If she had done nothing, her mother would have died.

It was a Saturday night and her parents ordered subs from the local sandwich shop. Maureen's mother ordered her favorite, a steak and cheese sub loaded with all the fixings, but on that night, there was no joy in it. Accidentally, her mother swallowed a large unchewed piece of steak which became lodged in her throat, blocking her airway.

She rushed to the sink and reached into her mouth, trying to remove the blockage. Each attempt was unsuccessful.

The seconds ticked past like minutes. Maureen watched as her mother turned around with eyes bulging with fear and held her hands to her larynx, displaying the universal sign for choking.

Maureen raced to her mother's aid and began administering the Heimlich Maneuver just as she learned in Health Class. Unable to clear the obstruction, Maureen looked to her father for help, but he just sat there taking bites out of his sandwich.

"Help her!" Maureen screamed, staring at him.

He put his sandwich down, stood up, and wiped his shirt before strolling over nonchalantly.

She assumed he would take over, so Maureen released her grasp and stepped back. Her father walked over, but instead of helping his wife, he raised his hand and backhanded Maureen in the face. The force of the impact caused her to lose her balance, and she fell backward against the countertop and slid to the floor.

Stunned, Maureen stood up and reached to help her mother again, who was turning blue. Before she could even get her arms around her mother, her father threw a hard-right jab which landed just below the ribcage on her left side. The pain was immediate and intense, which caused her to double over, and she felt sick.

Maureen looked up and saw the evil in her father's eyes as he stood there staring at his wife. His look was disturbing, like he wanted to watch her choke and die.

Sucking up the pain, Maureen stood up again, grabbed her mother around the waist, and thrusted upward with all her might. A wet, chunky sound escaped from her mother as the dislodged piece of steak sailed into the sink.

"Are you okay?" Maureen asked and rested her head on her mother's shoulder.

"Yes, dear," her mother replied, wiping her mouth and breathing hard.

Her father sat back down and started eating his sandwich again.

"We need to leave," Maureen whispered as she draped her arm over her mother's back.

"I can't," her mother sighed, tears in her eyes.

"Mom, he's going to kill all of us if he gets a chance," Maureen said before glancing over her shoulder at her father.

He glared back at her, chewing his sandwich. Her mother touched Maureen's already swollen face, causing her to flinch from the pain. It would leave a bruise for sure.

Maureen had enough of her abusive father, so she packed a bag and ran away to her friend Cathy's house. Paula, Cathy's mother, took one look at Maureen's face and told her she could stay. Paula told the girls she had an abusive boyfriend years ago, and that she understood the predicament Maureen found herself in.

Cathy stole two cigarettes from her mother's pack and handed one to Maureen and told her it would help calm her nerves. That was it. After the first drag, she was hooked.

The next morning, after discovering Maureen had run off, her father called the police.

Later that evening there was a knock at Paula's door. Cathy peeked out the window and spotted a police cruiser along with Maureen's father's car out front.

Paula told Maureen to run downstairs and hide in the basement behind the water heater.

Maureen heard Paula talking to the police and told them she was not there. One police officer said he knew Maureen was inside and told Paula she would be in trouble for lying to the police.

Again, Paula denied Maureen being in the house.

"I know she's in there!" Maureen heard her father yell.

"She's not here!" Paula said, raising her voice.

"Well, we're searching the house," one officer said.

Not wanting to get her friend's mother in trouble, Maureen decided it best if she left.

She crept out the bulkhead, careful to close it quietly behind her, and made her way across the backyard. A tall, white picket fence surrounded the property and the only gate led straight out to the driveway.

Her heart pounded away in her chest as she feared being captured and brought back home. Unable to scale the fence, her only escape was to climb the oak tree in the back corner.

The thick bark dug into her skin as she clutched and shimmied up the trunk. Grabbing onto a branch, she hauled herself up branch after branch until she was above the top of the fence.

Frantically, she kept looking over her shoulder, fearing being caught at the last minute.

She crawled out onto the branch that jetted out over the fence. Maureen glanced back one last time and saw her father step out onto the back porch. Fearing being caught, she was left with only one option; she let go of the branch.

She hit the ground hard but caught herself before falling over into the fence. Then she adjusted her shoe before running off into the darkness of the night.

Penniless, Maureen made her way to the local diner. Once inside, she headed straight toward the bathrooms but went to the payphone beyond. Pretending to be on the phone, she waited for a large table to leave. Maureen hung up the phone and made a beeline for the empty table. She snagged the cash tip as she walked past and caught up to the group leaving and walked out right behind them.

Hitchhiking, she caught a ride to the nearest bus station. With the stolen tip money, she bought her first pack of cigarettes from a vending machine.

Maureen sat in a bathroom stall smoking and biting her nails. She didn't have nearly enough money to buy a one-way ticket to nowhere and even contemplated going home, but instead prayed to God.

In that instant, an opportunity walked right in and presented itself.

A woman came in and sat down in the stall next door and accidently tipped over her pocketbook, sending her purse tumbling out while relieving herself. Maureen picked it up, grabbed all the cash, dropped the purse and bolted before the woman could wipe and pull up her pants.

A large map of the country hung inside the terminal, and an idea hit while standing before it. She closed her eyes and spun around three times. With her index finger out in front of her, she walked over to the map until she touched it. Opening her eyes, she smiled and headed to the ticket counter.

Three bus transfers, forty-eight hours, and sixteen hundred miles later, Maureen arrived in Nebraska.

Chapter 36

Crescent City, Florida

Billy woke up to the sound of cheers and clapping. The little boy rubbed the sleep from his eyes and trudged his way downstairs.

Just before reaching the bottom of the stairs Billy stepped on the squeaky tread and his mother, Betty-Sue, turned and saw him coming down the last step.

"Did we wake you?" she asked apologetically.

After a few steps into the living room, Billy realized his mother and grandparents were standing around the TV, while his uncle Dave was asleep on the couch.

"What's all the excitement about?" Billy asked.

"The TV is working!" his mother said gleefully.

"It is!" Billy said excitedly.

"Yes, it is dear. Your Uncle Dave got it working!" Grandma said, looking over at him passed out on the couch.

"Are my cartoons on?" Billy asked.

"No, not yet. It's just the news for now," Betty-Sue replied.

"Oh," Billy said, deflation in his voice.

"Breakfast is on the table," Grandma said, turning towards Billy. "I made your favorite, French Toast."

Billy went into the kitchen, made himself a plate, then came back and sat down in the living room to watch TV.

"Where's dad?" Billy asked, licking syrup from his fingers.

"He, Uncle Arthur, and Uncle Ralph took the produce into town to barter with Cap," his mother replied.

"Oh yeah," Billy said and then asked, "Are things going back to normal?" He sensed something he hadn't felt in a while, hope.

"Hopefully so," Grandma said.

"William, you sure do ask a lot of questions," his grandfather chimed in, annoyed with all the interruptions.

"Sorry Grandpa," Billy said before stuffing a forkful of French Toast in his mouth.

Henry parked out back at the loading dock behind Caps. Ralph and Arthur hopped out and removed the tarp covering the back of the truck. Then they started loading the produce onto a dolly from the loading dock, while Henry went inside the store.

Snaking his way through a corridor, Henry stepped into the back of the store. Instantly he noticed a small group of people congregating around the register and spotted Cap on the other side of the store.

"Hey Cap!" Henry said, walking over to him, removing his hat and pointing to the group of watchers.

"Oh, hey Henry! Here to drop off your produce?" Cap asked.

"Yes sir, my brothers are unloading it now," Henry said. "What's going on over there?" he asked, pointing his hat toward the group of customers.

"You haven't heard?" Cap asked.

"No!" exclaimed Henry.

"The news is on! One of the major studios in New York is up and running!"

"Really?" Henry said, striding over and joining the group in front of the TV.

It felt strange watching TV as it was something he hadn't done in what felt like forever.

"When did this start?" Henry asked, turning toward Cap.

"Sometime this morning. When Doug tried the TV this morning it was on."

Henry recalled seeing Doug, Cap's brother, working on the TV the other day when he was in.

"What are they saying?"

"Well, they said the sickness is gone."

"Gone?"

"That's what he said. Said we shouldn't be afraid to go outside. Said to help one another."

"Anything else?"

"Said the message is on a loop and they'll be back on later today with news about rebuilding."

"That's good news! Damn good!"

"What's good?" Ralph asked, poking his head into the store.

"Dave was right," Henry said, turning toward his brother.

"Our brother?" Ralph asked.

"Since when has Dave been right about anything?" Arthur asked jokingly, joining his brothers in the store.

Henry told them about the recent developments and how Dave was certain he had heard something last night while tinkering with the TV.

Cap wheeled over a cart loaded with the supplies he agreed to exchange for the produce and said, "I believe you specifically requested this," and handed Henry a four pack of toilet paper.

"Oh, how my ass has missed you!" Henry said, squeezing the package of Charmin, causing everyone to laugh.

"See you back in a week?" Cap asked.

"Yes, sir," Henry replied.

Chapter 37

Stoughton, Massachusetts

That night, Susan climbed into a cold bed with an empty stomach. She stared at the ceiling for hours before sleep finally found her. As she drifted off, a warmth slowly crept into her bed. It started at her feet and pushed upward. The freezing cold sheets thawed and felt warm, like when she laid on a towel on the hot beach sand. Her pillow was cold and hard, but it softened, becoming fluffy like a cloud on a summer day.

It had been years since she slept so cozy, not since before her husband passed. As time passed, she found it hard to recall his face, which had become blurry in her memory of him, and no matter how hard she tried, she could not remember his face. But now she could recall his facial features, and she even swore she felt his touch.

Susan's eyes fluttered open, and a smile washed over her face. She found herself back in her honeymoon suite again and felt a presence in the room with her.

"Henry!" she joyfully cried out.

Yes, my dear, answered a voice.

"Where are you?"

I'm here with you, my love.

"I can't see you."

I'm here with you in spirit.

"Are you… dead?"

I'm free of my body.

"I miss you so…" Susan said, tears welling up in her eyes.

Don't cry, my dear. We will be together soon.

"Soon?" she asked, wiping away her tears.

Yes, but I need you to do something.

"What?" she asked.

Winter is coming. I need you to pack up and head south.

"You want me to leave our home?" she asked, not understanding.

Yes.

"Why? We've lived through cold winters before."

Annabelle and Stephanie.

"Are they in danger?" she asked, concern in her voice.

Yes.

Susan sat up and looked around. She noticed that beyond the sliding glass door there was a wall with strange carvings on it.

"Where am I?" Susan asked, getting out of bed. Her feet touched the floor, and it felt cold. Standing up, she was shocked to find the bed was a slab of stone.

"Stephanie?" Susan said, confused at the sight of her granddaughter lying on the slab. Her mind was racing and then suddenly stopped. Susan's face went flush, and her mouth gaped open as the feeling of dread washed over her.

"No!" Susan screamed. "Not my granddaughter!"

Susan woke up trembling and startled to find Stephanie sleeping next to her like she had been in her nightmare. Instinctively, she reached out to ensure her granddaughter was alive and a wave of relief came when she felt her little chest rise and fall. She moved strands of hair that hung over the sleeping child's face and leaned over, gently kissing her forehead.

Susan climbed out of bed into the freezing room. She covered Stephanie with an extra blanket and headed to the kitchen, hoping to find something to eat.

Just before dawn Annabelle arrived back at her mothers. She slipped in the front door and into the kitchen.

"Was that the wisest thing to do?" Susan said from the kitchen.

"Oh mom, you're awake," Annabelle said startled.

"Yes, and I found your letter. What the hell were you thinking?"

"We needed food," Annabelle said, holding up the pillowcases.

"Annabelle," Susan said, taking a bag of food from her. "We need to have a serious talk about what we're going to do!"

"I know mom," Annabelle replied.

"My god!" Susan exclaimed. "Is that blood?" she asked at the sight of Annabelle's stained clothes.

"Yes," Annabelle said, putting the pillowcases down and began sobbing.

"Are you hurt?"

Annabelle shook her head no. Her bottom lip curled in as she cried.

"Whose blood is it?" Susan asked, trying to console her daughter.

Not wanting to tell her about the men who tried to rape her, knowing it would make her mother's anxiety go through the roof, so she lied and said, "A dog attacked me. I stabbed it before it could bite me."

"You were smart to bring a knife with you."

Annabelle nodded, trying to compose herself.

"Well, you need to get out of those blood-soaked clothes and washed up before Stephanie wakes up and sees you like that."

"Okay," Annabelle sobbed.

"Why don't you go wash up in the bathroom and I'll bring you some clean clothes."

Susan began putting the groceries away while Annabelle was washing up and started a pot of water on the stove.

"Thankfully, the gas still works," Susan said, opening the oven door, releasing much needed warmth.

Annabelle stepped over in front of the oven and rubbed her freezing hands in the heat emitting from it.

"All the food you brought from your house won't last long," Susan said, sitting down at the table.

"Mom, I know," Annabelle said, with a worried look.

"I think we should consider heading south. We won't survive a long harsh winter here."

"And you think it will be easier out there?" Annabelle asked, nodding her head toward the window.

"No, but a month from now the snow will be flying. Then what?"

"I don't know mom." Concern was visible across Annabelle's face.

"I say we pack up what we can for food and clothing, load up Stephanie's red wagon and head south."

Annabelle looked out the window, knowing snow would cover the ground soon. She also knew the temperature would plummet to the single digits, or even worse, negative.

"In a month's time we could be far enough south and away from the snow."

"But mom, where will we go?"

"Well, it's funny you should ask. I've been having dreams lately of Florida."

"Really?"

"Yes. In my dreams we're at the Disney resort that your father and I stayed at on our honeymoon. It's so beautiful and warm there and has all the accommodations. Plus, there's a man in my dreams."

"A man mom, really?"

"Yes, dear, but it's hard to see his face. It's always blurry, like a shadow, but he is in charge and he cares for everyone. He's like the Mayor or something."

Annabelle sat there recalling her trip to see the Mouse back in college, and she remembered how sunny and warm it was. Then, as if on cue, Stephanie called out, "Mommy, I'm cold." A moment later she rounded the corner adorned with a blanket around her which trailed down the hallway.

Chapter 38

Mystic, Connecticut

"Is anyone else concerned why this man has a mattress in the back of his truck, or is it just me?" Cass asked.

"Well, given that he drove from Nebraska and there are no hotels open, I assume he used it to sleep on," Sara said, stating the obvious.

"Oh," Cass said, looking down.

Grant squeezed his wife's hand and whispered into her ear, reminding her of what had happened to Cass's friends, so she was probably looking at the mattress through a different prism.

Drew sat in the front seat and it felt good seeing a familiar stretch of road.

Breaking the silence between them, Stan asked, "Where in Stoughton do you live?"

"Do you know where the Target is?" Drew asked.

"Yeah, right off of Route 24."

"I live about a mile down on the left."

"So, do you think it's quicker to go straight up I-95 to I-93 then?"

"No."

"Really?"

"Yes."

"Which way do you recommend then?"

"I-95 to 295, back onto I-95 and then get off at exit 9 for Foxboro."

"Why would we go 295? That's longer."

"It will add about fifteen to twenty minutes, which is better than driving right up 95 straight through the heart of Providence. There are a lot of tall buildings right next to the highway, including the Providence Mall, which provides dozens of ambush sites."

"True," Stan said.

"Plus, with all those interchanges, I bet it's clogged with a ton of cars. Going 295 seems longer, but it will be the fastest."

"Wow, you've really given this some thought. I bet you got the entire trip planned out in your head."

"Yup!" Drew said, turning his head, and looked out the window. He didn't feel like explaining what it was like growing up with an abusive father and always having to plan around his temperament. It was one of those things that just stuck, and Drew applied it to everyday life. See the issue before it arises and avoid it or try to have a plan if it does.

An uncomfortableness filled the cab of the truck that didn't sit right with Stan.

The miles passed as they made their way north straight up I-95 until they reached Warwick, Rhode Island where Stan moved the truck over to the far left lane and prepared to get on 295 which was one of those unusual left-sided exits in New England.

After making the turn, Stan thought about what Drew had said. Blinded by the desire to get home to see Carol, Stan acknowledged that he had overlooked that stretch of I-95, recalling how traffic usually backed up there when he had to travel to and from Pennsylvania for work. Breaking the silence, Stan told Drew that taking 295 was the right call, and the tension seemed to ease immediately.

In less than an hour they were back on I-95 and crossed over into Massachusetts, and a palpable excitement filled the cab.

Within minutes they reached their exit. Slowing, Stan snaked the vehicle down the offramp and onto the main road.

An eerie feeling washed over Drew as they made their way through the desolate streets, and anxiety replaced his excitement.

Twenty minutes later they arrived at Drew's house.

"It's up here on the right," Drew said as they rounded the corner and passed beneath the high-tension power lines. Drew's Spidey sense was in full swing and he had butterflies in his stomach.

"Right here," Drew said, pointing to his driveway, sweat forming on his palms.

Stan pulled into the circular driveway just after the brick wall adorned with decorative lions.

"Fuck!" Drew shouted, hopping out of the truck before it stopped.

Stan threw the truck in park and yelled to the group in the back.

Steve looked up just as Drew ascended the front steps with his rifle at the ready and stormed into the house.

"Oh, no!" Cass said at the sight of the busted open front door.

Chapter 39

Stoughton, Massachusetts

Drew charged up the stairs. Using his foot, he pushed the door open and entered the house with the rifle at the ready. His heart was pounding in his chest at the sight of the pair of legs sticking out from the kitchen doorway.

Storming into the kitchen, Drew scanned the area for any threats. Looking down, he felt relieved when he saw that the individual on the floor was a fat bald man. It was apparent by the amount of blood on the floor that the man was dead.

Stepping over the body, Drew made his way down the hallway and stopped when he spotted another pair of legs sticking out of Stephanie's room. Drew could tell it was another man, deceased, with a knife sticking out of the back of his neck.

Proceeding slowly, Drew stepped over the legs and peeked into his daughter's bedroom. Seeing it was empty, he looked down at the man and recognized his face. It was one of the Reynold's brothers, known troublemakers in the town.

"Annabelle!" Drew shouted, making his way down the hall into their bedroom.

Empty.

Drew ran back the way he came, stopping to whip open the basement door and shot down the stairs.

Outside, Steve jumped over the side of the truck and chased after Drew. Entering the house, Steve heard Drew screaming for Annabelle and stopped short when he noticed the pair of legs next to the refrigerator.

Cass hopped down from the truck upon hearing Drew shouting his wife's name and raced into the house. Steve turned as Cass came running in and stopped her from entering any further.

"Don't go in there," Steve said, holding onto Cass.

"What is it?" Cass asked. "Is she dead?"

Steve fought to hold her from going past and tried pushing her back outside.

Cass leaned hard to the right and caught a glimpse of a pair of legs on the floor with blood pooled around the body.

"Oh, God!" Cass said, her shoulders slumping down at the sight of the body.

Drew quickly searched the basement and noticed blood in the sink behind the bar. He stood there a moment staring at Annabelle's wedding rings sitting on the counter next to the sink covered in dried blood.

Back outside, Grant and Sara stood talking to Stan in front of the truck when Steve and Cass came out.

"Everything okay?" Stan asked.

Steve shook his head no and wrapped his arm around Cass.

"This isn't good," Sara said.

"I guess Drew was right, something bad happened," Grant said.

"Are they both dead?" Sara asked.

Just as Steve and Cass reached the truck, Drew came sprinting around the corner from the back of the house. Stunned, the group stood there staring at him.

"Let's go!" Drew shouted, running around the truck, and jumping into the driver's seat.

Steve released Cass and jumped in the front seat, leaving the others to scramble and hop into the bed of the truck.

Drew glanced over his shoulder, checking to make sure they were all safely in, then floored the gas.

Chapter 40

Stoughton, Massachusetts

Stephanie stood in front of the bay window playing with her dolls when a black pickup truck came barreling into the driveway and skidded to a halt on the front lawn.

"Daddy! Daddy!" Stephanie started shouting while jumping up and down.

"What?" Annabelle called from the kitchen table.

"Not this again," Susan said. "The poor girl."

"Mom, she lost her father."

"I know that."

"Look, Momma! It's Daddy!"

Just then there was a loud pounding from the front door.

Susan got up from her seat and stood at the top of the stairs and yelled, "Who's there!"

"Mom! Don't let people know we're in here," Annabelle said, making her way over to the window.

"Sure," Susan said. "Just go stand in front of the window, because they'll never see you," she said sarcastically.

More pounding came from the front door.

"Daddy! Yippie!" Stephanie shouted. "My Daddy's home, Grandma!"

Annabelle was in shock when she saw the black Toyota sitting on the front lawn with people climbing out of the back.

"Mommy, Daddy's home!"

Annabelle was about to grab Stephanie and head for the backdoor when Drew stepped back from the front door and into view.

"Oh my God!" Annabelle cried out.

"What is it?" Susan shrieked.

"It's Drew!" Annabelle screamed with excitement in her voice as she took off running. She was going so fast she nearly knocked her mother over before bolting down the stairs to the foyer and whipping the front door open.

Their eyes met, and a smile washed over both of their faces. Drew sprinted up the steps, grabbing Annabelle, lifting her off her feet, kissing her passionately.

"I can't believe you are alive," Annabelle said, her hands trembling as she held his face, her thumb rubbing the stubble on his cheek.

"Daddy!" Stephanie shouted from the top of the stairs and made her way down one step at a time, the way children do, putting both feet together before taking the next step.

Drew stepped into the house, scooping her off the stairs and into his loving embrace.

Laughing, she said, "Daddy, you need a shave," as he planted kisses all over her face and head.

"Hi Drew!" Susan said, with a smile and a wave from the top of the stairs.

"Hi Susan," Drew responded as Stephanie wrapped both of her arms around his neck and gave him a tight squeeze.

"I can't believe you're here," Annabelle said, putting her hand on his shoulder.

Turning his head, Drew leaned over and kissed his wife again.

Accustomed to checking his breath for booze, she took a little sniff.

"No booze," he said.

She looked into his eyes, which appeared clear, and the smile on her face grew before kissing him again.

"I'm so glad you're safe. I was so worried," Drew said, slipping his arm around Annabelle's waist and pulling her in close.

"Group hug!" Stephanie shouted.

"Friends of yours?" Annabelle asked, looking over his shoulder.

"Yes," he said. "Come meet them."

After they made introductions, Susan invited everyone in.

"My, it's colder inside than it is outside," Steve said, walking up the stairs.

"The flue's stuck closed, so we can't use the fireplace," Susan responded.

"I can look at it for you before I take off," Stan said.

"Take off? You just got here," Susan said, turning toward Drew.

"Stan lives in Quincy and he wants to get home and check on his wife," Drew said.

"Oh, you poor thing. You haven't been home yet?" Annabelle asked.

"Next stop," Stan said before asking for a towel.

Susan grabbed a kitchen towel and handed it to him. Reaching up inside the fireplace, Stan used the towel to grab the broken piece of the handle and with a little applied brute force opened the flue. Chunks of soot came raining down, landing at the base of the fireplace.

"There you go," Stan said, wiping his hands clean and rising to his feet. "It's all set. I opened it all the way up."

"Thank you so much," Susan said, shaking his hand and taking the towel back from him.

"Well, I should get going," Stan said.

"Someone should go with you," Susan suggested.

"No, that's okay," Stan replied.

"Are you sure?" Steve asked. "I can go with you."

"Thank you, but my wife isn't a big fan of having strangers over at the house."

"You're more than welcome to come back and stay here with us," Susan said, before thanking him again.

"It was nice meeting you," Annabelle said.

"Bye-bye, Stan," Stephanie said.

"Thank you for the ride," Grant said, shaking Stan's hand.

"Yes, thank you," Sara said, giving him a hug. "Take care of yourself."

"I'll walk you out," Drew said and followed Stan down the stairs with Steve and Cass in tow.

Once outside, Drew thanked Stan for stopping and giving them a lift. "If you need a hot meal or a warm bed, you're always welcome here," Drew said, shaking Stan's hand.

"Thank you," Steve said again.

"Yes, thank you," Cass said, giving the older man a hug.

Stan climbed into the truck, waved, and drove off.

The three companions stood there and waved, watching Stan drive off.

Chapter 41

Quincy, Massachusetts

Stanley McKnight arrived home around three o'clock in the afternoon. At this time of day, the little cul-de-sac he lived on was usually full of children riding their bikes and playing with their toys. But today there was nothing. The house looked deserted as he pulled into the driveway. Carol always had the house decorated for whatever season it was, making the house look open and inviting. But today it appeared gloomy.

After a short walk up the walkway, Stan reached the front door and found it unlocked. Well, that's not good, he thought.

"Carol honey, I'm home," he announced, stepping inside.

Once inside, it felt colder inside the house than outside, just as it did at Drew's mother-in-law's house.

"Carol! Are you home? It's me, Stan," he shouted.

It was unlike her not to come running out and greet him. He quickly realized something was wrong. His wife was a neat freak, always had been since they met, but the house was in complete disarray. Trash covered the living room floor and a foul stench hung in the air. Stan followed the stench into the kitchen where he found the trash barrel overflowing. Not only that, but bags of open garbage also sat on the kitchen table. Looking around the kitchen he noticed the kitchen cabinets were open and worse, they were empty.

"Oh, no!" he said out loud, realizing Carol must have resorted to going through the trash searching for scraps of food.

She's probably out scavenging for food, he thought, and made his way down the hall towards their bedroom.

He opened the door and almost vomited. A rancid smell wafted out and hit him like a ton of bricks. The room was in shambles, with discarded trash strewn everywhere. The bed was disgusting, and the sheets were grimy. It took his brain a minute to process Carol's decomposing body lying on the bed.

Feeling sick, Stan ran outside and threw up. After, he sat on the front stairs holding his face in his hands and cried. Stan's heart broke. He lost his best friend and the love of his life.

My effort to get home was futile, he thought. *If I hadn't been so afraid on my first attempt home, she might still be alive today.*

The hours passed as he sat there remembering Carol and their life together before getting up and going back inside.

He wrapped Carol up in the sheets and blanket from the bed, then dragged her body out back and buried her near her flower garden.

He spent the rest of the day cleaning the house. Out of habit, he brought the trash bags out to the curb, forgetting no one would be coming to pick them up.

After using up most of the cleaning products Carol had stored under the sink, he cracked opened a few windows as the house smelled like a chemical factory.

Stanley laid on the couch exhausted. Most nights he usually fell right to sleep, but not tonight. His mind was wide awake. On his wedding day, he envisioned growing old with Carol and never in his wildest dreams did he ever imagine he'd bury her in the backyard like a family pet.

I should have been here for her, he thought, tossing and turning.

Memories came flooding back, and he recalled when they first met. Having just received her graduate degree in

Political Science, she was determined and ready to take on the world. She was so damn sassy and smart.

He then remembered the time they spent the whole day at an amusement park. It was her first time riding the Ferris Wheel and how she loved it, especially the view from the top. It became their tradition to ride it whenever they were at a fair or carnival. He remembered paying the ride operator twenty dollars to stop their car at the top, allowing him time to propose to her, where she said yes. Later, when he dropped her off, she invited him in to spend the night.

At twenty-four, Carol was still a virgin. She told him she'd been holding out for the right person, which he now assumed he was. Once inside her apartment, she went to take a shower while he waited on the couch.

He dozed off and woke up when he heard the water shutoff. A minute later, Carol appeared in the living room wearing a bathrobe and a towel on her head.

He sat up full of excitement, hoping tonight would be the night they made love. Drops of water ran down between her inner thighs and he couldn't help but stare. When he looked up, she smiled, catching him looking at her wantingly. With a look of desire, she slowly tugged on the tie of her robe. Stan's eyes widened as the robe separated, exposing her cleavage and pubic hair.

"Is that for me?" she asked, looking at his erection.

At a loss for words, he swallowed and nodded his head.

"Care to join me in the bedroom?" she asked, turning and dropping the robe. "Well, come give it to me!"

Part of him knew he was dreaming, but he didn't want it to end. It had been one of the best nights of his life. Plus, the smell of her shampoo and body wash smelled so good.

"Are you coming?" she called from down the hall.

Stan stood up and took a step, but his legs seemed weighted down and pins and needles ran up his legs. He tried lifting them, but they wouldn't budge.

"Don't keep me waiting, Stanley!"

"Come on feet, get going," he said under his breath as he picked up his leg and shook it. Whatever was wrong with his legs disappeared.

"Stanley, I want to feel you inside me! Come to me!"

"I'm coming," he said, and noticed his breath hung in the air. *When did it get so cold?* he thought, making his way down the hall.

That's different, he thought, noticing a blue hue illuminating from Carol's bedroom.

Making his way down the hall, he could see one of the windows in her bedroom. *How odd*, he thought as the light diminished, exposing something outside the window covered with strange carvings. When he walked into the room, his mouth dropped open. Carol stood there with nothing on except for a towel wrapped around her head. *My Lord!* he thought, upon viewing her nakedness for the first time.

Just then something moved around his ankle, causing him to look down.

"What the hell!" Stan shouted at the sight of his shoelaces slithering up his legs.

Reaching down, he lifted his pants.

His laces were very thin, elongated snakes with tiny tongues darting in and out of the heads.

"Come on, baby! What are you waiting for?" Carol asked.

Stan looked up and then back down. All the snake's mouths opened, exposing their fangs, and then as if on cue, all struck at once, digging their fangs into his flesh.

Stan screamed out in agony.

"Do you still want me, baby?" Carol asked, laughing.

Stan looked over at her, and she was smiling at his predicament. The heads of the snakes started wiggling like they were trying to burrow into his skin, while the rest of the snake bodies constricted around his boot.

Stan took a deep breath and reached down, trying to remove the snakes, but they were too tight against his legs.

"Do you like it, baby? Does it feel good?" Carol asked.

The snakes tightened their grip, cutting through his boot. Stan could not believe the amount of pressure those miniature snakes applied and cried out from the discomfort.

"Oh! Does it hurt?" Carol asked.

Stan looked over at her and grimaced.

"I'm sorry," Carol said, then yelled, "Stop!"

The snakes removed their fangs and released their grasp, going limp, allowing Stan to slip his fingers underneath them.

He sighed as the pressure reduced and began tugging, trying to remove them from his legs.

Better? asked a mysterious voice.

Stan glanced around, searching for the origin of the voice. A dark silhouette of a man with red piercing eyes replaced where Carol had been. Outside the bedroom window, the blue hue pulsated and grew in intensity.

The beings mouth opened and inside swarmed thousands of tiny sparks. The form leaned forward, and several sparks shot from its mouth, landing on Stan's shoelaces.

Simultaneously, all four snake heads lurched backwards and then lunged at his upper calf. Sharp fangs tore into the meaty portion of his leg.

Stan screamed, trying to pull the snakes free, but they constricted so fast, pulling his fingers tight against his legs.

Now! an evil voice boomed.

The snakes glowed red hot and twisted.

Stan felt an immediate searing pain.

His instincts kicked in and he tried to yank his hands free.

A blood-curdling scream escaped his lungs as the molten hot snakes cut through his fingers.

Each finger was severed below the tip at the first knuckle. They fell to the floor and began sizzling like bacon in a frying pan. An awful smell wafted up to his nose, and he knew it was his own flesh burning.

Stan's face turned pale white when he brought his hands up to his face as he was not prepared to see his fingers divorced from his hands. Stunned, he couldn't do anything except stare at the bloody, cauterized stumps before him.

Will you look at that! the sinister voice said laughing. *They'll be no more jerking off for you!*

"Oh my God!" Stan shouted.

"Sorry sweetie, God can't help you anymore!" Carol said.

Holding his hands out in front of him, Stan turned towards his wife's voice. She stood there with nothing but a towel wrapped around her head.

"Why?" Stan cried.

"Hahaha!" Carol laughed as she removed the towel from her head. Water dripped from the ends of her long black hair.

In shock, Stan stumbled about.

"Hey hot stuff! Where are you going?" Carol asked.

Stan looked over at Carol, who said, "Why don't you cool down, my hot lover!"

Out of the corner of his eyes he glimpsed her as she leaned back and whipped her head around toward him, slinging water off the end of her hair at him.

Stan's eyes widened as his wife transformed back into the shadow creature who yelled, *Liquid fire!*

The drops of water turned into flaming globs of hot lava.

Stan focused in on the molten rock hurling towards him, paralyzed with fear.

The flying pieces peppered him, creating hissing sounds as each drop melted and penetrated his clothing, burning down to his skin.

Frantically, Stan tried to wipe the molten rock off, but his clothing caught fire and spread to his hands and arms.

It hurt so bad and the pain caused him to fall over onto his back.

"Please God, help me!" he screamed as fire consumed him.

Maybe you missed the memo, but God no longer cares about you anymore. He gave up on his pet project, hence why I'm here.

The dark entity stood over Stan and opened its mouth.

Sparks began shooting across the darkness of the opening and began spinning.

An appendage grew out of the middle, heading straight for Stan's face.

As it grew closer, Stan held his hands out in front of himself. The sight of his hands missing his fingers made Stanley scream again.

Stanley awoke on the couch to the sound of his own screams. His breathing was heavy, and his heart pounded in his chest. It took him a moment to notice his hands in front of his face.

Once he realized, he wiggled his fingers, counted them, and made sure they were all still attached.

Chapter 42

Stoughton, Massachusetts

It felt great to be home. For a while there, Drew wondered if he'd ever see his family again. But he made it.

Everyone took turns getting washed up while Susan and Annabelle made a smorgasbord out of the food that Annabelle retrieved from her house along with the food the group had with them.

After dinner, the group sat around the table, except Stephanie, who had fallen asleep on the couch.

Drew explained what had happened in Florida with his mother and then his return flight. He told them how he met Steve and then Cass, who cried as Drew told what happened to her boyfriend and their friends. Then he told them about how they met Grant and Sara. He even told them how he almost pissed himself jumping out of the plane. Annabelle looked shocked to hear this, as she knew Drew was scared to death of heights.

They all laughed at how Steve described both Cass and Drew's reaction to hearing they had to jump out of the plane.

Drew told them everything except for the shadow man both he and Grant saw.

Sara told the group why she and Grant were at the retreat. She explained how their marriage had stalled out because of their business. The stress of spending every minute together combined with the stress of working together took its toll on their relationship. But the one good thing about the pandemic was that it brought them closer together. It shined a light on what really mattered, each other.

Steve went next. He told them he was in southern Florida for a seminar on alcohol and drug abuse. Getting choked up, he told them how he had lost his family because of his habit and how he turned his life around and began working with other alcoholics and addicts to overcome their addictions. "I've even taken this one under my wing," Steve said, slapping Drew on the shoulder.

Annabelle mouthed, "Thank you!" with tears in her eyes.

Steve nodded.

Drew felt uncomfortable being talked about in front of everyone. He wasn't one for sharing his own feelings as he didn't know how to handle them. Living under a hair trigger his entire childhood and being criticized for every decision he made, he buried his feelings and when they rose to the surface; he didn't know how to handle them. The lack of knowing how to deal with his feelings usually led to anger and became his normal response to his feelings.

Susan went next, telling them how the police had closed all the roads when she tried to go into town. Then she told them about Tommy Welch and his little friends stealing their food and generator. She smiled, telling them about Tommy's house burning down in the middle of the night with him and all his friends inside. "Serves them right for stealing," she said.

"How about you?" Sara said, nodding toward Annabelle.

"Who, me? Not much. I was here the whole time."

"Well, except for your little adventure last night," Susan said.

"Mom, please!"

"What adventure?" Drew asked.

"She slipped out last night and went home for food," Susan said.

"Wait, you went home last night?" Drew asked.

"Yes," Annabelle said. "Anyone want dessert?" she asked, trying to change the subject.

"She was even attacked by a dog!" Susan exclaimed. "She came home covered in blood."

"Mom!" Annabelle shouted, getting up and heading to the sink.

The group exchanged glances around the table.

"What?" Susan asked, catching the looks.

"Did they hurt you?" Drew asked, standing up.

"There was no dog, was there?" Susan asked.

"No," Cass said.

"What was it then?" Susan asked.

"Not a what. A who," Steve said.

Drew walked over behind Annabelle, who was washing her hands in the sink, scrubbing them.

He put his hands on her hips and asked her again, "Did they hurt you?"

She looked up at his reflection in the window. "No, I killed them before they could do anything."

"That's my girl," Drew whispered into her ear.

"You did what!" her mother screamed. "You took another life?"

"Two. Two people," Grant said.

"Hey!" Sara said, slapping her husband on the arm.

"You killed two people!" Susan shouted.

"Well, technically it was three, if you count the one in the woods who tried to rape me!" Annabelle screamed.

Susan frowned at her daughter. "I thought I raised you better than that!"

Drew could feel his blood boiling. "Weren't you just happy that the kids who robbed you died in a fire?"

Susan sat up straight with a fire in her eyes and said, "Beloved, never avenge yourselves, but leave it to the wrath of God, for it is written, "Vengeance is mine, I will repay, says the Lord." — *Romans 12:19*." Susan seethed.

Steve stood and pushed his chair back, so it scraped across the floor.

"Oh great," Drew muttered under his breath.

Steve glared at Susan and waited until she looked up at him. When she finally looked up and their eyes met Steve said, "Beat your plowshares into swords, and your pruning hooks into spears; let the weak say, "I am a warrior." — *Joel 3:10.*"

"Why I've never…" Susan said, her face reddening as she stormed out of the kitchen. A moment later, she slammed her bedroom door.

"Well, that's a first for me. I've never seen the whole bible verses battle before," Drew said.

Annabelle snorted and then started laughing. "I've never seen someone else piss my mother off like that before!" Annabelle said with a chuckle.

"Although murder is not acceptable by God, neither do I believe He wants the wolves to slaughter His sheep. Nowhere in his son's teachings does he say to lie down and willingly be slaughtered," Steve said.

Annabelle turned to Drew and kissed him gently, then walked over to Steve and gave him a hug. "Thank you," she said, releasing him.

Steve nodded and said, You're welcome."

Wiping the tears from her eyes, Annabelle said, "You all must be exhausted."

"I'm pretty beat," Grant said, stretching and putting his arm around his wife.

"My mom made up the spare bedroom for you earlier," Annabelle said to Sara and Grant.

"Thank you," Sara said, standing up.

Annabelle turned to Steve and said, "I hope you don't mind the couch? My mom put out a pillow and some blankets for you."

"This is perfect! A roof, a couch, and a warm fire to fall asleep next to. It's my own little personal heaven," Steve said.

"Were going to turn in," Sara said.

"Okay," Annabelle said, pointing. "Go down the stairs and turn right."

Sara turned to Drew and padded him on his arm and said, "I'm glad you made it home to your family."

Drew smiled at her, "Me too!"

"Good night big guy," Grant said shaking Drew's hand and he and Sara disappeared down the stairs.

"Are you ready for bed?" Annabelle asked, scooping up Stephanie.

Drew scratched the weeks' worth of growth under his chin and said, "Yeah, after I shave."

His face itched something fierce, and scratching was the only way to stop it. Drew, like his father, was also bald on top with patches of hair remaining on the sides and back of his head. Drew vowed never to do the comb-over like his father had. It looked ridiculous. It was like putting plastic on a broken car window. It screamed, look there's nothing here! He opted to shave his head bald and had done so since his mid-twenties.

Once done, Drew's face felt naked and cold. It always amazed him how a good shave could revitalize him. Now, with that annoying itch gone, he was ready for bed.

He lifted the covers and slid into bed next to Stephanie and Annabelle. The memory foam mattress felt incredible. Compared to what he had slept on, it felt like a cloud.

Laying there, he let his body relax.

"Feel nice?" Annabelle asked.

"Oh God, yes," Drew replied. "There's just something amazing about a freshly made bed."

"Cozy."

"Yes! Cozy."

"I'm proud of you," she said.

"For what?" he asked.

"Well, for starters… You saving those people."

"It was the right thing to do."

"And I'm proud of you for quitting drinking."

"You were right. It needed to be done," he said, "because I am an alcoholic."

Although Drew couldn't see her face in the darkness, she had a smile from ear to ear.

"Steve told me the first step in recovery is admitting you have a problem."

"He's right," she said.

"I'm not going to lie, I drank on the way home. But I was able to stop with Steve's help, even if I did relapse once or twice."

"That's okay. What's important is that you're trying," she said, reaching out and putting her hand on his arm. "You don't want Stephanie growing up seeing you like that."

"I dreaded this moment the whole journey back."

"Why?" she asked.

"Well, because the last time I saw you, you weren't happy with me."

"I'm sorry for what I said. I've had nothing but regret over the things I said to you during our last conversation," she said with tears rolling down her cheeks. "I thought I'd never see you again," she said through her tears.

He reached out and took her face in his hand and wiped away her tears with his thumb.

"You have nothing to regret. What you said was the truth, and I needed to hear it," he said getting choked up.

"I'm sorry for how I acted when I was drunk. I'm sorry for how I treated you, you didn't deserve that. And I'm sorry for all those horrible things I said. I didn't mean it. I hope you know how much I love you and Stephanie."

"I know," she said.

"This whole thing has changed me. All I wanted was to get home. You are my world. I can't believe I let the bottle control my life, but no more."

"It's okay," she said, reaching out and touching his face. "We're all together now and I have my old Drew back."

He leaned over, trying not to smush Stephanie, and passionately kissed his wife.

"I love you!" he said.

"I know. I love you too," she said and kissed him. "You must be exhausted. Get some sleep, my love."

Drew put his head on the pillow, and a minute later he was snoring.

He was home.

Chapter 43

Stoughton, Massachusetts

His eyes fluttered open, and he saw Annabelle asleep next to him with Stephanie sandwiched in between them. His eyelids grew heavy, and he fell back to sleep.

He awoke sometime later to the sound of sizzling. When he opened his eyes, he no longer found himself in bed with his wife and daughter, but in a strange place.

It was a round chamber that reminded him of the inside of Gravitron, a popular ride at fairs and carnivals back when he was a child. On the outside, the ride looked like a flying saucer. Once inside, the rider made their way around the control booth and stood in front of a padded panel attached to rails mounted on the outward slanting wall.

The operator sat inside a control booth at the center of the ride. The booth had colorful lights covering it that the operator controlled, along with music that played through speakers attached to the booth. Once everyone was leaning against their panel, the operator would start the ride, causing it to spin. As the ride gained speed, the spinning created a centrifugal force pulling the rider against the pad. Spinning faster and faster, the force pulled the panel up toward the ceiling, lifting the rider's feet off the floor. Bold riders would spin their body and hang upside down, the centrifugal force holding them in place. The operator would announce when the ride started to slow down, allowing the bold riders time to recover. As the ride slowed, the panels slid down, bringing the rider's feet back to the floor.

That ride was one of the fondest memories Drew had of his older sister before she ran away when he was still young. One morning she kissed him goodbye and left. She disappeared and Drew never saw her again.

The memory faded, and he found himself held down on something hard by that same centrifugal force as the Gravitron, except he was not on a ride with his sister having fun.

Fighting the invisible resistance, Drew lifted his head up, trying to find out where he was. His eyes widened in disbelief at what he saw. Both of his legs were dangling over an open flame. Frantically he tried pulling his legs away from the flames, but he had no control over them.

He watched in horror as the skin on his legs began cracking and splitting like a sausage on a barbeque. Blood boiled and oozed out of the splits on his legs. The under part of his calf muscles charred and turned black.

POP!

His right leg exploded, and a large crack formed, sending scalding blood sailing up into the air. Drew watched in terror as the boiling liquid headed straight for his face. Closing his eyes in anticipation of the scorching body fluid landing on his face. He waited and waited, but his own sizzling juices never landed on his face. Slowly he opened one eye and found that he was no longer lying over the flames.

Now he lay on a cold, thick slab of granite. Sitting up he reached down and grabbed his legs and let out a loud sigh of relief, feeling his legs underneath his jeans. After his panic waned, he looked around the large chamber that reminded him of the Gravitron ride, minus the control booth and panels on the wall. Instead, strange carvings covered the circular brownstone wall.

Scanning the carvings, one in particular caught Drew's attention. Goosebumps formed on his arms as he recalled watching this depiction live on the morning of 9/11. Carved into the wall was the "evil face" inside the billowing smoke that rose from the World Trade Center building on that frightful morning.

Further down on the wall was a carving of two mushroom clouds. Drew assumed it was a depiction of the atomic bombs dropped over Hiroshima and Nagasaki. Over two hundred thousand people died instantly during the bombings, which ended World War II.

"Jesus!" Drew said. "Where the hell am I?"

Just then he felt a presence. The same presence he felt back in the retail store when he saw the strange shadow form sniffing his drink. Then again when Chad tried to kill him.

Where do you think you are? A beastly voice asked.

"I'm dreaming," Drew answered.

Are you? Asked the voice.

"Yes."

Then wake up.

Drew tried to wake up.

Sill here!

"Wake up! Come on, wake up!" Drew shouted, slapping himself in the face.

Well, are you awake?

Drew sat there, getting mad that he couldn't wake up. He took a deep breath, dug his fingernails into his thigh and yelled at the top of his lungs, "Wake up!"

Every muscle in his body twitched, startling him awake. Drawing in a deep breath, he opened his eyes, finding Annabelle staring at him, and Stephanie squirming between them.

"You were having a nightmare," Annabelle said. "You were shouting at yourself to wake up."

Drew laid there breathing heavily, sweat covering his body.

Furious, the sparks inside the entity spun faster and faster. It wasn't strong enough yet to maintain the connection. But soon it would be. Once the second horseman released War, everything would change.

Chapter 44

Quincy, Massachusetts

Stan sat there trembling. Never had he had such a visceral dream before, whereupon waking up he believed it was real. The image of his fingers being severed from his hands was hard to shake. Every so often he'd look down and wiggle them, ensuring himself they were still there.

There was no food in the house and his stomach was grumbling. He had food out in his truck and headed out to grab it. When he opened the truck door, he discovered another problem. There wasn't much left.

He let his options play out in his mind, and there was only one.

Stan knew Carol would want him to continue on and survive. With nothing left for him there, he decided to leave. He loaded clothes into a duffle bag and a minute later he was in the truck heading back towards Stoughton.

Drew was up early the next morning stoking the fireplace. Although he would have loved to have slept in and cuddle with Annabelle, he couldn't as the fire needed tending. With the poker, he poked at the pile of gray ash in the fireplace, exposing the red-hot layer underneath. Air met with the smoldering embers, giving it the vitality needed, which produced a small flame. By adding a few pieces of kindling, the flame began consuming them, making it grow. After a few moments, he added larger pieces of wood that crackled from the direct heat and flame. Soon warmth replaced the chill.

With the fire going Drew stood in the bay window watching the gray clouds pass overhead while listening to Steve snore behind him on the couch. In his mind, Drew thought of places they could search for food, hoping scavengers hadn't picked them all clean. Annabelle mentioned they still had food in their pantry, so his first stop would be at home.

There's a nursing home down the street that Drew wanted to check out. As an EMT, he visited many nursing homes and knew that they had industrial sized kitchens used to feed all the residents. He also knew they had large refrigerators that could hold a ton of food. But, if the power was out, and the food spoiled, hopefully they had stocked canned goods. It was worth checking out, and Drew hoped scavengers didn't dare venture in with all the infected bodies inside. He decided to check it out later, once the others were awake.

Off in the distance, a sound caught Drew's attention, and he reached for his rifle. The whine of an engine grew closer, and he feared whoever it was would see the smoke rising from the chimney and stop. *Would someone be brazen enough to try attacking in broad daylight?* Drew wondered.

Given everything that has happened so far, he didn't doubt it.

Expect the unexpected, he thought, standing at the ready with the rifle.

A wave of relief washed over him when he recognized Stan's truck, which was slowing, and turned into the driveway. Grabbing his coat, Drew headed outside.

The driver's side door swung open and Stan stepped out.

While making his way down the walkway, Drew noticed there was no one else inside the truck. Combined with the look on Stan's face, Drew knew.

With his head low, Stan made his way around the front of the truck.

"That bad?" Drew asked.

"Yeah," Stan replied, choked up.

"I'm sorry, Stan."

"Me too."

The front door behind them opened, and Steve came out. His hair was a mess, and he wiped the sleep from his face.

"Hey Stan!" Steve said as he approached.

Stan did a flip of the wrist wave.

"What's wrong?" Steve asked, stopping next to Drew.

"Stan's wife didn't make it," Drew said.

"Well, maybe next time," Steve said.

Stan let out a weak cry and rubbed the tears from his eyes.

"I… don't think so," Drew said.

"Oh!" Steve said realizing. "I'm sorry! How?"

"Is that important?" Drew asked in a *'how dare you'* tone.

"She starved. My wife starved to death," Stan said, his shoulders heaving with sobs.

"Are you sure it wasn't the sickness?" Steve asked.

"You're unbelievable!" Drew said.

"What? How does he know it wasn't the sickness?" Steve asked.

Stan wiped his nose and said, "Because she was all skin and bones and surrounded by trash."

Describing her caused Stan to wail. "There were trash bags all over the house from our different neighbors."

"Jesus!" Drew said.

"*He* is with us always," Steve said.

"Not now!" Drew spat.

"But *He* is always with us," Steve reiterated.

"Well, *He* wasn't with my Carol, and she was a God-fearing woman," Stan said.

"Why don't we go inside and warm up. It looks like you could use a cup of coffee," Drew said.

Once inside the house, Annabelle and Susan stood at the top of the stairs.

"Oh Stan, you're back. Where's your wife?" Susan asked.

Stan's shoulders sunk, and his eyes welled.

Drew put his arm around Stan and said, "His wife didn't make it."

"Oh, no! I'm so sorry," Annabelle said.

Stan sniffled and wiped his nose.

"Was it the sickness?" Susan asked.

Stan shook his head no.

"It was starvation," Steve said.

Drew turned with a fire in his eyes and glared at Steve.

"How awful," Susan said.

"Yeah, she resorted to eating out of the trash," Steve said.

"What the fuck is wrong with you today?" Drew snapped, turning towards Steve.

"That poor thing," Susan said, grabbing a box of tissues off the table and handed them to Stan when he reached the top of the stairs.

Over coffee Stan described what he found at home and how he buried Carol out behind his house.

They offered Stan to stay with them, which he graciously accepted. He had been alone the whole ride from Nebraska except for the last leg home, and he didn't want to be alone anymore.

After breakfast, Drew informed the group of his plan to head home and gather the rest of the food there before searching a couple other locations. He reminded them they should try to stock up with as many supplies as possible because winter was upon them and that the snow would start flying soon.

They spent the next two days scavenging everything from convenience stores to industrial parks. They hit payday with the industrial parks as most buildings had a break room with vending machines. Drew also liked the businesses better than houses because they were less likely to encounter someone. But, if it came down to it, he would go house-to-house searching.

They hit the mother lode when Stan suggested they go to the town of East Bridgewater and check out the distribution warehouse for one of the local grocery chains. When asked how he knew about it, he told them one of his neighbors worked there.

"Wow!" Grant said, at the sight of all the food.

"Um… how are we getting all this food back to the house?" asked Stan.

Drew said he had an idea and told Steve to wait with Grant. Drew and Stan hopped in the truck and took off.

Twenty minutes later, they returned with a U-Haul box truck that Drew commandeered from a local dealership.

The next day they took the truck to a local landscaper's lot and loaded the truck up with firewood. They now had enough supplies to last them until Spring.

Chapter 45

Rockefeller Center, New York

WTFH was on the air for less than a week when people started arriving. At first a handful of survivors showed up who pitched tents outside the studio window. They held up signs with their names written on them, hoping family in other parts of the country would see them and know they were safe. Every day brought more and more people. Many brought tents, and by the end of the week the plaza transformed into a full-blown campsite.

Seizing the opportunity to get interviews with survivors, Chris grabbed a camera before he headed out to the camp.

The consensus was excitement and a feeling compelling them to be there. They told their stories of loss and hoped that by coming here it might afford them a new beginning. They all said they yearned to believe in something again.

Glen loved all the attention from those gathered outside the studio. He listened to them give him praise, and soon his ego was bloated. Finally, he made it to the top.

There was one thing Glen was not happy about though, his erectile dysfunction.

After dusk he would venture out to meet his female admirers and attempted to sleep with different women. But there was one problem, his penis would not become erect, it would just stay flaccid, no matter how much attention the ladies gave it.

He found it odd that his manhood only worked with Kendra. It would become thicker and harder than he ever remembered it getting before. He wasn't complaining, but he just wished he could use it on other women and not just one. Plus, fucking Kendra was getting old as she just laid there and didn't even move. Her eyes just stared up at him. Sometimes he thought he was having sex with a corpse because Kendra's eyes were glassy, like she was either high or dead. One time he had to turn his head in order to finish because her lifeless eyes freaked him out.

Glen's penis now felt numb and cold to the touch all the time. Even when he took a warm shower, it felt cold as ice. While washing one day, he noticed tiny brown spots on it. A couple days later he noticed sections that appeared rubbed raw and other sections where scabs had formed.

What the hell is going on? he thought.

With every passing day, his penis looked worse and worse. Boils formed on the sides and tip, causing excruciating pain when he urinated. It got to where he couldn't stand looking at it anymore, and no matter how much he washed it, it gave off this foul odor that made him want to vomit.

The weird thing was that he was still horny, super horny. It was a deep sexual lust that only having intercourse with Kendra cured. It amazed him how being inside her made it feel better. She never looked at it, or put it in her mouth, thankfully because it embarrassed him, but even that didn't stop his urge for coitus. He made it a point to turn the light off before undressing.

At night he would just lay there after Kendra left his bed and wonder.

What did I do to deserve this? he thought, looking at his gangrene penis. His manhood reminded him of a piece of fruit found in the back of the fridge months later.

The next morning Glen woke up and dreaded looking down when he went to relieve his bladder. Using his thumb to hook his waistband, he turned his head and pulled his pants down. Staring at a spot on the wall, he waited for the foul stench to reach his nostrils like it had days prior. A few seconds passed, and he heard his stream of urine strike the water inside the bowl. Still he waited, but there was no awful smell rising from his decaying penis. Inching his head forward, he looked down and was shocked. Besides a few little red spots, his penis looked almost back to normal.

"Oh, thank God!" he said out loud.

Once finished with his morning business, he stood there a few moments staring at it.

Glen hopped in the shower and couldn't help staring at it. With a hand full of lather and the primal urge to release his seed, he masturbated in the shower. Holding his face in front of the shower stream, he allowed the warm water to cascade down his chest and back as he pleasured himself.

Once done, he dried off, got dressed and headed downstairs to the newsroom.

Stepping off the elevator, he ran into Chris.

"Well, someone looks chipper this morning!" Chris said. "I take it you heard the good news?"

Glen had good news of his own, but he wasn't sharing that with his producer.

"Actually, I haven't," Glen replied. "What is it?"

"The old man has some big news story he wants you to tease."

"He does?" Glen asked.

"Yeah, he wouldn't tell me what it was. He said we'll have the big reveal this weekend."

Later that morning, Mr. Williams called Glen up to his suite. When he arrived, Mr. Williams seemed chipper than normal and offered Glen a cup of coffee.

"I ran into Chris downstairs and he said you want to tease a big story for this weekend," Glen said.

"I did," Mr. Williams said, taking a seat behind his desk. "Let's talk."

"Shoot."

"Now this will sound odd, but I'm not telling you what's going to happen."

"Okay," Glen said, skepticism in his voice.

"The reason being is when you announce the message, I want the world to see your facial expression which will help convey the message."

"I like that idea! Can you give me a hint?"

"It's going to change the world!" Mr. Williams said, looking over at the entity standing in the corner. "I need you to tease the hell out of it. Tell everyone to tune in in four days, this Saturday at 3pm.

"I'll start teasing it today!"

"I always knew you were the right man for the job!" Mr. Williams said, standing up.

Glen took to the airwaves an hour later, doing as he was told, and teased it several times a broadcast every day. The anticipation outside in tent city was palpable. Everyone was excited for the big reveal.

Chapter 46

Rockefeller Center, New York

Whatever was needed at the studio, the entity found someone with a particular set of skills and instructed Mr. Williams to contact them.

For starters, the news studio needed new glass windows. It found Richard Lispin, an older man who owned Invisible Barrier, a glass installer. Mr. Williams promised him money and glass contracts in exchange for replacing the glass. After measuring the windows, they drove to a glass distributer in upstate New York whom they knew had the size panes needed in stock. Two days later, new glass replaced the plywood that had covered the front of the studio.

Next, it found two sisters who had run their own grocery store delivery business in the city. The Hannah Sisters Delivery Service was similar to all the online grocery delivery apps, except for one key feature. Instead of having to go to different apps for certain stores or creating several lists, one per store, they would go to multiple stores for each customer picking up and deliver all the items at once from multiple stores. This provided the sisters with the knowledge of where to find specific requested items. Again, with the promise of protection, Mr. Williams tasked the sisters with collecting food and items for the studio.

Roger Santiago had owned a lucrative towing company but lost everything and everyone in his life to the virus. Roger contemplated suicide and the Shadow Man arrived as Roger was getting ready to commit the act. It provided Roger with an opportunity to be useful again. The entity tasked Roger with removing cars from the streets and highways.

The last thing that needed to be tended to, which came at the behest of Chris, was the removal of bodies from the city. It would be hard to document the rebuilding of society with dead bodies scattered everywhere.

It was decided that a large section of trees inside Central Park along with other parks would be cleared, followed by massive pits to be dug.

Crews went around with garbage trucks and collected the dead. They tossed the bodies in and crushed them like trash.

Arms and legs twisted grotesquely as the bodies were dumped into the pits. Gasoline was then poured into the pit and set ablaze.

The body disposal was a twenty-four-hour operation. A constant thick black smoke rose from the center of the city and ash fell miles away. The trucks backed up and emptied their cargo. Arms and legs twisted this way and that in a grotesque sight. Gasoline was poured into the pit and set ablaze.

The Entity began appearing everywhere, from small towns to large cities across all four corners of the world. It searched out people who could turn the power back on and restore communications.

Just before spring, Peter Bane and his crew finally restored the power to most of the city.

Chapter 47

Paxton, Nebraska

Maureen was sixteen, on the cusp of being seventeen, when she arrived in Nebraska. She didn't know what the future held in store for her but stepping off the bus at least now gave her a chance at one.

Her first priority was finding a place to stay followed by a job. Back home, she had picked up several babysitting jobs by checking the grocery store community board where people listed services they were either looking for or could provide.

Maureen approached an older gentleman sweeping up at the bus depot and asked him if there was a local grocery store around. The man stopped sweeping and rested his elbow on the end of the broom.

"Well," he said, a big smile flashing across his face. Using his index finger, he pointed to the side exit and said, "The Beehive Grocery Store is just a few blocks yonder that way."

She stepped out into the crisp, clean air. Above, the bright sun was high in the sky, which provided her several hours of daylight to find a place to stay. She found the store, and upon walking in she discovered the community board hanging just inside the front door. There were several potential leads posted, so she tore off a dangling tab from each one and stuffed them in her pocket.

Maureen used the store's restroom to wash up from the long bus ride. Looking at herself in the mirror, she wished she had brought some makeup with her so she could cover the hideous bruise on her face from her father's backhand.

While leaving, she noticed a large map of Praxton hanging next to the exit. Each of the various farms in town were highlighted on the map, and a legend listed the different produce items that the store carried from each farm. Maureen found it fascinating that wheat, soybean and corn were among the produce all grown in this one town. But it shouldn't have been surprising because according to the map, the town appeared to be massive farmland.

Removing the paper tabs from her pocket, she located the streets on the map and headed outside.

It took her almost two hours to reach the first address. The ad was for a babysitting gig three days a week. A petite blonde woman answered the door holding a little girl on her hip. When Maureen inquired about the job the woman apologized telling her it had already been filled and promised to take down the ad on her next trip to the store.

Maureen headed back the way she came, taking the first left down Central Street. The next house was a beautiful mansion surrounded by open fields. As she approached, she wondered how luxurious it was inside and thought to herself how wonderful it would be to work inside a palace. An older woman answered the door and dashed her hopes, telling Maureen rudely that the job was no longer available.

With her shoulders hung low, Maureen trudged on to the next place. Her feet were killing her, and the sun was about to set. Off in the distance was a white two-story house next to a huge red barn.

Walking up the long drive Maureen said a quick prayer asking God for a little help. By the time she reached the house, dusk was rapidly approaching.

As she stepped on to the porch, she removed the cross from her shirt that hung around her neck. She gave it a quick kiss and dropped it back into her shirt.

Before she even knocked, the door swung open and an old lady with silver hair stood hunched over, leaning on a cane.

Startled, Maureen said, "Hi!"

"May I help you?" the old woman asked.

"Yes, I'm here about the job posted down at the grocery store," Maureen said, pulling the paper tab from her pocket.

"Oh?" the woman said.

"Let me guess, the job's already filled," Maureen said, turning around and walking away. *What am I going to do now?* she thought. *Why did I even come out here?*

"Wait!" The old woman called out. "Young lady, come back."

Maureen stopped and turned around.

The old woman clutched her cane straining to stand up straight and stood there gazing at Maureen, giving her the once over.

Maureen felt awkwardly uncomfortable being gazed up and down.

"Would you like to come in?"

"Well, is the job still available?"

"No, deary. I figured I'd invite you so I could cook and eat you," the woman said sarcastically.

A smile flashed across Maureen's face.

"Come on in then," the woman said.

Maureen looked up to the darkening sky and whispered, "Thank God!"

Inside, the old woman offered Maureen a seat on the couch and plopped herself down in an old red chair. A bag of yarn with silver sewing needles sticking out of it hung from the arm of the chair, the fabric worn from years of use.

There was something about the house that made Maureen feel very comfortable inside.

"And what's your name?" the older woman asked, breaking the silence.

"It's Maureen ma'am, Maureen Normandin."

"Hmm... I don't know any Normandin around these parts," the woman said, spying her suspiciously.

Maureen felt her cheeks getting warm, and they began to get rosy.

"What brings you to my part of town?" the older woman asked, leaning back in her chair.

Maureen removed the tab from her pocket again and said, "I'm here about the caretaking job."

"And where do you live?"

"On the other side of town."

"Little lady, I've lived here my entire life and I know the name of every person in this town."

"How can that be?" Maureen asked.

"Simple. Because I used to teach school here. I started teaching school in 1947 and I taught everyone until just a few years ago."

"But you wouldn't know if someone new moved in," Maureen retorted.

"Well, deary, I would. You see, this is a farming town," the woman said, leaning forward. "And my son is on the farming commission, which means he knows every farm owner and no one new has moved out, nonetheless moved in."

Maureen's eyes widened at being called out.

"So, why don't you tell me the real reason you're here. Are you part of some scam to rob the elderly?"

"No, ma'am. I'm honestly here about the job."

"How 'bout you tell me how you got that bruise on your face?"

Maureen tilted her head, allowing her bangs to fall over her face.

"No sense trying to cover it now, I've already seen it, girl. Spill the beans."

Maureen began crying. She told the woman everything, except the part about stealing. She told her about her abusive father and how she ran away.

When asked about her age Maureen's first instinct was to lie, but something inside told her to be honest, so she told the truth.

The front door swung open, startling Maureen, who jumped when a man and a teenage boy walked in. Maureen held her hand to her chest from the fright, which instantly passed when the boy caught her attention. He appeared to be around her age and Maureen couldn't help but notice his muscular arms and build drenched in sweat.

"Who's this, Momma?" the man asked.

"This is Maureen. She's my new caretaker and she'll be staying in the backroom," the older woman said.

"Hello Maureen! I'm Bill Sr. and this is my son Bill Jr."

"Hi!" Maureen said with a smile.

Bill Jr. smiled back.

"Go wash up for supper, boys," the older woman said. "While I show our new guest to her room."

The woman stood up and stopped. "How silly of me. I forgot to introduce myself. My name is Claire."

"Hi Claire," Maureen said. "It's nice to meet you!" and stuck out her hand.

The two women shook hands and Maureen couldn't help but notice Claire's knotted, arthritic hands.

"Don't get old, dear," Claire said, noticing Maureen looking at her hands.

Claire trudged through the house using her cane for support leading Maureen to a small bedroom off the back of the house.

At first Maureen helped with the cooking and dishes. Then she started helping with different chores around the house, including keeping it tidy and tending to Claire. It wasn't her first time working in a kitchen as she helped her mother from time to time, but her mother never taught her how to behead a chicken or pluck feathers before. Claire sat at the table and talked Maureen through it as the arthritis in her hands prevented her from doing it. The two women hit it off and enjoyed each other's company. The next two years were the best. Finally, she felt like she belonged and no longer lived in fear. Living on a farm provided her with isolation from the rest of the world. She was content with working the land and the quiet life it provided. Every couple of months when Bill Jr took the truck into town, she would ask him to buy her a pack of cigarettes. She didn't know it, but he'd do anything for her. Bill Jr. loved everything about her except for her smoking. He didn't care for the smell of it or the stench that clung to her clothes.

Claire's health started to deteriorate, and she spent most days in bed. With the extra time, Maureen began assisting in the barn. She never went far, always staying close to the house so she could check up on Claire. Bill Jr. showed her how to clean the stalls, milk the cows, and feed the animals.

Soon, a friendship between the two flourished, which soon blossomed into more.

That spring, two days before Easter, Claire passed away. After the funeral, Bill Jr. took her by the hand and kissed her. He told her he loved her from the first day he'd laid eyes on her. She smiled and told him she loved him too. That summer they told Bill Sr. about their relationship, to which he responded that he already knew. He told them he had been in love before with Bill Jr.'s mother until her passing from breast cancer.

The years passed on and together they all worked the farm, ensuring their goods made it to market.

One Spring morning, Bill Sr. suffered a heart attack and died out in the backfield. They buried him next to Claire and his late wife.

That summer Bill and Maureen wed.

The next several years they enjoyed being with each other as husband and wife. Eventually they discussed starting a family and the following year they welcomed their first son, Caleb, into the world.

Two years later, they welcomed their second son, Eben.

Chapter 48

Stoughton, Massachusetts

Winter had come and gone. Finally, the days were getting warmer, and the sun was staying out longer.

Susan continued to dream of her late husband Henry nightly, and in every dream he insisted she head south to Florida for safety.

Susan spoke to Annabelle daily, hounding her to consider heading south. Each time Susan told Annabelle that this was something her father insisted they do. Annabelle spoke to Drew, who was against it, which left her in a pickle.

Realizing she was getting nowhere with Annabelle, Susan started talking privately to Sara and Grant. Neither opposed the idea as they didn't enjoy the cold nor the several feet of snow that old man winter had dropped on them a few weeks back. Which made being from the south downright miserable in the northern winter months.

And without a snowplow it made leaving the house damn near impossible.

Now Annabelle faced their added pressure to head south too.

Susan tried digging her claws into Cass, which was a mistake from the start, since her loyalty lied with Drew and wherever he went, she went.

Next, Susan went to work on Steve. She quickly found out he was only interested in talking about God and how he believed He put Drew in his path for a reason. Steve informed her that like Cass, he too was sticking with Drew, whether it was staying here up north or heading down south. Steve finished each conversation regarding the matter by telling her that God works in mysterious ways and to pray for the answer.

Finally, Susan started in on Stan, who told her he could use a change of scenery. Although he loved having four seasons, his body could no longer handle the cold. So, he threw his two cents in, telling Annabelle his vote was to head south.

Over dinner Annabelle brought up heading south, which went just as she expected.

"We're not heading south," Drew said, and continued eating.

Susan threw her napkin onto her plate and stormed out.

"What's her problem?" Drew asked.

"See, I told you he doesn't want to go," Annabelle said to everyone.

"Does everyone want to go?" Drew asked, stopping mid-forkful.

No one answered.

"Cass, do you want to go south?" Drew asked.

"I'm going wherever you go," she replied.

"Steve?" Drew asked.

"Ditto," he said.

"Can I just ask, why the big push to go south?" Drew asked the table, looking around at everyone's face.

"Susan," Stan replied.

"Oh," Drew said and went back to eating, ending the conversation.

Later that night in bed, Annabelle snuggled close to Drew. "Don't be mad at my mother," she said.

"I'm not," Drew replied.

"Yes, you are," she said, running her fingers through his chest hair.

"Why does she want to go so bad that she's enlisting others to campaign on her behalf?"

Annabelle told him about her mother's repeated dreams of Henry and how in her dream he keeps warning her about food and survival in the north. She told him how Florida has a special place in her mother's heart because many wonderful things happen there when she got married. "My mother is an old woman who's nearing the end of her life. She fears all of her good times are behind her and all she has left, especially of my father, is memories, so going to Florida is keeping her dreams alive," Annabelle said.

Memories of his mother's lifeless body came flooding back to him along with the pain of not arriving in time to say goodbye. Plus, the deaths of Brad and the college kids weighed heavily on him, never mind the fact that he was shot twice there. Drew pulled the covers close, let out a big sigh and rolled over. Closing his eyes, he said, "Yeah, I don't want to go back."

Chapter 49

Stoughton, Massachusetts

Drew rubbed his head, which felt like he'd been up all-night drinking. Looking around, he discovered he was surrounded by a group of unknown people. A thick fog hovered just above the ground that encompassed the entire area. The earth was soft under his feet and dirt clung to his boots.

Jesus, did I tie one on last night and forget all about it? he thought.

Half awake, Drew felt like the group was being corralled and herded towards a mound of earth. Located at the center of the mound stood a large wooden door with a round top. Getting closer, he noticed thick granite steps leading up to the door.

Drew noticed the numbers 627 carved into the wood and thought, *How strange. That's the same number of the house I grew up in.*

The metal hinges creaked as the door swung open. The sound of metal on metal cut right through Drew, who closed his eyes and winced as the sound was painful to his ears.

The lead man stepped up and proceeded into the doorway.

When Drew reached the step, he felt a small hand wrap around his fingers. Looking down, he stared into familiar eyes. "Billy!" he exclaimed.

"Drew, I'm scared," Billy said with fright in his eyes. "Where are we?"

Glancing around, Drew watched in awe as the fog swirled like a vortex on its side.

"I'm not sure," Drew replied, feeling the small child's hand trembling in his.

The people behind Drew started pushing forward, causing Billy to trip and fall. Drew bent down and grabbed the boy, lifting him up in his strong muscular arms, then stepped up and walked through the door.

Once inside, they found themselves on a small landing. Burning torches hung on the stone walls, reminding Drew of some sort of medieval castle. The light from the torches danced and flickered on the walls, providing barely enough visibility. Beyond the landing was a darkened stairway leading down into the ground.

"Drew, I'm scared!" Billy said again, clutching his arms around Drew's neck, squeezing tightly and burying his head into Drew's shoulder.

Making their way down the steps, the group descended deep into the earth. The temperature seemed to rise with every step, and condensation dripped down the gray stone walls.

They arrived at another landing where two old men stood dressed in Nazi uniforms. One held a rifle trained on the group while the other passed out candles. Drew took the metal holder which had a long white candle in the center. The old man struck a match and laughed when Billy hid his face when it illuminated the old man's face, exposing his rotten and yellow teeth.

The man lit the candle, and the wick caught. Drew watched as the blackness before him disappeared as the flame danced to life, exposing a tight stairway carved out in the stone. The man behind Drew refused to take the candle, creating a commotion. Drew looked over his shoulder as the sentry swung the butt of the rifle, striking the man in the stomach, causing him to collapse, gasping for breath.

The next man in line looked nervously over his shoulder toward the way they'd come before, suddenly turning and bolting up the stairs.

Gun fire erupted. The sound was so intense as it reverberated throughout the confined passageway. Billy began screaming, covering his ears with his hands. Cries from the man who'd been shot grew louder as his bloody body tumbled down the stairs, rolling past the man on his knees and stopped with blood pooling around it.

The man on his knees jumped to his feet and began hysterically screaming. The old man nudged him in the back with the barrel of the sub-machine gun, forcing him toward Drew.

The group made their way down the steps, delving deeper into the darkness. The candle danced and flickered brighter the further they descended. Sweat formed on his brow as fear tugged at every fiber of his being, telling him not to go any further. Pausing for a brief moment, Drew pushed the fear aside and continued downward.

The stone steps were slick with condensation, and the only sound besides the clack of their boots was that of each man's heartbeat as they descended deeper into the blackened void.

Something indescribable hung in the air, and the feeling grew the further they descended. The candles melted faster, but not from the flame that danced atop of them, but from the heat radiating upwards from the darkness below. The candles disappeared before their very eyes.

The old man pushed them below faster as the temperature rose and the men in the group became visibly scared. Reaching the bottom, another old man, also in a Nazi uniform, greeted them. He sat on an old wooden ammo box and his skin sagged and hung over the SS on his Nazi uniform collar. Years below ground left his skin pasty white, the wrinkles of time betraying the man's hidden youth.

"You are here because it has summoned you," the old Nazi said, getting to his feet and pointing to the far wall.

The men looked around at each other.

"Move in closer," the Nazi who brought them down said from behind the group.

"Come and see," said the Nazi who greeted them and waved them closer toward eight darkened holes in the wall.

"What's in there?" asked one man.

"Your greatest evil," answered the guard who had led them down.

The older Nazi at the bottom of the stairs picked up his sub-machine gun and chambered a round. Letting out a wicked diabolical laugh, he used the barrel of the gun and pushed the first man toward one of the holes in the wall.

Drew stood at the end of the line and watched the first man enter. Almost immediately upon stepping through the wall, a blood-curdling scream escaped from the hole.

After that the others were relenting to step through and one dropped to his knees, covering his face, and wept.

"Please, I can't go in there! I'm afraid!" he said, sobbing.

"Jetzt!" the German soldier screamed. "Now!" shouted the other.

The man continued to sob and shook his head in his hands.

The Nazi soldier put the barrel of the rifle to his head. "Jetzt!" he screamed as he pushed.

"No. I can't," the man sobbed.

The men jumped at the crack of the rifle and watched the man's lifeless body collapse, blood spilling from the gaping wound in his head.

The old German soldier stood behind a third man and screamed, "Jetzt!"

The man made his way down the line shoving the barrel of the gun into each man's back forcing them toward the blackened hole.

Drew glanced to his right and saw hesitation on each man's face as they contemplated facing the unknown evil that waited for them in the blackened hole or being executed where they stood.

Billy clung to Drew's neck, sobbing.

Fuck it, Drew thought and grabbed the sides of the hole and stepped in.

The darkness was cold, freezing cold, and a faint blue hue dimly illuminated the chamber. A thick, musty smell hung in the air and the temperature between the two rooms was staggering. One room was so hot it caused condensation to drip from the walls and the next room was so freezing cold that ice clung to the walls.

Stepping into the room, something in the far-right corner called to Drew, drawing him near.

As Drew approached, a large metal box emerged from within the darkness. A bronze hue emitted from the metallic box. Its gaze was intoxicating, drawing him nearer.

Looking around, Drew noticed the man standing to his right stepped through the opening and headed straight toward the box. Drew began having visions of his childhood and of the abuse he'd endured at the hands of his father. Rage swelled within him, and the hypnotizing effect of the box seemed to lesson. However, the box seemed to control the other man who appeared unable to stop its effects.

Drew had visions of drinking and bottles of booze appeared on the walls, backlit by tiny lights. Feeling himself becoming drunk, Drew felt his anger waning, and the box calling to him again.

Drew watched the other man approach the box and couldn't believe what he was seeing. Every muscle in the man's body appeared to tremble and shake. The man's teeth were clattering together, which became so violent that blood and chunks of teeth shot out. Dropping to his knees, the man attempted to raise his hands to his face, but they just trembled and shook. Jerking gave way to full-blown seizures. Suddenly, the man's neck twisted hard to the left and a loud snapping sound rang out, followed by his body falling to the floor with a thump.

A sound escaped the body that sent shivers down Drew's spine. The man's jerking stopped as quickly as it had started and his body lay there rigid with a pool of blood forming around his face.

Drew found his gaze back on the metallic box and the ominous shadowy figure standing next to it.

"Hello, Drew," the figure said.

Drew stood there, staring into its eyes.

"Did you know a man's anger controls his descent into his own hell? Face your demons. Or are you too scared?"

Drew was about to answer when suddenly Billy looked up and began trembling. "Oh no!" Billy said. "It's the evil man!"

"You know the evil man?" Drew asked.

"Yes, he's trying to kill me." The little boy clung to Drew and spoke into his ear. "Save me, Drew. Save me!"

Drew felt his body jostle, like he was falling, and he awoke covered in sweat.

"Another bad dream?" Annabelle asked.

"Yes," he replied, putting his hand on her thigh.

"They're happening more and more now."

Taking a deep breath, Drew slowly let it out and said, "I think your mom's right, we should head south."

"Are you serious?"

"Yes."
"Thank you, Drew! Mom is going to be so happy!"
And I can stop and check in on Billy on our way, he thought.

Chapter 50

Stoughton, Massachusetts

Right after Annabelle informed the group of Drew's change of heart, the group went to work preparing for their trip.

Stan enlisted both Grant and Sara to help find enough gas for the trip south. He told them how he'd rounded up enough gas for his journey back from Nebraska and suggested they do the same. They agreed, and the three spent the day harvesting gas.

Drew and Steve checked the oil in three of the vehicles. The U-Haul's looked good, but Drew didn't like the look of the oil in Susan's car or Stan's truck and needed changing. They raided a local automotive store and brought back enough oil for both Susan's car and Stan's truck.

"Just curious," Steve said, turning and pointing toward the car Annabelle had commandeered. "But why aren't we taking that one?"

"Have you looked inside it?" Drew asked.

"No," Steve said.

"Go look inside."

Steve walked over to the car, looking inside. "Is that...?"

"Blood," Drew said. "Yes."

"Whose blood is it?"

"The guy who tried to rape Annabelle. Apparently after she stabbed him, his two friends, the ones we found at my house, had put him in the car. By the looks of it, he bled out and died."

"Your wife is a badass!" Cass said, sitting on the front steps.

By sundown both oil changes were complete, and Stan topped all three vehicles off with gas.

After dinner they finished loading up the U-Haul and Stan pulled Drew aside and asked if he would take a ride with him, explaining he wanted to go say goodbye to Carol. An hour later they were back and ready for bed.

Everyone was excited at finally having something to look forward to except for Drew, who was running all the potential dangers of their trip in his head. He had this unrelenting feeling that the shit was going to hit the fan.

Over breakfast, Drew pulled out a set of walkie talkies that Stan had collected from his house last night. He bought them for the kids in his neighborhood for checking up on Carol while he was away.

After breakfast they loaded up into the vehicles. Drew was driving Susan's car, which would be the lead car with Annabelle, Susan, Stephanie, and Cass. Sara and Grant followed behind in the U-Haul, and Stan and Steve were pulling up the rear in the pickup truck.

The walkie talkies crackled to life followed by Drew's voice saying, "Let's go."

By noon they reached Connecticut. Stephanie slept for most of the ride, and Drew noticed in the rearview mirror that Cass's eyes were getting heavy. I-95 South had been smooth sailing until the pickup got a flat just north of New Haven. The spare tire was a real bitch to remove from underneath the truck and cost them three hours of daylight.

Night had fallen by the time they reached New York City, which infuriated Drew.

"I don't understand why you're so upset," Susan said.

"Well, Susan," Drew said, slamming his fist against the steering wheel. "Because if we run into any problems, we're gonna have to deal with them in the dark instead of the sunlight."

Shortly after their brief argument they came across a pileup of cars which forced the convoy to do a U-turn.

Using his atlas, Drew planned a way around the blockage and got off at the next available exit. They found themselves on city streets and something didn't sit right with Drew and then it happened — the shit hit the fan.

Chapter 51

Rockefeller Center, New York

All around the country and world, people gathered to watch Glen's special report. The people of New York City especially looked forward to some good news since they were the hardest hit area.

Jack Denton sat on his worn-out couch and shifted his weight to adjust the spring that was poking his left buttock. The Silverline Trailer he called his home, consisted of the couch, a grungy bed, a filthy toilet, a sink with a busted spout and a TV from 1989. He never yearned for much in life except for cigarettes, they were his only vice, and the sickness provided him with an unlimited supply.

Before the virus, Jack worked for Phillip Morris at their Henrico County manufacturing plant in Richmond, Virginia. Once the virus hit, Jack never returned to the plant to work. Instead, he loaded his truck up with as many cartons as he could and made several trips home.

His robe hung open, and a smoke dangled from his lip. He spent each morning watching the news, and Glen Daniel's was the only face Jack had seen in months. Talking to him every day through the television, Glen was his only friend and like any loyal friend, Jack tuned in every day.

Jack was excited the day had finally arrived. Glen promised monumental news and really built up the suspense for today. He felt a bit sad because he was going to miss the anticipation. The countdown timer on the TV screen had less than five minutes to go.

Hopefully, it will be something great, he thought, sparking up the butt hanging from his mouth. For some reason, Jack couldn't help eying his .44 magnum revolver sitting on the side table next to the couch.

Ahmad Hadid moved to the U.S. ten years ago to provide a better life for his family. When he arrived, he used his life savings to purchase a small two-story building with a store on the first floor and an apartment above. A staircase in the back of the building connected the two floors. Ahmad turned the empty space into a liquor store and moved in above. Business stopped when the virus hit and he rode it out in the apartment. Slowly, things started getting back to normal, and he opened the store again. He kept a little portable TV near the register on the counter. Customers would stand and watch Glen with him and would talk after the broadcast. Ahmad could feel a sense of hope rising in his customers who said they looked forward to Glen's upcoming important message.

David Sanders worked as a tire mechanic for a local service shop on the outskirts of New York City. Every day he used a heavy mallet to knock tires free from the rim, and a ball peen hammer to put weights to help balance the new tires. Even when the owner, Ralph, laid him off when the pandemic hit, David kept returning.

He had no friends or family and had considered Ralph his family as he spent more time at the shop than anywhere else. He loved it there and found it cozy. He enjoyed the smell of the rubber along with the gas and oil combination.

Ralph used to sit at the front desk and watch the TV mounted to the wall at lunchtime. The TV was constantly on once the sickness hit. Once business dried up, they both sat around watching the news all day. One day a sick woman walked into the shop asking for help. The woman caught both David and Ralph by surprise. Ralph, always the chevalier one, assisted the woman and came too close to her, sealing his own fate. The sickness hit Ralph fast and before the end of the next day, he was dead. David buried his friend behind the shop with half a tire as a grave marker.

The smell of the decomposing bodies in the apartment next to David's became unbearable and before long he started sleeping at the shop on a makeshift cot.

Time ticked on. David ventured out to different stores to find food once the vending machine out back was empty except for the granola bars. He hated those.

One day while puttering around in the shop, he heard a strange sound coming from the front desk. Making his way towards the customer area, David grabbed both the heavy mallet and hammer. Once inside, he realized the sound was coming from the TV. He never turned the TV off once the last news broadcast aired.

Over the months he sat and watched as Glen Daniel read the news. David was excited over the possibility of the country rebuilding.

That morning David got up early, made his coffee and put on the TV. Sitting with his feet up, he sipped his coffee, watching as something was happening to Glen.

Lisa Thompson came down the stairs and walked into the kitchen. Her husband Keith sat at the breakfast nook watching their two little girls play dolls in the living room.

"Good morning!" she said, walking to the fridge.

"Hey babe," Keith replied.

"Have the girls been up long?"

"Probably about an hour," he replied. "I went downstairs earlier and checked the basement for water."

"Was there any?"

"Yup! There were torrential downpours the other night."

"I'm so tired of this happening. When do you plan on cleaning it up?"

"I was hoping to do it now."

"Okay, I'll keep an eye on the girls."

"Thanks babe!" he said, walking over to her and wrapping his arm around her waist. "I see you're wearing that white ruffly shirt I love seeing you in," and gave her a kiss.

"I know, I love teasing you!"

"Alright, I'll be downstairs if you need me," Keith said, and disappeared down the basement stairs.

"Girls! Are you hungry?" Lisa asked, starting coffee.

"Yeah!" they both screamed.

"Omelets?"

"Yes, please!"

Lisa grabbed the eggs, cutting board, vegetables, and a knife. Next she turned on the stove and grabbed her cup of coffee.

While taking a sip, she looked up at the TV mounted above the nook. Remembering Glen Daniels was supposed to make a special announcement yesterday, she grabbed the remote and turned on the TV above the nook.

Chapter 52

Rockefeller Center, New York

The day was here. Glen sat at the news desk watching the clock hanging below the camera count down. Glen noticed Mr. Williams and the shadow form both in the control room. Mr. Williams talked to Chris while the Shadow Man typed on the keyboard for the teleprompter.

Suddenly he was hit with an overwhelming feeling that something was wrong. Usually he had a hard copy of the transcript to read from in case the teleprompter stopped working, but not today. At first Glen didn't think anything of it because of the conversation he had with Mr. Williams. But watching the entity type on the computer that displayed the words for him to read on the teleprompter raised some serious concern.

Chris started counting down into the mic that relayed directly to Glen's earpiece.

Glen looked at the clock which was almost to zero, and felt the specter's eyes on him. When he looked up, he saw it staring at him, its eyes burning red.

The light on top of the camera turned green and words began scrolling up the teleprompter screen.

Staring into the camera, Glen read the words on the one-way glass to himself.

"No!" Glen said, shaking his head. "I won't read it!"

The shadow figure began typing again. Glen looked up at the words flashing on the screen.

****READ*****NOW!!!!!!

"No!" Glen yelled from his seat.

*************** P A I N ******************

Flashed on the screen.

"Never!" Glen screamed, standing up. Glen knew his defiance would be met with pain, but he didn't care. He would resist for as long as he could.

Glancing back over at the control room, Glen found its eyes glowing a dark crimson red and swore he could feel them trying to bore through him.

One bright yellow word repeatedly flashed on the screen.

Suddenly a searing pain shot up through Glen's penis all the way to the opening for his urethra, which felt like it was on fire.

Glen's body jolted and his eyes widened as he winched and screamed out in pain. His penis felt like it was trapped in a vice grip and being cut with razorblades all at the same time.

The blood drained from his face, which then turned pale. Tears streamed down his face from the pain. He had never experienced pain like this.

Instinctively both hands shot to his crotch, but the slightest touch hurt so much. Sweat appeared on his forehead and the nape of his neck dripped with perspiration. The collar of his shirt became soaked and beads of sweat began running down his back.

Clenching his jaw Glen let out a low guttural groan when his manhood starting to become engorged. It was the slightest of growth, like he was starting to get aroused, except Glen himself was not aroused. He couldn't stop himself from writhing in his chair, trying to take the pressure of his pants off it. Thankfully, it wasn't a full-blown erection, as that would have had him doubled over in pain, possibly killing him.

Glen stood up, bit down, and fought through the pain. He ran to the bathroom and barged through the door. The pain was so intense now that it was taking his breath away. He ran into one of the stalls and he fidgeted, trying to undo his pants. Finally he was able to get his belt open and his pants unzipped.

Reaching down, he slipped his hand into his underwear. His penis was freezing cold to the touch, and he felt a wetness on his hand. Pulling his hand out, Glen saw pink and brown moisture on his fingertips with tiny pieces of dead skin.

He brought his fingers to his nose and sniffed them. Bile rose in his throat and he began gagging. The foul stench on his fingers smelled like decomposing flesh. It smelled horrible. Something he'd never forget.

Beads of sweat formed on his forehead and he felt dizzy. *Is my dick going to shrivel up and fall off?* he wondered.

With that thought, his mind started racing. "I'll never be able to have sex again! If it falls off, I'll have to sit like a girl to pee!" he said to himself out loud.

The pain was constant and throbbed. He walked over to the sink and washed the stink from his hands. Then he splashed some water on his face. With eyes wide, he stood staring at himself in the mirror. Drops of water dripped from his nose. "Is it going to spread inward?" he asked himself. "How do I fix this?"

Staring at his reflection, he noticed the shadow man behind him.

Read the message. Everything will go back to normal, Glen heard in his head.

"It will all go back to normal?"
Yes!
"Will I be able to have sex with women again?"
As many women as you want!
"Do you promise?"
Yes!
"Will you make the pain stop?"
Of course!
"Can you do it now? It hurts so bad and I can't focus."
Done!

Glen felt an immediate difference and reached his hand down into his pants and his penis was warm and snuggled nicely in his underwear. He pulled out his hand and looked down and smiled. There was nothing on his fingers.

Read the message!

"I'm going right now," Glen said, quickly doing up his pants, adjusting his tie, and headed back out to the studio.

Glen sat down at the desk and positioned himself so he was facing the camera.

"You okay, Glen?" Chris asked.

"Better now, thanks!" Glen responded.

The entity was back in the control booth in front of the computer terminal.

Chris asked Glen if he was ready to go. Glen gave the thumbs up and adjusted his tie again.

"Alright, here we go! 3...2...1," Chris said.

Glen took a deep breath and began reading the teleprompter.

Chapter 53

New York City, New York

Drew and Susan finally stopped arguing and Cass started falling asleep. It had been a long day yesterday preparing for the trip today, plus not sleeping well left her feeling exhausted. The thought of heading south made Cass think of her family, and she couldn't help but wonder if they were dead or alive. She laid awake most of the night wondering if she should ask Drew to deviate off course. Her hometown of Cottonwood, Alabama, was just over the border from the panhandle part of Florida. Growing up in a small southern town, Cass yearned for the big city life, but after having had a taste, all she wanted to do now was go back home.

With the motion of the car and thinking of home, Cass nodded off.

Cass felt the car come to a stop and opened her eyes. To her surprise, she found herself in complete darkness. She tried rubbing her eyes but couldn't move as something was holding her down.

"Oh my god! We must have been in an accident and I'm pinned inside the car," she said. After a minute with no response she tried again.

"Drew!" she cried out, but the darkness seemed to just swallow up her voice.

Panic set in as she struggled to free herself, except she was met by a forceful resistance restraining her. Whatever was holding her, cinched tighter with even the slightest movement.

Behind her a torch flickered to life, and the flame danced around a chamber, exposing the cold, stone slab upon which she lay. Four thick straps bound her to the table. One across her forehead, one across her chest and arms, another across her hips, and the last one across her ankles. She tried to move, but the binds tightened.

Closing her eyes, Cass tried to relax her body in hopes she could wiggle her hand free from the binds that held her down. What happened next was one of the scariest moments in her life.

Hello, my darling, a sinister voice said, its words booming and bouncing around in the darkness.

"Who's there?"

I am the darkness, the voice answered.

Cass trembled with fear. Inside her chest, her heart raced and her breathing quickened. She felt the twang of adrenaline as it hit her bloodstream. She knew she was sleeping and wanted to awaken from the nightmare she found herself in, but she couldn't wake up no matter how hard she tried.

"Wake up!" she screamed while flailing her body. The straps holding her down tightened even more, and she gasped out in pain as they pulled her into the hard coldness beneath her.

Sorry, still here, the voice said, causing Cass to sob harder.

There, there, the voice said. *Tell me about your friends and I'll let you go.*

Cass immediately thought about Greg, Jessica, Jim, and the others.

No, not them. They're all dead. Your new friends.

Cass instantly knew the voice meant Drew and Steve. As soon as their names popped in her head, the voice spoke again.

Yes, those friends. Tell me about them, the voice commanded.

Cass tried to clear her mind, but the harder she tried, the more she thought about Drew and Steve.

Drew. Steve, the voice repeated. *And which one is the big man?*

Again, Cass tried to think of something else, but her mind answered.

A pair of red glowing eyes stepped out of the darkness. *Drew,* the voice said.

Cass closed her eyes and groaned as she fought the straps.

Now be so kind as to open your eyes and show me where you are.

Cass's eyes fluttered open and off in the distance was the skyline of New York City skyline.

Ahh…I see you're almost here. Well, you better wake up dear, for soon it will be time to die.

"No!" Cass shouted and sat up straight in the backseat.

Drew slammed on the brakes, bringing the car to a sliding halt.

"What's wrong?" he yelled.

"Are you okay?" Annabelle asked, turning in her seat.

Cass held her hands up to her face and sobbed.

Sara stopped the truck and pulled to the right to avoid hitting the car in front of them. Grant hopped out and ran up to Annabelle's window and knocked.

"Everything alright?" Grant asked, bending down and looking into the car window.

"No, it's not," Cass replied.

"It's okay," little Stephanie said, reaching out from her car seat and putting her hand on Cass's arm.

"You're alright, Cass. It was just a nightmare," Drew said.

"No!"

"Cass, you fell asleep," Drew said, turning in his seat and looking back at her. "It was just a dream."

"No!" Cass said. "There was something in the darkness and it's searching for you."

"Searching for Drew?" Annabelle asked.

Grant and Drew exchanged looks, which Annabelle caught, prompting her to ask, "So, which of you two wants to fill me in on the big secret?"

"Should we tell them?" Grant asked.

"No," Drew quickly replied. "They won't understand."

"Won't understand what?" Annabelle asked, staring at her husband.

Chapter 54

New York City, New York

Glen sat looking at the red light on top of the camera. The shadowy demon thing, whatever it was, stood in the control room hunched over the keyboard and a minute later words appeared on the teleprompter.

He could feel liquid trickle down the shaft of his penis and over his scrotum. He knew if he didn't read what that demonic thing wanted to him to read, it would cause him excruciating pain again.

The words made their slow crawl upwards and Glen followed them with his eyes.

This wasn't news that thing wanted him to read. It was a message.

Not just a message, but instructions.

Glen pursed his lips. He wanted to hold back, but he knew it would be met with instant penial pain, so his eyes darted over to the teleprompter and he began reading the message.

Behind the camera, Glen spotted movement in the control room. Looking up, he saw Kendra standing next to the evil entity.

In that instant Glen knew. His sexual addiction came back to haunt him, just as his ex-wife warned.

I never should have had sex with Kendra, he thought. *But I just couldn't resist. She was like a forbidden temptation which I couldn't pass up. Plus, she felt so good.* Suddenly he felt angry and a wave of arousal came over him and that's when it dawned on him.

That ice-cold pussy did this to me! That explains it because ever since I put it in her, my piece hasn't been the same.

Glen felt a twang of pain and began reading from the teleprompter.

"We are at war," Glen read, and the pain waned.

Chris knew something wasn't quite right with Glen. When he looked up from behind the control board, it appeared Glen was fighting with himself to read the script.

Why the hell would he be talking about war? Chris thought to himself as he pushed off with his feet, sending the office chair soaring across the control board toward the screen for the teleprompter. Suddenly the chair bumped into something, sending it in the opposite direction. Chris turned himself around and wheeled himself back to the screen, grabbing onto the control board and started reading the words on the screen.

"What the hell?" Chris said out loud, reaching for the delete key. As his finger reached across the keyboard, he felt an incredible jolt of pain down his entire left side. The nails on Chris's hands and feet shot off from his fingers and toes, leaving the nail beds exposed.

Glen peered into the control room window and saw the Apollyon with its hand on Chris's shoulder, and he stopped reading.

Sweat formed on Chris's forehead and his cheeks turned red. Tiny blisters began forming all over his body and grew in size. The outside of the blisters looked like bubbles that form on pizza.

The blisters filled with liquid and started sagging like water balloons, and the skin around the blisters dried up like a prune.

One by one the blisters burst and the liquid from inside his body spilled out, puddling on the floor.

All of Chris's precious life fluid dripped, oozed, and ran from his body. His tongue and eyeballs shriveled up. It sounded like a waterfall inside the control room as all of his bodily fluids escaped his body. Chris's shriveled up body fell from the chair and landed in the puddle of its own fluids.

Mr. Williams stood there in utter shock as his young friend dried up like a prune and died in front of him.

Taking a moment, Glen cleared his throat, wiped the tears from his eyes and adjusted his tie. He took a deep breath, sat up straight, then tapped the scroll back button for the teleprompter and began reading again.

Suddenly a blinding flash of light filled the studio. Everyone, even those watching on TV, shielded their eyes from the intensity of it.

Looking around with white spots in their vision, a loud, booming and commanding voice filled the studio, shaking it. *Come and See!*

Glen almost fell out of his seat and held onto the desk for support. With his ears ringing, he looked around the studio.

The ominous entity no longer looked like a shadow. It now looked translucent and had a well-defined human shape.

Glen felt something churn inside his head. It came from deep within his brain and washed over his body the same way a chill does, leaving goosebumps in its wake. His mind felt like a computer being reset, except not all the systems rebooted.

He sat straight up in the chair, and a feeling of despair overcame him. Chills rippled throughout Glen's body and he felt his ability to think fading.

He heard talking, which sounded muffled and strange. After a moment Glen realized he was hearing his own voice, except he was not controlling it. He felt trapped in his own body.

"We are at war! There is no time to hide. The world has gone mad and everyone is trying to kill you. Find a weapon and kill them before they kill you," Glen read, before pausing a moment. He couldn't believe what he was hearing or the fact that the words were coming out of his mouth. What he was saying went against every part of him. Yes, he was a sex addict, but it was always with a willing participant and he never hurt anyone, well, except for his wife, but that wasn't intentional, but he caused it, nonetheless.

"The world is at war with itself and you must stop it. Kill them where they stand, cut them down. Kill them in their beds while they sleep. Bash their brains in. Kill them all. Men, women, and children. Do not stop. Do not tire. Not until they are all dead. For I am with you as you vanquish the sinners from this world. Fear not killing nor death when it comes for you, for killing is thy word. Let it be done as it has been written. Kill in thy name, for I am War!"

Glen's words were picked up by the microphone pinned to his lapel while his image was captured by the camera and broadcast out through the dish on top of the roof. The message was received by TVs and radios around the world.

The message did not discriminate. It was sent in closed caption displaying the words on the screen. Anyone who saw or heard the message instantly became trapped inside their own body and turned into a crazed psychotic killer.

Glen looked out the window at tent city. People stood there staring at the large screens with blank expressions on their faces.

Movement in the back of the group caught Glen's eye and his mouth kept reading even though he wasn't looking at the monitor.

Glen watched as people in the plaza started attacking and killing each other. One man jammed a metal tent stake into the face of a woman standing next to him. People started hitting people with chairs and one man swung a grill propane tank around, striking people with it.

Glen watched in horror, even as his voice continued to carry on. The woman with a newborn baby, whom he spoke with a few days ago on his last visit outside, was swinging her baby by the legs using its head as a mallet. After a couple of swings, it was unrecognizable. A man ran up and clotheslined her and began stomping on her head. The baby killer died clutching a tiny leg in her hand.

Glen wanted to throw up at what he was witnessing.

An immediate feeling of terror washed over Glen as he recognized the look on everyone's face outside. He'd seen it many times before and had stared directly at it every time he had sex with Kendra.

Glen didn't know what exactly caused the bright flash of light or loud voice earlier, but he had an inclination. Growing up Catholic, he was forced to read the bible, and his mother always feared the Book of Revelation coming true. She died several years ago, but he remembered how she associated every news story with the End Times. She even swore the "Man would come around" like the one suggested by the Johnny Cash song written before his death titled, *The Man Comes Around*.

Both Peter and Mr. Williams heard the message but were not affected by it. They were under the control of the Diabolus being and could not be controlled by anyone or anything else.

Peter Bane was standing off to the side of the news desk, watching everything as it unfolded, and he couldn't believe what he just saw happen to Chris. Realizing that the message Glen was reading was causing all the violence, Peter knew he had to turn the power off to stop the message.

Running as fast as he could, Peter sprinted down the hallway towards the power room.

A large pit formed in his stomach knowing he had restored the power which allowed this evil message to be transmitted throughout the world. He had provided a means for that dark evil piece of shit to kill thousands, possibly even millions of people.

Entering the power room, he looked at the gauges as the power increased. A monitor mounted in the corner displayed a live feed from the control room. Peter glanced up and noticed the shadow man was no longer there.

Peter knew he had to stop it and placed his hand on the kill switch. There was no way he could live knowing his actions helped kill millions of people.

He applied pressure to the kill switch when he heard a man's voice behind him. It wasn't like before when he'd heard it in his head. Now he heard it in the room.

Peter turned and found himself staring at a five-foot-nine translucent man. Smooth muscle and bone were visible, and blood circulated throughout the form.

Right away, Peter knew. He knew deep inside that it was the dark man. It was no longer a shadow but appeared to be coming human. Pale skin and blonde hair formed right before Peter's eyes.

"Now, now Peter. All that we've been through and now in my finest hour, you decide to bail on me? What a shame. I would have shown you everything. How it began. How it will end. Hell, I would have shown you the darkest reaches of the universe.

Peter knew he was fucked. He had already out lived the normal parameter by surviving the plague.

In the back of Peter's head, a familiar voice started growing. It questioned everything he had done in the past several weeks, and his head hung low. It had disappeared, but now Peter's conscience was back.

"Do you think you can bail on me?" asked the blonde-haired man.

"I can't do this!" Peter shouted.

"Do as you must," the man said. "It's your freewill after all."

Peter grabbed the handle and thirteen thousand and eight hundred volts of electricity started coursing throughout his body. Peter screamed out in pain as his muscles violently twitched and melted away and his clothes caught fire. Within minutes, all that was left of Peter Bane was fused unrecognizable charred remains.

Chapter 55

Rockefeller Center, New York

Word of Glen and the news being back spread. People passed the word on to tune in for a special message Saturday night.

It had been awhile since Glen returned to the airwaves reporting that the sickness was over and people were finally feeling safe again. Some speculated a cure had been discovered.

Viewers at home watched with intense anticipation when Glen stood up behind the news desk and stepped away. Then they heard commotion off camera but were unable to see it.

Glen finally returned and started speaking again when suddenly there was a bright burst of light and a booming voice.

Come and See!

Lisa saw Glen Daniels sitting at the news desk with the Channel 29 backdrop behind him and turned the volume up. Putting the remote down, she walked over to the stovetop and cracked three eggs, dropping them into the bowl. Whisking the eggs, she poured them into the skillet, then went to the fridge and pulled out the orange juice. She closed the fridge door and yelled for the girls to washup for breakfast before turning to watch the news.

Keith found the shop vac under the basement stairs, plugged it in and started vacuuming up the water. With the amount of water on the floor, it took mere seconds to fill the six-gallon capacity. He already made several trips to the backdoor, dumping the water outside.

On his way back over to the flooded section he heard a loud commotion from upstairs followed by blood-curdling screams from his children.

Running to the stairs, Keith heard his children's screams moving from one side of the house to the other.

Keith bolted up the stairs and slipped on something covering the kitchen floor. The substance was thick, warm and red. "Oh my God!" he screamed upon realizing it was blood.

His adrenaline was pumping, and his heart raced while he fought to get up off the slick floor.

Did someone break into the house? he thought. Looking around, he noticed a blood trail that winded around the living room table and towards the bedroom stairs.

"No momma!" one of his daughters yelled, followed by screams of pain.

Racing up the stairs, he followed the blood trail, not knowing what he would find. His heart jumped into his throat as he rounded the top of the steps and saw a small arm lying out of the bathroom. He shot down the hall and dropped to his knees, cradling the lifeless body of his daughter. His vision blurred as the tears welled. Then he heard it, a muffled scream. Keith was quickly to his feet and darting down the hall.

He entered his bedroom and was taken aback by what he saw. Lisa was on their bed straddling their daughter, plunging a knife over and over into her abdomen.

Keith ran and lunged at his wife, but she turned, swung the knife, and slashed him right across the throat.

He fell to the floor, his hands shooting up to his neck. His mind raced as blood spilled between his fingers. He felt his body go weak and then was stunned by a burning, stinging pain that shot through him as the knife pierced his stomach. Grasping his throat, he was unable to do anything to protect himself from his wife, who plopped down on his abdomen and slashed at his face and chest.

Keith's vision became blurry and soon the light faded, and the darkness enveloped him.

Calmly Lisa walked down the stairs, her white ruffly shirt soaked in blood, and walked out into the street.

Ahmad stood behind the counter of his liquor store cutting up his shirt into strips and dipped them into bottles of alcohol to be used as Molotov Cocktails.

Out back he had an old twelve-speed bike, with its super thin tires, curled handlebars, and a milk crate zip-tied to the front. Back when he first opened, he used to deliver alcohol to the surrounding neighborhoods for an added price. Customers seemed to love the service, especially if they ran low during games. The bike made it easy to get around the constant heavy traffic.

He took a red lighter from the stand on the counter and carried the bottles outside. With the bottles secured in the basket, he hopped on and started peddling down the street.

Seeing people milling about, Ahmad stopped, lit one of the rags on fire and started peddling again. Bearing down behind them, he hurled the flaming bottle, firebombing the people. Flaming liquid covered those he targeted and most succumbed to their injuries.

If Ahmad saw someone in a car or window of a house, he attacked them, setting their concealment on fire. Half of the neighborhood was now burning because of him.

David sat watching Glen when suddenly a bright flash filled the screen and he heard a beastly voice from the TV.

Gears inside David's head started clicking and his mind became foggy and sluggish. It felt like he was becoming detached from himself, like his conscious was drifting away from his body and he was trapped inside his head.

Before long, his body was moving by itself. Scared, he tried to stop himself but could not. He watched himself pick up the mallet in one hand and ball-peen hammer in the other. Then his body walked out the front door.

David watched in horror as he chased people down, swinging the hammers wildly, beating his victims to death. He cried out, trying to warn people to run, but to no avail. Running from street to street, his body attacked and killed anyone it saw.

Jack couldn't believe it. His body was moving all by itself. The feeling of pins and needles covered his entire body and he felt disconnected from it.

Like everyone else who encountered the message, he tried stopping himself but could not.

Grabbing the .44 Magnum off the side table, his body went into the kitchen and retrieved the box of ammo from the drawer and filled his bathrobe pockets with bullets.

Jack's body then left the trailer and climbed into his truck and drove off towards New York City.

When his body spotted someone, the truck slowed down, and he aimed the handgun out the window and began firing.

A young man tried attacking his truck with a fiberglass hockey stick. The guy swung hard and connected with the driver's side mirror, which exploded and the end of the hockey stick broke off. Using the broken end of the stick, he jabbed at the window trying to break the glass.

Jack shot the man in the face. Most of the guy's head instantly vaporized, and he was dead before his body hit the ground.

Once he reached the city, Jack parked the truck. He got out and started hunting people down and executing them.

One woman was playing cat and mouse with him, running from street to street.

Anyone around the world who heard or watched the message became altered.

People within ear shot of the anchorman stopped and picked up whatever weapon they could find and started attacking people at random.

Mothers beat and killed their children. Some stabbed them to death with knives, forks, or whatever they could get their hands on.

Fathers dragged their family out to the pool and drowned them.

Husbands attacked their wives, and wives attacked their husbands. Sons and daughters attacked their parents and then turned on each other.

People in cars veered off the road, running people down.

A fear to survive crippled them, causing them to kill their most beloved family members. Within hours, the death toll was staggering. In the blink of an eye, Glen's message killed more people than all the world wars combined.

And there went out another horse that was red: and power was given to him that sat thereon to take peace from the earth, and that they should kill one another: and there was given unto him a great sword.

-Revelation 6:4

Chapter 56

Paxton, Nebraska

Bill finished loading up the truck with produce and moved it into the barn. He had Everything set and ready to go for his trip into town tomorrow.

For dinner Maureen made fresh chicken and vegetables. After eating, the boys helped Maureen clean up while Bill brought some of his guns into the living room. After the boys were done cleaning, Maureen led them into the living room where Bill was waiting for them. Both boys were eyes wide open when they spotted the guns on the table.

"Are they empty?" Maureen asked.

"Of course they are," Bill responded. "I checked each one twice."

"Okay, good. Because you know how I feel about them."

Bill gave the boys their first lesson in gun safety and taught them to always treat a weapon as if it were loaded, even when it is not.

The lesson went better than expected, and both boys listened intently. Bill told the boys they would have their first shooting lesson and sent them off to bed to get a goodnight's sleep.

Bill was up at the crack of dawn and set up several practice targets. Maureen came downstairs and found both boys dressed and sitting on the couch. Bill came back in and gave the boys a refresher course in gun safety while Maureen cooked breakfast.

After breakfast, the boys went out for their first shooting practice. Caleb was good, but Eben had an eagle eye.

"I'm older, so why is he doing better than me?" Caleb asked.

"It's not about age, son," Bill said.

"It's easy. All you do is point and shoot," Eben said, taunting his older brother.

"Yeah, so is making a fist and swinging," Caleb responded.

"Alright, you two," Bill said.

"But Dad!" Caleb cried.

"Don't whine, Caleb," Bill said. "Like anything else, you'll get better with practice."

They continued shooting for another hour. Bill locked the guns in the safe and got ready to head into town. He said goodbye to Maureen and the boys and drove the truck into town to barter.

When he arrived in town, he found several people in the store talking about how some townsfolk had gone crazy trying to kill people.

"Must be all that cabin fever," one old man said.

"Yeah, I'd try to kill you too if I was locked up with you for months on end," a man replied.

Bill made his trade and was on his way. Leaving town, Bill saw something strange. Passing the Old Man Crawford's place, he saw a man dangling from a rope hung from a tree.

I guess we're back to punishing criminals ourselves again, he thought.

Bill arrived home late afternoon and when he kissed Maureen, he slipped a new pack of cigarettes into the front pocket of her apron.

After dinner Bill removed a pistol and rifle from the gun safe. Maureen looked at him quizzically.

"I'll tell you later," he said.

Once the boys were asleep, Bill told Maureen what he saw out at Old Man Crawford's and how it was probably a thief. "But to be on the safe side, I want to keep a pistol on me," Bill told her.

"Okay," she said. "If you feel that strongly about it."

And for the first time since she could remember, Bill locked the front door.

Chapter 57

Crescent City, Florida

Henry couldn't wait to get home and poop. Real toilet paper was going to feel great, and he looked forward to not having his ass rubbed raw like it did with the other materials he'd used to clean his backside.

When the three brothers arrived home, they were surprised to find everyone sitting around the TV. Even more surprising was Dave asleep on the couch.

"Daddy! The TV works again!" Billy shouted when Henry walked in.

"I know. Cap had his on down at the store," Henry said.

"How d'you make out?" Betty-Sue asked.

Henry couldn't contain his excitement of having real toilet paper and held out the package like a child who just received a new toy.

"I'll be back," Henry said, disappearing into the bathroom.

The rest of the day they watched Glen. He reported on news from New York City and other parts of the world.

"Alright," Henry said, getting up and turning the TV off. "That's enough TV for one day. We still have chores to tend to before dinner."

An hour later Betty-Sue rang the dinner bell, and the men returned from tending to the fields.

"Billy, go wash up," Betty-Sue said.

The family all ate together in the kitchen except for Dave, who was sound asleep on the couch.

After dinner Billy asked if he could be excused.

"Hi Uncle Dave," Billy said, running through the living room and shooting upstairs to his bedroom to play with his toys.

Dave waved hello and rubbed the kink in his back from sleeping on the couch.

Grandpa walked into the living room and sat down in his recliner. Looking at Dave he said, "Welcome back to the land of the living."

"I guess so," Dave said, getting up and putting the TV back on.

Grandma and Betty-Sue started cleaning up after dinner while Henry, Arthur and Ralph discussed the game plan for harvesting the next shipment for Cap.

Dave stood there watching Glen at the news desk and witnessed the bright flash and heard the commanding voice.

Dave stood there in front of the TV in a trance-like state.

"Son," Grandpa said. "You sure do make a better door than a window."

Dave continued to stand there blocking the TV.

"Well!" Grandpa said after a few moments.

Dave suddenly grabbed the long flat common screwdriver he had used to fix the TV, turned and charged at his father.

"Agh!" Grandpa screamed as Dave began plunging the screwdriver repeatedly into his father's neck.

Blood pumped from the wound and the screwdriver dripped with blood.

"Dad!" Arthur shouted and ran into the living room.

Dave spun and slashed Arthur with the screwdriver. Arthur stepped back and bumped into the TV stand. He held his arms out in front of him, trying to stop his brother from attacking him. Dave did a softball type pitch with his right hand plunging the screwdriver into Arthur's stomach.

Arthur screamed out in agony as his brother drove the screwdriver into his abdomen repeatedly. Arthur's shirt was soaked with blood and littered with puncture marks.

Henry and Ralph stood in disbelief. Ralph finally acted. Grabbing a frying pan off the stove, he ran into the living room and began swinging wildly. One swing connected with Dave's head, making a loud *thud* sound.

Stunned, Dave dropped to a knee before Ralph kicked him onto his back.

Henry and Betty-Sue went running into the living room to tend to Grandpa and Arthur, while Grandma hobbled into her bedroom.

Dave clutched at his head. His face void of emotion as he tried to get back to his feet.

"Dad!" Henry shouted, tending to his father.

"Do something!" Betty-Sue sobbed.

"He's gone!" Henry said, turning to check on Arthur.

Blood covered the living room floor and arterial spray ran down the walls. It looked like one of those Hollywood Detective murder scenes, only worse.

Ralph stood over Dave with the frying pan in case he tried anything.

"What the hell happened! Why did you do this?" Ralph shouted at his brother lying on the floor, still clutching his head.

"He's gone too!" Henry said, kneeling over Arthur's body.

"They're both dead?" Ralph asked, looking over his shoulder at the carnage.

Before Henry could speak, Dave lunged at Ralph with the screwdriver, stabbing him in the knee. Dave wiggled it around, inflicting damage to the bone and cartilage.

Ralph dropped the frying pain and bent over, clutching at his knee.

Betty-Sue stood there shocked at what she was seeing.

Dave picked up the frying pan and quickly got to his feet. He brought the pan high over his head and brought it violently down, smashing into the back of Arthur's head.

Arthur crumpled to the floor, his eyes wide open and lifeless.

Upstairs Billy heard shouting and fighting and ran into the hallway. *Don't go downstairs,* he heard in his head.

Dave swung the pan in a wild arch and the bottom of the pan crashed into Henry's face and his nose instantly exploded.

Dave got to his knees and raised the pan over his head again.

"No!" Betty-Sue screamed as Dave brought the heavy cast iron pan down onto Henry's head.

Dave repeated the blow several times, crushing Henry's face. Blood spattered everywhere and pooled from the large gaping wounds.

Blood flung from the frying pan, leaving tiny spots all over the room.

Betty-Sue trembled as her brother-in-law stepped over her husband's lifeless body. The twang of the frying pan striking Henry's head repeatedly rung in her ears. The loud hollow thud and the cracking of his skull. She felt sick. One hand covered her stomach and the other her mouth.

Dave stood there breathing heavily. His shoulders were slumped, and his head hung low. Henry had landed a hard right jab on Dave's chin, which clearly left him dazed.

Billy had paused, but he couldn't ignore the screams from his mother below. The sound of Billy running across the floor above snapped Dave out of his confused state. He spun the handle of the frying pan in his right hand. Tiny globs of crimson blood shot off in every direction.

Betty-Sue stood there trying not to breathe when she heard her son's galloping footsteps across the second floor. Billy reached the top of the stairs and stopped. His eyes widened, and he started down the stairs when he saw his father's lifeless body lying on the floor.

Slowly Betty-Sue held up her hands trying to stop Billy from coming downstairs, but Billy's foot was already in motion and his foot landed on that step, the one that always creaks and lets out an audible squeak.

"Billy, no!" Betty-Sue screamed.

Grandma grabbed her husband's double-barrel shotgun from their bedroom closet and flipped it open. She looked down at the two shells and flipped it close. Tucking the shotgun under her arm, she heard the thudded twang of the pan followed by the screams. She made her way into the hallway, but with all the commotion she forgot to grab her glasses, which she needed for distance. Watching TV without them was like watching a football game from a blimp. The end of the hallway was just a blur, but she continued hobbling on.

"Please! No! No! No! No!" Betty-Sue screamed as Dave turned and made his way towards Billy.

Billy was rife with fear. His young brain was still trying to process what was happening. His muscles tensed and were ready to get the hell out of dodge, but the signal from his brain telling him to run hadn't been received yet.

Grandma quickened her pace even though she could barely see.

"Billy! Run!" Betty-Sue screamed.

Dave turned towards Betty-Sue and swung the frying pan. She shot her arms up like an X to block the incoming blow.

Grandma feared her grandson was in danger. As she reached the end of the hall, her foot stepped in a warm substance, which she knew was blood. She raised the shotgun up, holding it straight out, and rounded the corner just as Betty-Sue's body hit the floor.

"Momma!" Billy screamed before running back up the stairs.

Grandma's eyes widened and for a minute she could see clearly. She saw her son's bloody body on the floor and caught her grandson running up the stairs just as her daughters-in-law's body hit the floor. Her cataracts shifted and her vision started to blur. She couldn't tell who was standing over Betty-Sue.

Grandma aimed the shotgun and pulled both triggers. Dave's body was severed in half and went sailing across the room from the force of the impact. His upper torso bounced off the wall about waist high and fell to the floor, his intestines spilling out across the floor. His lower half careened across the living room and hit the TV stand, knocking the TV off. It crashed to the floor with a loud pop as the tube inside the old TV exploded and pieces of the glass screen went everywhere.

Chapter 58

New York City, New York

"Bravo-Two Lima!"

"Bravo-Two Lima, do you read?"

"This is Bravo-Two Lima," answered the Army Captain.

Captain Todd Rayburn was an Army Reservist from upstate New York. Bravo-Two Lima was their designated call sign given to the unit upon activation. They had been activated and given orders to assist local and state police in an effort to lock down New York City. No one in and no one out.

"Oh, thank God! We worried your unit might have been wiped out," the voice over the radio said.

"We're still here, sir. We were given orders to fall back and wait for command once the sickness died down," Captain Rayburn said.

"Please standby while I connect you with command."

The radio squeaked as the connection to command was made. "Bravo-Two Lima, how do you read?" asked a deep raspy voice that sounded like it just finished smoking three packs of cigarettes.

"Loud and clear, sir."

"Strength?" the voice asked.

"Seven-teen sir," Captain Rayburn replied, making sure to use the correct military pronunciation of numbers as he had been taught.

"Jesus!" replied the voice. "All casualties?"

"Mostly sir and a few deserters."

"Alright Captain, that will have to do. We have a mission of the utmost importance."

Captain Rayburn looked around at each of the sixteen remaining men's faces. Most were young men in their late teens to early twenties. They were all good men. Smart men. Men who had signed up to defend their country.

"Send your traffic," Rayburn said into the mic.

The men of Bravo-Two Lima gathered around listening, waiting for orders.

A few seconds later the radio crackled back to life. "Captain, we need you to make your way to New York City. We have reports of a mad man broadcasting a message from WTFH news studio that is making people kill one another."

The sixteen men all looked at their Captain in unison with furrowed brows.

"Your orders are to kill everyone in that studio and then blowup the studio. How do you read, over?"

"Sir?" Captain Rayburn said. He had heard the order, but it didn't make sense.

"I know how it sounds, Captain. We believe there is something embedded in the broadcast. Everyone who sees or hears the broadcast goes completely crazy and starts attacking anyone they see."

Rayburn looked around at his men, trying to gauge their body language.

"You'll need to proceed in radio blackout. Have your men use earplugs so you won't be effected by the broadcast."

Captain Rayburn looked up to his NCO Sergeant Mills and asked, "Thoughts?"

Sgt. Mills rubbed the stubble on his chin and looked back at Captain Rayburn. "Well sir, we still don't know what caused the sickness. Was it nature, was it God, or was it a terrorist attack? If it was terrorists, could it be some sort of second wave attack?"

Rayburn looked around at his men again. He searched their eyes, looking for any sign of hesitation or doubt. They would be going into an unknown situation facing an unknown force in a communications blackout. Every man would be critical in completing the mission.

"Fuck it. Let's go kill some terrorists!" one soldier said.

The other men cheered.

No matter what it was, Captain Rayburn decided to stick with the broadcast is a terrorist attack because it seemed to motivate his men. No need to add doubt to their mission.

"Alright men, weapon and gear check. Get an ammo count and make sure you have your ear plugs," Captain Rayburn said.

"Time for some payback!" Sergeant Mills shouted.

The men cheered again.

Captain Rayburn picked up the radio mic and said, "Send the address, sir."

Chapter 59

New York City, New York

The voice on the radio sent the coordinates and Captain Rayburn acknowledged them.

A lengthy pause left the Captain wondering if the call was over.

"Rayburn?" the voice said, finally coming back over the radio in a fearful tone.

"Go ahead, sir."

"This message is affecting citizens too, Captain. Consider everyone a potential threat," the voice said.

"ROE, sir?"

"There are no Rules of Engagement. You are weapons free."

"Received. Weapons free," Captain Rayburn repeated.

"And Rayburn,"

"Yes, sir?"

"Good luck!"

"Thank you, sir. We'll let you know once we accomplish the mission," Rayburn said hanging up the mic.

"Alright boys, you heard the Captain. Weapon, ammo, and earplugs. Go!" Sergeant Mills barked.

The men took off running to carry out the Captain's orders, leaving both Mills and Rayburn standing there together.

"Are you kidding me?" Mills asked, looking into his Captain's eyes. "They're really sending us into New York City weapons free?"

"That's an order we won't be following, Mike," Rayburn said using the sergeant's first name.

Once the sun set, Rayburn gave the order for the soldiers to form up.

"Alright boys, we're going into Manhattan. As you heard, our objective is to cut the enemy transmission and wipe out those responsible for it. You all heard we're cleared weapons free, but we will *not* be going in there shooting everyone we see. I will not have our unit disgraced by shooting unarmed citizens. If attacked or fired upon first, you may return fire," Captain Rayburn said, looking around at all of his men's faces.

"Just to reiterate what the Captain said. You will *not* shoot anyone who is not holding a weapon or trying to attack you. Once we reach our objective, we will clear you weapons free," Sergeant Mills said. "Understand?"

"Hooah!" the men cried out.

"Mount up!" Mills yelled.

They climbed into their five Humvees and headed into the city.

They drove past the checkpoint they had manned, restricting citizens from flowing in or out of the city. But their efforts had been futile. A city with so many exits and entry points it was inevitable someone broke through, unfortunately whoever broke out took the virus with them.

The convoy drove south through deserted streets and everything seemed quiet, but that would soon change.

Chapter 60

New York City, New York

Annabelle was looking back and forth between Grant and Drew, "Well?" she asked.

"Can we talk about this later?" Drew said, clearly not wanting to talk about it right now.

"No, now!" Annabelle demanded.

At that precise moment, the truck horn behind them started blaring.

Grant looked back to find Sara frantically pointing and waving at something behind him.

"Oh, shit!" Drew said, grabbing the rifle and hopping out of the car.

A woman wearing a white shirt covered in blood charged toward Grant with a knife in her hand.

"Stop! Stop! Stop!" Drew shouted, but the woman kept charging, her brown hair swaying every which way.

Grant stood there stunned and couldn't believe what he was seeing. The woman coming straight toward him had a blank look on her face.

Grant focused on her lifeless eyes when the side of her head exploded, and her body cartwheeled to a stop.

"Jesus, Drew! Why did you do that?" Annabelle screamed from inside the car.

"Oh, my god!" Susan screamed. "What the hell just happened!"

Stephanie held her hands up to her ears and began crying from the loud noise and the shouting.

Drew slung the rifle and walked over to the woman's body.

"He just killed her!" Susan screamed from the backseat. "And in front of his daughter, too!"

"Mom, please!" Annabelle screamed.

"Annabelle, I can't look!" Susan said, holding her hand up to her mouth. "I think I'm going to be sick."

Stan and Steve exited the pickup, made their way past the U-Haul, and headed for the car to see what happened.

"Your husband just murdered that woman!" Susan screamed hysterically.

"Is that a knife?" Annabelle asked, watching Drew kick something from the lifeless woman's hand.

"What?" Susan asked.

"Did you see that?" Grant asked, leaning into the car window. "That lady was crazy!"

"Crazy?" Susan said.

"Did you see the size of that machete?" Grant asked.

"Calm down, honey. It was just a butcher's knife," Sarah said, walking over next to her husband.

"You ladies alright?" Stan asked through the open driver's door.

"Did she really have a knife?" Annabelle asked.

Steve ventured over to Drew as he was flipping the body over.

"Yes, and her shirt was already covered with blood," Drew said.

Steve looked down at the body and clearly the blood covering the front of her shirt was dry, unlike the blood pooling next to her head.

"Excuse me," Annabelle said, opening the door trying to avoid hitting Grant and Sara and made her way towards Drew.

"Did she really have a knife?" Annabelle asked, staring at the body.

"Yeah, right there," Steve said, using his foot to point to the knife.

"Guys!" Cass suddenly shouted from the car.

"What is it?" Susan asked.

"Guys!" Cass shouted again, stepping out of the car, pointing.

The group turned and saw a man throw a lit Molotov cocktail toward them.

Chapter 61

New York City, New York

Drew turned and raised the rifle, but it was too late. The man had already launched the bottle of flaming liquid toward them. It was a long shot, but Drew aimed for the hurtling bottle and fired twice.

Both rounds missed.

The glass bottle smashed into the side of the U-Haul just behind the driver's door, sending liquid fire everywhere.

Turning his attention back to the man, Drew spotted him pull another bottle from the basket of the bike and tried to light it. Drew fired two more shots, both finding their intended target. The man fell holding the lit bottle, which smashed on the ground igniting him instantly on fire.

"Drew!" Annabelle screamed.

Drew turned with his rifle ready to shoot another possible attacker, when he noticed the back of the car was on fire.

Susan hopped out and tried freeing Stephanie but was having no luck with the buckle, which was on the other side of the seat.

Cass jumped back in the car and pulled Stephanie out just as the gas tank blew.

Annabelle ran toward them and helped Cass to her feet before taking Stephanie in her arms.

Drew's Spidey sense was in overdrive when suddenly people started coming out of the woodwork, like cockroaches.

People were attacking each other with all sorts of weapons. Whatever could be picked up and used as a weapon was.

"To the pickup!" Stan shouted.

Annabelle took off running with Stephanie cradled in her chest.

"Come on, Susan!" Grant said, grabbing her by the arm and escorting her to the pickup. Sara was right on their heels.

Drew's adrenaline was pumping. People were rushing toward the vehicles, but they were attacking each other as well. It looked like an unorganized group.

Drew took a fighting stance and started engaging targets as they approached the group fleeing toward the pickup.

Stan pulled his pistol from his waistband and shot an old man who was trying to grab Annabelle and Stephanie.

"Get in!" Stan shouted, as he turned and shot a middle-aged man wearing sweatpants and a sweatshirt carrying a crowbar. The man and the crowbar hit the ground at the same time. A young man in his late teens grabbed the crowbar and started swinging at Stan.

Drew turned and saw his wife get into the truck with their daughter while Stan held off an attacker who appeared to have the upper hand against Stan.

Pivoting, Drew fired, dropping the young man with the crowbar.

"Drew!" Cass shouted, as she made her way next to him, carrying the shotgun and bag of ammo that she retrieved from the car before it was completely engulfed in flames.

"Go! Go! Go!" Drew yelled, waving to Grant.

Stan jumped into the bed of the truck as Grant hopped into the front seat of the pickup and threw it in reverse. Flooring it, the tires screeched as the ass end of the truck skipped and hopped across the pavement until the tires caught. The truck rocketed backwards toward the intersection several hundred yards away.

"Has everyone gone mad?" shouted Steve, picking up the knife the woman had dropped after being shot by Drew.

"What does your bible say about people going crazy?" Drew yelled, before shooting another person running toward them.

"It doesn't!" Steve shouted.

"Well, I guess this isn't God's doing then!" Drew said, reloading.

"Maybe it's not God," Steve replied.

"Isn't that what I just said?"

"You said, 'God's doing'. I'm saying it's the devil's doing."

"Okay, so what does your bible say about the devils doing?"

"Well, we had a plague of biblical proportions."

"Yeah, so!"

"And now it seems everyone is attacking each other, like it's a war."

"Not seems! *Is*!" Drew shouted.

"I think it's the second horsemen!" Steve said.

"Like the Four Horsemen?"

"Yes, exactly."

"And what are the Four Horsemen again?"

"Pestilence, or plague."

"Well, put a check in that column."

"Then its war."

"Check."

"What the hell is next?" Cass asked, both scared and intrigued at the same time.

"Famine," Steve said.

"What?" Cass yelled.

"Starvation."

"Oh good, I can afford to lose a few pounds," Drew said sarcastically.

"Do I dare ask what the last one is?" Cass said.

"Death," Steve said.

"Yeah, I think we got that covered already between the virus and these crazy fucks," Drew said, shooting another individual.

Chapter 62

New York City, New York

The lead Humvee's headlights stopped on three cars sitting across the bridge, rendering it impassable.

"Hey Capt.," Sergeant Mills said into the radio mic as he exited the Humvee and made his way over to the cars blocking the bridge.

"Send your traffic," Rayburn responded.

Mills used the car's fender to climb up onto the hood to get a better view and noticed barricades at both ends of the bridge. "Should we find another way around?" Mills asked, telling the Captain what he discovered.

"I think we're gonna find every bridge this way," Rayburn replied.

"What's your pleasure Captain?"

"Mike, let's take a midnight stroll."

"Roger that," Mills replied, and returned to the Humvee to pass along the order.

A minute later, the soldiers formed a tactical column and set out on foot. They moved in complete silence and the only sound they produced was the occasional pitter-patter of their boots hitting the pavement as they ran. Before the sickness hit, they completed the Army's intensive and rigorous Close Quarter Battle (CQB) training at Fort Carson in Colorado. The training they received prepared them for combat in an urban setting, but it did not prepare them for what lay beyond in the city.

They crossed over the bridge without incident. When they reached the other side, Captain Rayburn sighed in relief. He was nervous crossing the bridge because the abandoned cars on each end created a perfect chokepoint for an ambush.

They made their way block by block but had yet to meet any resistance. A short time later they discovered the first fresh body. It appeared to be that of a young man in his mid-twenties, but it was hard to determine his age because someone had bashed in his face.

None of the soldiers believed people were going crazy and killing others. They thought it was an exaggeration, kinda like the one you'd hear around Christmas time regarding parents who would kill to get their hands on one of the *must have sold out* holiday season toys.

The column reached the halfway mark without incident, but before they reached the next block, they lost two men. As the column passed by two trash barrels, a man with a knife lunged from the shadows and slashed one soldier's face before slicing another's throat. Four soldiers opened up on the man, riddling him with bullets.

A woman wearing broken stilettos hobbled down the front stairs of an apartment building toward them. In one hand she held a bloody knife, and in the other she held the broken heel to her shoe.

She started making her way across the street, heading straight for them. Her face held a blank expression, as if she was in shock. When she did not comply with one soldier's orders to stop, he leveled his weapon and shot her dead.

Further up the road, three men appeared. One began attacking another, killing him with a fire axe, while the third man made a beeline straight toward the column.

"Weapons free, Captain?" Sergeant Mills asked, standing next to the medic tending to the injured soldier's face.

"Jesus, Mike!" The Captain said, turning towards Sergeant Mills. "I didn't think the guy on the radio was fucking serious!"

"Me neither Capt.!" Sergeant Mills said while nodding his head in agreement. Mills checked on his soldier, seeing how he was doing, who had a nasty gash on his face. Then he stared at the dead man who tried killing him.

"Mike," Rayburn said, but he noticed Mills was staring at the dead man they just shot. "Mike!" Rayburn shouted.

Mills looked up and found Captain Rayburn staring at him.

"Weapons free. Pass the order," Rayburn said.

"Yes, sir!"

"Oh, and Mike."

"Sir?" Mills said, looking back.

"Call me Todd."

"You got it, sir," Mills said and went to pass on the order.

The pointman lead the column at a steady pace with Captain Rayburn and Sergeant Mills in the middle. Sporadic shots rang out as the soldiers engaged and neutralized potential threats.

A few blocks later, the pointman stopped the column and signaled the Captain to the front. When Rayburn arrived, the pointman told him that someone had blocked the road up ahead with cars and other debris.

"What's your preference, sir, left, or right?" the PFC asked.

"Neither."

"Sir?" the PFC asked, confused.

"I want you to take us over that obstacle."

"Over it, sir?"

"Yes," Rayburn said, putting his hand on the young specialist's shoulder. "Because they're trying to prevent us from going that way."

"Roger that, sir," the PFC said and made his way toward the obstacle.

A few minutes later the column cleared the debris and was back on track.

As they grew closer to their mission objective, the sound of shouting came from a block over and Captain Rayburn gave the order for the column to stop.

"Mike, take two men and check it out," Rayburn ordered.

Grabbing two men, Sergeant Mills headed out.

Rayburn told the remaining men to take a knee and to drink some water, reminding them they needed to stay hydrated.

An eerie silence filled the night air, and the city no longer resembled what once had been the busiest metropolis, as Captain Rayburn recalled.

Gun shots shattered the silence, followed by screams and the screech of tires. Rayburn peeked around the corner, making sure Sergeant Mills wasn't in need of help.

"Thank God," he muttered with a sigh of relief when he spotted Mills and the other soldier approaching the next block. Another cluster of shots rang out, which Rayburn assumed was one shooter and judged them to be active or former military by the sound of the shot cluster.

From his vantage point, Rayburn could see flames reflecting off the windows of the building at the next cross street. Along with the fire, there was thick black smoke billowing down the street, with the buildings acting as a wind tunnel.

The sound of a racing engine echoed and bounced off the buildings, making it hard to determine where the vehicle was heading.

A moment later, a loud crash caused Rayburn to turn around and look back. As he did, he heard a woman scream, followed by gunshots. Whatever happened was off in the distance and out of his sight. When Rayburn turned back around, he watched Mills turn the corner and disappear.

"Sir," one soldier said, tapping Captain Rayburn on the shoulder.

"What is it, Specialist?"

"Sir!" the Specialist said with an urgency in his voice. "You need to see this!"

Looking to his right, Rayburn noticed several people in the street. It appeared to Rayburn that when one person saw another; they began attacking that individual, fighting them to the death.

What did we get ourselves into? Rayburn thought watching these people fight to the death.

Several of the soldiers moved up to get a better look, leaving their rear flank exposed.

Gunfire erupted from Rayburn's left, where Sergeant Mills's last known location was.

Jesus, Mike must be in heavy contact, Rayburn thought based upon the vast shots being fired.

Rayburn contemplated sending more men to assist Sergeant Mills when one of his men behind him started screaming.

Turning his head, Rayburn saw a skinny woman stabbing a soldier in the neck. The soldier clutched at his neck as he fell to the ground, blood pumping through his fingers.

The woman's face exploded as the soldiers open fired on her.

Rayburn turned to find a fat man carrying a plastic gas can, who was wearing a white t-shirt that appeared more like a tube top on his massive girth.

In one fluid motion, the man swung his arm back, then hurled an open container of gasoline toward the soldiers. The man then reached into his back pocket, produced a road flare and removed the cap, exposing the striker on top.

Gas sloshed from the can as it slid across the pavement, coming to a halt against one of the Specialist's feet where it tipped over, spilling fuel on the black asphalt.

Rayburn and several other soldiers raised their weapons and fired, but the fat man had already used the striker to ignite the flare and was in mid-toss when the bullets tore into his flesh, dropping him to the road dead.

The flare came in low, skidding across the ground. It cartwheeled upward, and the soldiers stood there watching the flare as it spun upward. The flare went several feet into the air, before falling straight downward.

Grabbing the PFC next to him by his shoulder straps, Rayburn flung the young man around the corner of the building, then jumped on him.

The burning flare met the gaseous fumes, igniting the air around the men.

An explosive fireball engulfed four of the soldiers, catching their uniforms and gear on fire. Several remaining soldiers tried to save their comrades but had to abandon their efforts as more crazed people started attacking.

Erupting gunfire drowned out the screams of those soldiers who were burning to death.

Getting to his feet, Rayburn began engaging targets, and they started dropping like flies. Even with his adrenaline pumping, the smell of gunpowder mixed with blood and burning flesh turned his stomach, and he thought he might get sick.

Crazies charged at them from every direction, and Rayburn knew he needed to retreat and take up a defensive position.

Looking over his shoulder, Captain Rayburn saw Sergeant Mills waving to him from down the road.

"Men, on me!" Rayburn shouted, and the soldiers took off running toward Mills with crazies on their heels.

As Rayburn approached where Mills was standing, a large muscular bald man stepped out from behind the corner, raised his rifle, and began shooting.

Chapter 63

New York City, New York

Grant reached the intersection and slammed on the brakes. Then, turning the wheel hard to the right, he floored the gas.

"Take the next right!" Stan shouted from the bed of the truck.

Grant jammed the brakes hard and turned the wheel to the right and screamed, "Oh shit!" as the front end collided with a wall of abandoned cars and debris.

Susan started screaming when a man reached into the truck and grabbed her. Stan turned around and saw Susan fighting with an old man. He had her by the arm, tugging her out of the truck. She was on her back using her feet kicking at him. Stan pulled the pistol from his waistband and aimed it at the disheveled gray haired man's face and pulled the trigger. The man stood there a moment with a large gapping void where the left side of his face used to be. The man's lone lifeless eye stared back at Stan before his body crumpled against the truck and fell to the ground.

"You all good?" Grant shouted from the window.

"Go!" Stan shouted, slapping the roof of the truck, noticing a woman charging the truck with a fire axe.

Grant hit the gas hard, shooting the truck backwards and tossed Stan out of the truck.

Stan hit the ground hard on his left shoulder. The woman brought the axe high over her head and charged at Stan. She was making no sound and her face was void of any emotion.

Stan got to his knees and aimed the pistol at the woman's chest and fired. The axe slipped from her hands and the metal head clanged off the pavement. The wooden handle bounced as her body fell to the ground. The woman lay there, blood drooling out of her mouth.

Stan turned around, hoping to see the truck stopped, but it was gone. Stranded all alone with limited options, Stan decided to head back toward Drew and the others and hoped they were still there.

Grant drove as fast as he could. Once on a straightaway, Grant floored it and the truck sailed down a main street. As they approached an intersection, Grant took his foot off the gas and hovered it over the brake. They blew through intersection after intersection, and Grant stopped in the middle of a bridge.

"You guys good?" Grant yelled out the window.

No answer.

Sara rolled down her window and called out.

Still no answer.

Sara flung open her door and ran to the back of the truck. Sara found Susan rubbing an egg sized bump on her forehead from slamming her head into the side of the truck.

"Hey guys! Susan's hurt," Sara said, appearing in the door.

"Mom!" Annabelle cried out as she made her way out of the back seat.

"Where's Stan?" Grant asked.

"He's not back there. He must have fallen out," his wife answered.

"Are you fucking serious!" Grant screamed. "He fell out?"

Annabelle ran back to the front of the truck. "My mom said Stan fell out right after telling us to go," Annabelle said. "She said the woman with the axe killed Stan."

"Damn it!" Grant shouted, slamming his palm against the steering wheel.

"How's your mom?" Sara asked.

"She's fine. It wasn't blood, it was dirt from the side of the truck."

"That's good," Sara said.

"What the hell do we do now?" Grant asked.

"Well, we sure as hell can't go back that way!" Annabelle said.

"But what about Drew?" Sara asked.

"He made it all the way from Florida to Boston, he'll be fine."

"So, that brings us back to the original question. What do we do?" asked Grant.

"Did Drew tell you what we should do if we got separated?" Annabelle asked.

"No," Grant replied.

"He told me," Sara said.

"He told you! But not me?"

"Yeah, get over it."

"Well, what did he tell you that he didn't tell me?"

"He said to head to SOTB."

"South of the Border the fireworks place in Dillon, South Carolina? Or south of the border like as in Mexico?"

"Which do you think, Grant?" Sara asked sarcastically.

"The fireworks one," Grant replied, shaking his head.

"That's what he told me too," Annabelle said.

"I wish I had known that, now that we've driven north and away from I-95," Grant said. "Oh, wait! There's an atlas under the seat, why don't you pull it out," Grant said.

"We have an atlas?" Sara asked.
"Yeah, Drew put it there," Grant said, making a face at Sara for knowing something she didn't.

Chapter 64

New York City, New York

"Where's the rest of the men?" Sergeant Mills asked.

"They didn't make it," Rayburn said.

"So, what, were down to..." Mills said. Quickly counting, "Seven men, sir?"

"Well, you make eight, Mike," Rayburn said.

"What are we going to do?" one Specialist asked, his voice trembling.

"We continue the mission!" Rayburn snapped.

"How can we possibly continue on? We're not even there yet and we've already suffered over a fifty percent casualty rate," a PFC piped in.

"Zip it, Private," Sergeant Mills said, giving the youngster the stink eye for speaking out of turn.

"If you don't mind me asking, what's your mission?" the big man asked.

"Who are you again?" Rayburn asked.

"I'm the guy who just saved your ass!" the big guy responded.

"Captain, this is Drew. He's a former Marine and he not only saved your ass, sir, but he saved mine too."

"Marines," the Captain said. "Well, that explains the deadly accuracy with that rifle."

"Thank you, sir," Drew said. 'So, what's this mission? Does it have anything to do with all these crazy fuckers running around killing each other?"

Cass and Steve looked from Drew to the Captain.

"Actually, it does," Rayburn said, and filled Drew in on what command told him.

"What?" Drew asked in disbelief. "You have to be kidding me."

"It's true. I was standing right there when it came over the radio," Sergeant Mills said. "I didn't believe it at first either. But I do now."

"You're saying that whoever hears this signal turns crazy, is that correct?" Steve asked, injecting himself into the conversation.

"You guys are fucking with us, right?" Drew asked.

"Hey, listen, if you have a better explanation why these people are going crazy then I'd love to hear it," Captain Rayburn said.

"Well, good luck with that," Drew said. Then he turned and walked away.

"Be right back. Don't leave," Steve said, holding up his index finger, implying they give him a minute.

Steve caught up to Drew and put his hand on Drew's shoulder. "Hold up a minute," Steve said, getting in front of Drew.

"What?" Drew said.

"What if it's that shadow figure again?" Steve asked.

"Not this again?" Drew said, rolling his eyes.

"What if it is true? Seriously, think about it!" Steve said, staring into Drew's eyes. "What if what they're saying is true? At some point the girls are bound to turn the radio on. And then what happens if they're right," Steve said, pointing at the soldiers. "Then the girls might go crazy too!"

Drew took a deep breath and closed his eyes.

"What's going on?" Cass asked.

Drew opened his eyes and shifted them towards her but continued to hold his breath.

"I think we should go and help them stop it," Cass said, looking down.

Drew slowly released his breath. "Why?" he asked.

Looking up, Cass flipped her hair from her face and looked Drew directly in Drew's eyes. "Because I think they're telling the truth, and I think Steve is right. This is the second horseman," she said.

"Why?" Drew asked.

"Why!" she yelled. "Look around! Everyone is going fucking crazy and killing each other! It's like humanity is having a full-blown war with itself!"

Drew's eyes shifted to Steve.

"I agree with Cass," Steve said.

"Me too," Drew said.

"What?" Cass asked, taken back by his response.

"Is this what you want to do?" Steve asked Drew surprisingly.

"I'd really like to have a drink, but that won't achieve anything," Drew replied.

"I'm proud of you," Steve said, placing a hand on Drew's shoulder. "Not only did you survive a global pestilence, but you did it while overcoming your addiction."

"Yeah, I've faced my demons and now we just need to stop this war," Drew said.

"Both literally and figuratively," Steve said with a chuckle.

Chapter 65

New York City, New York

They turned around and headed back towards the highway. The plan was to find the quickest route and go like hell. Annabelle, Susan, and Stephanie all crammed in the backseat. They didn't want to risk anyone else falling out of the back. Thankfully Stephanie's stroller was in the back of the truck, which Susan found when her foot hooked on one of the handles. Annabelle moved it to the front of the bed in case they had to exit the truck quickly.

"You're going to take the next right," Sara said, holding the atlas.

Grant slowed to take the corner, then slammed on the brakes. A mob of people filled the street from sidewalk to sidewalk, and every person had that blank deer in the headlights look on their face.

Grant threw the truck in reverse and stomped on it. Empty store fronts zipped past in reverse as the truck raced down the street.

"Hang on!" Grant shouted as he jammed on the brakes and cut the wheel hard to the right. The rear brakes locked up and smoke poured from the tires. There was a loud bang, and the truck jostled to a halt. Their bodies whip lashed around the inside of the truck.

Grant groaned and rubbed his neck. He put the truck in drive and stepped on the gas, but they didn't move. His eyes shifted to the side mirror. "Fuck!" he shouted, slamming his hand down on the steering wheel.

"What is it?" Sara asked, rubbing her head.

"We're hooked up on a car back there."

"Can we get free?" Susan shouted, clutching her chest.

"I'm trying!" Grant said through gritted teeth, shifting the truck back and forth from drive to reverse.

"I'll go take a look," Annabelle said, hopping out. The smell of burnt rubber hung in the air. She ran to the back of the truck and found a crumpled Honda Civic. The truck's tow hitch was buried deep in the frontend of a Honda Civic and Antifreeze poured from the radiator, pooling on the ground. Annabelle shot her legs apart trying to keep the raining fluid from splashing on her shoes and ran back to tell Grant.

"The tow hitch is hung up," she said, appearing in the rear passenger door.

"Get in, Annabelle!" Susan shouted at her daughter.

"I'm gonna try to rock it free," Grant said, as Annabelle started stepping up into the truck. At that moment Annabelle noticed someone outside Grant's window and screamed, "Grant!"

Suddenly the driver's side window shattered. Chunks of tempered glass went flying everywhere in the truck.

Grant held up his arm blocking the glass, then something smashed into his forearm and he felt the bones inside break and his left arm now looked deformed.

"Oh my God!" Susan screamed, watching the man outside the truck swinging his hammers widely into the truck.

Instinctively Grant pulled his arm in close to his body in a guarding posture, which left his head fully exposed. Before he could fully grasp the situation, Grant received multiple hammer blows to the head and his skull cracked open like a coconut with pieces of his brain exposed.

Susan sat in the back screaming hysterically.

Annabelle opened her door and hoped out. With both feet planted on the ground, she reached in and undid Stephanie's seatbelt, yanking her from the vehicle.

"Mom! Let's go!" Annabelle screamed, holding Stephanie on her left hip and reaching into the truck with her right arm, helping her mother out.

Sara opened the glove box and pulled out the 9mm handgun. She opened the door, jumped out and raced around the truck. The crazed man turned and swung the hammer just as Sara pulled the trigger.

The hammer connected with Sara's jaw, shattering it. The impact and sheer pain knocked Sara to the ground.

Hammer Man stumbled, dropping one hammer and looked down at his chest. Blood trickled out of the hole below his left nipple. He fell to both knees, dropping the second hammer before falling face first onto the pavement and died.

Annabelle reached into the bed of the truck and pulled out Stephanie's stroller and put her in it. She then turned toward Susan and said, "Mom, stay here!"

Annabelle slowly made her way around the front of the truck. As she came around the driver's side, she spotted Sara's lifeless body lying on the ground. There was a large pool of blood in front of Sara's mouth with tiny white chunks of bone and teeth inside.

Annabelle reached down and picked up the handgun. She checked the hammer wielding man for a pulse and felt nothing. She then checked on Grant, whose chest awkwardly heaved up and down and blood and brain matter streamed from the wounds on his head.

There was nothing she could do for either of her friends now. It was only a matter of minutes, if not less, before Grant would expire.

Annabelle tucked the gun in her coat pocket and made her way back to her mother and daughter.

Annabelle could feel her mother's eyes on her and she shook her head no.

"Neither of them?" Susan asked.

"No."

"What do we do now?" Susan asked, rubbing the cold from her hands.

"We get the hell outta this city. That's what we do!"

Annabelle climbed into the bed of the truck and rounded up some blankets and clothes to keep Stephanie warm.

"Ready?" Annabelle asked.

"I guess," Susan said.

"Oh wait!" Annabelle said and reached into the front seat and retrieved the atlas.

"Thankfully the stroller wasn't in the car or it would be a puddle of melted plastic now," Susan said, taking the atlas from her daughter and putting it in the storage area under the stroller. *Sometimes God works in mysterious ways,* Annabelle thought.

Susan and Annabelle made their way through the deserted streets. Stephanie was sound asleep in the stroller. The city seemed eerie, and it wasn't what they remembered when they were here last Christmas for the tree lighting at Rockefeller Center.

It had been the first trip Susan had taken in a long time since her husband became sick. Annabelle saw an ad in a magazine offering discounted trips to New York City during the holiday season and thought it would be good to get her mother out of the house. Plus growing up her mother always mentioned wanting to see the Rockefeller tree lighting and do some Christmas shopping. Annabelle told Drew of her plans, and he thought it was a great idea. Susan loved Christmas, but for the last few years she had a real struggle catching the Christmas spirit.

They caught a bus and a few hours later they arrived. They were in awe of the tall buildings which were beautifully adorned in the holiday spirit. They went to an expensive restaurant where they enjoyed a great meal. They sat and talked over a bottle of wine. They discussed their future and Stephanie. She was Susan's only grandchild, and she wanted to spoil her for Christmas. They laughed and told stories. They giggled with each glass of wine. The hotel was around the corner and neither was driving.

After dinner they took a stroll doing some window shopping and stopped to check out a few stores. One they came across was an old toy store which seemed to be alive. It was filled with the laughter of children who ran and played while parents watched with cautious smiles. Susan found the perfect present for Stephanie, a new woobie. It was a pink bear atop a small blanket. The bear wore a red bow above its left ear. Both Susan and Annabelle knew Stephanie would love it. The price was a little steep, but Susan knew that every time she saw her granddaughter snuggle with the blanket it would remind her of this wonderful night. They cashed out and made their way further down the block. There was a chill in the air, but it was expected for late December and the wine kept them warm. They walked arm in arm, enjoying the moment together. They reached the end of the stores with shoppers inside and passed empty concrete buildings that housed workers by day and laid dormant at night.

They crossed the street and made their way back along the opposite row of stores. One of the stores they came across had two mannequins dressed in long sleeve flannel shirts in the display window. Susan stopped and clutched Annabelle's arm tight at the sight of the mannequins. Annabelle leaned over and put her head on her mother's shoulder. They stood there for a minute staring at what reminded them of him. Wiping tears from her eyes Susan said, "Your father is here with us."

Annabelle cracked a smile and laughed as a single tear ran down her cheek. She patted her mother's hand. They stood there another minute before turning and walking away. Suddenly one of the wheels of the stroller got stuck on something hidden by the darkness and the handle dug into Annabelle's chest, instantly yanking her from the memory. She pulled back on the stroller, removing the broken piece of asphalt that stopped the front wheel, which caused Stephanie to jostle in the stroller.

Susan reached out and grabbed Annabelle's arm and asked, "Is everything alright?"

"Yes, mom. Let's keep moving."

Annabelle was starting to regret the decision of leaving home. She thought of how vast the city was and how on their trip they had gotten lost after leaving the toy store. How are we supposed to get through the city in complete darkness? Hell, we couldn't even find our hotel last year and the city was lit up. She asked herself.

They made their way across the city. The air was becoming colder and Annabelle stopped for a moment, ensuring Stephanie was covered with the blankets. She imagined her daughter kicking the blankets off in the darkness, and then they would be screwed. Stephanie stirred as she tucked the blankets around her.

Up ahead, streetlights appeared to be on. Looking up, they noticed some lights were on in the buildings above them.

Susan turned and looked at Annabelle who couldn't believe what she was seeing.

"Mom, if the power is back on," Annabelle said in a hushed tone. "Then the heat should be on too!"

"Let's go see. Maybe we can warm this little one up," Susan replied, her breath visible.

Annabelle turned the stroller towards the lit area of the street and skirted around an abandoned car. Susan was rubbing her hands together, thinking about the warmth inside the buildings.

"Maybe we can find some food, too," Annabelle said as she quickened her pace. Both women hurried towards the sign of life and returning society.

Reaching back, Susan felt the can of beans she put in the side pouch of her pack and the thought of having a nice hot meal to warm her bones excited her.

"We'll have to try to find an apartment building or restaurant. Someplace we can heat up a meal," Susan said.

"An apartment building has beds and what I'd give to sleep in a bed right now," Annabelle replied.

"And a shower!"

Both women laughed and were now jogging towards the lit area of the city.

When they reached the first streetlight, they heard a woman screaming. They both instantly froze and looked at one another.

"What was that?" Susan asked.

They stood there for a moment, listening.

"Maybe we should turn around," Annabelle said.

Susan was about to respond when they heard shouting from up ahead. Annabelle tightened her grip on the stroller and turned it 90 degrees, preparing to bolt if need be.

They heard more screams followed by the sound of something metal being dropped. It rang aloud and reminded Annabelle of an aluminum bat.

"Mom, let's go back."

Suddenly a woman ran from behind a building up ahead. A man chasing after her caught up and pushed her down. The woman fell onto her face beneath a streetlight and quickly scurried to her knees. The man walked up to her and kicked her in the ribcage, causing her to flip over onto her back. The woman raised her hands up in an effort to defend herself and used her feet to scooch backward.

Both Susan and Annabelle stood there horrified.

The woman frantically searched for something to defend herself with. Her head whipped from side to side as she searched and suddenly stopped when she saw Annabelle and Susan.

"Help me!" the woman screamed.

The man turned and saw them both. Opening his bathrobe, he reached into his waistband and withdrew a .44 Magnum handgun. The woman lying on the ground was begging for her life when he pointed the gun at her and shot her in the head.

Susan stood there with her hand covering her mouth, overcome with fear. She watched the man reach into his pocket and pull a pack of cigarettes out, then using his teeth he pulled one from the pack and lit it.

"Mom, run!" Annabelle shouted as she turned the stroller and took off running into the darkness.

Chapter 66

Rockefeller Center, New York

Glen glanced out of the corner of his eye at the control room and couldn't believe what he was seeing inside.

Whatever it was, it was no longer a shadow. It became translucent and started taking on a human form. Bones and organs appeared within the translucent form. Blood started snaking its way through it. Muscle and cartilage formed. Skin began covering the body and blonde hair sprouted from its scalp. Bright blue eyes the color of the ocean appeared in the sockets.

The man stood there holding out his arms, staring in awe at his new vessel. He rotated his hands and bent his arms. A smile appeared on its face and it reached up, touching its cheeks. Glen looked from the control room to the front window. He couldn't quite understand how he was looking one way and his body the other. He felt trapped inside his own body with no way to interact with anyone else. The other him, or whatever controlled his body, continuously read the same message over and over. Looking out the window was hard for Glen and his soul hurt. Complete strangers traveled to see him and put their trust in him, expecting to be led out of the darkness. They came in search of a better life, but he failed them. He did no such thing for them, instead he led them all to their deaths.

Outside, they all lay dead out in the plaza. Glen couldn't help but think of the irony. The demonic being used the act of creating life against him, using it to deal death instead. All those people outside committed violent and unspeakable acts on each other. That thing brought them here for the sole purpose of killing them.

Glen, like Kendra, had nothing left except his own conscious. It dawned on him why Kendra acted the way she did. She too was under its control. Glen's heart broke for her, and he wondered how long she'd been like that.

In that moment, Glen prayed. *Dear God, please forgive me for what I have done. I have committed sins of the flesh, but I never intended to harm anyone, let alone have people get killed. Oh Lord, please make it stop. Please forgive me!*

Outside, Rayburn's team lined up against the wall and prepared to breach the front door of the WTFH studio.

"Ear plugs in and weapons free," Rayburn ordered.

An explosion rocked the front of the building and debris sailed across the studio.

Captain Rayburn was first through the door. Rushing into the studio with his earplugs in, all he could hear was his own heavy breathing. Smoke lingered in the air from the explosive device used to breach the door.

Rayburn had never been inside a newsroom before, and the large floor cameras hindered his view of the studio.

The remaining enlisted men followed Captain Rayburn into the studio, weaving around the cameras. Sgt. Mills and Drew hung to the right side as they entered.

Upon seeing the soldiers rush into his studio, Mr. Williams stormed out of the control room, shouting and pointing at both Drew and Mills.

Remembering the orders to shoot anyone inside the studio, Sgt. Mills aimed his rifle at the old man and squeezed the trigger. After, Mills shot the beautiful woman standing in the control room.

Still in the metamorphosis process, the entity could not protect Kendra or Mr. Williams, whose chests were riddled with bullets.

The camera captured the muzzle flashes around the studio.

Captain Rayburn and the men following him found themselves standing right in front of Glen Daniels, who was sitting at the news desk.

Glen's body continued reading from the teleprompter as troops stood to each side of the camera surrounding him. In the control room, the metamorphosis process was complete. The shadow man now had a full human form with wavy blonde shoulder length hair. An evil grin flashed across the man's face and he pointed at Glen. Suddenly time seemed to stop and the soldiers in front of him froze. Glen felt heavy and the feeling of his body returned. Laughter rang out through the studio and Glen saw the man laughing at him and covering his crotch, mocking him and his pain. "What do you want from me?" Glen shouted.

"Death!" the man replied. Slowly, he raised his arm and extended his finger toward Glen.

"Bang," the man said. Time slowly resumed and the soldiers surrounding Glen open fired.

Glen's eyes opened wide at all the muzzle flashes and he saw all the bullets leave the barrel heading straight for him.

"No!" Glen screamed as bullets tore through him, creating an immediate searing pain, violently jolting his body. Each bullet strike violently jolted his body as they passed right through him, the back of the chair, and shattering the WTFH labeled glass partition behind the news desk. Shards of colored glass scattered across the floor.

Glen sat in a wheeled office chair behind the anchor desk, which was built atop a raised platform. The force of the multiple impacts forced the chair to roll backwards. Glen felt the wheels come off the platform, and he started falling backwards. Glen looked at the blonde-haired man who still had his arm outstretched, pointing at him. Laughing at him. Laughing at his death.

The birthmark on Drew's forehead burned, which was odd as it would sometimes feel puffy. Also, his Spidey sense was tingling and that little voice deep inside was screaming for him to take cover. Having learned to trust that voice, Drew dropped to the ground and shielded his face with his hands.

Suddenly time resumed and Glen fell backwards. Falling, Glen noticed the blonde-haired man had turned and had his face tucked into the crook of his elbow. As Glen's back hit the floor, another bright flash of light filled the studio.

All the monitors inside the studio shattered and the camera lenses cracked. TV screens around the world burst. Screens that were left intact had the flash burned into them, rendering them useless.

Screams and moans filled the studio. Soldiers lay on the ground clutching at their eyes. Their retinas were destroyed, and their eyeballs fused inside the sockets. In the blink of an eye, their vision was gone. The skin on their faces was the color of lobster, and blisters formed on the exposed skin.

When the light dissipated, Glen's body was gone.

Kendra had been shot multiple times in the chest and her body was sprawled out on the floor. The wavy blonde-haired man kneeled next to her, placing his hand on her chest. A dark void emitted from the blonde man's hand, causing Kendra's body to writhe. Slowly he lifted his hand from her chest and the bullets began rising to the surface of her skin, followed by several loud sucking and popping sounds as the bullets came out of the wounds. Kendra's eyes opened and her body drew in a large breath. The man smiled at her and said, "You're my bitch and my bitch can never die."

Lying on the floor, Drew felt the presence of the shadow man. Slowly, he opened his eyes and looked around. He found everyone sprawled out on the floor except for two people. Inside the control room stood a beautiful woman and a man with blonde hair. The man smirked and waved at Drew.

Suddenly, there was a loud pop behind Drew. Turning around, he saw the camera in front of the news desk sparking and watched it catch on fire. Soon smoke began filling the studio.

When Drew turned back toward the control booth, he discovered both the man and woman had disappeared.

The fire quickly started to spread and with help from Steve and Cass they dragged the soldiers from the studio one by one. Most of the soldiers had succumbed to their injuries except for Rayburn, Mills, and one PFC.

Outside, they all watched as the fire consumed the building. The three surviving soldiers felt like they had fallen from a ten-story building onto concrete.

"You guys okay?" Drew asked.

"Yeah," Captain Rayburn said, shaking his head. "You saved our lives. We owe you."

"Pay me back later," Drew said. "Right now I need to find my wife and daughter."

"We're heading to South of the Border if you want to meet us there," Steve said.

"The fireworks place?" The PFC asked, touching the blisters on his face.

"That's the place, kid," Drew said and walked away.

Chapter 67

New York City, New York

Annabelle was running as fast as she could go. All the tossing around woke Stephanie, who sat up.

"Wee!" she shouted as the stroller plunged forward into the darkness.

Susan wasn't sure which way her daughter went, and her heart raced as she ran through the darkness. In her late sixties, it felt like she hadn't run in forever. She could hear the loud steps of the man running behind her. Her face became flush and her skin itched all over. Her old heart was pumping as fast as it could, but she was becoming winded and was losing speed. A thick film formed in her throat and mouth, causing the urge for her to spit.

Annabelle fumbled through her thick clothing and found Sara's pistol that she'd dropped. Using her gloved hand, she cocked the hammer back like Drew had shown her years back. She placed her finger on the trigger guard and tried to slip her index finger onto the trigger. The thick material of her glove wouldn't allow the glove to fit in between the guard and trigger.

"Shit," she said out loud as she brought her gloved hand up to her mouth and clamped her teeth down on the extra material on one fingertip. Yanking her head up while pulling her arm down, the glove slipped right off.

The clouds above broke and the light of the moon illuminated the street. Annabelle could see her mom running. The look on her face stunned Annabelle. Never had she seen that amount of fear on her mother's face.

"Mom, over here!" she shouted.

Susan heard her daughter's voice and turned her head, searching for her. She spotted the stroller off to her right and her daughter crouched down. She ran towards them when a cloud passed in front of the moon, blocking its light. Her foot fumbled, and she tripped over the curb. She fell hard. There was a distinct snap sound followed by a searing pain from her left hip.

The clouds passed again, illuminating the area in a soft light.

"Mom!" Annabelle screamed when she saw her mother lying on the ground.

Susan tried to get up, but her left leg just hung there and pain coursed through her body.

Annabelle looked at Stephanie in the stroller and back at her mother sprawled out on the ground.

The man was sprinting towards Susan and was screaming something that was completely unintelligible.

Annabelle didn't know what to do. She couldn't leave Stephanie all alone, and she couldn't let her mother get killed by that psycho. "God, tell me what to do!" she screamed, looking up.

Just then thick clouds passed overhead throwing the area again into complete darkness.

Susan lay on the ground clutching her hip as the man bore down on her. His arm was stretched out, pointing the gun at her, ready to shoot her just like he did the young woman down the road.

Suddenly shots rang out. Multiple muzzle flashes lit up the area off to Annabelle's right. It sounded like fireworks, but in rapid succession.

The clouds above broke as Captain Rayburn and his men stepped out of the shadows. The three men removed their night vision goggles as one man shot the already dead gunmen again. His body jostled and the gun fell from his clutches.

Annabelle stood there stunned as one man ran over to attend to her mother while another started making his way towards her.

"We're going to be okay," Annabelle said as she leaned over the stroller peeking in on her daughter whose big, beautiful eyes were illuminated by the moon.

"Thank you so much!" Annabelle said.

"Excuse me, Ma'am," the third soldier asked, heading toward her. "By any chance is your name Annabelle?"

Chapter 68

New York City, New York

Annabelle stood there stunned. What were the chances of running into people her husband had just helped? It was hard to fathom and she couldn't help but think it was divine intervention.

"How did you run into Drew?" Annabelle asked.

Captain Rayburn told her the whole story, from receiving the radio call to storming the studio. He told her how Drew had saved his life and that he was one tough son of a bitch.

"Yes, he is," she replied.

Captain Rayburn asked how she was doing. She told him she wasn't looking forward to the long journey south on foot with a child and injured mother in tow.

"Well, the men and I spoke, and we'd be honored to drive you south," Rayburn said.

Annabelle looked around and asked, "Drive?"

Rayburn laughed and informed her that their Humvee's were parked a few blocks over.

Sgt. Mills and a PFC went to grab the trucks and returned thirty minutes later.

They loaded Susan up and made her as comfortable as possible, which is damn near impossible inside a Humvee.

With the adrenaline of tonight's events worn off, the pain in her hip really started to set in. Combined with the exhaustion from being up for almost twenty-four hours, Susan passed out. Every so often when they hit a bump, she would groan a little.

Annabelle looked over her shoulder and saw her mother had passed out. "I think she fell asleep," she said.

"I think they both did," Rayburn said with a chuckle, looking at Stephanie sleeping in her car seat.

"Thank you again for doing this," Annabelle said.

"Sure, no problem," Rayburn replied. "So, why Florida? If you don't mind me asking."

Annabelle looked at him, confused.

"Why not South Carolina or Georgia?"

"My mother."

"Oh!" Rayburn said, lifting his eyebrows.

"Well, according to my mother, my father who's deceased has been visiting my mother in her dreams and told her to head south to Florida where they went on their honeymoon.

"What part of Florida?"

"Disney."

"And the firsts just keep rolling!" he said laughing.

"What?" Annabelle said, sitting up straight.

"It's a first," Rayburn responded, not sure if she misheard him.

"You've never been to Disney?" she asked.

"Never. My parents never could afford it."

"Firsts," she repeated, looking out the window.

"Do you want to fill me in on the joke?" Rayburn asked, looking at her.

"Oh, I'm sorry," Annabelle said, moving strands of hair from her face to behind her ear. "It's just that my mom asked the same exact thing."

In the back seat Susan dreamed of the man with blonde hair. He told her he would take all the pain away if she promised to bring the group to Florida and meet him at the Grand Floridian hotel.

She promised she would, and a soothing warmth came over her and the pain in her hip washed away and she fell into a peaceful sleep.

Annabelle checked the lock on the door and leaned against it. She closed her eyes and wondered if she'd ever see her husband again. Within minutes she was asleep.

Chapter 69

New York City, New York

Drew started back the way they came, fuming over losing Annabelle and Stephanie. He hoped they had returned, though he doubted it. Plus, Drew wanted to check the vehicles for anything salvageable.

Steve and Cass were a block behind, trying to catch up. When they arrived at the vehicles, Drew was standing there shaking his head. Both the car and U-Haul were nothing more than smoldering chassis.

The three stood there in disbelieve. They barely made it two-hundred and fifty miles and they already lost all of their stuff.

"What do we do now?" Cass asked.

"We walk until we find new wheels," Drew said.

Steve was half listening as his eyes darted from body to body that littered the streets.

"And standing here is doing us no good," Drew said.

"What?" Steve said, being drawn back into the moment.

"I said its time to go."

The three of them trudged through the city streets.

Cass had fallen behind, so Steve slowed his pace and walked with her. Drew pushed on like a robot, leaving block after block behind him.

The pair caught up to Drew, who had stopped and was standing in the middle of the street staring at a storefront.

Steve walked Cass over to the curb and sat her down and then went and stood next to his friend.

"You know that won't help you?" Steve said, looking at Drew.

"I know," Drew replied, looking into the liquor store window.

"Don't listen to that little voice telling you to have a drink."

"I won't," Drew said, continuing to stare at the bottles in the window.

"1 Peter 5:8 says to, *"Be sober-minded; be watchful. Your adversary the devil prowls around like a roaring lion, seeking someone to devour.""*

"Tell old Petie thanks for the advice!"

"Remember, the right side of an alcoholic's brain is selling bullshit and the lift side is trying to buy as much as it can."

Drew turned toward Steve and smiled.

"You like that one?" Steve asked.

"I do."

"I have another one for you."

"Hit me."

"I find strength and protection in the lord."

"Really?" Drew said, rolling his eyes.

"Hope!" Steve said.

"Okay," Drew said. "What's next, wishing?"

"Sure, why not?"

"Well, you know what they say about wishing, don't you?"

"No."

"Wish in one hand and shit in the other. Then wait and see which one fills up faster."

"Then why would you stop here then. Clearly it's for the booze?"

"No!" Drew said.

"Are you sure?"

"My life is like a shit sandwich," Drew said.

"What do you mean?" asked Steve.

"Think of a sandwich. Any kind. It could be a ham and cheese or even a fluffernutter."

"Fluffernutter?" Steve asked.

"You are from New England, right?"

Steve raised his eyebrows. "Never heard of it."

"I have to explain this to you?" Drew asked.

"Guess so."

"You don't know, fluff? The marshmallow stuff. It was invented in Lynn Massachusetts by a couple of World War I Infantryman. People combine it with peanut butter in a sandwich, hence the name Fluffernutter. It was the cornerstone of every kids' lunch who grew up in New England."

"Oh, wait. You mean a marshmallow and peanut butter sandwich?"

"Ding! Ding!" Drew said. "Welcome back to earth."

"How does that relate to a crap sandwich? I'm confused."

"So, think of a sandwich and how you spread the mustard, mayonnaise, fluff or peanut butter. You evenly distribute the condiment or whatever, but you miss the corners. You know, the place you hold the bread while spreading it," Drew said, miming the process with his hands. "Now think of those condiments as shit. Nasty, stinky corn filled shit. You take your knife and spread it across the bread. It's thicker in some areas and thinner in others. Now that shit covered bread, that's my life. The corners without shit, that's the good stuff in my life."

"How can you say that?" Steve asked.

"Look! There's no society left. There's limited food. I got all the way home only to lose my family again," Drew said.

"I can see why you'd think that."

"Yeah, well, it's kinda hard to miss the big shit sandwich constantly being forced down my throat."

"Well, removing booze from your life will help take away that poop from the sandwich."

"Why do you think I'm standing outside the store and not inside it?"

Behind them, Cass yawned. Steve looked over his shoulder and said, "We should find her a place to sleep."

"Turn around."

Slowly Steve turned around and noticed the Sporting Good shop behind Cass.

"I already went in and checked it out. They have two tents and sleeping bags."

"Tents?" Steve asked.

"Yeah, there's a park over there with a thicket of trees and some scrub brush. I figure the crazies are less likely to go trekking through the trees."

"Whatever is fine by me, I just need some sleep."

Thirty minutes later Drew had the two tents erected, and they bunked down for some rest.

Chapter 70

New York City, New York

Drew tossed and turned in his sleeping bag. Sleep was not his friend tonight, nor the last few nights. If he hadn't stopped drinking, he would've passed out long ago and been in la la land by now.

Steve's heart was in a good place; *shit he was right, drinking won't help find Annabelle and Stephanie,* Drew thought. I should be thankful for a friend like him because I ruin everything when I drink.

Finally, sleep found Drew, and he awoke to find himself in that same crypt-like chamber from the other night, the one adorned with carvings of heinous moments in mankind's existence. Again, he found himself strapped down to a cold, hard stone slab.

Upon the wall there were new carvings, or at least ones he hadn't seen.

One was of Hitler, standing over a pile of bodies, each wearing striped pajamas, with his arm extended out in front of him, almost as if saluting the chamber.

Drew was able to shift his eyes to another carving and saw a horse-drawn cart where people were placing their loved one's lifeless bodies onto it. Drew assumed it was the time of the Bubonic Plague, Black Death, which hit Europe hard back in 1347, killing anywhere from seventy-five to two-hundred million. If it weren't for the garb and horse-drawn cart, Drew could have mistaken it for recent times.

Farther down the wall he saw an American Indian receiving blankets from a group of white Union soldiers.

Drew followed the carvings with his eyes, which read like a picture book of history. The last depiction ended with the crucifixion of Jesus Christ. Drew's heart wept at the sight of the pain and anguish that Jesus had endured.

Being strapped to the table limited Drew's ability to see the entire room. Shifting his eyeballs, Drew looked over at the other wall of the circular room. It was then that he noticed the other slabs, each with someone on them. The strap across his forehead didn't allow him much wiggle room, but he noticed Steve's shirt on the slab to his right. Straining the muscles in his neck, he was pretty sure he caught a glimpse of Cass's boots over his right shoulder.

"Cass, is that you?" Drew asked.

Cass turned her head slightly towards the sound of his voice and instantly a pain shot across her forehead as the strap holding her head down tightened. "Yeah," she whimpered as hair clung to the tears that streamed down her face. "I can't move."

"I know. Me neither," Drew replied.

"Where are we?" Steve asked. "And how did we get here?"

"You haven't been here before?" Drew asked, surprised.

Fear washed over Cass and her body began to tremble. She tried fighting the restraints, but they wouldn't budge. They never budge.

Fighting the straps, Drew tried to search the room for anyone else.

"How the hell are we all having the same dream?" Cass asked, holding back her tears.

"Wait, this is a dream?" Steve asked.

Drew felt a presence in the room and a chill ran down his spine. Instantly he knew it was the shadow man.

"Hello, all!" came a sinister voice from the back of the chamber.

"This fucking guy again?" Drew said.

"Be nice," the voice said. "I have your friend Grant and his wife Sara over here with me."

"Why are you doing this?" Cass gasped out through the pain.

"Silly girl! Because now is the time for the darkness to consume the light," the voice said, before returning to the task at hand.

"You're a sick fuck!" Sara shouted, spittle flying from her mouth as tears rolled down her cheeks and her chest heaved heavily.

"I'm glad you're all here, because man, this one right here, she's a real piece of work. Annoying as Hell too!" the voice said.

"Eat shit!" Sara shouted. "Take these straps off and I'll show you!"

"Oh, please. You're just a useless barren womb," it said, walking over to Sara jabbing its dark finger straight into her chest and piercing her heart. Sara's color faded and her body turned an ash gray color. She let out a gasp, and the light escaped from her eyes.

"Whoa!" it said, tilting its head back, shaking it. "Damn, consuming a soul straight like that is like a drug! What a rush!"

"Sara!" Drew cried out.

Both Cass and Steve began weeping.

"Well, at least we won't have to listen to that annoying voice of hers anymore," he said. Then, grabbing Grant by the hair, he lifted up Grant's head and spoke into his ear. "I really don't know how you put up with her. She must have had some serious voodoo punani."

"I'm going to kill you!" Drew screamed, fighting the straps.

"Sure, you are!" it said in a mocking tone. "Now, where was I?" it said, looking around. "Oh, that's right. I was ripping out Grant's memories. It's such a shame, really. His whole life will change, and he won't even remember who he was. He'll just sit around and drool for the rest of his pathetic existence."

Drew tried to move, but the several straps holding him down tightened with every move, like a boa constrictor squeezing its prey.

"What are you?" Cass screamed as the dark figure grabbed Grant's head.

"I am *Neque Sanctiores Animarum*," the man said, transforming from its shadow form into a muscular built man with blonde shoulder length hair. Reaching out, it took Grant's head in its left hand. The index finger on his other hand turned black and sparks formed inside it, which started to spin.

"What does that mean?" Cass cried out.

"Its Latin. He said he's The Destroyer of Souls," Steve said.

"That's right. I am a star killer. I come from where light goes to die. And I am here to collect the brightest of His stars, the human soul."

"You're a sick fuck, that's what you are!" Cass shouted and spat towards the blonde-haired man.

Drew relaxed his breathing, taking in a long, slow breath. Slowly he exhaled, letting it out, and he felt his body sinking closer to the cold stone beneath him. He wiggled his feet, trying to gauge how much movement it took for the straps to tighten. It didn't take much as the strap around his ankles instantly constricted. A sharp pain coursed through his right foot, causing Drew to grit his teeth, as the wound had not completely healed yet from being shot.

"Almost there!" he said, releasing Grant's head. It made its way around Grant's lifeless body and headed for Drew.

"Grant here told me that you have a wife and young daughter. Is that true?" the entity asked as it circled Drew.

Drew's body went rigid at the mention of his family, and the straps tightened.

Remembering what it was like to be squeezed and held against his will, Drew took a deep breath and tried to relax his body. It was a trick he'd learned as a child when his father would grab him from behind. *Go limp*, he would tell himself, and would relax his body, fighting the urge to resist the panic that would set in from lack of air. Drew closed his eyes, took another deep breath and asked, "What are you? Why are you doing this?"

"I'm glad you asked," the entity said. "You see, I am the darkness of space. I come from a place where light goes to die. I am known as a star killer."

"You're fucked up, that's what you are!" Cass yelled.

"No, I'm doing exactly as the Creator wants, well sorta," it said chuckling.

"What the fuck are you? Drew snarled, not satisfied with that answer.

"I am the darkness. I consume light," it responded.

"What does that mean?" Cass cried out.

The man raised both of his arms and quickly brought them down, causing the burning torches inside the chamber to go out.

Cass whimpered as she hated the dark.

Suddenly, as the man spoke, the chamber filled with hundreds and millions of stars.

Drew searched the room with his eyes, everywhere he looked there were tiny dots of light.

"You see, I am the darkness."

Then, on cue, the stars dimmed and the darkness between them became darker and more pronounced.

"You silly humans always look to the light and never the darkness. I come from the place where light goes to die."

"Yeah, you said that already fuck nuts!" Drew spat.

"What does that even mean?" Cass shouted again.

Suddenly the chamber went dark, and a single light appeared in the middle of the ceiling.

Cass's eyes locked onto the light, which seemed to grow in size. She watched as the single dot of light turned into many tiny lights and soon, she recognized what it was.

"Our galaxy," Cass whispered.

"Yes, my dear."

"I don't understand," she spoke aloud, sounding like she was in a daze, as if it mesmerized her.

"Do you see how it spins?" the man asked.

Drew noticed the scaled model of the galaxy was spinning.

"Do you notice the black center?"

The model zoomed in close and in the dead center of the spinning mass was a massive black hole.

"The time of the light ruling this planet has ended. Once I extinguish enough of the bright souls on this world, the rest will quickly burn out, eventually becoming extinct, and my dark souls will take hold. When they look up at the night sky, they will no longer see the lights of heaven, but the darkness of hell."

While the entity was describing where it came from, Drew was relaxing his body.

"I come from beyond gravity's grasp. Your Laws of Physics do not apply to me as the Creator made me Himself."

Bringing his elbow and wrist close to his body, Drew slowly rotated his right wrist into the void next to his hip, while his eyes focused on the black hole devouring the light of the galaxy in the visual model above him.

"Why are we here?" Steve demanded.

Steve's voice startled Drew, but not by the question but by his tone. It was a commanding tone.

"So, the quiet one finally speaks," he said. "And you are again?"

"Oh, that's Steve. He's our Bible thumper," Drew said sarcastically.

"So, you're the religious one in the group?" the man asked.

"Yes, I am a Godly man!" Steve replied.

"Is that so?" the blonde hair man asked.

"Watch out! He's really good at zinging Bible verses. Aren't you, Steve?" Drew said.

"You still haven't told us why we're here," Steve said.

"Yes, you're right. How rude of me," the man said. "You're in my private chamber. Using time and gravity, I have separated your consciousness from your body and transported you here."

"But why?" Drew asked.

"You see, everyone is filled with what you call, good and bad. Or what I call, light and darkness. The creator provided one percent of each in every soul upon birth, and as that individual grew, their soul was filled based upon their upbringing and life experiences. Love and happiness grew the light in their soul, while fear and hatred filled the darkness. Every person is filled with a certain amount of each. A scale that fits to humanity. Checks and balances, if you will. I mean, how would it be if everyone was nice? Who'd want that!" it said, followed by a diabolical laugh.

"Oh boy! Someone drank the Kool-Aid!" Drew said.

"Funny!" it said. "But there are consequences, which either fill one or deplete the other. And let's face it, many people today are filled with darkness. People witness injustices being perpetrated against their fellow man and do nothing about it; they lose light and gain darkness. People constantly argue with each other and have zero regard for anyone else. Then we have this massive heap of a man. He always acts. He always intervenes," the man said putting a hand on Drew's shoulder. But sometimes he does evil things to stop bad things from happening. You see, people like your friend Drew here have exactly fifty-fifty. He has the same amount of light as he does darkness, which gives him true free will. He doesn't tip one way, or another based upon the percentage inside his soul, he literally makes the decision."

Just as it lifted its hand off of Drew, it saw something. Something from Drew's past. Something he could use against him if things didn't go the way he planned. He put the information in the back of its mind and continued speaking.

"And all the others," he said pausing. "Well, they exercised their free will by choosing to do bad things. And by doing nothing at all, they filled their soul in the wrong way. Hardly anyone does what's right anymore. They do what's best for them and not their fellow man. I am here to wipe the slate clean. A new world I will control by using the darkness. I will eliminate the rest of the light in people's souls and rule earth. Mankind will become my minions. Light, or God as you call Him, had his chance and your kind chose darkness, so here I am!"

The birthmark on Drew's forehead hurt from the strap rubbing against it, and he could feel it becoming raw. It made him think of his mother, who told him he had been blessed at birth by his guardian angel with a kiss on his forehead.

"I hate to interrupt," Drew said. "But is this a joke?"

"Look at you!" the man snapped. "You cry and become upset because I killed your friend, yet your kind does nothing to stop itself from killing each other. That's all your kind seems to do, attack and kill each other with either words or weapons.

"Your generation is so concerned about words and so perturbed over what words are used, when words carry no weight. Action carries weight. Words are empty, just like the souls who fret over them. You should fear those who speak with actions. People who sling words are cowards. Your kind is afraid of a bunch of words and too scared to deal with them."

"How did you cause the war?" Steve asked.

"Ooh, a great question! You see, I control the darkness using gravity. With my message, I was able to draw one's own inner darkness to the surface of their mind and control it. I instructed the darkness to destroy the inner light and by doing so it drove that person crazy. I then told the darkness to kill anyone it saw. I am the war that rages inside their head."

"You're a pussy!" Drew said with a laugh. "I see you're a little too full of yourself."

"You dare question me?" asked the man. "Some call me the Boogie Man, others call me the Sandman. I've traveled the world, making nightmares come true. I am the fear in children's hearts. I am the black in the light. I am the home of evil. I am torture. I am Rape. I am blood lust. I secrete hate. I am Death. I am the reaper of lost souls."

"Yeah, ok. You sound like a fucking loon to me," Drew said.

The Dark Figure's eyes grew darker and a pale look washed over his face. He grabbed Drew by the neck and began squeezing, crushing Drew's throat.

"Did you think you'd live forever?" the man said, continuing to squeeze. "Your reign is over! The human race is done. You were given your chance, and you failed. And now it's time for something else to have its reign. Someday they'll dig up your bones, like you did the dinosaurs and they'll be like, oh, look how these creatures lived. You'll become non-significant, just a memory in the past, something buried in the dirt. That's all you'll be!"

"Why can't we wake up?" Cass shouted, trying to fight the straps. "God, please help us!"

"Awe sweetheart, God doesn't care about you, that's why He sent me," the man said releasing Drew's throat.

"I believe in our Lord and that he truly saves. Oh God, please protect this young woman!" Steve shouted.

"Well, speaking of women" he said. "Our Father wants you to believe that all women are perfect and can do no wrong. Hell, He even made them think that they're always right. Yet I know the truth, women are vile creatures! They use that hole between their legs to manipulate men to get what they want because they lack the strength to just take it. They use sex, the gift from our divine creator, meant to express true love and to create life and use it as a tool or a weapon. Yet they belittle it by whoring themselves out to achieve personal gain. They wield it with precision to get whatever they want with no fucking concern. And if the seed of life gets planted, Poof, they kill it with no remorse.

Heck, most of your kind are infatuated with sex and can easily be manipulated by using it. Your women have discovered this and hate whores because of it. Women cannot be controlled by other women, because of their disdain for each other. So instead, they degrade them in private to other women, all secretly wishing they could be like those they vilify. But they all understand they can control men by using sex. That's why two women will fight one another over a man. It's about the need to control. Sex controls."

"All women aren't like that!" Cass hissed.

He cast a look at her and said, "Come on, silly girl. Everyone knows it's true."

"She's right." Drew said, said with a raspy voice and breathing heavy. "Not all women are like that!"

Rolling his eyes, the man ran his hand through his hair and his gait changed from one of toying to that of seriousness before lunging at Drew.

"No! It is all women! I know this, for I was there! I was in the garden. I seduced her. I tempted her. And she took the bite."

Cass gasped. She didn't know much about religion. Shit, she couldn't tell you why she celebrates Christmas. But this, this she knew.

"Cassidy," Steve said, using her full first name. "Don't get worked up. Don't play into his trap. If he is who he says he is, then he's a liar and a manipulator. Don't believe a word that comes out of his mouth."

The man turned towards Steve, "I'm touched. We just met, yet you know me so well!"

"You, sir, are a liar!" Steve spat.

A smile a mile wide formed on the man's face. "Maybe not all women, but definitely most!" he said, followed by a diabolical laugh. "But I was really there."

The man snapped his fingers and the hologram of the universe disappeared. Then the man's voice became dark and beastly. "And it was *I* who set it all in motion."

The mood in the room instantly changed, matching the lighting and fear began to set in.

Members of the group tried to free themselves, but the binds would not break.

"Isn't this wonderful," the man said. He began golf clapping and skipping around the room like a child excited at receiving a new toy.

"Why are we here?" Steve shouted.

"Oh, come on! You just ruined my moment," the man shouted while raising his hand and twirling his index finger.

Suddenly, the binds holding them tightened.

Cass cried out in pain, but her scream ran out of sound as the bind across her chest squeezed the breath right out of her.

Drew grunted as he tightened his ab muscles, hoping it would stop the straps from crushing him.

"You know, life is one big experience and people make it worthwhile. But people come and people go. And now comes the darkness."

"Subterfuge!" Steve shouted.

"What? Stop using five-dollar words, please!"

"It means, something intended to misrepresent the true nature," Steve said.

"Really? For entertainment, you watch people pretending to be someone else. You fill your lives with lies!"

"You're a rambling madman," Steve said.

"Am I?" the man asked. "Look at Drew here, why do you think he's an alcoholic? Let me tell you," the man said, patting Drew on the shoulder. "Because he knows drinking makes the darkness enjoyable. Isn't that right, big fella?"

"You're just pissed because our Heavenly Father gave you the boot," Steve said.

"Oh, I know, He is pissed! But not with me this time. This time it's with you!"

"Why us?" Cass asked.

"You see, you squandered His gift. He gave you something precious and all you do is waste it," he said, making his way around the room between the slabs.

"He gave you a higher intelligence. You are aware of yourself and others. He gave you the ability to figure things out, to question things and seek answers. But what do you do with it? You become imbeciles who only care about what someone is wearing or who's fucking who. Hell, you all care more about sex than anything else. Your kind will throw away their lives and everything they have for a few minutes of physical pleasure. What intelligent creature does that? You imbeciles, that's who!" he said, shouting, waving his arms around.

"You once strived to go further. You ventured across the lands. Then the oceans. You even invented your very own time travel machine!" it shouted as it twirled around.

"Wait, we have a time machine?" Cass asked.

"Yeah, kid. The airplane," Drew said.

"That's right. It's very primitive, but it works," it said walking over to Cass. "So, congratulations!" it shouted as it clapped its hands together.

"Ouch, not so hard!" it yelled at its hands, rubbing them, not used to feeling pain in this new form.

"So now that we've educated the little one here," he said, flicking Cass in the cheek as he walked by. "Let's move on, shall we? Good!"

'You're so full of shit and lies!" Drew said.

"Pardon me?" the man asked as if it couldn't believe someone would question it.

"That's some mumbo jumbo story you got there, Starman," Drew said with that sarcastic Boston tone of his and began laughing.

Drew wanted a chance to escape and needed to redirect this thing's attention.

"Some souls burn brighter than others and need to be extinguished before they cause others to resist and grow in intensity," it said as it stepped towards Drew.

"You will never extinguish our souls!" Steve said, in that same forceful tone as earlier.

The galaxy hologram disappeared, and the torches came flickering back to life. They cast the room in a light that danced across the floor and walls.

The blonde-haired man made his way around the room towards Steve. As he passed Drew, he looked down and looked him in the eye. Tapping Drew on the shoulder, he said, "I'll be back to you in a minute."

It made its way to the end of the slab and stood at Steve's feet. The man began to swirl his index finger in a small circle, gaining speed as it spun. Sparks began to appear at the tip, which also began to spin.

"Do you think you're tough? Does your soul burn bright?" the man asked Steve as it began to move down the side of the slab towards Steve's head.

Drew saw the man's finger emitting a bright light just before he walked past.

"Go back to hell, you demon!" Steve shouted.

Appearing as the dark entity now, it took a step closer to Steve and outstretched its arm and said, "Oh, I'm going to enjoy this!"

Drew was fighting his body from tightening up. He knew if he could get his right hand loose, he would be able to free himself and his friends. The only problem was the straps would tighten with the slightest movement.

Cass shifted her eyes and saw the evil man with his illuminated finger pressed up against Steve's head.

Steve started to groan in pain, which quickly turned to screams and the smell of burning flesh filled the chamber.

"Steve!" Cass yelled.

"Fuck you!" Drew shouted, causing his body to tighten briefly.

The thing held its finger against Steve's head and pushed harder, but it was meeting resistance.

Taking a few quick deep breaths, Drew tried to relax his body as he felt the strap tighten when he shouted.

"You're a tough nut to crack," It said, bringing its other hand up and placing it on the top of Steve's head.

"My, my!" it said. "Someone is not whom they are pretending to be, now are they!"

Steve groaned in pain.

"Steve, fight it!" Cass shouted as she fought against the straps, which zipped tighter around her.

"Stop! You're killing him!" she screamed, remembering what had happened to Grant.

Steve began to scream louder as the being tried to tap into its mind.

"Why, that's the whole point," it snarled, now appearing as the blonde-haired man, looking up at her with his mesmerizing blue eyes.

"It's not every day I get one like you," Blondie said, as it worked harder to drill into Steve's head.

Drew closed his eyes and remembered back to his childhood and how great it felt when he was able to get an arm free and use it to help free himself by punching and swinging towards his father's face.

The evil creature was focusing all of its energy onto Steve, trying to get in.

Drew opened his eyes and with every ounce of strength, pulled his right arm as hard and fast as he could, freeing it from the strap just as Steve cried out in excruciating pain.

"Steve!" Drew shouted as he shot his arm up to the strap holding his head down. Slipping his thumb underneath the strap, he lifted up, fighting the strap which was tightening.

Using both applied and opposing force, Drew lifted the strap up and at the same time, he kinked his neck towards his shoulder and jammed his arm hard back towards the end of the table. The strap, unable to resist being pushed in the opposite direction of its applied force, slipped off Drew's head and went completely taut against the stone slab.

The Dark Man looked up in disbelief as Drew sat upright, breaking free from the straps.

"Get the fuck off of him!" Drew shouted, jumping down.

The entity released its grasp of Steve and took a step towards Drew.

The Dark Man didn't know what to expect when he became human. It was something he wanted to become upon learning the Father had taken on a new pet project. He witnessed the love the Father gave to its creation called mankind and felt like he was left behind in the dark, literally.

"Take this!" Drew said as he threw a right haymaker.

"Drew!" Cass shouted as she watched the man turn back into its shadow form and disappeared just as Drew's fist was about to impact its jaw. Drew put all his weight into the swing, expecting to connect with the man's jaw. When his arm did not connect, Drew shouted, "Oh shit!" as his forward momentum sent him sailing across the chamber and landing hard on the floor.

"Drew!" Cass shouted again as the blonde-haired man appeared behind Drew and grabbed him from behind. Clamping down over Drew's nose and mouth, pulling him in tight to his own body, just as his father had done to him as a child, suffocating him. The distinct pungent smell of his father's fingers filled his nostrils.

The man brought his index finger of its other hand up to Drew's head, the tip glowing white hot. The skin on Drew's ear reddened, causing a burning pain, and the skin started to bubble and blister from the intense heat.

Drew tried to scream, but the man's grasp tightened over Drew's nose and mouth. Unable to breathe, Drew's consciousness began to fade. He felt the darkness creeping in, as he did as a child.

Flailing his arms and legs, Drew tried to free himself from the Dark Man's grip.

Leaning over, he brought his face close to Drew's and said, "I am your fucking God now!" Then he let out a low gruffly laugh and his breath reeked of decay, which burned Drew's eyes.

Fear started to overtake and staring up into the dark, endless eyes of the Dark Man, Drew actually feared he was going to die.

His lungs burned, starving for oxygen, and his face turned a bright purple. Drew was petrified he was going to die.

Just as Drew felt death taking him, a surge of energy hit him and his will to live kicked in.

Clenching his fist, Drew jammed it over his head and drove it hard into the Dark Figured Man's face. The cartilage in the man's nose exploded.

Drew pulled his fist back and fired a second jab. Again, he struck the Dark Figured Man's face, catching him under his right eye, and felt the man's eyeball socket shatter.

The Dark Man never felt pain before; it overwhelmed him causing him to release his grasp, allowing air to rush into Drew's lungs providing life back to his body. The Dark Man stood and staggered around. Pain was something he needed to adapt to. He was having trouble breathing through his nose and could no longer see out of his left eye. He took a few steps and fell to his knees with his back toward Drew.

Drew laid there and just breathed. His body was so starved for oxygen he could do nothing but breathe. After a moment he rolled over, coughing, breathing in fresh air. Drew started to stand up, his body exhausted from lack of oxygen.

Blood poured through the Dark Man's fingers, running down his forearm. Pinching his nose, he stopped the bleeding and said, "The drawing of your number is now!"

Drew stood up with a fire in his eyes, having stared down death and lived to talk about it.

"Not if I pull your number first!" Drew said, approaching the man on his knees.

The Man let out another low gruffly laugh as the chamber began to spin.

The light inside the chamber started to dim and fade. A black hole began to form in the chamber causing the room to start spinning and Drew's body became heavy and felt like he was back on the Gravitron ride.

The room began spinning faster and faster, and Drew was pulled off his feet. He hit the floor hard, headfirst, and momentarily blacked out.

Drew's eyelids slightly opened, and he saw Steve standing atop the stone slab.

Something began glowing inside the chamber with an increasing intensity. Drew brought his hand to his face to protect his eyes and his skin felt like it was on fire, which instantly reddened and began to blister.

Suddenly, a blinding light exploded with the intensity of a star going supernova and the chamber walls turned white hot.

"No!" the Dark Man screamed as cracks began to appear in the walls, and instantly everything was gone.

Chapter 71

New York City, New York

Steve awoke early that morning and his body hurt all over. He unzipped the tent and stepped out. The air held that distinct smell of snow, and it felt cold and refreshing on his naked body. Taking a deep breath, he filled his lungs, replacing the stale air from the tent.

His bare feet crunched on the fresh blanket of snow. The sun, just a sliver on the horizon, broke through the barren trees. The days were becoming shorter and colder, and it reminded him of winters back home in Maine. A smile washed over his face, knowing he had been able to save his friends last night.

You should not have done that, said a voice from within the light. It reflected off the snow, surrounding him. Steve looked down and found his body translucent, and the light inside him was dim. His body absorbed the light encompassing him and his soul began to glow again. Steve basked in the light for a few moments longer and returned to his tent.

They had collected firewood the night before at Drew's behest because he thought it might snow. Steve had looked to the cloudless sky above and asked Drew if he was studying to become a junior meteorologist. Cass had snorted at Steve's sarcasm. For some reason it was funny coming from him.

Now Steve was happy that he heeded his friend's warning, as it would have been difficult to find branches with the ground covered in snow.

Steve started a fire and thought about what he wanted to say to Drew. First, he'd have to get Cass out of the way so they could talk. He knew Drew wouldn't talk about his drinking in front of her. She had put her life in Drew's hands, and she might get upset if she thought Steve was attacking her guardian.

Drew awoke with one hell of a headache. He remembered everything that happened, including the blonde-haired man who tortured Steve by trying to drill into his head with its rotating and glowing finger.

Cass stirred in the sleeping bag next him and woke up. They both got dressed, putting layers on to fight the cold, and emerged from the tent at the same time.

Drew went to do his morning business and Steve capitalized on his absence. Once Drew was out of sight, he walked over to Cass.

"Hey kiddo," he said.

"Good morning, Steve."

"I was wondering if you could hang back a little today when we set out."

Cass tilted her head, wondering what was up.

"I'd like to talk to Drew about something privately, if that's okay?"

"Sure," Cass said, as she put her head on his shoulder. "Manly stuff, huh?"

"Yeah," Steve replied, as he gave her a kiss on the top of her head.

"I have to pee," Cass said, as she grabbed her bag and headed off.

After breakfast they packed up and headed out down the tracks. Cass took the lead and gave Steve the space he asked for.

"Wow! Someone has a little pep in their step this morning," Drew said as he pointed to Cass, who was already a good fifty yards ahead of them.

"I asked her to give us a little time alone," Steve said.

"Oh man, we're not gonna have one of your talks again, are we?"

"You've been doing great lately, but I'm afraid you'll relapse. I just wanted to teach you a few things that helped me and hopefully they'll help you too."

"Okay."

"Have you ever heard of HALT?"

"As in stop?" Drew said with that sarcastic tone of his.

"No. H.A.L.T. it's an acronym. Hungry. Angry. Lonely. Tired."

"Nope. Never heard of it."

"For us addicts, we have to watch out for triggers. If at any time we feel more than one of those four, it can trigger us and can cause us to pick up and use again."

Drew thought about it for a minute and definitely could see that happening to him. He was already a moody prick to begin with without any of the four. Add booze and it created an instant firestorm.

"How long has it been since your last drink?" Steve asked.

"A couple months."

"That's amazing. I'm so proud of you, Drew."

"Thanks," Drew said, as he rolled his eyes. He wasn't one for praise. He didn't need other people's acceptance or positive reinforcement. He provided that to them. Not the other way around.

"Do you want to talk about what drove you to drink?"

"Um, no."

"Drew, you need to face this problem head on because what are you going to do later when whatever it is rears its ugly head?"

"Touché," Drew said, who was still uncomfortable in his own skin. He didn't like himself. He didn't like that he was weak. He was tough now, but as a child he was weak.

He thought about his father and he felt an anger swell within him.

"You're getting mad," Steve said.

"No, I'm not."

"Yes, you are. Your face turns red when you get mad."

"Poke a bull and you'll get the horns."

"Drew, I'm trying to help. You saved my life and I want to help save yours."

"Speaking of saving lives. What the hell was that last night?"

"What?"

"What, what? You were there last night. I saw you in the chamber."

"Did you bump your head?" Steve asked, finally giving Drew a taste of his own medicine.

"Steve," Drew said, stopping. "Cut the bullshit."

"Seriously, what are you talking about?"

"Never mind," Drew said. *It must have been a dream,* he thought.

"I just want to help," Steve said.

"I know. This is tough for me. You're asking me to look back at a point in my life that hurts when I think about it. A lot of mean and violent things happened to me as a child. I was helpless. I cried and screamed but that didn't help nor did it make it stop. The only thing that helped was letting those feelings turn into anger. It kept me warm. It gave me the ability to push on and accept everything that was done to me."

"I understand."

"Do you? Because most of the people I know who look back on their childhood feel happy. Most people are happy. I'm not."

Steve put his arm around Drew, slowing their pace. "It's okay. Let it out."

"If someone you loved died and when you think about them, you feel sad. The sadness is brought on by memories and the fact that they are no longer with us. Some people get trapped in that sadness. When I was a child, I flipped a switch on my emotions and now I don't know how to handle them. I turned everything to anger. It was my defense mechanism. Whenever I'm faced with an emotional situation, my brain senses those emotions, and it turns them to anger. I'm always on a heightened alert. Even during times of great happiness, I am on edge. I don't know what to do with my emotions. I can't get the switch to flip back. It's my demon."

Steve felt happy. He was finally getting the breakthrough he needed. Now he could truly help his friend.

Drew thought back to his childhood. That constant fear of his father. Those big hands clamping down over his mouth and nose, suffocating him. The constant abuse.

Steve wasn't ready for it when Drew collapsed to his knees. He kneeled down next to him as Drew sobbed and tears streamed down his face.

"It's going to be okay. We're safe now."

"No, we're not."

"Yes, we are," Steve said with a reinforcing tone.

Just then, Cass screamed.

Cass walked the tracks thinking about Greg and felt a great sadness inside. She loved him and he was the only boy she had ever slept with despite what her mother and father thought. For some reason they thought she was out 'sleeping around' when she was not. Possibly because she was beautiful and used her looks to her advantage. She was planning on saving herself for marriage, but she couldn't resist Greg's charm. Her friends in high school would sleep with just about anyone and each other. She didn't care for that. She was attracted to men.

She loved Greg, and he had tried standing up for her, but those evil men shot him like a dog. Forced him to his knees and shot him execution style. His body twitched and lurched before landing face down. She couldn't shake the vision of his lifeless eyes as they looked up at her or the blood that ran from his nose and mouth. She felt sick.

She glanced over her shoulder and saw Steve had his arm around Drew. She wished one of them was holding her right now, like her father did as a child. Her thoughts drifted, and she wondered if her parents were still alive. It didn't matter. They didn't seem to care for her anyway. All they did was yell. Her mother was constantly on her about the dishes not being done, laundry on the floor, trash overflowing. It never seemed to stop.

My parents are kinda like Drew, she thought. *Maybe they did love me?*

Tall grass covered both sides of the tracks, which curved up ahead and beyond the curve was a road.

Cass was looking down in deep thought as she stepped on each railroad tie.

If Drew barely knows me and wants to keep me alive yet acts the way he does, did my parents really love me? she thought. She never looked at it that way. She never thought they were being too overbearing because they loved her. She always thought they hated her.

My God. What did I do? Did I turn my back on those that loved me? she thought, as her mind swarmed with questions.

She reached up and wiped away her tears. *My family did love me.*

Cass was about to head back when something caught her eye out on the road. It was a man walking toward her. Cass noticed he was covered in something, and it took her brain a minute to realize he was covered in blood. The man had salt and pepper hair and appeared to be about forty years old. Suddenly he went from walking to a full-on sprint toward her.

She froze.

The man ran at her hard and he had a crazed look about him. And he was carrying a metal pipe.

Cass didn't know what to do. She just stood there and screamed.

Drew was wiping away the tears when he heard Cass scream.

"What the fuck!" Drew shouted as he rose up and sprinted down the tracks. He felt an anger swelling inside himself that provided him fuel to propel him down the tracks.

Steve was stunned. One minute Drew was sobbing like a baby and the next he was barreling down the tracks.

The tall grass on the right side of the tracks started rustling. A man emerged and his left leg dangled as he hobbled toward Cass.

"Arrgghh," Drew shouted as he ran, trying to get the man's attention. But it didn't work.

The man running with the pipe was closing in on Cass fast.

Drew skidded to a stop, dropped down onto one knee, and brought the rifle stock up to his shoulder and aimed.

He squeezed the trigger.

The man stumbled. He clutched at his left side where the bullet entered but he still continued on.

Drew aimed and squeezed the trigger again.

Click.

It was empty.

Drew took off in a sprint toward the man approaching Cass. Muscle memory kicked in and his body rocketed down the tracks. He felt like he was back on the cross-country team in high school.

The man swung the pipe at Cass. The hole Drew put in the man's side didn't seem to slow him down or diminish his determination. At the last-minute, Cass jumped out of his way. The man's momentum sent him sailing across the tracks and he landed hard and lost his grip on the pipe which bounced off the track with a loud clang. He rolled down the slight embankment and ended up in the long grass.

Drew adjusted the rifle in his hands as he ran. He had a good strong grip on the barrel of the rifle. Cass was breathing heavily, and her heart raced in her chest. Adrenaline coursed through her body as her outstretched arms held the man with the injured leg at bay.

He was wearing a white sweater that was smeared in dirt and blood. The man was trying to get his hands around her throat, but she was a wiry little thing. They were in a constant struggle and she was growing tired. She was no match for the man's two-hundred-and-fifty-pound frame, and soon her arms gave out. She felt herself falling back and in a desperate move she shot her right leg out and up.

Her foot caught the man square between the legs, causing him to double over. Cass lost her balance and fell onto the tracks.

Running up behind the guy, Drew butt stroked him as hard as he could. The impact from the stock slammed so hard into the base of the man's head it severed his spine and drove him into the ground.

The first man crawled over toward the pipe and picked it up. Clutching his side, he attempted to get up. Using the pipe, he pushed himself off the ground.

Drew spun the rifle around and hit the release for the magazine. He reached into the side pouch of his pack, pulled out a full magazine, slapped it in and pulled the bolt back chambering a round.

The man charged at Cass again, holding the pipe, and all she could do was scream.

It was life or death, Drew thought, as he aimed and squeezed the trigger.

A fine red mist appeared from the man's head.

A slight breeze blew, which peppered Cass in blood and brain matter as the man's body crumpled and landed half on and half off the tracks.

Cass stood there screaming. In light of recent events who could blame her?

Steve ran down the tracks towards Cass and passed Drew, who was scanning the area for other potential threats.

After several seconds, Steve reached Cass.

"Are you okay?" he asked, with his arms stretched out, pulling her into his full embrace.

Cass just stood there crying and clutched at her arms where the man had grabbed her. They were sore, and her triceps and biceps burned from the vigorous workout.

Drew was searching the body when Steve said, "Drew, here comes another one."

"Did the whole world see that fucking message?" Drew asked, standing up.

"Maybe," Steve replied.

"Oh look," Drew said. "It's a woman this time."

"Haha, very funny," Steve said.

"She's got that crazy look, doesn't she?" Drew asked, not wanting to shoot her.

"Afraid so."

The shot reverberated through the woods and the woman fell dead.

They sat on the tracks for a while, letting Cass get it all out of her system.

"How you doing, kiddo?" Drew asked.

"I'm okay," Cass replied.

"Are you ready to go?"

"Yeah."

"Steve?"

"I'm good," Steve replied.

They walked the tracks in silence and after a few miles Cass spoke up.

"Drew?"

"Yeah, Cass?"

"When we get down south, do you think we could check on my parents?"

"Of course."

"Thank you, Drew."

"You're welcome, Cass."

"Thank you for everything."

"It's what family does."

Chapter 72

Newark, New Jersey

They spent most of the day walking the tracks and hunger was setting in.

"I think we should turn back and check out that last street we crossed. Maybe we can find some food," Drew said.

Both Cass and Steve agreed, so they stopped and turned back.

Cass stepped up onto the one of the rails and putting one foot in front of the other started balancing herself on the rail. A moment later she started giggling and reached out for Drew's hand. Holding onto Drew's hand, Cass started picking up the pace with Drew right beside her. He was looking down, making sure he didn't trip over a railroad tie, and laughed with Cass.

Suddenly Steve called out. "Guys!"

Both Cass and Drew continued on laughing and enjoying the moment.

"Guys!" Steve shouted again.

This time Drew heard him and turned around, letting go of Cass's hand, who lost her balance and stepped off the track.

"There's someone coming!" Steve shouted.

Instantly Drew whipped around and had the rifle off his shoulder.

Off in the distance, a man approached. He was too far away to tell if he was crazy or not.

"Drew! Shoot him!" Cass said.

"No! Wait!" Steve shouted. "We don't even know if he's crazy."

Drew stood there like a statue; his sights locked onto the man approaching.

A minute passed, and the man continued towards them. Then something strange happened. The man began waving.

"Is he waving at us?" Cass asked.

"Jesus!" Drew said, lowering his weapon.

"What?" Steve asked.

"I think its Stan," Drew replied.

They quickened their pace and soon they discovered it was Stan after all.

Before they were even done embracing and saying hello Drew asked where Annabelle and Stephanie were.

Stan told them how he fell out of the truck and when he turned around, they were gone.

"You did tell them that if we got separated to meet at South of the Border, right?" Stan asked.

"I did," Drew responded.

"Well, what are we waiting for? Let's go find them!"

Chapter 73

Crescent City, Florida

Grandma and Betty-Sue scrubbed the blood from the hardwood floors and rung it out into buckets. Yesterday they buried their husband and son out back.

Billy sat in his room and cried. The pain he felt was indescribable, and he missed his father terribly. Remembering back to the dream he had of the little boy who warned him not to go downstairs and wished he'd warned his father. If he had, would his father still be alive today? It was such a heavy weight to bear for a child. The pressure was so draining that Billy couldn't even think straight. He just wanted to go to sleep.

Grandma and Betty-Sue finished cleaning and rearranged the furniture to hide the stains they could not remove.

With glasses of lemonade and heavy hearts, the two women retreated to the front porch. They sat in silence and mourned together.

Lying in bed a warm glow surrounded Billy and he fell into a deep sleep. A man in white appeared at the foot of his bed and whispered, "For he will command his angels concerning you to guard you in all your ways."

The warm glow grew, encompassing the room and a voice came from within the light.

Angel of God,
my guardian dear,
to whom His love entrusts me here,
ever this night be at my side,
to light and guard,
to rule and guide.
Amen.

The man bent over and gently kissed Billy's forehead, leaving a small puffy mark. The man and the light dissipated leaving Billy's spirit to mend.

A few hours later Billy awoke and headed downstairs. He avoided looking at the spot where his uncle murdered his father.

"We're out here!" Betty-Sue shouted, hearing Billy come down the stairs.

Billy lumbered out onto the porch and collapsed into his mother's lap, burying his head into her chest. She held him and they both cried.

"What's this?" she asked, noticing the mark on his forehead as she wiped away his tears.

"I don't know, Momma," Billy said, burying his head into her chest and cried again.

Grandma rocked slowly in her chair, her eyes wet with sadness. The three of them all alone.

The tears stopped, but not the pain. They sat there together in silence and a cool breeze swept in across the field from the west. Goosebumps formed on Grandma's arms and she pulled her sweater tight around herself.

Billy asked his mother if he could ride his bike, and Betty-Sue said yes.

The two widows sat watching Billy ride in circles around the house, and every so often he'd get a little unstable and the handlebar would wobble and shake. But round and round, he went.

Another chilly breeze blew and Grandma stopped rocking, staring off into the distance.

"What?" Betty-Sue asked.

"Someone's coming," Grandma replied.

"Who?"

"Don't know."

Betty-Sue got up and went inside and retrieved the shotgun.

They waited with anticipation to find out who was coming their way.

As the stranger grew closer, more details about him emerged. He wore an all-black tee-shirt, blue jeans, a baseball cap and had shoulder-length blonde hair.

"Howdy!" the stranger said, walking up to the base of the stairs.

Just then Billy came zipping around the house on his bike. He stood on the brakes, skidding to a halt a foot from the man.

"Hey there, kiddo!" the stranger said.

Suddenly Billy froze, his face flushed.

"What is it, Billy?" Betty-Sue asked.

Billy didn't answer. He just stood there looking frightened.

"Can we help you, mister?" Grandma asked.

The stranger tousled Billy's hair and used his thumb and touched the center of Billy's forehead. There was a singeing sound, and the man quickly pulled his hand away and stuck his thumb in his mouth.

Betty-Sue and Grandma exchanged glances.

"Well, I came to see Billy here. But it looks like somebody already beat me to it," the man said.

"Mister, step away from my son," Betty-Sue said, brandishing the shotgun.

"Well now! Is that very lady like?" he asked.

Betty-Sue racked the shotgun.

He held his hands up and took a step backward. "I see he bears the mark, so that makes him untouchable. But you two don't have it, so I guess that makes you fair game."

Grandma leaned forward in her rocker and said, "You're no longer welcome here."

The man whistled and said, "Alright lady!" He then looked down at Billy and said, "You remember what your daddy told you now. Stay away from those trees out back."

"You heard her, leave," Grandma said, getting out of her chair.

The man tipped his hat, turned, and walked away.

They watched him go until he was almost gone.

Grandma ambled into the house and returned with her bible and sat back down. Flipping through it, she finally stops, flips another page and runs her finger across the page and stops.

"What is it, Grandma?" Billy asked.

Chapter 74

Paxton, Nebraska

Maureen stood at the sink washing the potatoes that the boys plucked from the earth earlier this morning. The dirt instantly turned to mud and washed away down the sink. Bill and the boys finished putting the hay in the animal quarters in the barn. She looked up from the sink at the sound of her boys' laughter. She watched out the window as they raced towards the house, each jockeying to be first. Maureen couldn't help but smile at the boys' laughter. Her mind drifted, and she thought back to her little brother. The scrawny little kid who used to pull her hair and run away. She wondered where he was now or if he was even alive. Her hands scrubbed the potato as Bill emerged from the barn, slid the big heavy door closed, and started towards the house. The memory of her brother faded when she noticed Bill had stopped halfway back to the house. Bill stood there with his hand to his brow, blocking the setting sun. Maureen felt something in that instant. She wasn't sure what it was. Call it a woman's intuition or some other form of perception, but Maureen felt it and something was wrong. Very wrong.

She dropped the potato into the sink and hurried to the screen door. The boys were just reaching the porch when Maureen stepped outside. "Go inside and wash up for dinner," she ordered.

"Yes, Ma'am," both boys said in unison.

She glanced to her left as she walked out onto the porch. Off in the distance she saw a man's silhouette cresting the horizon. She turned toward Bill, who still had his hand to his brow along with a thousand-yard stare. Hurrying down the porch steps, she made her way over to her husband's side.

"Who is it?" she asked as she stood next to him.

"No clue," he replied.

The man with the shoulder-length blonde hair walked up the long drive. With each footstep, the first few feet of vegetation along the sides of the drive started to turn brown and wither. Each step left a wake, like a boat moving through the water. Each step brought him closer to the two people standing off in the distance.

"Howdy," the blonde-haired man said as he approached.

"Can we help you, mister?" Bill asked with his head cocked to the side and one hand on his pistol and the other held up to his brow, blocking the setting sun.

"I know you, don't I?" asked the blonde-haired man.

"I don't think so, mister," Bill replied.

"No, not you. Maureen," the stranger said.

Bill looked at Maureen, who was staring at the strange blonde-haired man.

Maureen felt like she knew the man. Like he was someone from long ago but just couldn't place where from. Her mind raced, trying to place the man's face and voice. She searched back. A memory from a lifetime ago came flooding back. It was from when she was a little girl and she and her younger brother shared a room. Suddenly she felt very afraid.

"Do you remember me?" the stranger asked.

Bill watched as Maureen's face went from a blank look to one of sheer fright.

It was something she blocked out. A nightmare both she and her brother shared when they were children. She was seven or eight years old and her brother was two or three at the time. The memory came flooding back, and she found herself in her childhood bedroom. It was pitch dark. There was a strange noise, like sheets rustling. She awoke and turned on the light. She found her brother talking to a sheet that hovered in the middle of the room.

"See, I'm an old friend of your brother, Drew," the blonde-haired man said.

Bill watched as a look of terror washed over his wife's face.

"He's one tough mother fucker to kill. That damn free will thing keeps getting in my way. I wish He never provided that," the stranger said. "But I'll get him, one way or another."

If you enjoyed this book, please feel free to leave a review:
https://www.goodreads.com/book/show/58966575-war

Visit me at:
https://emkellyauthor.com/

Or drop me an email at:
emkelly@emkellyauthor.com

Available Now!
Pestilence
A Drew Murphy Post-Apocalyptic Thriller

A Journey Through Hell
Book 2

Coming Soon!
Famine
A Drew Murphy Post-Apocalyptic Thriller

A Journey Through Hell
Book 3

ABOUT THE AUTHOR

E.M. Kelly lives in Massachusetts with his wife and their daughter